Vietnam took his legs.

A murderer took his father.

Somehow, Jason Crow has to take a stand.

"My father had no reason to kill himself," I said. "On the contrary, he had every reason to live. I was coming home. We had plans to do things together. Plus, there's no way he'd kill himself using my gun."

Burker picked up a screw driver, went through the motions of examining it. "Look, Jason, we're not friends. Never have been. Probably never will be, but I've always respected your talent on the football field and your intelligence. You were good. Damn good. What's happened . . . well, it's a shame."

"I don't want your pity, Burker."

"Good, because you won't get any from me, but I will tell you I'm disappointed in you. You're smart. That's why I expected you to be more objective about what's happened. Let me give you another tidbit of information, another fact for you to consider. There were powder marks on your father's right hand. He pulled the trigger."

Jason Crow comes home to Texas on clumsy, prosthetic legs—a double amputee, struggling with his lost dreams and the pitying curiosity of friends and strangers. But there's no time for him to brood, because his father has just been shot to death.

Unable to convince the police that his father was murdered, Jason begins his own investigation. In the process he uncovers family secrets that shake him to his core and make him question everyone and everything around him, including the love of Michiko, the beautiful Eurasian-American nurse he met in Japan.

While fighting his own insecurity as a double amputee, Jason must challenge forces capable of destroying him and those he loves to pursue the person who robbed him of his greatest hero: His father.

This debut book in Ken Casper's Jason Crow series treats readers to a powerful new voice in mystery fiction.

As the Crow Dies

by

Ken Casper

Bell Bridge Books

This is a work of fiction. Names, characters, places and incidents are either the products of the author's imagination or are used fictitiously. Any resemblance to actual persons (living or dead,) events or locations is entirely coincidental.

Bell Bridge Books
PO BOX 300921
Memphis, TN 38130
ISBN: 978-1-61194-008-4

Bell Bridge Books is an Imprint of BelleBooks, Inc.

Printed and bound in the United States of America.

We at BelleBooks enjoy hearing from readers.
Visit our websites – www.BelleBooks.com and www.BellBridgeBooks.com.

10 9 8 7 6 5 4 3 2

Cover design: Debra Dixon
Interior design: Hank Smith
Photo credits:
house/windmill (manipulated)- © Vicki France | Dreamstime.com - wall texture (manipulated) © Azathoth973 | Dreamstime.com - crow © Lhfgraphics | Dreamstime.com

:Ltac:01:

Dedication

To Mary Casper, first and foremost
To Roz Fox, Jan Daugherty and Connie Marquise
To Ken and Rita Hodgson
Thanks to all of you for your insights and encouragement,
For your wise counsel.

A very special thanks to Pres Darby
Who has been and will ever be
An inspiration and a friend
In secula seculorum

CHAPTER ONE

Set me a seal upon thine heart, as a seal upon thine arm:
For love is strong as death; jealousy is cruel as the grave:
The coals thereof are coals of fire,
Which hath a most vehement flame.
—Song of Solomon, 8:6

Saturday, August 22, 1968

The physical recovery from the loss of my legs in Vietnam was uncomplicated and relatively painless. After all, aside from the nearly fatal trauma of getting shot and buried alive for three days without food or water, I was young, healthy and in good shape. My phenomenal progress—I was pumping iron and playing wheelchair basketball within six weeks—fooled me into believing I'd overcome the biggest obstacles. What I didn't realize was that the hospital was an artificial world, a temporary haven, where I was just another twenty-something war casualty, one of many.

Home, however, is by definition permanent, the place where you belong, where people accept you the way you are, where you feel comfortable being yourself.

On my initial visit to Coyote Springs over the long Memorial Day weekend, old friends, neighbors and fans came by to welcome me home. That said, they quickly ran out of words or babbled incoherently, all the time pretending to avert their eyes from the shrouded remnants of my legs or to not glance with guilty curiosity between them. *Is he still . . . Can he . . .?*

My friend Zack Merchant brought me home every weekend after that, but nothing really changed, except that some people simply stayed away. My funk didn't improve when the therapists at Willy—Wilford Hall, the Air Force Medical Center in San Antonio—told me my residual limbs—their polite code for stumps—were too short for me to use prostheses effectively. In other words, I'd never walk again. I'd spend the rest of my life in a wheelchair—stared at, pitied, isolated emotionally as well as physically.

“Face it, big guy,” Zack said nonchalantly, “your strolling days are over. So what? Living without legs is better than not living at all.”

He was my best friend. He’d saved my life. But there were times when I wanted to strangle the little runt. Still, I understood where he was coming from. Insisting on pursuing the impossible was setting myself up for a reservation in the booby hatch.

It was Dad who insisted I could walk—*if I really wanted to.*

Want to? At this point in my life I’d expected to be playing football for the Cowboys, signing autographs, driving fancy sports cars and partying on Greenville Avenue in Dallas. If I was going to be driven around, it wouldn’t be in my father’s aging Packard with my former college roommate behind the wheel. I’d be in the back of a chauffeured limo with a cheerleader on my lap. That was before I met Michiko, of course.

I kept hearing my father’s words. *You can walk if you really want to.*

Dad knew me better than the experts. If he said I could walk, I could. I would. I trusted his judgment. He’d never led me astray, never let me down. The therapists were more skeptical, but they accepted the challenge. First came the stubbies, strap-on balsa wood extensions for my stumps, then longer extensions, then articulated extensions, then . . .

The atmosphere home in Coyote Springs was dramatically different, when I showed up wearing full prosthetics for the first time. I was several inches shorter than I’d been, but even at six-two I was taller than average. No one seemed to care that I needed crutches to move about. I had legs. That they weren’t real didn’t make any difference. That I couldn’t cross my knees or kick a can wasn’t important. *The illusion of normalcy* was all that mattered. The transformation in their attitudes settled any lingering doubts I might have had that the struggle to use the steel-and-plastic contraptions was worth the effort.

That was Sunday. Monday afternoon Zack drove me back to San Antonio for my final week of resident physical therapy, and on Friday afternoon I walked out of Willy. Clumsily but unaided. No crutches. No canes. I’d done what everyone—except Dad—said I’d never be able to do. I was walking. Yes, I was still a double amputee. I’d always be a double amputee, but for a few hours a day I could make the world believe I wasn’t. Now it was time for me to get on with the rest of my life.

"Your dad's going to be impressed," Zack said. "He never doubted you'd learn to walk, but I don't think even he expected you to be doing it so soon. He’s very proud of you, Jason."

The words brought a warmth of emotion. My father's approval had always been important to me. The prospect of seeing his smile, of starting the vineyard and getting back to productive work—the anticipation of

Michiko's touch—made me more eager than ever to move on.

I'm coming home. Some things will be different, but I'm still a man. I'll be all right.

Zack turned left on Davis Street, passed churches and banks, a motel and several shops, then crossed the meandering Coyote River. On its west bank, just beyond the bridge, stood the *Crow's Nest Steakhouse.* Mauve-gray clouds forming in the southwest were filtering the sun so that the chalky whiteness of the Victorian hulk assumed a ghostly luminescence. Intensely green patches of neatly trimmed grass, the dark crooked fingers of towering pecan trees, the gray tones of pavement, each took on three-dimensional qualities that made the picture seem artificially rich. My heart thudded. Home.

But there was something wrong with this perfect picture. The semi-circular red-brick driveway in front of the mansion, normally used only for discharging and picking up guests, had cars parked in it: police cars.

My palms grew clammy as Zack motored slowly up the narrow blacktop that skirted the east side of the house, around the porte cochere under which another police car sat, and turned left into the parking area between the back of the *Nest* and the carriage house. Ahead of us, an ambulance was pulling solemnly into the side street on the west. Its lights were not flashing, nor was its siren blaring. As it glided noiselessly past, the sun caught the shiny bottom of a beer can being tilted back by the driver of a faded blue pickup.

The courtyard was a mix of bustle and lethargy. Men carried bags and cases in no discernible pattern of activity, while several lawmen stood on what had once been the house's back porch but which now served as a loading dock. They interrupted their conversation to gaze silently our way.

Dark, portly George Elsbeth, Dad's business partner, rushed to the Packard even before it came to a complete stop. Great beads of sweat were poised in the ebony ripples of his shiny forehead. Zack lowered the electric windows on his side of the car.

"What's happened, George?" I asked across the length of the back seat. "Somebody get hurt?"

"I'm sorry, Jason, your pa . . . your pa . . . he's dead, Jason."

CHAPTER TWO

Time stopped. "Dead? That's ridiculous. I spoke to him just yesterday." Dad couldn't be dead. I was home now. We had plans.

"I'm sorry, Jason," George said. "I don't understand what could have happened. I'm so sorry. I'm so sorry."

The man was babbling. Was he drunk? Did I smell liquor?

The car rocked as Zack climbed out from behind the wheel. He opened the sedan's rear door and stood in front of me, his expression blank. For a moment I wasn't sure what I was supposed to do. Dad dead? I must be having another nightmare.

But the one I wake from to find my legs have been cut off always turns out to be true.

"How did it happen?" Zack asked. "Heart attack? Stroke?"

George mumbled a reply I didn't catch. At last something in my brain clicked. I glanced around. "Why are the police here?" I'd counted three patrol cars in the front driveway, one under the canopy on the side of the house, and an official vehicle parked just a few yards from us. Cops didn't show up for heart attacks or strokes.

"Shot," was the only word George said that penetrated.

Even then a moment went by before it registered, and I began to shake. I'd seen a man get shot, watched the utter surprise flash in his eyes an instant before searing pain took over. I'd watched helplessly as his life's blood gushed from his body.

I had no memory of being shot myself, no recollection of that jolt of awareness or pain. Zack had questioned me a dozen times in as many ways, but I had no idea who was with me in the bunker, who had applied the tourniquets that kept me from bleeding out, and I still didn't know if I ought to thank that person or curse him.

"A robbery?" I heard Zack ask now. "Did somebody try to hold Theo up? Did he walk in on someone?"

Why would a robber shoot Dad? He wouldn't have resisted a thief, certainly not one wielding a gun. "Do they know who did it? Have they caught him?" George didn't answer, and I wondered if I'd spoken the questions out loud.

"Clyde Burker's here," he warned. "He's a detective with the police department now. I told him you'd be home soon. He wants to talk to you."

Clyde Burker. We'd gone to high school together, played football. He'd been a bulldog of a lineman. We'd been on the same team, but we hadn't exactly been buddies.

My natural impulse was to bolt from the car and charge up the stairs of the carriage house to my father's office, but the motor commands my brain sent to my lower limbs had nowhere to go. In my angry attempt to shove what was left of my legs across the back seat's leather upholstery, my trousers rode up.

George stared at the shiny pink plastic prosthetics. "I'm sorry, Jason. I'm sorry," he kept muttering. Whether he was referring to my lost limbs or the death of my father was unclear.

I made the mistake of glancing beyond him. I recognized one or two of the cops standing with arms crossed or smoking cigarettes. Only a few years ago they'd slapped me on the back and shouted their congratulations for my athletic prowess. That was then. Now they didn't see a promising college athlete, a tall young hero to be praised and applauded. They saw an alternate reality, a freak who both fascinated and revolted them.

Don't look at me that way, I wanted to shout. *Don't pity me.* But of course they did. I did. My self-loathing intensified when Zack squatted in front of me and casually tugged down my pants legs, like a mother grooming her child. He didn't do it to humiliate me, but it did. With trembling hands I positioned each of my booted feet on the pavement, braced my elbows against the car's doorframe, and hefted myself upright.

"Where's Burker?" I demanded of George.

"Up in the office."

Aware that I looked like Frankenstein as I moved forward, stiff-legged, my arms flapping to keep balance, I struggled around the back end of the fin-tailed Packard and crossed the baking pavement. I could feel Zack watching, ever prepared to grab hold of me if I started to fall. At ground level the carriage house was comprised of six garage bays, three on either side of an open-arched central breezeway. The full upper floor was divided into two apartments by a central foyer and kitchenette.

I struggled through the passage, wishing there were handrails for me to grasp, but this was the real world, not rehab. The real world didn't come with handrails. I stopped in front of the free-standing elevator my father had installed only six weeks ago. Automatically I glanced to my right, at the underside of the wooden stairs I used to sprint up three at a time. I'd never run up those steps again. I'd never run again. Then it hit me: I'd never speak to my father again either. Suddenly my missing legs weren't so important.

My throat tight, I punched the button. My hand shook. The door opened. I shambled inside, rocked like a penguin as I rotated around, and slammed my sweaty palm against the Up button. The whine of the motor reminded me of my hospital bed being raised and lowered—the mournful groan of helplessness. When the door opened again, Zack was standing on the covered landing, waiting for me.

I strode across it, but before I reached the opposite door, a uniformed policeman opened it from the inside. He raised a hand to stop me. "Just a minute. You can't—"

I lurched past him, my arm swing forcing him to jump back out of its arc. My father's office on the left spanned the width of the building. Midday sunlight streamed through the south windows.

Clyde Burker was bent over the desk. He had to have heard me coming—I couldn't tiptoe—but he took his time straightening up.

"I'm sorry, Detective—" the cop peeked around the corner behind me "—but—"

"What's happened to my father?" I took an unsteady step into the room.

Speed had never been Burker's forte, and he showed no inclination to rush matters now. He offered neither a greeting nor a handshake. "Leave us," he instructed the uniform, then acknowledged Zack who'd slipped in behind me. "Merchant."

"Answer me. What happened to my father?"

Burker flexed his jaw. Old animosity showed in his brown eyes. "He's dead. His body's on its way to the Clover Hospital morgue."

Heat rose to my face. I grew lightheaded, felt myself sway and instinctively tightened what was left of my leg muscles. "I know that, damn it. Why is he dead?"

"Umm—" Burker studied me for a moment, then motioned to the chair beside the doorway "—do you need to sit down?"

"God damn it," I bellowed. "Answer my question. Why is my father dead?"

"Jason," Zack muttered, "calm down."

"I want this son of a bitch to answer my question."

The cop stuck his head in from the hallway again. "Is everything—?"

Burker waved him out dismissively. "Let's get something straight, Crow. This isn't a football game. You aren't the quarterback. You're not in charge here." He paused for effect. "I am."

If I had legs, I'd kick your fat ass.

Add ass-kicking to the list of things I'd never do, like skating, dancing, weaving across a football field to make a touchdown, or jumping for a hoop shot. Enough self-pity. I took a deep breath and counted to ten, then took another breath. My rage marginally under control, I enunciated, "Then answer my question."

His eyes hooded with thoughtful indecision, Burker scrutinized me another minute, then finally dropped his shoulders, as if the scrimmage wasn't worth the effort. "Elsbeth called at 10:15, claimed he'd just found your father dead of a gunshot."

Claimed . . . just found. Was he accusing George of lying? I refused to go for the bait. George wasn't the issue. "Shot? Who shot him?"

"Shot himself."

"What?" I heard Burker's words, but I couldn't conjure up a mental image. "You mean accidentally? I don't believe it. My father wasn't careless. If he was cleaning a gun—" But there wasn't any gun-cleaning paraphernalia in sight, unless the cops had already removed it. Why would they?

Burker deliberated a moment, then declared. "From all indications your father committed suicide."

CHAPTER THREE

"No-o-o." Strength abandoned me. I teetered and would have fallen flat on my face if Zack and Burker hadn't leaped forward, grabbed me by the elbows and eased me into the armchair by the door. Sweat broke out, trickled down my spine. In a minute I'd wake up. I'd have two strong legs and Dad would be sitting at the desk talking to me about being named starting quarterback for the Cowboys.

"He couldn't have," I mumbled. "That's impossible." I gaped at Zack. "If we'd come home yesterday like we planned, Dad would still be alive."

"That's ridiculous. Your father didn't kill himself because we didn't come home last night."

I glared at him. "Don't you dare patronize me, not you. That's not what I meant and you know it. If I had been here, I could have prevented it."

"You can't be sure of that." Burker added his rebuke. "Suicide isn't a spur of the moment decision, no matter how it might appear. If a person really wants to kill himself and has the means, there's not much you can do to stop him."

"But there was no reason—"

"We all have our limits," he insisted, his tone unrelenting. "We think we know other people, but we don't. We know about them. Everybody's got secrets. Like it or not, your father did too. Maybe you'll never know what they were, and maybe that's just as well. One reason people take their own lives is so they won't have to face others when those secrets come out."

Hot rage swept through me. He was calling my father a coward, making him sound like some sort of con-artist or pervert. I wanted to stand up, grab the obnoxious bastard by the collar and pummel his fat face. He had no idea what he was talking about. He had no right. He didn't know my father. Theodore Crow wasn't a secretive man, not the way he was implying, but I'd be wasting my breath arguing with this narrow-minded prig. "How did he . . ." I couldn't bring myself to say *kill himself*. "Not an accident or a break-in?"

"It's an unattended, violent death, so I'm required to investigate it, and I will. But I can tell you now, Crow, it was suicide. Accept it and move on."

My fists tightened.

"How can you be so sure?" Zack was standing beside me now, a hand resting on my shoulder. To restrain me or to console me?

Burker leaned his rump against the side of the desk facing me. "I'm just looking at the facts." He ticked then off on his fingers. "No evidence of forced entry or a scuffle. The gun was still in his hand. Single bullet through the head. One shot fired. He'd been drinking. Nobody around. The middle of the night. All fits a pattern."

"Drinking?" I asked.

Heaving himself fully upright and stepping aside, he pointed to a bottle of Dom Perignon and the solitary champagne glass beside it. "One of the boys says that's real expensive bubbly."

But my eyes were drawn past the crystal stemware to the brown stain in the middle of the desk blotter. My father's blood? My stomach clenched, and a wave of nausea rose, burning my throat.

"What time did he . . . did it happen?" Zack asked.

"Can't say right now. We'll know something when we get the results of the autopsy. He died instantly. I can tell you that. No suffering, if that's any consolation."

"You'll do an autopsy?" Again Zack was ahead of me with a question that seemed obvious.

"Have to in the case of violent or unexpected death." Burker crossed his arms. "It's the law. Should have the results back Monday, Tuesday at the latest."

"Did he leave a note?" I asked.

"Haven't found one."

"That doesn't make sense," I muttered to no one in particular. "Dad would have left an explanation, a letter, something—"

"It's a common misconception that people who kill themselves leave notes," Burker said. "Truth is a lot of deaths aren't even recognized as suicides. One car accidents, pills and booze, things like that. I reckon your daddy's been under considerable pressure these last few months . . . with the business and family and . . . well, what happened to you."

I fumed. "Are you suggesting my father killed himself because of me?"

Burker glanced at my legs, then looked away. I'd seen it before in people's eyes. The morbid curiosity, the guilty fascination, the revulsion and pity.

"What I'm saying is—" for the first time he seemed flustered "—all the evidence points to suicide. Nothing else. When was the last time you saw him?"

"Monday afternoon. Zack and I had a late lunch with him before we left for San Antonio."

"Was he in good spirits?"

"In very good spirits. He had every reason to be."

"That was the last time you saw him too?" Burker asked Zack.

"Yes, I drove Jason back to Wilford Hall Monday afternoon. While he was in therapy I did reserve duty in one of the training squadrons there at Lackland."

"Either of you talk to him during the week?"

"I called him Wednesday," Zack said, "to check on some business details."

"Problems?"

"No. Mr. Crow and I went to the courthouse Monday to file some legal documents. There was a small discrepancy on one of the forms. I wanted to make sure he was able to resolve it without me. He was."

"How did he sound?"

"He sounded fine, wanted to know how Jason's rehab was coming along. I told him he was doing great."

"That was the last time either of you spoke to him?"

"I called him yesterday afternoon," I said, "to let him know Zack and I were stopping off in Austin to see some friends before driving home. I called him again later to say we'd be spending the night with one of them and would see him today."

I clenched my jaw and squelched the taste of vomit. Dad had said he was glad I was getting out and meeting people. I'd been avoiding public places, irritated by the way people looked at me, or pretending not to, and the problems presented by the wheelchair itself. But oh, God, what difference did missing legs make now? My father was dead.

"Does my mother know?"

"I'm fixing to drive out to y'all's ranch from here to inform her."

"I'll do it."

His tone softened. "Sometimes it's easier coming from an outsider."

"I said I'll do it." My voice had risen. I lowered it, realizing his solicitude might actually be genuine. "She's my mother. It's my responsibility. I'll take care of it."

He shrugged his thick shoulders. "If that's what you want. Just trying to help."

When I didn't respond, he snatched a paper bag from the far corner of the desk. "Before you go, Elsbeth said the revolver your father used looked like one that was in the gun case." Taking a pencil from his breast pocket, he removed the weapon by the muzzle and held it up for me to see. "Can you confirm that?"

I instantly recognized the custom-made mesquite hand grip. Without thinking I glanced over at the glass-fronted cabinet. The peg where it should have hung was empty.

"Yes." It was my .38 Smith and Wesson. *Even if Dad were going to kill himself, he'd never have done it with my gun. Never.*

"Did he sometimes keep it in his desk?" Burker continued to dangle it in front of my face.

"No," I answered in a whisper. "It was always locked in the cabinet with the others."

"Who, besides him, has a key?"

It was an old piece of furniture I'd found in a junk shop and refinished for him when I was in high school. "There's just one," I admitted. "My father kept it on his key ring."

"In his pocket." Burker returned the weapon to the bag and moved over to the tall piece of furniture on the other side of the doorway. "Quite a collection y'all have here. A couple shotguns. A pair of 45s. Target guns. Rifles." He peered closer. "Real nice scopes on them too. But then the Crows always did have the best, didn't they? I didn't realize your father was a hunter."

"He wasn't. They were my grandfather's. He left them to Leon and me."

I waited for him to make a comment. He must know my twin brother was back in town. But he said nothing.

"Real beauties." He continued to examine the collection. "Look well-maintained too."

"If you have something of value, you take care of it."

He glanced at me with a fleeting sneer. "I'll keep that in mind."

I knew what—or more precisely who—he was referring to. The girl he'd gone steady with through most of high school was elected homecoming queen in our senior year. Being the star quarterback in what proved to be a shut-out season, I escorted her to all the school events. We made what people referred to in nodding whispers as "a lovely couple". Blissful smiles and platonic hand-holding in public soon proved insufficient in private. She was beautiful and willing; I was a healthy teenage male and eager. Clyde became a laughingstock.

She and I continued to date off and on in college. I certainly enjoyed the pleasures of her company, but she was more interested in commitment than I was. For me those years were fun and games.

When I entered the Air Force immediately after graduation she promised to wait for me, though I hadn't asked her to. It was nice having a "girl back home" while I was in basic training. From there I was sent to

Japan, where I met Michiko Clark. I wrote a Dear Jane letter, explained that I'd found someone else and hoped she'd understand. She wrote back saying she'd forgive me, which wasn't the response I'd expected—or wanted. I shipped out to Vietnam shortly after that and stopped writing. Then came Tet. A month after word reached Coyote Springs that I'd had both my legs blown off—an exaggeration, though the net effect was the same—she married Clyde Burker.

Now, arms folded across his massive chest, the former lineman stood in front of me. "I'll get back to you with the autopsy results soon as I receive them." He studied me a long moment. "I'm sorry for your loss."

It was a dismissal, but I remained seated, drained of energy. My shirt collar was damp with sweat, as were my armpits. I looked down at the dark patches on my trousers, where my hands had been clamping my legs.

Zach went to the refrigerator in the compact kitchen off the entryway and returned with a glass of cold water. "Here. Drink this."

I shook my head impatiently. "I'm not thirsty."

"Drink it anyway," he commanded.

Too depressed to argue and knowing he was right, I straightened my shoulders, accepted the tumbler with shaky hands, took a deep breath, and downed the contents. "We need to go out to the ranch so I can tell Mom."

CHAPTER FOUR

I wanted to call Michiko. I wanted to hear her voice. I needed to talk to George and my sister, to contact my brother, to figure out what the hell was going on. My father was dead, and I didn't understand why.

First though I had to freshen up. I'd been sweating profusely from nerves and the summer heat. Only a few months ago I could have stripped out of my clothes, jumped into the shower and been dressed again in ten minutes. It wasn't that easy now and I couldn't afford to borrow the time my new ritual would take. Undressing was the easy part. Then I had to remove the prostheses, hand-walk into the bathroom and shower in the tub. Putting the artificial limbs on again was still a matter of trial and error.

A sponge-bath would have to do. I worked myself up onto my feet. The cop standing guard in the entryway glanced at Burker for his approval to let me pass, then in silence the two men watched me cross the hall.

Like my father's office, our old room spanned the width of the building and had windows in the four corners. The blinds were drawn, casting it in somber shadow. Dad would have reset the thermostat that morning in anticipation of our arrival. Since he hadn't, the air felt thick and stuffy. Zack adjusted the AC and opened the blinds, letting in daylight.

The room resembled a standard college dorm, except it was bigger. Single beds on the right and left as you entered. At the foot of each, a desk and bookcase. Beyond them, at the far end, two closets separated by a bathroom. School banners and posters still decorated the walls. Our records, albums, photographs and books, though dusted, remained undisturbed. The only changes my father had made were to widen the doorways to accommodate my wheelchair and modify the bathroom to include handrails.

I entered it, shucked my tacky shirt, tossed it in the hamper, washed up and made my way to my closet for a clean shirt. I checked my watch. Already past one. I had so much to do, so many questions, so much to think about.

What had happened after my second call to Dad yesterday? He'd been positive and upbeat when I spoke to him last, said he was proud of me. He'd encouraged me to spend the night in Austin. Now he was dead. It didn't make sense.

Was Burker right? Did Dad have a secret I didn't have a clue about?

My world was spinning out of control, and I was shuffling along in slow motion.

"Do me a favor," I said to Zack as we rode down in the elevator together, "run over to the *Nest*, let George know where we're going and tell him I'll see him when we get back if he's still here, otherwise ask him if we can all meet at his house around six."

As soon as we emerged from the breezeway on the other side of the carriage house, a small mob charged toward us.

"Damn," I muttered.

Reporters used to jostle against me when I was in school, eager for hype about my scoring the winning touchdown in the last thirty seconds of play or slam-dunking the crucial two points on the basketball court just as the buzzer sounded. They didn't come close enough to touch me now. Instead, as I lumbered like a giant on stilts across the blacktopped courtyard, they formed a bubble around me and spewed out questions.

"What can you tell us about your father's death?"

"Did you know he was planning to take his own life?"

"No comment." I rocked my hips higher to quicken my pace. They widened the circle around me, watching, curious but also embarrassed. I wondered if one of them would ask what it was like to lose both legs, to walk on artificial limbs.

"Did he leave a note?"

"Why did he decide to end his life?"

I gritted my teeth.

"Was he experiencing health problems?"

"Did your injury in Vietnam have anything to do with his depressed mental state?"

The implication was clear. I burned with a frustrated impulse to shove my way through these bastards. "No comment."

"What's going to happen to the *Crow's Nest* now that your father's gone?"

"Is there any indication the steakhouse is in financial trouble?"

I stopped on the driver's side of the Packard. Where the hell was Zack? I held up my hands. "Ladies and gentlemen, I have nothing to say."

I turned away from them, braced one hand on the vehicle's broiling roof and bent cautiously to clasp the rear door handle. A camera clicked, then another, sending a scalding wave of anger surging through me. I used to enjoy having my picture taken.

I opened the car door, rotated around and lowered myself onto the warm leather. Since Zack was only five-two, he needed the front seat pulled all the way forward. If I wasn't wearing my prostheses, I could sit in front with him, but wearing them, I had to settle in the back where I could extended them across the seat. This time, as I positioned them in the available space, I resisted the temptation to look up. Taking a deep breath, I slammed the door.

A mistake. The inside of the car was sweltering. The windows were electric, and Zach had the key to the ignition. Feeling helpless and trapped, I sat perfectly still, sweated and waited.

Zack scurried behind the wheel a minute later. "Sorry to take so long." He removed his wire-rim glasses and wiped his brow with a handkerchief from his hip pocket. "George's pretty upset. He's called Debbie and Aaron. They'll be here in a few minutes. You want to wait for them?"

I needed to see my sister and George's son, but not yet. "Just get me out of here."

The moment we were beyond the driveway, I opened the window closest to me. The air rushing in was hot but dry and evaporated my new perspiration. By the time we crossed the river and were approaching Coyote Air Force Base, the air conditioning was beginning to kick in. I raised the window. The world outside didn't make sense anymore.

I dreaded this meeting with my mother, dreaded having to tell her Dad was gone, dreaded even more telling her how he'd died. I recoiled from the look in her eyes whenever she saw me sitting legless in my wheelchair. Pity? Fear? Revulsion? But I had two legs now. Maybe the illusion of normalcy would temper her reaction.

It wasn't just Mom though. I thought back to a discussion Dad and I'd had shortly after I was told I might never walk again. We were sitting in the hospital sun room. At a table not far away, two patients about my age were playing checkers. One was missing his right arm above the elbow, the other had lost an eye and an ear. In the far corner near a window a teenage paraplegic was being visited by his parents. His mother couldn't stop weeping.

The late afternoon heat made me drowsy, yet the memory was so real, so vivid.

"I don't want to live this way." *I pound the arms of my wheelchair. "I don't want to be a cripple." The bitterness in my voice makes me ashamed. I wish Dad would go away. I don't want him to see me cry.*

He shakes his head. "We're not quitters, you and I. We make the best of the hand fate deals us."

"But what am I going to do without—"

"Whatever you want to do, son." The reply is sympathetic, but there's no pity in it. Dad doesn't believe in pity, and he's taught me not to give it or accept it.

"Actually, I was thinking about playing professional football." Then I add, "But I suppose that's out now."

He grins wryly. "You told me once you were Superman. Do you remember what I advised you?"

I can't help smiling. I was in the fifth grade. "That if I intended to leap off a tall building, I do it from the high-diving tower at school when the pool is full of water. And be sure to land right. A belly-flop from fifteen feet up can be really painful."

Dad chuckles. "Good advice is ageless." He lets a minute go by in silence. "Do you remember Sasha?" Sasha had been in Dad's army company when they helped liberate Dachau concentration camp. Just before he was due to rotate home for discharge, Sasha had sustained a head injury that severed his optic nerves. "You knew he was blind before he came to visit us, but when you met him, you froze. He tried to get you to talk, but you were shy all of a sudden."

I'd never met a blind person before. It seemed like everything I wanted to say involved the words "see" or "look" or "appear" or some other reference to vision. The dilemma left me tongue tied.

"You suggested we play chess," I remind him.

"You were good at chess," Dad says, "even then. You started to agree, until you realized it would be unfair to play against someone who couldn't see the board."

I cringe at the memory. "Sasha trounced me every game. No matter how hard I tried, I couldn't beat him."

"Remember what he said when you finally worked up the courage to ask him how he could keep track of all the pieces?"

"He said he'd lost his eyesight, not his ability to see."

Dad takes my hand, presses it between both of his. "You've lost your legs, son, not your ability to go places." He looks me square in the eyes. "We're not quitters, you and I. We make the best of the hand fate deals us. We're not quitters. We're not . . ."

CHAPTER FIVE

My head popped up when Zack nearly bottomed out as the Packard vaulted from the blacktop onto the caliche county road. My God! How could I have fallen asleep at a time like this?

We're not quitters . . .

Zack pulled up at the ranch gate, got out, opened it, jumped back in, crossed the cattle guard, got out and closed the gate behind us. Had I been quick on my feet, we could have done it in half the time. I braced myself as we swayed and bounced up the narrow, rutted drive toward the house. Our spread was twenty miles south of town, ten sections—64,000 acres—of good pasture and fertile meadows, but there were also tracts of caliche and rock, expanses of mesquite and prickly pear cactus, cedar and live oak—rugged ranges only goats could love. Cattle was king, however. Much of the beef raised here found its way onto *Crow's Nest Steakhouse* platters.

As a kid I'd spent my summers here with Mom's dad. Gramps taught me to hunt and fish, all the time recounting the legends and lore going back to the Texas Republic. Fond memories. I was a junior in high school when he died, about a year after my father opened his first steakhouse on North Heyward with George Elsbeth. Gramps wasn't pleased about Dad having a Negro partner, and he'd said so. Woolworth's had separate drinking fountains for whites and coloreds in those days. I don't remember my father ever answering Gramps back—at least in my presence—except that one time. After the old man's rant, Dad said, "Now that you've gotten that off your chest, don't ever bring up the subject again." As far as I know Gramps never did.

The following year Dad and George bought the derelict Victorian mansion overlooking the river, renovated it and called it the *Crow's Nest.* My father had to sell our house on Quincy Street to help finance the venture, so we all moved out to the ranch.

Between Dad's extended working hours at the *Nest* and the long school bus ride my brother, sister and I had every day, the family didn't spend as much time together as we had when we lived in town. Dad's partial solution was for us to have dinner with the Elsbeths every Sunday afternoon in the *Nest*'s private dining room. My mother was her father's daughter so she wasn't thrilled at sharing the table with colored people. Unlike her daddy, however, Mom kept her objections to herself, and in time she and George's wife became good friends. By my sophomore year in college, Dad, Zack and I had completely renovated the carriage house and Dad took up periodic residence there. Rather than stay in the college dorm, Zack and I'd moved into the other half of it, while my brother and sister continued to live out at the ranch with Mom.

Our world had shifted. We just hadn't understood how much.

I loved my grandfather's ranch. I cherished the land and my happy memories there. But my heart was in the carriage house.

Gaping out the car window, I could see the fences and cross fences were mended, but haphazardly, not with the diligence Gramps had taken. Errant mesquite was reclaiming grasslands, and the house and barns could use fresh coats of paint.

"The place needs work," I commented, as we approached the squat, unpretentious clapboard house.

"Yeah, well, you take the roof and I'll do the painting. I hate heights." Which was true. Could I still climb a ladder?

My mother's ten-year-old Ford pickup was parked in the shade of a centuries-old live oak tree. The front porch ran the width of the house, but it was four steps high, and there was no handrail. Zach pulled around to the kitchen door, which was only one small step above ground level. I caught sight of my mother peering through the window over the sink, watching me approach. She met me at the door.

How little she resembled the woman of a few short years ago. Her blonde-rinsed hair had given way to a mousy brown with a considerable streak of gray. Her blue eyes had lost their luster, along with the mascara. Anxiety was written in the webbing beside them. The crepe skin of her neck made her appear older than her mid-forties. The lines and wrinkles seemed as much a gift of bitterness as the dry West Texas wind, a bitterness I didn't understand.

"You're walking." Her expression brightened. "I'm glad, Jason."

I braced my hand on the door jamb as I moved in from the summer heat. The blast of chilled damp air from the evaporative cooler refreshed me. Until I looked around.

The place resembled a junkyard, though some of the clutter was far from worthless. Antique china and silverware covered the porcelain-topped kitchen table on their way into or out of the double sink of soapy water. I wondered what had brought on this spurt of domestic industriousness, but I wasn't there to discuss housekeeping.

I moved into the corner between the stove and refrigerator, then rotated around to face her. "Mom, I have bad news."

She gaped up at me. "What . . . what's the matter?" Her hands went to her mouth. "What's happened?"

"Last night," I began, "Dad—" there was no way to cushion the blow "—he's dead, Mom."

Her eyes went round, and she became absolutely motionless, so still, I was afraid she'd stopped breathing, until she moaned. "Oh, no." I extended my arms. She slipped between them and clung to me. I stroked her back, trying to soothe her. She was so rigid. So bony. She rested her head against my chest and murmured, "The Lord giveth, the Lord taketh away. Blessed be the name of the Lord."

That wasn't exactly my sentiment at the moment, but I let it pass.

"There's something else you need to know," I said softly. "The police think he shot himself."

She pulled back, her red-rimmed eyes filled with fear, then she tore herself away, fingertips again pressed to her mouth. "No," she shrieked. "No. No, he couldn't . . ." Tears rolled down her cheeks. "You've got to believe me, Jason. I didn't mean for this—"

I opened my arms once more, prepared to hold her for as long as she needed, but when I took a step toward her, she all but cringed at my laborious shuffle and backed away, almost knocking over a stack of clean dishes behind her. My heart sank. *She's in shock*, I told myself. *She's not rejecting me.*

Nevertheless I continued to approach her, aware of my clumsy gait, uncertain of my balance, fearful of falling and bringing everything crashing down with me. "Mom, do you believe Dad would take his own life?"

She shook her head, but I wasn't sure if it was in response to my question or denial.

"Was he sick? Did he have some illness he didn't want to tell me about?"

"Sick?" She looked bewildered. "He wasn't sick."

But would she know? They didn't talk to each other much these days. Could he have developed cancer and not told her, not told anyone? Could the pain last night have become suddenly so excruciating that he couldn't bear it even long enough to welcome me home? Was that possible? I understood pain, but I couldn't imagine him giving in to it, not like that.

"Did he leave a note?" she murmured, head bowed.

"No." I waited for her to comment further, but she didn't.

"I'm sorry." She covered her face with her hands. "I'm so sorry. I never meant . . . I didn't know . . ."

I limped forward and pulled her into my arms.

Zach, who'd remained a silent witness to our exchange, went to the water cooler across from the stove and filled a glass. He held it out to me.

"Take this," I instructed her. "Drink it."

She gulped it down. I handed the empty glass back to Zack. "I didn't know this was going to happen," she repeated in a monotone, eyes downcast. "You've got to believe me, Jason. I didn't know."

"Nobody's blaming you, Mom." But she was obviously blaming herself. Why? What did she know? "When was the last time you saw him? Did he say anything—"

She'd withdrawn into herself and didn't seem to hear me. My questions would have to wait until she'd calmed down. I followed her eyes. Through the front window I saw a stranger standing on the porch, a blond, blue-eyed young man of Aryan coldness, leaning against a wooden pillar, unabashedly studying us.

"Who's that?" I asked.

"The church is here, Jason," she said in a whisper that was almost serene. "The church is my comfort and my salvation. I will seek my solace in the bosom of the church, for there dwelleth the Lord who giveth all peace and redemption."

I glanced over at Zach who'd positioned himself behind an overstuffed chair and was quietly observing. With a shrug he indicated he didn't recognize the stranger either. As for the catechism lesson, I'd heard it all before. I'd spent part of my first weekend home here at the ranch and been miserable. My father had taught me to be neat and orderly, habits my mother didn't share. I soon found the cramped, cluttered space an ever-changing obstacle course, not at all suited to a wheelchair. The solution had been to abandon it, but that only made matters worse. The look in my mother's eyes and her tearful wringing of hands whenever she saw me hand-walking from place to place added to my demoralization. She was my mother, yet we'd become strangers.

By the following weekend the installation of the elevator on the outside of the carriage house had been completed, so I could stay there when I returned "home." I used the convenient explanation that it was more accessible to the local military hospital where I'd be continuing physical therapy. My mother must have realized it was an excuse, but she raised no objection. I suspected she was relieved that she wouldn't have to watch me struggling just to cross a room.

Then there was her "church." My brother, sister and I had attended her Baptist church as children, but none of us, including Mom who accompanied us dressed to the nines, as her father would say, would have described ourselves as particularly devout. After I entered the Air Force, however, Mom joined the Evangelical Church of the Sacrificial Lamb. I might have accepted her conversion, were their doctrines not so rigid and intolerant. I told her and the deacon with her that surrender was not for me, that I wasn't ready to give up my God-given free will just yet. The deacon condemned me for blasphemy. My mother cried.

"I'll live here with you until we get things settled," I told her now, though it wouldn't be easy, isolated, dependent on her to drive me places. Maybe I could persuade Zack to stay with me, at least for a few days. After all, we still had plans to make for our vineyard.

"No." Mom stepped back before turning away from me. "This isn't where you want to be. You're not comfortable here. Go back to the carriage house. That's where you belong. I have the church. They're my family now, my comfort and consolation." She peered up to me. "You are your father's son, Jason, but be careful for your eternal soul. Be very careful."

Her dismissal was like a slap, an indictment, the warning ominous, yet I was also grateful for the reprieve, and that filled me with shame. I wished I could understand my mother. She hadn't always been like this, sad, fatalistic, afraid. I wanted to help her. I just didn't know how. I'd have to find a way, I resolved. But she was also correct. I needed to return to the carriage house. I had to figure out what had taken place there.

A climate of exasperation and helplessness enveloped me on the drive back to town. I wanted to talk about Dad, to ask questions. Would I ever know what happened the night he died?

The road was mercifully empty of traffic, even farm vehicles. When we pulled into the courtyard, the police cars were gone, as were the reporters. Zack and I shared the elevator.

"I need to call Michiko," I said.

We returned to the rooms my father had lived in for the past seven years. I settled into the swivel chair behind the desk—his chair—thankful that someone, probably George, had removed the blotter, soaked with his blood. I was just reaching for the telephone when I heard the clatter of feet on the outside stairs.

CHAPTER SIX

"I'll get rid of them," Zack called out from the tiny kitchen off the entryway, where he'd gone to get us cold drinks and something to eat. We hadn't stopped for breakfast on our trip home or eaten lunch. It was now after three, and still I wasn't hungry.

I figured more reporters or maybe friends or neighbors were coming to offer condolences. The voices I heard, however, were those of my sister and Aaron Elsbeth, George's son.

I was standing by the time Debbie barged into the office. Her jade-green eyes were at the point of tears, but she was in control of herself, if only barely. I was suddenly aware that my kid sister wasn't a kid anymore.

She'd been sixteen when I went into the Air Force, a bouncy, very much aware girl, generous when it pleased her, aloof when it didn't, and every bit as strong-willed as the men in the family. In the three years I'd been away, the awkward teenybopper had evolved into a poised and beautiful young woman.

"How did you get here?" I shambled around the side of the desk, "I didn't see your car when we drove up."

"The place was packed with cop cars and TV-news vans. We parked on the side street. We've been with Aaron's dad." She glanced around, then with a frown, waved her hand. "What's all this?"

I surveyed the room. The furniture was covered with smudges. Had they been there earlier? I didn't remember them. "Looks like the police dusted for fingerprints." Did they take the blotter too? *Maybe Burker wasn't totally convinced it was a slam-dunk suicide after all.* Or maybe it was standard police procedure at the scene of violent death. He'd said he was obliged to investigate.

"The fuzz are acting like pigs," Debbie raged. "That fat guy, Burker, the way he talked to George . . ." She growled.

Coyote Springs was no hotbed of racism. Desegregation had taken place peacefully. That didn't mean there wasn't prejudice. Burker and my grandfather would have gotten along fine.

Aaron, tall, broad and lean, stood in the doorway. "I'm sorry, Jason. I had no idea . . ." The words trailed off.

Debbie paced the sun-filled room. Her long, straight, light-brown hair was draped over her shoulders. It glowed with golden highlights.

"I can't believe he did this. I hate him. I hate him." She burst into tears.

I extended my hand, stopped her and turned her to face me. "No, you don't, Deb, or you wouldn't be crying. You loved him too."

She threw her arms around me, almost knocking me off balance, and I realized that for the moment she'd completely forgotten about my legs. It was grim satisfaction.

"Who'd ever believe he'd do this?" she muttered. "I still can't. What're we going to do without him?"

I led her to the conversation area across from the desk. The couch was too low for me, so I settled into the armed leather chair at one end of the coffee table. Aaron sat down beside Debbie, and Zack took the other chair.

"How could he do this?" she railed. "We were counting on his support."

Support? For what?

Aaron reached for her hand. She gave it to him eagerly. Her golden tan took on a creamy whiteness intertwined in his chocolate-brown fingers. With a jolt, I realized what kind of support she was referring to. They were . . . My head reeled with questions.

"Tell me what's been going on. When I was here last weekend, everything seemed fine. Now he's—" I had a hard time saying dead "—gone."

Her voice caught. "He changed after you left home."

"Changed? What do you mean?"

"My whole life, I saw him cry only once. Not when he learned you were missing, or even when he found out what happened to you."

"When?"

"The day you went into the Air Force. I stopped in to see him right after you left. Tears were streaming down his face. I backed out. I don't think he ever knew I was there."

I was stunned. Our parting had been so upbeat and positive.

"You must have noticed now much weight he's lost," Debbie continued. "He hasn't been himself this last year, and Mom sure hasn't been any help." Her fingers tightened in Aaron's. "Dad seemed to give up on her."

"Give up? In what way?"

"She stopped coming to Sunday dinner, and after you . . . were hurt, he didn't press her."

Mom hadn't joined us last Sunday either. My brother had, everybody else had, but not Mom.

In Vietnam, whenever I thought about home it always included our Sunday dinners, Dad at the head of the table, leading, orchestrating, sometimes instigating lively discussions. No subject was off limits. There were so many things I wanted to talk to him about, so many questions to ask, experiences to relate. I'd thought I had time.

"Have you been out to see her yet?" I asked. Debbie had just started her sophomore year and had elected to stay in the dorms on campus rather than drive to and from the ranch every day. I couldn't blame her.

She averted her eyes, almost in a sulk. "No."

"Deb, she's our mother. Maybe we don't agree with her, but she deserves better from us than to be left with strangers—" Yet I too avoided her company.

"Yeah, well, it's a two-way street. Don't you wonder if Dad would have done this if she'd been a better wife to him?"

"That's enough, Debbie." But I understood her frustration.

She heaved a heavy sigh.

"He's right." Aaron squeezed her hand and turned to her. "You need to be with your mom."

"Only if you come with me."

He shook his head. "You know I wouldn't be welcome. Besides, right now my dad needs me."

Debbie's lips trembled. "I need you too."

He brought her fingers to his lips and kissed them. "It'll just be for a few days, until after the funeral."

"I'll go," she murmured, "but I don't think she'll let me stay."

"Maybe not," I said, "but you have to make the effort, show her you care."

She nodded without enthusiasm.

"I left word with your dad," I told Aaron, "I'll be at his house at six. I'd like both of you to be there too. Bring Mom if she'll come," I told my sister.

Debbie snorted. "Fat chance."

Aaron gave her hand a gentle tug. She looked at him with love in her eyes. They rose. I levered myself upright.

"You're walking well," Aaron commented as I started across the room.

Debbie's voice quavered. "Jason, he was so proud of you." There it was again, unsolicited, the contradiction of Burker's conclusion.

In the foyer she gave me a watery-eyed smile of encouragement. "In no time at all you'll be out dancing."

I used to like dancing.

Aaron offered me his hand. "I'm sorry, Jason," he said. "I . . ."

I shook it. "I know." I accompanied them to the door. "What about Leon? Has anyone told him?"

"George said the police didn't ask about him," my sister replied, "and he—"

Aaron's father wouldn't volunteer information to a white policeman, especially about someone who might be a fugitive.

"I'll go see him," I said. "I just hope he hasn't heard the news over the radio or on the street."

Debbie hesitated. "Jason, he worries me."

Me too. "Why?"

She paused. "He and Dad didn't always get along. You know that. When he finds out what happened . . . Suppose he blames himself. I'm afraid he'll do something stupid. You know his temper."

"Leon takes his rage out on things, not people. He won't hurt himself or anyone else, if that's what you're worried about." I hoped it was true. We were twins and twins were supposed to share a special bond, a peculiar empathy. Maybe we had once, but that time was long past. We were brothers who barely knew each other anymore.

"Maybe not intentionally, but . . ." She didn't finish.

A minute later I watched them go down the stairs, a black man and a white girl, and I shook my head. How long had they been together? I'd missed the bond between them all these months. How much more had I failed to see?

CHAPTER SEVEN

I closed the outside door. "I want to call Michiko, but first I need to find my brother."

"Go ahead and call her," Zack said. "I'm going to take a couple more aspirin, then gas up."

"Your head still hurting?"

"Like a pile driver."

We'd had a nightcap after dinner last night in Austin. I felt fine, but Zack woke up this morning with a splitting headache that didn't seem to want to go away.

He started to turn, then stopped. "You want your wheels?"

For once I would have welcomed my wheelchair. At best I could expect to wear my legs about six hours a day. I'd already been wearing them nearly four. My back ached. My stumps felt sweaty and sore. I needed to massage and soak them in a warm bath for twenty minutes, but there wasn't time.

I want to be the way I was, I carped to myself for the millionth time. *I want to be whole again.* But I never would be. *I don't want to be a cripple.* But this was the rest of my life.

"Not now, after I see Leon."

Zack nodded. I followed him to the door and shot the bolt behind him. Returning to the office, I settled again into my father's chair and picked up the phone. Since Coyote AFB was on the same exchange, I only had to dial the last four digits. I gave the base operator the three-number extension for the hospital.

"Lieutenant Clark, please," I told the male voice that answered.

Two years had passed since I'd met Michiko in Japan, an Air Force nurse and just about the most beautiful woman I'd ever seen. Sloe-eyed, with the peaches-and-cream complexion the Japanese prized, she had the quiet grace and exotic allure of a Geisha.

Whatever happened to the ring I'd had in my pocket, the one I'd bought for her in Saigon? It didn't matter. I could never ask her to be my wife now, never dance with her or pick her up in my arms again, never run laughing with her along the beach or trek beside her up a long flight of steps to an ancient Shinto temple.

I heard the rustle of a starched white uniform over the phone and could almost smell her delicate jasmine scent.

"It's about time you called me." My pulse skipped until I realized the sparkle in her voice meant word of my father's death hadn't yet reached the base. "How did your therapy go? Are you still using crutches or just a cane now?"

I had to interrupt her happy interrogation to break the news.

"Suicide? Your father? Why would the police think that?" A moment of silence, then, "Oh, Jason, I'm so sorry. Where are you? At the carriage house? I'll be there in twenty minutes."

"No," I practically snapped, then softened my tone. "I won't be here. I have to see my brother and tell him." She started to object. "Michiko, listen, please. We're all getting together at George's house at six. Meet me there."

"I want to see you now." She sighed. "Okay. George's at six. I love you, Jason." A long pause. Then an empty dial tone.

I should have told her I loved her too. That was what she was waiting for. I did love her, but she deserved better than me.

I stared at the telephone in my hand, pictured her beautiful face, swallowed hard, began to place the receiver back in its cradle, then changed my mind. I dialed zero and asked for the long distance operator. It seemed only right that I inform the guys I'd been with the day before of what had happened.

Ned Herman had been my hooch mate at Tan Son Nhut. He'd also been with Zack when Zack found me in the rubble three days after the rocket attack that had started the Tet offensive. Ned was now taking courses in viticulture and geology at the University of Texas in Austin.

Cole Wainton had been Zack's instructor at Officer Training School. I'd met him two years ago in Japan, when we were all there on temporary duty en route to Vietnam. Zack, Cole and I would have gotten together again in Tokyo for R&R, if the Lunar New Year attack hadn't intervened. Like Ned, Cole attended UT, but in the law school.

I was able to reach Cole at his home, where we'd stayed the night before, not far from the campus, and told him about my father's death.

"Suicide? Are the police sure?" Then the inevitable comment: "I'm so sorry, Jason."

I was getting tired of people's pity, until I remembered my father's advice not to confuse it with sympathy. I agreed to keep Cole posted, thanked him for his offer of help and promised to let him know about funeral arrangements when they were finalized. I hung up and made the second call but had to leave a message with Ned's landlady. Not convinced the elderly-sounding woman had the message straight, I told her to just have him call me as soon as he returned. I left my father's number.

A key clicked in the outside door. I spread my hands on the desktop and raised myself to my feet. It was time to visit my brother.

CHAPTER EIGHT

Zack drove east into the heart of the city. Most of the stores had closed at one o'clock, giving the downtown district an air of dozing.

"How long have Debbie and Aaron been going together?" I asked.

"Several months."

"Why the hell didn't you say anything to me about them?"

Zack kept his eyes focused on the road ahead and answered with infuriating calmness. "It seemed pretty obvious."

Obvious to everyone but me. I'd been so preoccupied with myself that I'd failed to notice what was happening in the lives of the people I cared about. When Debbie and Aaron had visited me at Willy, they were always together, but it had never occurred to me they were anything but friends who shared the two-hundred-plus-mile trip down from Coyote Springs. When Zack and I were in the bar in Austin the evening before, Ned had asked me if Debbie and Aaron were still doing their thing. I'd assumed he was referring to their involvement in the civil rights movement and wondered why Cole had an amused expression his face. Now I understood.

"I suppose Cole picked up on it during his visit here last weekend. Why the hell didn't I?"

Zack stopped for a red light. "Because you see them as family. Ned and Cole see a black guy and a white girl."

I felt off-balance, the way I used to in the last minutes of a close game, when conventional wisdom said to throw a pass and my instincts told him to run down the middle. "Have there been any incidents?"

"A few raised eyebrows." The light turned green. Zack applied the gas. "Debbie still has her room in the college dorm, but she spends most of her time at Aaron's garage apartment behind his father's house. George isn't too happy about it, but your dad convinced him to let them be."

"Does my mother know?"

Zack shrugged. "They've been discreet but they haven't been secretive. I imagine your mother's spies in the church have kept her fully informed of their sins. The so-called high priest has probably condemned her as a bad mommy for letting it happen." He turned right off Davis onto Travis.

In spite of his sarcastic tone, Zack was probably right. I had the feeling a showdown was coming with the Church of the Sacrificial Lamb. I'd have to play Knight in Shining Armor, except it wouldn't be a damsel in distress I'd have to rescue, but my mother. I almost laughed. A legless knight charging the fiery dragon of bigotry and superstition. Could I even still ride a horse?

My brother lived in a converted single-car garage on South Travis, in a barrio where mostly Mexicans, legal and illegal, led lives of not always quiet desperation. A group of children, scantily clothed in the summer heat, stopped their games to gawk and point fingers at the giant gringo. There was a time when I would have invited them over and talked with them in Spanish about sports, maybe even kicked a soccer ball around with them. Not today.

I marched stiff-legged past Leon's battered, pea-green Volkswagen and the red '65 Mustang Zack had bought after his return to Coyote Springs. Maybe it wasn't a lemon like Cole's Volvo, but it turned out to have more things wrong with it than Zack had bargained for. In a gesture of good will, he'd offered the job of overhauling it to my brother, who was an expert mechanic. There it now sat, disemboweled in the driveway, presumably awaiting parts.

I knocked on the peeling wooden door. A man's hand pulled the curtain aside from a high sliding window on the right. A moment later Leon opened the door, but blocked entry.

He had a smug smile of amusement on his face. "Out for a drive?"

We were fraternal, not identical twins. In fact, we didn't physically resemble each other at all. Usually described as pleasant-looking, my brother was not quite six-feet tall and had hazel-green eyes. His blond hair touched his threadbare plaid shirt, the cuffs rolled back above the wrists. Washed-out, ragged jeans, frayed at the pockets and torn at the knees, hung loose on his lanky frame. A wispy yellow mustache and beard exaggerated his gauntness. He was a hippie his old friends wouldn't have recognized.

"May we come in?"

His jocularity melted. "Oh . . . yeah, sure . . . but . . . give me a minute to straighten up."

The door slammed shut, and I was left standing in the bright sun, the dry wind making the hundred-degree temperature feel like a convection oven.

Two minutes passed before the door again squeaked open and a skinny Mexican emerged, clutching a manila envelope bulging with photographs. Avoiding eye contact, he brushed past me without a word, practically sprinted to the Indian motorcycle parked under a mesquite tree at the curb, kick started it and roared away.

Leon swung the door wide. "Come on in."

In spite of a rattly window air-conditioner high in the blank left wall, the room was hot and clammy. It reeked of body odor and pot overlaid with air spray. The furniture was cheap junk, long past its prime. Why my brother chose to live here baffled me. Maybe because no one would ask questions or complain about a torn-apart car in the driveway.

Leon searched for something to say. "Hey, you're walking real well."

"Listen, we have to talk. I have bad news, Lee. Dad . . . It happened last night. He's dead, Lee."

"Dead?" He gaped at me open-mouthed, then crumbled into the scruffy easy chair at the foot of the twin bed, his jaw slack. "What happened?" His voice was hoarse, husky with emotion. "Heart attack?"

"George found him this morning at his desk. It looks like he shot himself."

It took a second for the words to sink in, then Leon sat bolt upright, eyes wide. "Shot himself? You mean like suicide? He committed suicide?"

"That's how it appears."

He jumped up and began pacing past me in the narrow area between the bed and the wall.

"Can't be. He couldn't have. He wouldn't have." He stared at me, confusion shining in his watery eyes. "All his talk last weekend—" his voice went hollow with despair "—I thought it was his way of saying he'd forgiven me."

At dinner Sunday afternoon, the discussion had migrated to the U.S. Constitution. Dad noted it had only one significant flaw—since corrected—slavery, then added there was still one misinterpretation that needed to be reconciled—the draft.

"You mean you think the draft is unconstitutional?" Leon had asked, stunned by the comment.

Cole Wainton, our surprise guest, had challenged Dad's premise. "The Constitution specifically authorizes the raising and maintaining of an army and navy."

Dad had agreed. "Yes, raising and maintaining. That doesn't give the government the authority to impress men into service. The constitution authorizes post offices and post roads. Does that mean it sanctions forcing citizens into road gangs?"

"Are you saying," Leon had asked in disbelief, "that Jason was wrong to go into the Air Force, and I was right to refuse to be drafted?"

Dad had shaken his head. "It was wrong for Jason to be drafted, but it wasn't wrong for him to serve. It was right for you to resist the draft, but it wasn't right for you to run away. The point of civil disobedience, son, is that you're willing to accept the consequences of defiance."

I had come to my brother's defense. "The price he paid was exile from his home and family."

Leon gave me the same disbelieving stare now. "He must have left a note. What did it say?"

"There wasn't any."

Bafflement darkened his fair features. He continued to pace. "So this is how it ends. It's over. I suppose you think this is my fault."

I looked at my brother's glistening eyes. "You know I don't, Lee." In spite of the friction between my father and brother, I knew they loved each other.

"All I asked for was time to prove myself, make up for . . . But he didn't trust me. You can blame me if you want, I don't care."

"There's nothing to blame you for."

"Isn't there?" He stopped and peered up at me. "But I suppose it was his choice." He snorted. "Choice. He put a lot of stock in that, didn't he? We have free will. That's what makes us different from animals. Free will, and if our choices are logical we'll be happy, no matter how ugly those free, logical choices might be."

He took a step back, then spun around, his fists clenched. "Tell me, Jay, do you still believe that? Is this the best of all possible worlds?" He didn't wait for an answer. "Desires aren't logical or even a matter of choice. What's so damn great about being logical?" His voice became shrill. "Is what happened to you logical? Is it logical that I—" He stopped. "Is there any consolation for him now that he's dead?" A sob choked his voice.

"Lee, I'm sorry." I extended my arms for a brotherly embrace. I searched his face and saw the need there, but he turned away. "Look, we're all getting together at George's place at six. Join us and—"

"Maybe I'm the one who should be dead."

"Knock it off, Leon!" Zack exploded. "Think about someone else for a change. Jason insisted on coming here to tell you personally about your father, so you wouldn't have to find out about it from the radio or the police. Why don't you think about what he's feeling?"

"Zack . . . " I said in a warning tone.

"Police?" Leon asked. "And I suppose Jay's little puppy came along to watch the bad boy squirm." He began a childish mimic. "Oh look, Leon. Now see what you've done? You've made your daddy kill himself."

I closed my eyes, defeated, exhausted, in danger of toppling over.

"You can go now, Jay," Leon shouted. "You don't have to pretend anymore. You can hate me. Oh, leave me alone. Get out, both of you, get out, get out, get out."

I rocked around in place to face him. "Blame you, Lee? I don't blame you. You're not responsible for what happened to Dad last night, and neither am I." I took a deep breath in despair. "I wish things had turned out differently for both of us—and for Dad. But I'm not going to spend the rest of my life feeling sorry for myself—or for you."

I opened the door and stepped into the broiling sun.

Zack probably thought I was beyond earshot, but I heard him say, "Keep your distance, Leon. He doesn't need to see you destroy yourself. He's been through enough."

"Get out!" Leon screamed after him. I turned to see great tears running down my brother's face. His hands were shaking as he tried to brush them away.

I gathered my legs onto the back seat of the car and recalled my sister's earlier comment about Leon's erratic behavior.

George had recounted with annoying regularity an incident that had taken place not long after our grandfather had died. Gramps's will contained a long list of bequests. To Debbie he'd left the china and silver his grandmother had brought to Texas in the days of the Republic. He'd divided his guns and rifles between my brother and me. Leon had never showed any particular interest in hunting or in firearms—until he became an owner. Then, all of a sudden, he started acting like a kid with a new toy playing quick draw. The revolver went off. The bullet barely missed Dad's head.

Hearing George tell the story for the umpteenth time, I'd asked him if he really thought Leon was vicious.

"Makes no difference," he'd countered. "The slug could just as easily have gone into your pa's skull as the woodwork. Call him accident prone, wild or unbalanced, the end result's the same."

Which brought me back to my sister's remark that Leon didn't always realize what he was doing. I understood now that she'd been referring to more than lack of concentration.

I waited until Zack had started the car, turned on the air conditioning and driven a block away. "Why the hell couldn't you keep your mouth shut back there? You set him off." I knew I was being unfair. Leon was a powder keg in search of a spark. Whether Zack had said anything or not, my brother would have found an excuse to explode. To his credit, Zack didn't respond, but I could see his jaw working.

"What's he using besides pot?" I asked a minute later, this time non-confrontationally.

"There's no telling," was his toneless reply.

"Did Dad know he was on drugs?"

"Yes."

I could feel my temper rising. "You both knew and neither of you said a God damn thing to me."

"Look, your dad asked me not to, all right? What good would worrying you have accomplished? You weren't here. You had enough to contend with."

Pity the poor cripple. "You son of a bitch."

Zack's shoulders stiffened. His jaw clamped. He stared directly ahead without speaking.

Leon's drug addiction. Debbie and Aaron's affair. Mom's growing instability. What other secrets had Dad considered me too weak to handle? For a moment I was furious with my father. I thought he'd respected me, trusted me. Now I realized he'd been patronizing me too.

"If you'd been on the level with me," I said, appalled at the whine in my voice, "I could have talked to Leon."

"And said what? Reasoned with him?" Zack stopped for a red light, took out a cigarette, lit it, then cracked the window to release the smoke. "You saw how well that works. He's too high to listen." He looked back at me. "My God! You don't get it, do you?"

"Get what?"

"He feels guilty about what happened to you."

"That's ridiculous." I stared out my side of the car and wondered if I resented my own brother for being whole when I was not. "He had nothing to do with it. Some of my friends were there. My enemies certainly were. He wasn't."

"Exactly."

The signal changed to green. Zack turned onto Davis and crossed the river. The multi-gabled green-tile roof of the *Crow's Nest* loomed above the front of the mansion's four Corinthian columns. The pink-and-white periwinkles in the flowerbeds seemed to dance in the afternoon breeze. There were no cars in the driveway now, no indication that a man had died violently here a few hours ago.

"Did you notice who was with him?" I asked when we pulled into the courtyard, referring to the guy who'd fled Leon's hovel with the envelope full of photos.

"Kern Flores."

Flores had been a busboy at the *Nest* until the previous Sunday when Dad had caught him smoking a joint and fired him on the spot. It had prompted Leon to bolt from the dinner table and leave in a huff.

"Did you know they were friends?"

"No." Zack switched off the ignition, got out and removed my wheelchair from the trunk. He brought it to my side of the car and locked the wheels, while I worked myself up onto my feet.

"I don't need it," I said.

"Damn it. Shut up and sit before I knock you down. Not that it'll take much. You can barely stand, much less walk. So swallow your God damn pride and sit your ass down."

I stared at him, stunned.

CHAPTER NINE

I gripped the arms of the chair and lowered myself heavily onto the seat. At the top landing, Zack unlocked the outside door and swung it open. Somebody had slipped a folded piece of paper under it. He bent down, picked it up and handed it to me. A single sheet of loose-leaf with my first name written boldly on the top flap. I recognized my sister's scrawl.

"Jason, the newspaper wants an obit. I told them you'd send them one. I just can't do it. Debbie."

I showed it to Zack. He checked his watch. "It's a little after four. If you write it now, I'll run it over to the *Gazette*, probably still make tomorrow's edition."

"Let me take off my legs first." Now that I'd acknowledged they were uncomfortable, I couldn't wait to be rid of them.

He pushed me to our room. I locked the wheels, unbuckled and unzipped my pants, worked them toward the knees and released the prostheses. Zack pulled them away and stood the steel-and-plastic limbs, still inside the pants legs, in the corner at the foot of my bed. Other than doctors and therapists, Zack was the only person who'd seen my naked stumps. Even Michiko hadn't—so far.

"I need to bring up the luggage," he said. "I'll lock the door behind me."

Unencumbered now, I rolled to the bathroom and washed away the unpleasant odor of bound flesh. I emerged to find Zack bringing in the last of the suitcases.

Wearing only skivvies and a T-shirt I wheeled over to my father's office. The air conditioning felt glorious. Zack shifted the swivel chair out from behind the desk and I maneuvered into its place.

"Before we do anything, let's check around for a note."

"You won't find one," he said.

His thoughts apparently paralleled mine, but I decided to wait until later to discuss them.

The nearly square room served as my father's office and living room. Across from the desk was a sitting area. Behind the desk, floor-to-ceiling bookcases. The pecan desk was inlaid with green Morocco. I surveyed the familiar room. Nothing seemed out of place, and for my dad everything had its place.

"Check the safe while I go through the desk."

Zack didn't have to ask for the combination. Dad had given it to him when he'd moved back into the carriage house six weeks ago. The only things kept there were cash and papers on their way to the bank. Zack found money but nothing else.

I removed my father's day calendar from the top left-hand drawer. He didn't keep it in plain sight because some years before a visitor had deciphered an appointment scheduled on it and used the information to beat him to the punch in a business deal. For today only one notation was penciled in: 2 p.m. Spites.

Zack came up beside me. "I wonder what *he* wanted."

"Your guess is as good as mine." I shoved the book back in the drawer. "But you can be sure I'll find out."

I braced a hand against the top of the desk to keep from toppling over as I leaned forward to examine the contents of the wastebasket. Dirt, probably from one of the flower pots, a couple of business envelopes and a sprung paper clip. "Let's check the other room."

Dad's bedroom on the east end of the building was through a narrow passage between his bath and a walk-in closet. My chair wouldn't fit, so I lowered myself to the floor and entered on my hands. Doing so made me feel like both the freak I'd become and a violator of my father's personal space.

The furnishings were sparse. To my left, a twin bed, unmade, a nightstand with a brass lamp. On the right, an upholstered chair, a floor lamp, and a side table with a book on it. Zack picked it up and showed it to me. *The Lessons of History*, by Will and Ariel Durant.

The surprise came when I turned around.

Above the three-foot-high bookcases lining the inside wall were dozens of framed photographs, pictures of my sister Debbie, my brother Leon, our mother, George Elsbeth, his late wife Lavinia and their son Aaron. The one of Gramps in a wooden rocker on the porch of the ranch house, a shotgun leaning against the window frame at his elbow, brought back warm memories.

Prominent in the collection was a formal portrait of me in my dress blues, shots of me in rodeo gear, on horseback and in football jersey, barelegged in basketball shorts, swimsuit and casual cut-offs. I studied my legs, not sure what I felt or was supposed to feel. Those long, well-muscled limbs were foreign objects now, alien. It was as if I were looking at a stranger.

I took a deep breath and surveyed the rest of the collection. There were no pictures of me in my wheelchair. None of me without legs. But there was one taken just last weekend of me standing proudly on the front lawn of the *Nest* with my arm around Michiko's shoulders, the crutches I'd temporarily abandoned out of sight.

I stared. My father's bedroom wall betrayed a deep sentimentality.

"I'll go through his stuff later." I was hoarse and had to clear my throat. "No need to do it now. Dad wouldn't leave a note and then hide it."

"Maybe George picked it up when he found him."

Possibly. He might have pocketed it if it said something personal—or incriminating. Did George hold the key to my father's death? He was Dad's best friend as well as his business partner. Did he know secrets I didn't?

We returned to the office. I hoisted myself into my wheelchair and again moved behind the desk.

"I'm going to take another aspirin," Zack said, "then unpack our things."

I nodded, barely aware of him, as I gazed at the spot where the blotter had been. I could still picture it, soaked with my father's blood. I took a yellow legal pad and pencil out of the desk's middle drawer and started writing:

Theodore Crow was born May 16, 1917 in New York City, the only son of Alfonse and Birgit Crow.

I paused. Should I mention that the name had been changed from Krahe, that he grew up in the Jewish ghetto and spoke Yiddish, German and Polish fluently? I decided to leave those details out.

Theo earned a bachelor's degree in business accounting from Columbia University in 1939 and taught at DeWitt Clinton high school until the country's involvement in the Second World War. It was while stationed at the newly established Coyote Field that he met and married Julia Snodgrass, the daughter of a prominent Coyote Springs rancher.

After serving with distinction in the European theater of operations, Crow returned to Coyote Springs and settled down with his family, which included twin sons, Leon and Jason, and later a daughter, Deborah.

In 1958, Crow established a steakhouse on North Heyward Street in partnership with George Elsbeth. The restaurant was an instant success. The following year, they bought a decaying mansion on the Coyote River, refurbished it to its former charm, and opened it as "The Crow's Nest Steakhouse." It has since become a landmark in the city and is renowned for its excellent quality, generous portions and superior service.

The reputation for fine craftsmanship that Crow earned in renovating the Nest prompted him to establish "Restoration, Inc." which is active in rehabilitating and restoring old and historical structures.

Theodore Crow is survived by his wife, his two sons and daughter, his close friend and partner, George Elsbeth and son Aaron Elsbeth, as well as Isaac (Zack) Merchant. Funeral arrangements have not yet been announced.

I reread it, changed a few words, fixed the punctuation and transcribed a clean copy.

"I'm running you a bath," Zack announced from the doorway.

"You didn't have to do that."

"Damn right I didn't. Got the obit?"

I handed it to him. "Thank you."

"I'm going to walk this over. I need the exercise. So I'll be a few minutes. While I'm gone, you can go soak your . . ."

"My what?"

He came close to blushing with embarrassment. "Whatever you like."

After locking the door behind him, I returned to our room, got out of the chair and hand walked into the bathroom. My father had installed handicapped-friendly plumbing for me about a month ago. I soaked and massaged my *residual limbs*. The pencil-thin scars on the ends were already beginning to fade. Was the day coming when there would be no mark left of what had been removed? Would I forget what it was like to have two legs? Their loss was nothing compared with the loss of my father. Why was he dead? I had to find out. I had to know.

I dressed in a short-sleeve cotton-knit shirt and an old pair of jeans I found in the bottom drawer of my dresser. The knees were blown out, so I took a pair of scissors, cut off the lower parts and folded what remained under me. I'd sew them closed some other time.

The clock on my desk said 5:15. We weren't due at George's until six.

Zack probably wouldn't be back for another half an hour. Half an hour of solitude. I wheeled into my father's office. I was looking for something. I just didn't know what.

The desk offered no clues. The bookcases were crammed with volumes, any of which could hold a piece of paper with the secret written on it, but I doubted it. I parked my chair by the passageway, lowered myself to the carpet again and hand walked into my father's bedroom.

I ignored the volumes of fiction and nonfiction and pulled out one of the family photo albums. I was struck once more by the sentimentality they spoke of. I turned page after page of pictures of people I recognized, though some I'd never met, like my father's parents. I exchanged the album for one of the scrapbooks where I found yellowed clippings of birth and death notices, stories and articles about ranching, cattle raising and cotton farming in which my grandfather was at least mentioned. The second scrapbook contained articles and feature stories about me as an athlete—proud moments, bittersweet now and forever—news releases announcing my commissioning in the Air Force, my assignments to Japan and Vietnam, and my becoming a casualty there.

I also came across columns, some of which I hadn't seen before, about the only car accident I'd ever had. It happened at the end of my senior year at Coyote Springs College. I'd been nominated for the *Outstanding College Athlete of the Year Award.* The governor was to make the final presentation a month before graduation at a high-profile luncheon ceremony at the University of Texas, not far from the state capitol. I drove to Austin by myself the morning of the banquet. The team, family and friends had all gone ahead the night before.

I was on the outskirts of Llano just past the crest of a hill when a shiny red Corvette barreled out of a ranch road without slowing. I slammed on my brakes, but not soon enough, and crashed into the driver's side of the 'Vette.

Miraculously I was uninjured. Not a scratch. The driver of the car, however, was unconscious, her legs pinned under the dashboard. She was bleeding from a cut on her side. I knew enough first-aid to stanch the flow of blood by applying pressure, but I could do little more. My truck was inoperable and I didn't dare leave the injured woman alone to summon help, so I waited—almost half an hour—until another vehicle came by.

The young woman—she was nineteen—was taken to the hospital in Llano where she awoke two days later to discover she was paralyzed from the waist down. I went by to see her, to express my relief that she'd survived and to offer my best wishes for her future recovery. She told me to get out and never come back.

Her name was Daphne Higginsson, the only child of a wealthy local rancher and oil tycoon. She had an extensive record of driving violations, speeding being the most prominent. She'd been in three previous accidents, all minor, and had had her license suspended twice in three years for DWI. Her daddy had gotten it reinstated both times.

The official accident investigation had confirmed my account of what happened. My skid marks had been clearly visible on the pavement. She'd left none. I'd been exonerated. No charges were filed.

I won the athletic award in absentia, graduated from college a few weeks later and went into the Air Force. Six months after I arrived in Japan, I received a letter from my father telling me Daphne's fiancée had called off their wedding, and that she'd died a short time later. What Dad hadn't told me—which I read only now—was that she'd died by her own hand. It sent a shiver down my spine.

I crawled out through the passage, pulled myself into my chair and returned to my bedroom. Zack lay stretched out on his bed, one arm crooked behind his head, the other hand holding a cigarette over the ashtray propped on his belly.

Seeing me, he swung into a sitting position, planted his feet on the floor and stood up. It was time to go meet the others.

CHAPTER TEN

The Elsbeths lived on the north side of town. Just as Indian Heights was not on high ground, so Seacrest had no view of a sea. Many of the area's houses were about the same vintage as those in the Cottonwood district where we'd lived before Dad bought the *Nest*, but Negroes didn't reside in Cottonwood. They only worked there as domestics.

Michiko's red MG was parked at the curb. Zack drove past it and turned down the long dual concrete tracks beside the square, pyramid-roofed house. Zack pulled up next to George's gray Pontiac.

My pulse quickened when I saw Michiko step out onto the back porch of the house. She was wearing powder-blue bell-bottoms and a white cotton blouse. Her long, shiny hair fell like a veil across her shoulders. I opened the passenger door, uncomfortably aware of the tightness of the jeans tucked under me. She bent and kissed me on the cheek. Her scent taunted.

"You all right?" she asked.

Unwilling to admit I'd never be all right, I nodded. Zack insinuated my chair between us. I transferred to it and propelled my way toward the house and up the ramp Aaron had recently installed. The kitchen was warm and filled with the smell of fried chicken and biscuits. My sister gazed at me from the refrigerator, her lips drawn in. She possessed an infectious smile, but she wasn't wearing it now. Her green eyes were brimming.

"I wish I could understand," she muttered.

"Me, too." Not knowing what else to say, I asked, "Did you go out to see Mom?"

Her mouth sagged in a frown. "For all the good it did. Her church was there, Jason. I swear that high priest or whatever he calls himself must have graduated at the top of his class at Condescension U. I wanted to slap his smug face. Needless to say I won't be staying out there."

I rolled into the living room. George was sitting in his usual overstuffed easy chair, his head thrown back on a white lace doily. His left hand dangled over the arm. In his right he clutched a glass of red wine.

I didn't waste time. "George, when you found Dad—"

"He was dead." The words were slow, almost a moan.

"Did he leave a note? Did you take it so the police wouldn't find it?

He glowered at me. "No note. Blood. Just blood."

Debbie summoned us to the dining room.

"Tell me what happened this morning, George," I prompted, when everyone had served themselves from a cardboard bucket of fried chicken. No steak tonight. Debbie, taking after Mom, wasn't much of a cook in the best of circumstances.

George made no move to bite into the drumstick he'd taken. Instead, he gulped his wine and topped off the glass from the bottle he'd brought with him.

"Your pa was late." His tone was defiant, his words slurred. I'd known George to occasionally have a drink with my father at the end of the day, but I'd never seem him drunk. "We get together every morning at nine for coffee 'cept Sunday, when I go to church. He was late this morning, so I walked around outside, waiting."

His diction was deteriorating. "I know the names of every plant, bush and flower. Aaron's mama—" his voice choked "—taught me. One of the 'drangeas . . . under the stairs . . . We try to make things look nice . . . then people let their kids go digging. I watered it, went upstairs. The door to y'all's room was closed. Knew you and Zack was in Austin. Theo's door closed too. Reckoned somebody with him. I knocked but . . . Couldn't hear no talking. Opened the door. Your pa . . . at his desk. Gun in his hand . . . pointed at me."

George polished off the wine in his glass and tried to pour himself more, but the bottle was empty. Aaron told him he'd had enough. He didn't argue. I suspected he was glad someone had finally told him to stop.

"When I left here Monday," I said to everyone, "Dad was in high spirits. Now he's dead. Something happened in the meantime. What?"

Debbie plopped mashed potatoes onto George's plate. "Just the IRS showing up to audit."

"We're being audited?" I looked across the table at Zack. "Did you know about this?"

"Your dad told me Wednesday morning when I called him about the papers we filed at the courthouse."

"Why didn't you tell me?"

"What the hell for?" he snapped. "You're not the accountant. I am."

My father had always done the books for the *Nest*, the family ranch and any restoration jobs we'd accepted, but when Zack got off active duty and moved back into the carriage house, Dad offered him the job. It was only part-time and uncomplicated, but Dad said he'd take it in exchange for rent. It would also be good experience in preparation for the CPA exam. Our plan was for him to handle all the financial matters on our ranch and vineyard as well.

"An IRS audit sounds ominous," I noted. "Is this routine?"

"Never happened before," George murmured. "Came out of the blue."

"Did they say why?"

He groaned.

"They spouted the usual mumbo-jumbo about verifying accounting procedures," Zack explained.

"What was Dad's reaction?"

"He sounded more amused than annoyed. Wondered who'd set us up. Whoever it was, he said, was in for a disappointment."

"Set you up?" Michiko asked.

"Theo figured someone sent an anonymous letter to the IRS claiming an irregularity or cheating." Zack told her.

She scowled. "Who'd do a thing like that?"

"Spites," George muttered.

"Brayton Spite, the builder? But why?"

"There isn't much Dad wouldn't credit him with doing," I said. At her bewildered expression I added, "It's a long story. I'll tell you about it later. So Dad wasn't worried?" I asked Zack.

"I offered to drive back and help get things organized and answer any questions, but he said not to bother. He could handle it."

"We don't cheat people . . . don't cheat the gob'ment," George insisted, as if he'd been personally insulted.

Not everyone would agree. Dad saw nothing wrong with taking advantage of a situation. Some people regarded that as opportunistic, parasitical, though they couldn't point to a single instance where he'd created the circumstances he profited from. On the contrary he quietly helped a lot of people recover from predicaments they'd gotten themselves into, but he'd have spurned being called charitable. He considered charity, if it meant giving people something they hadn't earned, not only foolish but morally wrong. Generosity was another matter.

"What's the financial condition of the *Nest*?" I asked Zack. "Is it making money?"

"More 'n ever," George muttered, "more than I thought possible. If it wasn't for the *Nest*, never could'a sent Aaron to that music institute in Dallas. His mama . . . so proud." He gazed bleary-eyed at his son, who lowered his head in embarrassment.

Debbie started clearing the table. Michiko got up to help.

I persisted. "What else happened this week?"

"Might as well know." George's eyes were bloodshot, the corners of his mouth sagged. "Your ma showed up Monday afternoon."

Debbie was startled. "Mom? At the *Nest*?"

"What did she want?" I asked.

"A divorce."

CHAPTER ELEVEN

"What? Mom? A divorce?"

It was a bombshell. My sister and I stared at each other across the table. Was this what my mother had been referring to when she said she hadn't intended for this to happen? Surely she didn't seriously think my father would kill himself because she asked for a divorce. The sad truth was he was probably relieved.

"I didn't even know she was there," George explained, his words still slurred but more coherent, "'til I started into the parlor. Couldn't make out much of what they was talking about, 'cept your ma was real upset. Raised her voice. That's when I heard her say she wanted a divorce."

"Did she say why?"

"Not so I could hear."

"What about Daddy?" Debbie asked. "What did he say?"

"Reminded her that her church don't believe in divorce. She say the church don't have to. Enough the law do. They lowered their voices then. I couldn't hear . . . 'til she was leaving. Heard your pa say her and her church could do their damnedest, but it won't do 'em no good. He'd see to that."

"What did he mean?" Debbie asked.

George shook his head. Because he didn't know or wouldn't say?

"Did Dad have any other visitors this week?"

"No." He appeared about to pass out.

I had the impression I was missing something, that I wasn't being told everything. Because I wasn't asking the right questions? I kept hammering away. Was Dad sick? Was something else going on? What was his demeanor with everyone? Had anything changed? But I got nowhere.

It was well past ten when Zack and I left the Elsbeths. Twenty-four hours earlier I'd been sitting in Cole Wainton's living room in Austin sipping Courvoisier, while Zack was getting snockered on Grand Marnier. Twelve hours ago I'd been buoyant with hope and enthusiasm for the future. I was coming home. I'd achieved a major milestone, a giant step, so to speak, toward getting my life back. Dad was waiting to welcome me. Zack and I were going to plant a vineyard, raise cattle, and build our restoration business. Michiko was here, and she loved me. I'd never be the professional football player I'd dreamed of becoming, but I'd convinced myself it wasn't the end of the world. My life had taken an unexpected turn, and I was learning to deal with it. I was going to be okay. I'd make my father proud.

But I'd been fooling myself. I hated what I was, a legless freak. And now my father was dead. Nothing would ever be the same.

Michiko followed Zack and me to the carriage house in her MG, then stood by while I transferred to my wheelchair. Zack locked the Packard and disappeared through the breezeway, leaving Michiko and me alone.

She bent and kissed me softly on the forehead. The closeness of her breast . . . Did she realize the effect she was having on me? "I'm sorry about your dad, Jason. I wish . . ." She backed away. "I have to go."

"Why? Why can't you stay?" I felt panicky. Maybe she didn't want to be around me after all.

"I'm on the mid shift."

"But you worked today."

"I was filling in for someone."

"Can't you get someone to fill in for you tonight?" I'd been hoping with a mix of excitement and dread that she'd invite me to spend the night at her house. I was still a man, but would she see me that way? Would my mutilated body disgust her?

"I tried, but we're shorthanded."

So she was abandoning me too. I couldn't blame her. I wanted to tell her I wouldn't ask her to touch me. I just wanted to be with her.

We gazed at each other in the dim light cast by the security lamps on the side of the carriage house. Her eyes were moist. So were mine.

"I'll see you tomorrow," she whispered and slipped into her open sportster. The tinny sound of the foreign car had completely faded into the night by the time I rotated around and retreated to the elevator.

Zack was taking off his shirt when I entered our bedroom. I went to the bathroom and splashed water on my face. I felt weighed down with fatigue, but I knew I wouldn't be able to sleep.

He was sitting cross-legged on his bed when I emerged. He'd removed his high-heeled boots and was wiggling his toes. He stopped momentarily as I wheeled to my bed, as if he'd been caught doing something forbidden, then he pulled off his socks and massaged his feet.

I slid onto my mattress and maneuvered the chair out of the way. "What do you think of Dad's death?"

He stopped and stared at me. "You have to ask me that?" Dad had become a father to him.

"I mean what do you think about his suicide?" I paused. "I don't think Dad killed himself, Zack. I think he was murdered."

He calmly lit a cigarette. "You sure you've thought this completely through?"

"That's all I've been doing all day, thinking about it."

"And Michiko? What does she say?"

"I haven't told her."

He propped his pillow against his headboard, leaned back and extended his legs, ashtray in one hand, cigarette in the other. "We'll have a hard time proving it."

"We? So you agree with me?"

"My gut told me it was murder from the beginning. Your father had no reason to kill himself. He wasn't suicidal. He was excited because you were at last coming home."

I peered at the false limbs standing forlornly at the foot of my bed. "Dad always said feelings are the result of knowledge, not their cause. They can tell you if something fits or not, but they can't tell you why." I turned to face my best friend. "The trouble is my feelings and yours aren't going to persuade anyone, especially Clyde Burker, and they shouldn't. He has to work on facts, and right now the circumstantial evidence for suicide is very convincing. I can't deny it."

"So how do we convince him otherwise?"

I squirmed, stretching my tired back muscles. "I don't know. You, Dad and I talked about suicide a few times, remember? We even discussed it with Michiko once. He found the concept of hara-kiri or seppuku reasonable, to die for honor, though he thought the methods barbaric. For him suicide was an acceptable option if he were painfully, terminally ill, or in some way unredeemably dishonored. Pain and shame, he called it."

"The autopsy might reveal an illness we didn't know about."

I shook my head. "He'd have told us if he was sick. And why kill himself hours before I was due home?"

"Did you notice how many people asked if he left a note?"

I nodded. "Zack, am I calling it murder because it'd mean someone else is responsible for Dad's death. If he really did commit suicide . . . I must have failed him as a son."

"You didn't fail him, Jason. I've said it before, but I'll say it again. He was damn proud of you."

It was selfish of me to want to hear the words spoken, but I did. "My mental processes haven't been particularly objective these last few months—"

"Your father was murdered." He crushed his cigarette out.

The tension in my chest and shoulders subsided, as if I'd been holding my breath and didn't realize it. "How can we prove it?"

"Drinking, for one thing. Your father wasn't a solitary drinker. There must have been someone with him."

"Burker will counter that we didn't know about his drinking because he drank in secret. Even if we convince him Dad never drank alone, how do we know he didn't start while we were away? You heard Debbie say how much he'd changed. If you'd asked me yesterday, I would've sworn George wasn't a solitary drinker either, but he was sloshed tonight."

"He had good reason. He's just lost his best friend."

I snorted. "I don't think you'll sway Burker that Dad didn't have his reasons, too. Me being one of them."

Zack shot me an aggravated sneer. "Burker's an ass. A big ass. As for your legs . . . they were cut off five months ago, not last night." He lit another cigarette, sucked tobacco smoke deep into his lungs and blew it out. "Everybody's got it backwards. Your father wouldn't kill himself because of what happened to you. That was a reason for him to live, to make sure you were all right, to help you all he could."

Over the next three hours we traded the role of devil's advocate. When one came up with a feasible theory, the other shot it down.

"Do you think there could have been a struggle without leaving evidence?" Zack asked.

"Possibly—" it didn't seem very likely "—if the disturbance was contained and no physical damage was done that couldn't be hidden."

"You're implying the killer knew the room well enough to put things back correctly?"

"Nothing seems to be out of place," I pointed out.

"How do you think the murderer got the gun from the locked cabinet? You said yourself there's just one key, and Burker said it was in your dad's pocket."

I'd been trying to figure that out too. Then I remembered something. I grabbed my wheelchair rolled over to my father's office and reexamined the wastepaper basket beside the desk. Two business envelopes, both utility bill types, and . . . I held up a sprung paperclip. "Some old locks are notoriously easy to pick."

For several minutes we fiddled with the cabinet mechanism using paper clips, a pen knife and a letter opener—without success. We returned to our bedroom.

"The real question—" and the one I was sure was the key to finding the murderer "—is motive. Why would anyone want to kill Dad? Who'd have the most to gain by his death?" I paused. "Or what threat did Dad pose to the killer?"

"I reckon there are a few business people who think they'd be better off if your dad wasn't competing with them."

"You're referring to Brayton Spites. I agree he's the most prominent candidate. Except . . . they've been rivals for years. Why kill Dad now?" I tried to answer my own question. "Do you think it has anything to do with the mall project?"

Coyote Springs was contemplating building its first indoor shopping mall. As usual Dad and Spites had very different visions about it, including where to locate it.

"Possibly." Zack didn't sound convinced.

I wasn't either. "This execution was well thought-out, so well the police don't even suspect it was murder."

"The best way to avoid being a suspect in a crime is to disguise the fact that a crime has even taken place."

"It would represent a new level of sophistication on Spites' part. I see him as more sneaky than subtle."

"Do you think we know the murderer?" Zack asked.

"Not necessarily. In the three years-plus we've been away, I'm sure Dad's dealt with a lot of people we never heard about."

"Is there anyone we can eliminate besides you and me?" Zack asked, then added, "And Cole, since we spent the night with him?"

"Technically, no." I thought about Ned. When the four of us had met for drinks at a lounge in Austin the afternoon before, Cole had invited all of us to dinner. Ned had declined because he was driving to Midland, west of Coyote Springs, to talk to an oilman about exploration. He'd have to come through Coyote Springs to get to Midland, which technically gave him opportunity, but Ned had no reason to kill my father that I knew of. When Ned had proposed Zack and I start a vineyard on the old Schmidt place, Dad was the first to endorse it.

"Zack, I've been . . . distracted, self-absorbed these past months. Do you know of anything else going on that'd explain Dad's death?"

He wagged his head. "Your father was down a few months ago. Why wouldn't he be? He hated what happened to you, but once you'd made up your mind to walk, he snapped out of it. He was convinced you'd overcome your handicap and be a better man for it. Those are his words."

I didn't want to be a better man, I reflected. I just wanted to have two healthy legs again. I wanted my father in my life even more, but I wasn't going to get either wish.

We finally turned out the lights around two. I lay on my back, my hands behind my head, staring at the ceiling. Debbie said Dad had changed. Had he really? I'd found him a bit older, more patient, but there was also a contentedness about him that had surprised me, as if he'd accepted what I myself had not. But changed?

We're not quitters, you and I. We make the best of the hand fate deals us. We're not quitters.

Dad was still the same man who'd spent hours reading to me as a child about *Jason and the Argonauts* and *The Quest for the Golden Fleece*, the same dad who gave me a mongrel pup for my birthday and had tears in his eyes when we found the dog gut-shot in a field three years later. Together we'd buried Shep in the shade of an oak tree where he used to snooze on hot summer afternoons. I was sure Bubba Spites had killed him in payback for some forgotten schoolyard prank, but I could never prove it. Dad had talked me out of notions of revenge.

"Remember the good times you had with Shep," he'd said, "not how he died."

I'd have to do that again, I thought. But not yet.

CHAPTER TWELVE

Dad's standing in my bedroom doorway. "Heard Sean was elected class president today. I thought you were running, figured you for a shoo-in."

I shrug, then blurt out, "He betrayed me, Dad. I don't mind not being elected. It's the way he won."

He brings the chair from my desk over to face the bed where I'm stretched out and straddles it. "What happened?"

I'm glad he's here. I need someone to talk to. Mom's at her bridge club. Debbie's with her girlfriends, besides, she's too young to understand. And Leon's over at his buddy's house rebuilding an engine.

"Everybody expected me to run for president again. Sean even joked that he'd be my campaign manager."

I squeeze the undersized Nerf football I've been clutching, then roll to a sitting position on the side of the bed. "You were at the game last Friday night, Dad." He comes to all my home games and rarely misses an away event. "I messed up."

He gives me a lopsided grin. "It wasn't one of your stellar performances—" I got sacked three times—"but you did your best, didn't you?"

"I tried, Dad, I really did, but nothing seemed to work." Afterwards, the locker room was like a wake. Permian's our biggest rival and they whupped our asses. Again.

"Monday afternoon Leon told me some kids were spreading rumors that I messed up because I was hung over. I told him that's crazy. He said they're saying just because I was on the football, basketball and swimming teams didn't mean I was entitled to be president. Dad, I never said I was. But that's not the worst of it."

He tents his arms on the chair back and rests his chin on his joined fists. "Go on."

"Yesterday during lunch, Beth accused me of cheating on her, said one of her friends saw me parked out by the lake Sunday night, that Sally and I were going at it in the back of my truck. Dad, I . . . "

I look away, angry and embarrassed.

"So what did you do?"

I hang my head. "Something really stupid. I confronted Beth in the cafeteria where everyone was watching and listening. I shouldn't have done it, but I was mad," I say in self-defense. "I wanted to know who was spreading that bull crap. She insisted it didn't matter. I said the hell it didn't. I asked her if she believed it. She said since I hadn't bothered to deny it, it must be true. Then she walked away. She broke up with me, Dad, without ever giving me a chance to defend myself."

"I'm sorry to hear that. Beth seemed like a sensible girl."

It was humiliating, standing there speechless in the completely silent lunch room, everybody staring at me.

"Her mind was made up, Dad. I couldn't win."

He doesn't say anything, but I can see in his eyes he understands.

"Today at assembly," I go on, "Sean nominated me, like he said he would, but instead of applause, I got booed. Then one of his buddies stood up and nominated him. A few minutes later he was elected unanimously."

I study my hands, angry and confused. "Why'd he do it, Dad? Why'd he betray me? If he wanted to be president, all he had to do was tell me. I would've supported him."

"Maybe he didn't know that."

"I was president last year. It's no big deal."

"I guess it is for him though." He turns the chair around, sits down and faces me. "I expected better of Sean. He'll regret what he did for the rest of his life. But you learned a valuable lesson today, son, that sometimes good people do bad things. We all make mistakes. We're human. The challenge is being able to tell the difference between the ones who make innocent mistakes, simple errors in judgment, and those who do the wrong thing even when they know it's wrong. They're the ones you really have to protect ourselves against."

"How do you tell the difference?"

"The best way I've found is to compare what they say with what they do. It's not always easy, though. People do things in secret, like spreading rumors, and don't always own up when they're caught."

"What should I do now, Dad?" I know what I want to do. Get Sean alone and beat the crap out of him.

Dad smiles. He knows what I'm thinking. "The hardest thing of all, son. Let it go."

I'm disappointed in his answer, but I'm not really surprised.

"Let him get away with it?" I protest. "That doesn't seem right."

"It isn't. But you and I can't correct all the evils in the world. Confronting him might give you satisfaction at the moment, but what will you gain? People will just say you're a sore-loser, which'll give Sean another victory. Eventually they'll figure out what he did. Better for you to take the high road, be magnanimous."

"That's awfully hard, Dad."

He smiles again. "Yep, that's why so few people do it." He pauses. "You'll run into a lot of people like Sean, son, people who are jealous because you have things they don't. In a sense you have a handicap."

This time he's lost me. "Handicap? What do you mean?"

"You've been blessed with looks, talent and brains, Jason. Some people will admire you for those qualities. Others will be jealous. They'll say it isn't fair for you to

have advantages they don't. They'll want to cut you down to size."

There's compassion in his eyes as he gazes deeply into mine. "People let us down. Usually it's unintentional, but . . . "

He comes over, sits beside me and puts his hand on my shoulder. "We can't control what other people do, son. We can only act honorably in our own lives. We're not quitters, you and I. We do the best with the hand fate deals us . . . "

CHAPTER THIRTEEN

Coyote Springs, Texas, Sunday, August 25, 1968

The alarm clock went off at seven. I tried to ignore Zack putting on four pairs of sweat socks and oversized running shoes, a cushioning trick I'd taught him when we were in college. While quartered at Coyote AFB after returning from Vietnam, he'd kept up his regimen of running three miles every morning before work. After he moved back to the carriage house, I told him not to change his routine on my account. Just because I couldn't run with him was no reason for him to stop.

In college we'd jogged together every morning, an incongruous, comic pair. The natural assumption was that I, the consummate athlete with my long legs, could run circles around my diminutive companion. Zack didn't even come up to my shoulders, yet he was able to beat the socks off me in a sprint, and outdistance me in a cross-country endurance race. It had been his only claim to physical superiority then. Now, I was no competition.

Last night's dream lingered in my mind. Sean had served his year as class president. I hadn't said anything against him during those months, but we were never friends again. Beth and I hadn't gotten together again either. I'd run into each of them from time to time at CSC. We were invariably polite, but even more we were relieved when it was time to say goodbye. Neither of them came to welcome me home after I returned from Vietnam.

While Zack pounded the pavement, I did what I had to do. I'd never liked calisthenics, but since I spent most of my waking hours sitting, it was important for me to keep limber. As an athlete I'd pushed myself hard. Now I pushed harder, to maximum endurance. Stomach crunches. Legless pushups. Pull-ups, chin-ups. I rolled twenty-five-pound dumbbells out from under my bed and performed a series of curls and flies. Later in the day, if I had time, I'd use the weight room we'd improvised years ago in one of the garage bays downstairs to pump serious iron.

Forty minutes later, shaved and showered, I donned the blue hobi coat Michiko had given me before I'd deployed to Tan Son Nhut and took to my wheelchair. In the kitchen I poured half a mug of coffee and cautiously made my way back to the bedroom. I'd just settled at my desk when Zack returned, grunted a greeting, handed me the *Gazette* and headed for the shower. I unfolded the morning paper and stared at the headlines: *Theodore Crow Dead.*

The article announced that the owner and operator of the *Crow's Nest Steakhouse* had been found dead Saturday morning, apparently by his own hand. I was annoyed to see George Elsbeth mentioned in a tone that suggested he was an employee rather than a business partner. The writer went on to mention that Crow had suffered a series of setbacks in recent months, including the crippling of his All-American son in Vietnam. It summarized my records in basketball and football and lamented the loss of the six-foot-six athlete to the world of sports. There was no mention of my brother or sister. The obituary on page 2 was as I had written it.

I turned to the editorial page. Helga Collins's column was entitled "The Stature of a Man."

> *A man is not a man because of his height or the color of his eyes. Those are genetic and immutable. Manliness is not a given. It is earned. It is that elusive quality that makes each of us admirably human. Nor is it physical prowess or intellectual achievement, though these are desirable qualities gained only through hard work. Manliness is not found in what a man achieves but in how he goes about achieving it. It is his character as a human being.*
>
> *A man is always tall, made taller by looking ever up. He projects by his actions a will that shows his head is above his shoulders, not shrunken into them. He has pride in himself, is content with his humanity and is not intimidated by its potential. A true man is honest and determined in his pursuit of perfection, and with that confidence he fills the lives around him with inspiration.*
>
> *When such a man passes, we look not at his departure, but at the joy of his perpetual presence within us.*
>
> *A man departed from our midst yesterday. His name was Theodore Crow. He left behind great sorrow at his passing, but he also left us richer for his having lived. He had those elusive qualities of which great men are made. In time he will be remembered by only a few of us. But to those of us who knew him, he will be recalled with gratitude for having known him, and it will be with great love that we cherish his memory.*

It was an unusually emotional article for Helga Collins whose normal style was blunt and sometimes ruthless. I'd always admired her cold, clear logic, her uncompromising standards. That implacability was still there, but with an unexpected sentimentality.

I was scanning other headlines, other columns in the newspaper, when Zack emerged from the bathroom, his balding pate still damp. I folded the paper with Helga's column on top and edged it toward him.

"How's your head this morning?" I asked.

"Not aching, thank God. Remind me never to drink Grand Marnier again."

"I need you to stand by while I put on my legs. Then I'd like to go out to the ranch. It's time my mother answered some questions."

"Sure."

My "residual limbs" had shrunken in the short months since the amputations and would continue to shrink, requiring periodic adjustments to my prostheses. I pulled on clean compression socks, then slipped the form-fitted top of the false limbs onto each egg-shaped appendage. It took several tries before I was satisfied I had them right.

Zack stood within arm's reach, watching, prepared to catch me if I lost my balance.

The process had taken almost twenty minutes. Therapists assured me that with practice, I'd eventually be able to do it with the ease of putting on a pair of lace-up work boots. Maybe.

Zack took the stairs while I rode the elevator. He had the engine started and the air conditioning running by the time I reached the Packard.

"You sure your mom will be at the ranch?" he asked as he turned right off Davis onto Heyward and headed south. "Today's Sunday."

"Her church usually holds services at sunrise and sunset. In between seems to be pretty much improvised. I thought about calling ahead but decided I didn't want to alert whoever's with her."

There always seemed to be someone. I would have liked to throw them off the place, but this was my mother's home. She was an adult, capable of making her own decisions, whether I liked them or not.

What had happened between my parents while I was in the Air Force, I didn't know. I wondered whether Mom's joining the Church of the Sacrificial Lamb was a cause or an effect of their marital problems. In any event, the church seemed to have lured her away from the rest of the family by the time I returned home.

No decals or lettering identified the black Chrysler sedan parked in front of the house, but I had no doubt who owned it.

Zack was about to pull around to the back door when I asked him to stop. My mother, dressed in black, had come out onto the front porch, accompanied by a guy who bore an eerie resemblance to Popeye the Sailor—narrow shoulders, a lantern jaw, and a curly tuft of albino-blond hair in the middle of his forehead. His thick arms seemed about to burst out of the dark suit coat he wore in spite of the summer heat.

Mom stood at the top of the steps watching me labor toward her. I halted at their base and looked up at the bruiser in funereal attire.

Zack leaned against the front fender of the car and observed with crossed arms.

"You must be with the church," I said. "I'm Jason Crow. I don't believe we've met. Who are you?"

"I am a servant of the Lord." Even his gravelly voice matched the Popeye image.

"Well, servant, take a walk. I want to talk to my mother in private."

He didn't move. A year ago I could have shot up the steps and sent the jerk flying over the porch rail without even working up a sweat.

"Jason, what are you doing here?" my mother asked with more resignation than hospitality.

I was appalled by her frail, disheveled appearance in spite of her Sunday dress. She and Popeye had undoubtedly been on their way to a meeting or service. "We need to talk."

She nodded to the sailorman. He slinked inside, leaving the door ajar. I expected to see his fingertips and nose peek around the doorframe, a lop-sided Kilroy. They didn't, but I had no doubt he was listening.

"You'll have to come down, Mom," I said. "I can't climb the stairs."

Biting her lower lip, she descended the four steps. She'd been a positive force in my life once, a natural, patient teacher, maybe because she'd never completely lost a childlike quality that allowed her to understand a child's vantage point. She taught me to read when I was barely four and how to play the piano when I was six. I used to love the old pump organ in Gramps's parlor. At the moment, however, she didn't appear at all pleased to see me.

"You went to see Dad Monday and asked for a divorce," I said. "Why?"

I wasn't sure if it was my directness or the question itself that seemed to catch her off-guard, but her eyes widened. "To make him give me my father's ranch."

"You already have it."

"I wanted him to give me clear title."

The legalities of the situation were complicated. Gramps had left the ranch to my father in trust for my mother. In other words she inherited it, but he controlled it. That kind of old-fashioned paternalism wasn't uncommon, except that Texas was also a community property state, which meant Dad was entitled to half of what she'd inherited after their marriage. Dad had never laid formal claim to the ranch, since it would ultimately come to my brother, sister and me. I supposed a slick lawyer could argue that as her father's only child, Julia Snodgrass had de facto brought her entitlement to it into her marriage, and that if Gramps had wanted to convey joint title to her and Theo, he would've said so in his will. However, my father had never renounced any claim to the ranch either.

"Why?" I asked her, though I suspected I already knew the answer.

"So I can give it to the church."

I wasn't surprised, only outraged.

"He said no," she blurted out. "I knew he would, but I had to give him a chance to acknowledge his obligation to the Lord. Your father never understood the ways of the Lord, Jason, that we're not given things in this world to possess but to share in his name."

"Mom, you love this place. It's where you were born, grew up. Gramps wanted you to pass it on to your children, your grandchildren, just as his father passed it on to him. It's a part of you. It's a part of all of us. Why would you want to give it away?"

"You're just like your father," she flared. "You don't understand. I have to. It's the only way I can atone."

"Atone? For what?"

"I have sinned, Jason. I have sinned against the Lord, and I have failed you, failed to make you see his love. That's why all this has happened."

I closed my eyes, resigned to a distortion of reality I felt helpless to correct. Yet rage was also welling up, rage I had to fight to control. "Who told you that?"

"The Lord has told me, Jason, through his priest. He has made me understand it's only by giving up the evil of possessing that I can atone for my sins."

"What were you supposed to gain by giving away this ranch? Did your priest tell you my legs would miraculously grow back?"

Tears welled in her bloodshot eyes. "I can't change what's already happened, but maybe I can prevent something worse from happening. Maybe I can keep your brother and sister from suffering as you have."

Did she understand what she was saying? Was this cruel, ruthless God of hers going to chop off Leon's and Debbie's legs too? Feeling defeated, I took a deep breath and willed the pounding in my head to subside.

"I know you love me, Mom—" I started, but she wasn't listening. Instead she seemed to be reciting something by rote. A prayer, I presumed.

"Your father has paid for rejecting salvation, Jason. He's made you pay for it too, but there's still time. It's my fault the Lord has punished you. I'll give up anything for you, even this ranch, and I'll pray for you."

"And Dad? Did you pray for him too?"

She closed her eyes. "He's in the hands of the Lord now. Suicide is the Lord's way of reclaiming his wayward sheep, the sinners who have failed. The Lord's taken your father back to cleanse him. He knows now the Lord he rejected."

It was a hellfire of rage that burned within me.

"Is that a consolation to you, Mother? What a terrible God you believe in. Tell me, if Dad had given you the ranch to turn over to your church, would he still be alive now?"

"Sister Julia," Popeye called out before she had a chance to answer.

Zack straightened and moved toward me.

"Tell me, Mother, what would they do with the ranch if they owned it?"

"It's not my place to question the decisions of the Lord or his priest." Her voice was almost singsong. "He's a holy man, wise in the ways of the Lord, blessed by him, and inspired with his grace and goodness."

"No, he is not," I shouted. "He's a charlatan who's making a fool out of you." Before I realized what I was doing it, I put a hand on Zack's shoulder to brace myself. "Mom, what happened to me isn't because of some sin of yours, real or imagined, or of Dad's, or anyone else's. I was in a war." I wanted to ask her what had happened to the merciful Lord she taught me about when I was a child. But it was no use. She wasn't listening.

Using Zack as a crutch, I turned and strode stiffly to the car where I rotated around to face her once more. Her keeper appeared beside her, holding her elbow.

"I don't know what happened between you and Dad, Mom. Whatever it was, it's over now. But what in the name of a loving God has happened to you?"

She was a pillar of salt.

A minute later, as Zack was pulling out of the driveway, I looked back. My mother was still standing where I'd left her, tears now streaming down her face. I desperately wanted to help her. But how?

The solitude of the journey back to town was accompanied only by the crunch of tires on the dirt road and the blast of the air conditioner.

What part might the Church of the Sacrificial Lamb have played in my father's murder? Zack had asked last night who might have gained by his death. I instantly dismissed the notion that my mother had willingly participated in a plot to kill him, but I couldn't eliminate the possibility that she'd been used for that purpose, and what about her church? They obviously had something to gain.

When we pulled into the courtyard, Cole Wainton was leaning against the fender of his sun-bleached Volvo.

CHAPTER FOURTEEN

I was very much aware of Cole watching me as I maneuvered around in the seat and used my hands to position each of my legs squarely on the ground. I remembered the same curiosity on his face yesterday morning at his house when he barged into his upstairs guestroom carrying a coffee tray. It was only by luck that I was already on the bed and had a pillow readily at hand with which to hide my deformity. Fifteen seconds earlier I'd been hand walking across the floor from the bathroom. For a fleeting moment, Cole had fixated on the pillow before awareness and embarrassment compelled him to avert his eyes.

"How long have you been here?" I grasped the Packard's door frame and pulled myself upright. The church bells a block to the south were ringing for the eleven o'clock service.

"A few minutes." We shook hands. His grip was firm as usual. "I checked upstairs, but the door was locked. I wanted to see you and tell you personally how very sorry I am about your father. If there's anything I can do, you have only to ask."

While Zack took the stairs to the office, Cole joined me in the elevator. I had to smile at his get-up. Yesterday's dark-blue business suit had been replaced with tan bell bottoms, a wide belt and a flowered shirt. A silver peace medallion dangled from a heavy chain.

"Nice threads," I commented.

"Yeah, cool, huh?"

We walked into the office. I was shuffling to one of the high-backed chairs in the sitting area when I changed my mind, reversed course and took my father's place behind the desk. Cole seemed for a brief moment surprised, then parked himself in the seat closest to the door. Zack took the one against the opposite wall.

A moment of self-conscious silence ensued.

"I've been thinking about this vineyard you talked about." Cole hesitated. "You still planning to go through with it?"

"Yes," I answered. "Now more than ever."

"Good. Good." Cole pursed his lips. "Look, I'd like to help if I can. Business ventures have a way of costing a lot more than you expect. I didn't say anything earlier, but my mother passed away last year—"

"I'm sorry," I said. He'd never talked much about his family.

He shrugged. "She left a good-size insurance policy. It gave me the push I needed to get out of the Air Force. The irony is that with the GI Bill for school and my savings from 'Nam, I can get by without it." He paused again. "What I'm trying to say is that if you guys can use some extra capital, I'd like to join you . . . as an investor."

The offer surprised me. Friday evening at *Chambers*, the lounge where we'd met, we'd told Cole about our plans to start a vineyard on the Schmidt ranch. He'd been mocking. A vineyard in West Texas! Later, over dinner, Zack and I had continued to discuss it with Cole. Apparently we'd been more persuasive than I'd realized. I had to ask myself if it was out of conviction or pity. I hated doubting his motives, but I'd been patronized by a lot of well-meaning people over the last six months.

I was about to thank him and say we'd keep his offer in mind when we heard the clatter of hurried footsteps on the outside stairs.

Debbie again. This time alone. Her long chestnut hair hung loose. She was wearing jeans and a man's white oxford shirt knotted at the waist. The lack of makeup and the tension around her eyes gave her face a raw, tired look. It took a minute for her to recognize Cole from the previous weekend. She greeted him and turned to me.

"Aaron didn't come home last night. I've asked around, but nobody's seen him. After y'all left George's place, he took his bike, said he needed to think. He's real upset. All day yesterday he kept saying it was his fault. I tried to tell him it wasn't, but he won't listen."

"What was his fault?"

"Daddy's suicide." She looked away. "He thinks Dad did it because of . . . us."

"That's nonsense." Besides, it wasn't suicide, but I didn't tell her that. I rose and started for the door. "Let's go find him."

Cole proposed staying behind since this was a family matter.

I pooh-poohed the idea. "Come along. It'll give us a chance to talk about the vineyard."

We piled into the Packard. Zack drove. Cole sat in front, his knees cramped against the dashboard. Debbie sat in back with me.

We covered the same ground she had earlier, either in her car or by phone. The auditorium at the college, where Aaron sometimes practiced on the grand piano, was closed. He wasn't at the church where he played the organ on Sundays. We dropped by the homes of a few friends who might not have admitted on the phone he was there. No one had seen him, heard from him or had any idea where he might be. It was twelve hours since he'd disappeared. He could be anywhere from Lubbock to San Antonio by now.

"You and Aaron had dinner with Dad Friday night," I said to my sister. "How was he?"

"Fine." She kept peering out the window.

"What did you talk about?"

"Oh, I don't know. Nothing special."

"Debbie, you two could've talked to Dad anytime. Why go to see him at the *Nest* on one of the busiest nights of the week?"

"Can't I have dinner with my father without you being suspicious?"

She was hiding something. "Dad must have been suspicious too. How'd you explain your sudden interest in his company?"

She twisted to face me, angry. "All right, if you must know, we told him we wanted to get married."

She was nineteen, legally old enough. I had a feeling I knew what was coming. "What did he say?"

"That I'm too young. That I need to finish school first. That Aaron needs to work on his music career and get himself established before taking on the responsibilities of a family."

It sounded like Dad. "So he didn't actually say you couldn't get married. Just that you should wait."

"It sure sounded like no to us."

Zack turned down Hopkins Street on the edge of the campus. We were ready to give up the search and head back to the carriage house when we saw a police car, its red bubble-light revolving, in front of a student hangout called *The Joint.*

"Stop," Debbie shouted. "That's his ten-speed against the wall."

Zack pulled into the parking lot. Everyone got out of the car and waited while I hefted myself upright.

The Joint wasn't big. The customer section to the left of the entrance was divided into two rows of booths running parallel with the front plate-glass window. The second aisle had booths on the near side but only half way along the far side. The other half was a waist-high counter over which sandwiches, burgers and soft drinks were ordered and picked up. The kitchen behind it had a high pass-through window at one end and a swinging door at the other. The place smelled of greasy burgers and stale French fries. A gaggle of young people, badly dressed but "hip," blocked the aisle.

Beyond them I saw Aaron in the far corner booth, his head thrown back against the top of the bench to stanch a nose bleed, his long, bare brown legs stretched across the narrow aisle. A Mexican waitress was holding a cold compress on the side of his face. Debbie ran over and grabbed it from her. Only then did she notice what I already had, that his arms were pulled behind him.

It took a moment for its significance to sink in. Then came the outrage and fright. "Why are you handcuffed?"

"Well, lookee who's here!" mocked a spectator, dressed in a dirty, sweat-stained T-shirt and painfully tight jeans. "It's Plastic Man and his little Tom Thumb."

I'd known Harden "Bubba" Spites since elementary school. Brayton Spites' son had dropped out of CSC at the end of our first semester. Rumor had it he'd tried to intimidate one of the professors into giving him a passing grade and the prof, instead of capitulating, had turned him in. Since then, Bubba's beer belly had expanded considerably, practically swallowing the oval silver buckle on his wide leather belt.

As for the Plastic Man dig, despite a thick head of black hair, I have very little body hair. At a summer event in high school, a girl took a look at my bare chest and said I looked like a manikin. One of the guys then dubbed me Plastic Man. I'd always hated the moniker.

"What's going on here?" I asked the police officer standing wide-legged in front of Aaron. The room went still.

"I'll tell you what's happening, man," Bubba taunted before the cop could answer. "That nigger hit me, and I'm having his black ass arrested for assault and bat . . ."

The young, white policeman overrode him "According to this gentleman—" he nodded to Bubba "—the boy struck him." He pointed to Aaron. Gentleman? Boy?

"With or without provocation?" Cole challenged in his best commanding officer manner as he stepped around Zack and came up beside me.

"Well, I'll be damned. Who the hell do you think you are?" Bubba asked, adding "sir" sarcastically, the way crusty old non-coms addressed young, shave-tail lieutenants.

Cole stared him down.

"Apparently they had a disagreement—" the cop started.

"No nigger's gonna put his freakin' hands on me and get away with it," Bubba growled.

I addressed Aaron over their heads. "What happened?"

"He said some things I took exception to."

"I'll tell you what I said," Bubba snarled. "I said she—" he indicated Debbie with a tilt of his head "—was nothing but a nigger-loving whore. I told him he better keep his black paws, and the rest of his goddamn nigger body off white women, if he knows what's good for him."

The blood pounding in my ears was deafening. The impulse to lift fat boy up by the hair on his chest and toss him through the window was tempered only by awareness of my own vulnerability.

"Maybe you should ask the lady how she feels about it," I suggested with false calmness.

Bubba looked at Debbie bent over Aaron. "Lady?" He snorted. "She ain't no lady. Decent white women don't spread their legs for niggers. Just the sight of her touching that black bastard disgusts me."

"Then I hope you go blind," I said with a low-pitched intensity that drew everybody's attention.

For a moment it appeared nothing would happen. Whether Bubba realized I'd cursed him in the most primitive sense, or he only suspected he'd been insulted, the fear of losing face suddenly provoked him to action. His right hand shot up in a tight fist aimed straight for my face.

CHAPTER FIFTEEN

I deflected the punch easily. It landed on my forearm, but the force of the blow was enough to send me tumbling backward like a long-neck beer bottle. My instinctive reflex to grab at something for balance sent my left hand flying up towards Bubba's porky puss, and my school ring tore a bloody scratch across his left cheek. There was a heavy thud and clatter as I crashed sideways into a pedestal table. It collapsed and dirty dishes cascaded down on top of me. Tan Son Nhut flashed before my eyes. Tet without the rockets and gunfire.

Combat training took over. I cushioned my head with my arms.

Pandemonium broke out above me. I looked up in time to see Zack swing an angry fist, but Bubba was a good ten inches taller, and his barrel shape made the assault all but futile. In that split second, however, Aaron—hands still cuffed behind his back—bolted from his seat, almost knocked Debbie over and shot around the cop. Just as Bubba stepped back from Zack's swing, Aaron crouched behind him. Bubba stumbled, out of balance. Aaron sprang up and with perfect timing, flipping the fat guy in a spectacular cartwheel. Bubba landed with a thump.

On his feet now, Aaron threw a kick into his winded victim's side. The cop grabbed him by the scruff of his shirt and yanked him away. Bubba's shouting cohorts surged forward.

A whistle blew, followed by "Stop. Police!"

The room instantly froze. A man in civilian clothes stepped out from behind the kitchen door, held up a shield and ordered everybody to back off.

Clyde Burker. Great!

My face burned as everyone stared down at me. This was my worst nightmare, the humiliation of being helpless and laughed at.

Bubba picked himself up off the floor. Aaron was between him and the cop. Bubba was about to take full advantage of the manacled man's defenselessness, when the officer holding Aaron quickly reversed positions and interposed himself between the two. He ordered Bubba back. From my vantage point on the floor, I could see the rock hardness of Aaron's muscles. Adrenaline was pumping through his bulging veins, giving his lean body exaggerated strength. I saw too the potential for violence in his dark face—the seething anger, the rage. What I didn't see was fear.

Bubba was rubbing his side. I doubted he'd been seriously hurt. His assailant's rampage had been checked in time.

Debbie rushed toward Aaron, but the cop blocked her and shoved the black man roughly onto a booth bench.

Bubba wiped blood from his face with a dirty handkerchief and looked down at me. My pants legs had ridden up, exposing shiny plastic.

"That crip scratches like a girl," he said loud enough for everyone to hear. "They must have chopped off more than his legs."

His companions snickered. I clenched my jaw and wished I could disappear.

Zack handed me a fistful of paper napkins. While I wiped away the mayonnaise-covered lettuce and tomato and the greasy squashed fries my hand had slid into, he drew my empty limbs together.

"You okay?"

I bit my lip and nodded.

He tugged down my trouser cuffs, and with Cole's help, hauled me up onto a chair. I'd have other bruises where my ribs hits the edge of a table as I went down, but the mortification of being unable to get up, of having to sit on the floor amidst broken dishes and discarded food scraps was far more painful.

"You can take the cuffs off Mr. Elsbeth now," I told Burker. "He's through fighting."

"Bull," Bubba exploded. "That nigger's goin' to jail."

"My, what a brave man you are, Mr. Spites," Cole jeered. "You provoke a fight with racist remarks, beat up a man in supposed self-defense, then insist on preferring charges against him. To cap it all, you attack a legless cripple."

I froze, stung by his characterization. Cole, however, had his eyes locked on fat boy.

"I don't know how many of your buddies witnessed Mr. Elsbeth's alleged attack on you," the aspiring lawyer went on, "but we have a police officer and several other witnesses who saw you initiate physical violence against Mr. Crow."

"You son of a bitch," Bubba sputtered. "Mr. Fancy Mouthpiece."

"Be careful what you say, Mr. Spites," Cole cautioned. "There are laws against slander."

"Shut up, both of you." Burker motioned to the uniformed officer to move the others outside. They groused but did as they were told.

"Detective Burker, please take the cuffs off Mr. Elsbeth," I repeated. "Spites won't be pressing changes, will you, Bubba? Because if you take in

Mr. Elsbeth," I told the detective while I gazed at my assailant, "you'll be taking him in too. I'm prepared to press charges against him for assault, battery, violation of my civil rights, as well as slander."

"And I'll be contacting the press," Debbie added from the sideline.

After a pause, Burker nodded. The cop removed Aaron's manacles. Burker then proceeded to give everyone a stern lecture on behaving themselves. I wondered if the situation would have been handled with the same kid gloves if the belligerents were not Spites and Crow, or if I wasn't—to use Cole's words—a legless cripple.

The detective ordered Spites to leave. Bubba obeyed, but with a smug grin and a defiant swagger. Only the bloody streak across his pudgy cheek robbed it of its full effect. I almost wished I'd put it there on purpose. At the door he turned and faced me. "Just remember, your old man ain't around no more to take care of you and your nigger friends." He gazed at me, the gleam in his brown eyes viciously triumphant. "Plastic man, yeah." Then he left.

Burker studied Aaron for a long moment. "Mind telling me what that was all about?"

"Nothing."

"I can't help you if you won't let me."

Aaron lifted his head, his eyes narrowed, bitter. "Leave me alone." He started to get up, but exhaustion and anger made him shaky. Debbie's hand reached out for his.

"You all right?" I asked.

"Fine." He intertwined his fingers with hers, then looked at me. "Thanks for coming to my rescue. I'm sorry he knocked you down. You hurt?"

"Only my pride."

"He has a way of doing that, doesn't he?" We exchanged weak smiles.

"How'd all this start?" Burker pressed.

Aaron told him, "I was out riding—" he didn't mention it had been since the night before "—and was on my way home when I thought I—" he stopped, then resumed "—when I realized I was hungry, so I decided to grab a sandwich. Bubba was by himself in a booth. I got a glass of iced tea and waited for my order to be called." He rubbed his wrists where the cuffs had chafed. "The waitress told Bubba he had a phone call. He went behind the counter to answer it and was just coming out when I went to pick up my food. He brushed past me and started the 'who do you think you're pushing, boy' routine. I tried to ignore him, but his friends were coming in. Having an audience egged him on."

I listened. Something was out of kilter. I'd seen Aaron in similar spots a time or two and admired his ability to defuse tense situations without losing dignity.

"When he brought Debbie's name into it," Aaron said, "I took a swing at him. And missed. The next thing I knew, I was on the floor. Bubba was yelling the usual obscenities and about to kick me in the groin when the cop stepped in."

What concerned me was Aaron's ferocious reaction. He'd faced violence more than once—and had the scars to prove it—but he'd always staunchly followed Dr. Martin Luther King, Jr.'s philosophy of non-violence. It seemed inconceivable in this petty incident he'd throw the first punch. I wondered if there was more to the story than he was admitting.

"Look," Burker told Aaron, "take my advice and stay away from Spites. He's never been sympathetic towards colored people, and now he has a special reason to have it in for you."

When the five of us went outside a few minutes later, we found the spokes of Aaron's bike smashed. Zack stowed it in the trunk of the Packard and battened down the lid with the laces from Aaron's sneakers.

At the carriage house, Cole apologized for referring to me as a legless cripple. I wished he'd just let the matter drop.

"It was—"

"Thoughtless," Zack said, "and insensitive."

"Forget it," I said.

Pursing his lips, Cole looked from Zack to me to Zack again, then excused himself to gas up his car.

Under different circumstances I would have changed out of my soiled shirt and pants, but doing so now would take time and Zack's help, and I didn't want to give my sister and Aaron an excuse or an opportunity to leave. Still smelling of rancid grease, mayonnaise, mustard and catsup, I shuffled over to the office and settled into the leather armchair I'd previously occupied, while Debbie and Aaron sat together once more on the couch.

"Debbie says you asked Dad's permission to marry her, and he said no."

Aaron nodded.

I looked at my sister. "Debbie, are you pregnant?"

CHAPTER SIXTEEN

She had her legs tucked at her side as she leaned against Aaron on the couch. We stared at each other.

"That's why you want to get married, isn't it?"

She planted her feet on the floor. "We want to get married because we love each other."

"Don't play games with me, Debbie."

Aaron had bowed his head when I asked the original question. Now he raised it. "Yes." His tone was defiant, but also defensive and maybe just a little scared.

"And Dad opposed it?"

"I told you," she answered. "He kept harping on responsibilities, and before you ask why we weren't more careful—we were, but birth control isn't one hundred percent foolproof. You must know that."

"Foolproof." Aaron snorted. "That's a good one."

I looked at him and my sister. "You told Dad you were pregnant, and he still wouldn't consent to your getting married?" It didn't sound like my father.

"We didn't tell him," she admitted.

"Not then," Aaron said. "I told him later . . . in private."

"After we left Daddy—" Debbie started.

Aaron interrupted her, "I should've laid it on the line from the very beginning, been honest. We have to get married because I've been irresponsible."

"That's not true," Debbie countered.

"Your father was always fair and honest with us. We had no right to deceive him."

Debbie looked aggravated. I got the impression they'd had this conversation before. "I told him we could see Daddy together in the morning, but Aaron insisted on facing him man-to-man that night."

"What time was this?"

Debbie answered. "He left the house at a quarter after twelve. I know because I told him Daddy might already be in bed. He said he'd wake him if he had to."

"He was still up," Aaron said. "Friday's a busy night. He rarely leaves the *Nest* before ten-thirty, and there was a private party that evening in the Crystal Room." He kept rubbing his wrists, as if he were trying to erase marks that weren't there. "But when I was telling him about Debbie and me, about . . . I was nervous, almost afraid." He seemed to be talking to himself. "I remember staring at his tie. There was this pencil-thin violet line. You don't notice it. The pin stripes in his brown vest seemed to match it, yet I was sure they were gray, not violet. It's silly the things you notice sometimes." After a pause he continued. "Anyway, I told him everything."

"What was his reaction?"

"He wanted to know if we'd used birth control. I said we had." Aaron's voice took on a dullness. "He asked me if Debbie had considered getting an abortion, or if she was too far along."

Debbie interrupted again. "Jason, I'm not ashamed of loving Aaron, and I'm not afraid of having his baby. I know it'll be black and that there'll be more incidents like today. My God, don't you think I hear what they call me? I don't care. I love Aaron, and we're going to have our baby."

"But Dad wanted you to get an abortion?"

Aaron shook his head. "He said he just wanted to know if we were considering it, because he was opposed to it. Then he asked if we planned to stay here or if we wanted to go somewhere else, like California, where it might be easier." Aaron paused again, worked his jaw. "I told him this is our home. This is where our families are. I told him we wanted to stay here and raise our child."

Debbie clutched his hand and gazed at him with adoring eyes.

Aaron frowned and his tone became a tender whisper "That's when he seemed to melt," he continued. "I can't think of any other way to describe it. He said he always wanted to be a grandfather. He shook my hand, then put his arms around me." Aaron looked at me, his dark eyes glassy. "He never did that before. He insisted we have a drink, a toast . . . to new life."

The last words came out thickly.

"It sounds like he understood, accepted your decision and supported it," I commented.

"Man, don't you see? He must have killed himself right after that."

"Aaron, do you really think Dad would kill himself just because Debbie's pregnant?"

"God almighty! What's the matter with you? Are you blind too? Don't you see? She's not just pregnant," his voice was shrill, "she's pregnant with my black bastard."

She pulled back, her blue eyes wide, then threw herself against him.

"Don't ever say that," she cried out, hugging him. "Never, never, never. Promise me."

Aaron drew her to him, and they clutched each other. Then he gently eased her away. "You know I love you. But your Dad was right. You should get an abortion."

"No!" She covered her face with her hands. "I won't, I won't." The words were muffled with tears.

I looked at Zack whose expression mirrored the helplessness I felt. I waited for my sister's crying to subside.

"Aaron, how long were you with Dad?"

"Half an hour, maybe a little more."

Again Debbie furnished the precise time. "It was a quarter after one when he got back. He was gone exactly an hour. I know because I was watching the clock. I thought about following him over here, then realized I'd just upset him. I knew Daddy would understand once Aaron explained things to him."

"And he did." I turned to Aaron. "You said you even shared a toast?"

"He opened a bottle of champagne, Dom Perignon."

The one Burker had been examining.

"I took a sip to be polite, but I don't really like champagne. Besides, I wanted to get back and tell Debbie the good news."

They looked at each other. She murmured. "We were together the rest of the night."

I had no doubt how they had spent the time. I thought of Michiko. I'd seen that look in her eyes when we'd made love. I wondered if I ever would again.

"There's something I wanted to ask you," I told Aaron. "At *The Joint* I noticed you started to say something to Burker and changed your mind. What was it?"

I detected a moment's hesitation. "The reason I stopped there was because I thought I saw Leon outside. I called to him but by the time I was able to cross traffic he, if it was him, had disappeared."

I was glad he'd kept that piece of information to himself. I didn't have to ask why. Leon was a draft dodger.

Aaron shook his head. "He was ahead of me on the other side of Hopkins Street, walking toward the place, so I didn't see him from the front. I was sure it was him at the time, but I might've been wrong."

I wondered why Leon would be in that neighborhood. He could have been visiting someone, I supposed, but if he was, why did he disappear when Aaron called out to him?

Debbie and Aaron climbed to their feet, obviously antsy to leave, but

I couldn't let them go without some reassurance.

"You weren't responsible for what happened last night," I said. "I want you to know that."

Both faced me squarely. I could see hope and fear in their expressions.

"I don't know what exactly did happen, but I can assure you it wasn't because of either of you. Or me," I added.

Debbie bit her lips and nodded. Tears were close. Aaron put his arm around her. I didn't miss the gratitude for my words in his dark, glassy eyes.

I let them go. I didn't go so far as to tell them Dad hadn't committed suicide, that he'd been murdered. Why had I held back? Because their lives were complicated enough? Wasn't that why Dad had kept things from me? Would murder be a consolation to them as it was to me, or would it increase their paranoia? Were they in danger? Should I have put them on guard?

There was of course another reason for my not saying anything. I had to consider the possibility that Aaron had killed my father.

My first impulse was to dismiss the notion. George and my father had been friends for over twenty years, most of Aaron's life. Aaron's description of his conversation with Dad rang absolutely true. Dad would have posed those questions. To someone who didn't know him, they might have sounded insulting or like a rejection. At least until the punch line—the announcement that he always wanted to be a grandfather—and the emotional embrace.

He'd never see his grandchildren now.

As for Aaron's blaming himself for Dad's death . . .

Aaron was no coward, but I couldn't fault him for being scared. The social shunning from both races and the threats of physical violence that awaited them were likely to be all the more difficult without the strength and support of my father. It was then a new thought struck me, one that filled me with apprehension and doubt. Given my brother's status and my mother's fragility, I was now, for all intents and purposes, the head of the family.

Oh, Dad, a voice inside me cried out. *I'm not ready. How can I be when—*

But I could hear him as clearly as if he were standing directly in front of me. *We're not quitters, you and I. We make the best of the hand fate deals us. We're not quitters . . .*

CHAPTER SEVENTEEN

Zack put out a tray of cheese, crackers and fruit, while I cleaned up as best I could. Cole returned. I was filling him in on the circumstances surrounding my father's death, when I heard the outside door open and close. A knock followed and George came in. He epitomized a man suffering from a severe hangover, but the pained expression in his bloodshot eyes could as well have been interpreted as grief. He wasn't surprised to find Cole there; he'd seen his Volvo in the courtyard. He greeted him, then apologized to me for the previous night. I assured him no apology was necessary. But that was only part of the reason he'd come.

"Been getting calls all morning from folks wanting to offer their condolences, so I'm gonna open the Crystal Room in an hour for people to come by."

He and my father would have conferred about such a decision, but he wasn't asking my advice. Why should he? The message was clear, whether intended or not: I may be the head of the Crow family, but he was in charge of the *Nest*. I was glad, thanked him and agreed to join him and the others, then watched him leave. I'd been so focused on Dad, that I hadn't thought to ask Aaron if his father knew about Debbie's pregnancy. I suspected not. George wouldn't be happy when he found out, especially when he'd opposed their shacking up in the first place.

Michiko arrived a few minutes later, looking tired and tense. She shook hands with Cole, ignored Zack, kissed me on the cheek and settled onto the couch.

"Where have all of you been?" she asked. "I called earlier, but there was no answer. What's up?"

I told her about the incident at *The Joint*, about Debbie's pregnancy and Aaron's late-night visit with my father.

"It's going to be tough for them," she said. "Outcasts of both races. It'll be especially hard for the kid."

She knew from personal experience what she was talking about. Her father was an Army Sergeant Major who'd married a Japanese woman during the Occupation and retired in Japan afterward. Michiko had been brought up there, but she'd also spent summers in Alabama with her grandparents and cousins. More than once she'd heard herself referred to as a Jap or a slope or a slant-eye, while back "home" she was derided as *hambun-hambun*, a half-breed. She was as American as apple pie and as mysterious as the fabled Orient.

"I'm sorry about your father's suicide," Cole commented. "A terrible tragedy."

"It wasn't suicide, Cole. My father was murdered."

Michiko gasped and covered her mouth. The room became very still. Cole frowned and studied his hands.

"You met my father," I continued. "What did you think of him?"

"You mean did I get the impression he was self-destructive? Of course not. I liked him, but that doesn't mean I knew him. I don't suppose most suicides show their intentions except in retrospect."

"In retrospect then, did you see any indication he was unhappy?"

Cole rotated a nearly empty beer bottle in his hand. He'd taken Zack's offer of a Coors rather than iced tea, since the distinctive Colorado brew wasn't available in Austin.

"Jason, last Sunday the four of us spent a few minutes together here, before going down to dinner with a group of people I'd never met before. That's hardly enough time for me to evaluate a stranger's frame of mind."

Cole looked at Zack as if he were responsible for this aberration of my mental powers. He turned back to me. "Who would want to kill your father anyway, and why?"

"I don't know the answer to either of those questions right now."

"Do the police think it was murder? Is there some evidence of foul play?"

"The investigating officer's convinced it was suicide."

"Yet you think he was murdered?"

Michiko said nothing. I saw her skepticism, took a deep breath and recited the circumstances of my father's death in the same staccato manner Burker had used. One bullet in the head. The gun still in his hand. No signs of a struggle. The middle of the night. Drinking.

"But you don't believe it," Cole countered. "Why? Be specific." He asked for another beer, which Zack went to fetch.

"Several reasons," I replied. "I'll give you just three. First of all, there was no reason for him to kill himself. Second, he didn't leave a note. And third, the gun he used was mine."

Cole cocked his head to one side. "Yours?"

"I'm not saying my father would never have committed suicide if there was justification. But even if he'd been despondent over something—and he wasn't over what happened to me, if that's what you're assuming—there's no way he would have used my gun. It would have been unthinkable."

Zack returned with a fresh beer. Cole's usually bland features showed uneasiness. He took a sip from the already opened bottle. "You said yourself, Aaron and your father were drinking the other night."

"They shared a toast," I countered. "That doesn't constitute heavy drinking."

"I'm not suggesting it does. I'm just trying to put this in context. One drink leads to another. After Aaron left, what's to say your father didn't decide to have one more glass while he mulled things over, then another?"

"If you think Dad would become depressed over Debbie's relationship with Aaron," I told him, "you're wrong. He knew what was going on. My father wasn't a bigot."

Cole held his free hand up in surrender. "Jason, nobody's saying he was, but even if he wasn't upset about their affair, her pregnancy couldn't have been a pleasant surprise. Forget for a moment that Aaron is a Negro. Being told your teenage daughter is pregnant out of wedlock isn't exactly good news. It wouldn't be enough to kill yourself over, but it might be reason to take another drink."

"For somebody else perhaps. I know what you're leading up to. Okay, Dad might have finished his glass after Aaron left, but not the whole bottle. He had a little wine with dinner, as you saw on Sunday, and once in a while a nightcap with Zack and me, or with George, but he wasn't a heavy drinker, and he didn't drink alone."

"That you know of," Cole said. "I can see why the police are satisfied with suicide—unless you have some evidence you haven't mentioned."

"Damn it," Zack exploded, "isn't that enough? Jason's gun, the fact that he left no note, and that pesky little detail that he had no reason to kill himself?"

Cole remained calm. "Zack, everything Jason's said is easily explained. I don't think anyone, including the police, will give much credence to Jason's feelings, no matter how sympathetic they may be to him." Cole showed me his palm. "Wait, let me finish. You say your father had no reason to kill himself. I agree he didn't seem suicidal last Sunday, but that's not when he died. A man's attitudes can change dramatically between Sunday afternoon when he's surrounded by friends and family, and Friday night when he's all alone. Did anything happen, did he get any other bad news during that time?"

I told him about my mother's demand for a divorce so she could give away the family ranch, and the IRS audit.

"I'm sorry, Jason. You must see that taken altogether it's a pretty grim picture. As for not leaving a note, well, consider this possibility. Your father has insomnia and gets up. He starts reminiscing. I'm sorry to bring this up but it can't be ignored. What happened to you must have been a terrible disappointment for him. Your promising athletic career shattered . . . your prospects limited . . . anyway, he starts thinking about you and sees your gun. He picks it up while grieving about you and worrying about the rest of his problems, and . . . and on an impulse puts it to his temple and pulls the trigger."

"You're right," I said. "You didn't know him." I turned to Zack. "Do you accept that scenario?"

"No. For one thing, your father never took the guns from the cabinet except to clean them, and there was no cleaning stuff out. He also didn't keep them loaded, and he wasn't a man who acted on impulse, certainly not with a loaded gun in his hand."

Cole looked disappointed and impatient. I could appreciate his frustration. It was like arguing with a fanatic—the more logic you give him to prove you're right, the more he attacks reason.

"Michiko, you didn't know my father as well as Zack, but you knew him better than Cole. Do you think Cole's description is reasonable?"

For some time she had been looking at Zack, apparently sharing Cole's attitude that he was responsible for my distorted frame of mind.

"I could accept suicide if he hadn't used your gun," she said. "Not leaving a note bothers me too."

"So you don't think my father committed suicide?" I persisted. Her answer was crucial, not to my conviction that he'd been murdered, but in our relationship. If she accepted Cole's premises, she was saying I was a factor in Dad's death, and that'd be a hurdle I couldn't imagine leaping over—with or without legs.

"No." She was more decisive this time. "It couldn't have been an accident, so it must have been murder. But why, Jason?"

"Will you help me find out?"

"Any way I can."

"Cole, it's back to you. Do you still think my father killed himself?"

He'd played spoiler very well Friday night when we talked about starting a vineyard, but then a little while ago he'd offered to invest in the venture. I was expecting him to reverse himself this time as well. He shook his head. "From what you've told me, Jason, I honestly think he did."

My heart sank.

"You tend to idealize him, you know," he went on, "you and Zack. You saw him the way you wanted and ignored what didn't conform to your perfect image of him. That's natural. It's what everyone does with the people they love, defend them, protect their memory."

Cole could see he wasn't convincing anyone. "Look, sometimes people let us down. You remember General Dilworth? I worked for him here in the States and then again over in 'Nam. I admired and respected that man, and to be frank, I was hoping to ride his coattails. You asked me last Sunday why I got out of the Air Force. I'll tell you. Because I found out Dilworth was involved in the drug racket over there."

Cole scowled as he contemplated the pattern in the Chinese silk rug. "My shining star," he continued, "the leader I looked up to was dealing drugs in a combat zone. By the time Tet hit, I'd already made up my mind to leave the Air Force."

When Cole announced he'd resigned his commission after six years of active duty, Zack had been astonished. Cole seemed molded for full colonel, maybe general someday. But these were the worst of times. Service academies were having cheating scandals. Colonels, generals and sergeants major were masterminding slot machine rackets in combat zones. Red light districts were being run by military brass, and drugs were being used, not just behind the lines, but in combat itself.

"How can anyone take pride in the uniform anymore?" Zack wondered out loud. "Here at home, marchers and protesters are encouraging servicemen to desert. Movie stars are committing treason by giving aid and comfort to the enemy. Priests and ministers are burning draft cards or pouring blood on Selective Service files. GIs are being cursed and spat upon. The American flag, the very symbol of the freedom that allows them to carry out these desecrations, is being burned. America the Beautiful! The Land of the Free is befouling the Home of the Brave."

Cole broke the tense silence that followed. "Please don't misunderstand me, Jason. I'm not suggesting your father was doing anything wrong. What I'm saying is we all have our limits, and people disappoint us sometimes. Your father had his limits like the rest of us. I'm sorry he let you down."

I shook my head. "You're wrong. My father wasn't perfect, but he'd never have abandoned me. Not now when I needed him more than ever. Not like this."

"Okay, how's this for a compromise?" Cole said. "I think your father killed himself, but I also see it's important for you to understand why. So if I can help you figure that out, I will. Let me put it another way. You want to look into the specific causes of your father's death. Okay, count me in. I'll assist in any way I can. I just hope it doesn't hurt more than it helps."

In other words, Cole was warning me, dig too deeply and you'll find your father's feet were made of clay.

"I'll take that chance," I told him, "because I'm completely confident I knew my father."

"How long do you think the reception will last?" Michiko asked me a few seconds later.

The abrupt change of subject caught me off guard. "Oh, I don't know. An hour or two. Why?"

"My shift starts at six."

"You just got off mids," I protested. Would I never get to spend time with her alone?

"The IG hit us with a surprise visit this morning," she said. "Everybody's pulling extra duty."

As former military officers, we all knew how nerve-racking inspector-general visits were, how hectic it could be trying to steer nosy outsiders around things you didn't want them to see, or doing things twice to make sure they were done at least once. There would be the idiotic stuff that seemed to impress inspectors: dust mops that didn't have a speck of dust on them; water fountains that didn't show water marks. We all sympathized with her, knowing from experience how frustrating and stupid the game could be.

She also announced she'd received a package on Friday from her parents in Japan with some things for me. She asked Cole if he'd help her bring them up from her car.

"Have I miscalculated?" I asked Zack after they left. "Cole does make it sound convincing. Even Michiko's not sure."

Zack smirked. "He's practicing to be a lawyer."

Cole returned a few minutes later straining under a stack of books about Japanese art, history and culture. People were already arriving for the reception at the *Crow's Nest.* For some time, we'd been hearing vehicles pulling into the parking lot and car doors slamming.

Cole had just dumped the books on the corner of the desk when Ned Herman came bursting into the room. He stopped in front of me, the shock on his face turning to one of stunned disbelief.

CHAPTER EIGHTEEN

"But . . . But you're supposed to be—" Ned's dark eyes blazed. "If this is your idea of a joke?"

I knew instantly what had happened. The woman at Ned's rooming house in Austin had gotten my message mixed up.

Ned wilted into the armchair by the door. "I decided to stay in Midland to see a drilling operation tomorrow, so I called my landlady to let her know. She told me Mr. Crow phoned from Coyote Springs to say his son had died." He looked at me in embarrassment. "I called here but there was no answer."

"I'm sorry, Ned," I said, "I'm afraid she got it backwards. It was my father who died."

"Your father? Oh God, Jason, I'm sorry. What happened? Heart attack?"

"No." I was about to elaborate when Cole interrupted.

"I need to get going. I can never be sure how long the drive will take me in that clunker of mine." He turned to Ned. "I'm glad you're here. You were able to talk these guys into starting a vineyard, so you obviously have some influence on them. See if you can straighten them out this time. Jason has this crazy notion that his father was murdered."

"Murdered? Are you serious?"

"Jason's father killed himself the night before last," Cole explained. "Now Jason's got it in his head that he was murdered, and Zack here seems to be going along with him."

Ned gaped at Zack. "What in the name of God—"

"I appreciate your loyalty to Jason," Cole told Zack. "It's admirable. But I think you're doing our friend a disservice by encouraging him. Unless there's something he hasn't told me, he just doesn't have a leg to stand on." He winced. "Sorry, poor choice of words." He reached across the desk and shook my hand. "Remember, if there's anything I can do to help . . . "

"Thanks for coming," I said, then added, "and for your candor. It means a lot."

Ned kept staring at me. "You want to tell me what the hell's going on?" he said after Cole left.

Zack got him a glass of iced tea. A minute later we could hear Cole's engine catch on the third try, its rusted-out muffler reverberating between the walls of the *Nest* and the carriage house.

"What time did you leave Austin Friday night?" I asked Ned.

"Right after I saw you guys. Around six, six-thirty. I stopped at home to pick up some things, then hit the road."

"Did you go directly to Midland?"

"Yeah. Why?"

"I was wondering if you stopped off here. I'm trying to put together my father's last hours, find out what frame of mind he was in."

"I thought about coming by to say hello, but it'd mean a delay of at least an hour, and I didn't want to take the time. Besides, I knew your dad would insist on buying me dinner. I don't like to drive on a full stomach, especially at night. And . . . I didn't want him to think I was freeloading, so I gassed up and kept going."

Unlike Cole, who clearly had a healthy bank account, Ned didn't. His need for frugality occasionally made him overly sensitive about accepting the generosity of others. I'd wondered if his passing up Cole's invitation to dinner at *Chez Pierre* Friday night might have been one of those occasions.

"Boy, you really put the pedal to the metal," Zack commented. "I'm surprised you didn't blow that little engine of yours."

Ned awarded him a mocking scowl. "I was planning to stop by on the way home."

No help from Ned, unfortunately. Even if he'd come by the *Nest*, it would have been when Dad was having dinner with Debby and Aaron. Besides, Dad died well after midnight, not at nine or ten o'clock. Of course, Ned could have driven back from Midland later . . .

But why would he? He had no motive to hurt my father.

At a quarter past two, Zack, Michiko and Ned followed me, freshly attired, as I used the handrail to pull myself up the ramp to the back door of the *Nest*. George met us in the hallway outside what had been the mansion's original dining room, now called the parlor. He was dressed in a dark blue suit, white shirt and black tie, a sharp contrast to his usual happy plaids and colorful neckwear. His brown face was puffy with sadness and fatigue. He thanked Ned for coming.

Debbie and Aaron were also there. The side of Aaron's face was shiny and swollen from the battering he'd taken that morning.

"Were you able to get hold of Mom?" I asked Debbie.

"Yeah, I called her, offered to go out to the ranch and pick her up. She said her solace is in the bosom of her church."

I shook my head, disappointed. "And Lee?"

"He doesn't have a phone," Aaron reminded me. "I sent one of the busboys over to his place to invite him. He sent back word he might be over later."

Which meant he probably wouldn't show. Being marked as a draft dodger didn't make him very popular. Under the circumstances staying away was probably just as well. Still the situation depressed me. It also made me wonder why my brother had come back to Coyote Springs at all.

We proceeded down the central hallway, past the broad staircase, and turned left into the most impressive room in the mansion. The Crystal Room was paneled in native pecan. A crystal chandelier hung from the center of the medallioned ceiling, but that wasn't the reason for the name. The outside corner of the room was a full length curved window composed of hundreds of leaded panes. The beveled glass prisms twinkled with thousands of rainbow colors in the daylight. At night the reflection of the inside fixtures had a similar effect.

A long, German baroque buffet opposite the double entry doors was covered with plates, bowls and platters of food, all brought by friends and neighbors. It seemed ironic for people to bring food to a restaurant, but some customs were sacred. Besides, today the old house had reverted to its original function, that of a home.

About twenty-five people were gathered in clusters, a few blacks and Hispanics on the periphery. There was a hush when we walked in, all eyes initially focusing on me. Not an unfamiliar experience. My height had always drawn people's attention when I entered a room. Now they watched me for a different reason.

But there were other curiosities, as well. The forbidden liaison between my sister and Aaron. Michiko's mysterious, Oriental beauty. Ned drew a few glances too. At six-one, he was tall, but his big bones and bulging muscles made him impressive. The recent addition of a swirling handlebar mustache emphasized his Latin heritage and added to the macho image he cultivated.

The way people greeted me was understandably awkward. A death had brought them here. The perception of it being a suicide complicated matters. Many of them also seemed uncertain about how to react to my walking—ignore it or congratulate me on my achievement. Others were uncomfortable with Debbie and Aaron. A few even murmured comments behind their hands.

When formal salutations were finally completed and people began helping themselves to the generous spread of food, I found myself cornered by Ernest Scarphanian, the city's mayor. He was average in height but burly.

"As you probably know," he rumbled, "I'm not running for reelection. Been trying to talk your daddy into throwing his hat in the ring, and per usual, he didn't seem much interested. Leastways not at first. I thought he was coming round this time though."

I tried not to show my surprise. Dad hadn't said anything to me about it. Because he considered it not worth mentioning? Or was this another secret he'd kept from me?

"Look at this referendum he just introduced," Scarphanian went on, "turning downtown into a mall, closing off certain streets to motor traffic and putting in nice promenades with trees and fountains and things. It's a first-class plan that'll increase tax revenue instead of decrease it, and it'll save the heart of the city."

I knew one of the plan's chief opponents was Brayton Spites. He wanted the city to build a separate mall southwest of town on property he held a major interest in and to grant special tax breaks as an incentive for investors, mostly his friends.

While Mayor Scarphanian was expounding his views to the men, his wife, Glorianna, a large, square-framed woman of prodigious proportions, with dyed jet-black hair and a matronly demeanor, was discoursing with the womenfolk. She had the kind of voice that could be heard over a steam locomotive in a train station. Only a few feet away, I had no trouble hearing even her discreet asides.

"Your ma ain't here?" she asked Debbie. "Well, I ain't really surprised. She never was much good at handling a crisis. When her daddy passed years back, your pa had to practically carry her through the services. Mercy, your granddaddy would turn over in his grave to see what's going on now."

She helped herself to another heaping plateful of finger sandwiches, her fourth. Debbie caught my eye, smiled dolefully and sighed. Glorianna bellowed on in what she probably thought was a whisper.

"I remember when your pa proposed to her. Even then your ma couldn't seem to make up her mind—not that she had another offer waitin', mind you. You'd think she had all the time in the world and she was doing Theo a favor instead of the other way round. Your grandpa now, he was real pleased. Said it was nice to know someone was acting responsible, even if he wasn't a Christian."

She patted Debbie on the arm, then flicked breadcrumbs off her ample bosom. "I could just cry when I think of what's happened to him. He's doing real good though, ain't he?" It took a moment to realize the woman had changed subjects and was referring to me. "He's a remarkable young man," she went on without stopping for breath. "This must be 'specially difficult for him, after what happened."

Just then Helga Collins, the editorial page columnist at the *Gazette*, arrived. Somewhere between forty and fifty, a little gray showing in her auburn hair, Mrs. Collins dressed with simple elegance. English-born, she'd come to Coyote Springs as the young wife of an American instructor-pilot stationed at Coyote Field after World War Two. He'd been killed early in the Korean War.

She strode directly up to me and put out her hands. I bent, kissed her cheek and gently squeezed her fingers. As I did so, I noticed Zack staring at the young lady accompanying her.

"Jason, I don't believe you've met my niece, Nancy Brewster." Helga still spoke with a crisp English accent that seemed completely out of place in West Texas.

"I'm sorry about your father," Nancy said, looking up at me with pretty blue eyes. "I met him only a couple of times, but I liked him. I know you'll miss him."

I thanked her and glanced at Zack who couldn't seem to take his eyes off her. Helga hugged and kissed the others: George, Michiko, Debbie, and Aaron. Within minutes of taking a seat and accepting a glass of white wine from George, she was talking politics with one of the members of the city council. This was her milieu. She and my father had generally agreed on world affairs, but they often arrived at the same conclusions from different perspectives. It made for interesting discussions.

Grover Reed, our family lawyer, was the next to arrive. After the usual expressions of condolence he asked me if I expected the steakhouse to stay open.

"That'll be up to Mr. Elsbeth."

He looked up at me. "George is a good man and a damn fine waiter, but you can't expect him to run this place without your father. I'm sure you don't want to embarrass him. Or lose money."

It was a common sentiment, one I resented on George's behalf. I was also confident the future would prove them wrong. Reed moved off, but before doing so I overheard him ask Zack to come by his office at his convenience in the next day or two. Zack asked him something I couldn't hear. A moment later the group of women around Ned burst into laughter, no doubt at one of his vast repertoire of jokes. The mirth was cut short, however, by a surprise visitor whom, I realized, I should have expected.

CHAPTER NINETEEN

The room fell silent when Brayton Spites entered. We made brief eye contact, but his attention was instantly drawn to Michiko who was standing at my side. Were the man closer, younger or had his salacious gaze lingered a second longer than it did, I would have taken a swing at him. The memory of my earlier encounter with his son Bubba rankled, but legs or no legs I'd crawl through a garbage dump before I'd let any man threaten those close to me. I could wash off dirt, but I couldn't cleanse myself of the odor of cowardice.

As though he'd read my mind, Spites shifted his attention away from Michiko and focused on me. People cleared an aisle between us. He approached like an ambassador presenting his credentials. Along the way he bestowed a gentle pat on Debbie's arm, from which she flinched. He slanted Zack a nod of recognition, totally ignored the Elsbeths, and peered uncertainly at Ned who stood beside me, a member of the palace guard.

My father's antagonist was tall and lean, big-boned and loose-jointed with little spare flesh save for a slight paunch that was more the result of middle age and physical inactivity than overindulgence in foodstuffs. His shiny black hair was still thick. He'd let it grow over his ears and collar in the contemporary vogue. His high cheek bones hinted of American Indian. He had dark-brown eyes that could be uncomfortably piercing, and a full, expressive mouth. I'd heard women call him handsome. Perhaps he was in his younger days, but time and alcohol had taken its toll. His once-smooth complexion had coarsened over the years. Lines and wrinkles bracketed his features. In a long black frock coat he could have convincingly played the part of Simon Legree.

He shook hands with several people as he approached, then stood directly in front of me. Previously I'd been several inches taller than he. Now I was less than two. Still, he had to look up and did so with an appropriately somber expression. He extended his hand. I accepted it perfunctorily. His grasp was firm and leathery.

"I'm glad you're home again, Jason. I sincerely wish it were under different circumstances. Life isn't fair, but I don't have to tell you that. Please accept my condolences for all that's happened. If at any time I can be of assistance, don't hesitate to call on me."

"I'll keep that in mind," I said.

"And this beautiful young lady?" He turned to face Michiko.

I made a brief introduction and was gratified to see she didn't offer her hand, reverting instead to her demure Japanese feminine good manners. She joined her hands in front of her and awarded him a simple nod, not the deep bow that tradition demanded of a younger woman to a senior, more socially prominent male. I wondered if Spites was at all aware that he was getting the Oriental version of the cold shoulder.

Spites half turned to the crowd beginning to close in around us and in a clear, sonorously deep voice eulogized his dead competitor.

"Theodore Crow was a good family man as well as a worthy opponent. I always respected him for his integrity, civic mindedness and foresight. It's true he and I occasionally disagreed, sometimes strongly, but it was always an honest difference of opinion, devoid of bitterness and recrimination."

What I found so unsettling was that it was all true—on my father's part. That the largess hadn't been reciprocated was outrageously, even proudly implied.

The quality of Spites was that his listeners often found themselves believing him, trusting he meant what he said, since much of it was correct. What he was saying in this case was that my father was a virtuous man. What his presence implied was that the corrupt survive.

He was greeted by several sycophants as he wandered to the drinks table where he poured a generous double shot of Bourbon into an old-fashion glass and downed half of it in one gulp. Conversation in the room resumed.

I waited another ten minutes before I stood in front of the buffet facing the assembly.

"Ladies and Gentlemen," I called out. "May I have your attention please?" The drone of voices subsided. "I want to thank y'all for coming here today, for your kind words of condolence, and for the many nice things you've said about my dad. I know he'd be embarrassed to hear so many accolades heaped upon him."

A polite murmur of approval rippled through the room.

"Only a few of you have voiced the question I know has been on everyone's mind. Why did my father kill himself? Some of you have commented on how at ease he seemed to be lately, and a few of you have asked if he left a note."

There was a nervous suspension of breathing and an uncomfortable heaviness in the air. Most of my audience lowered their eyes in embarrassment. Few continued to look directly at me.

"My father didn't leave a suicide note for a very good reason. He didn't commit suicide. He was murdered."

Heads shot up. I watched the faces around me and saw the predictable expressions of shock and horror on most of them. A few shook their heads in pity. Their reactions didn't surprise me, nor did they make me angry. I wasn't seeking their approval or agreement.

"You don't really believe that," said the mayor.

"With all my heart." I glanced at Spites, who was standing alone near the main entrance with a curious expression on his face. He was sizing me up in a way that sent shivers down my spine.

"But why?" the mayor's wife asked in her not-so-quiet voice. It brought everyone's attention back to me.

"Because my father had no reason to kill himself. Mrs. Collins said it very well when she wrote that a man's actions are guided by reason and logic. She was describing my father. Have any of you ever known him to act impulsively, based purely on emotion? That wasn't how he did things. My father didn't run from problems. He faced them and met them head-on. He wasn't a quitter."

I sought eye contact with the columnist and was disconcerted when she too avoided it.

"But the police say—" someone called out.

"They're wrong," I stated categorically. I had to speak over the rush of voices now. "They didn't know the man. I did. Most of you knew him well enough to realize what I'm saying is true." I looked again at Helga Collins, but her face was downcast, intently examining the hanky in her hands.

"Why would anyone kill him?" another man asked.

"I don't know," I replied. "Not yet."

There were more questions from various quarters. Some I answered, a few I admitted I couldn't.

"What do you intend to do?" a councilman asked.

"Find his murderer and make him pay."

Was the killer in this room? It didn't matter. It wouldn't take long for word to spread that I was out for blood. Would that frighten him, spook him enough to do something stupid? Or would the killer go on the attack? Outmaneuvering what Cole called a legless cripple ought to be easy.

Gradually the uproar mellowed into social chatter. The room seemed split into three factions, those who agreed with me, those who thought I was nuts, and those who couldn't make up their minds.

Brayton Spites was among the first to leave. He made no reference to my declaration, simply thanked me for allowing him to visit and wished me the best of luck in my future endeavors. I would have liked to question him about his appointment with my father for the previous afternoon and to get his reaction to the episode with Bubba at *The Joint* earlier that day. But those matters would have to wait for a private discussion.

A few minutes later Helga Collins came up to me and took my right hand between both of hers. "That was a brave thing you just did. Theodore would be pleased." I saw tears in her eyes. She turned quickly away.

Nancy stepped up. "I'm glad to have finally met you, Jason. I wish it were under different circumstances. I liked your dad. If there's anything I can do to help you find the person who killed him, don't hesitate to ask."

It was a stunning, unexpected and unconditional vote of support. For a moment I felt speechless. "Thank you."

She turned to Zack. "Do you know where my aunt lives?"

He nodded.

"I'm staying in her rental cottage in back." She hurried off to join the older woman.

By four o'clock all the guests had left. I caught a glimpse of George over by the bar. No wine today. He'd been nursing iced tea all afternoon. He looked shaken by my declaration.

Debbie approached and kissed me on the cheek. "I'm glad, Jason. I'm glad it wasn't suicide," she said with tears in her eyes.

Aaron stepped up beside her. "What can I do to help?" I didn't miss the sense of relief with which he asked the question.

CHAPTER TWENTY

After Aaron and Debbie left, George shooed the rest of us out. I looked at my watch. It was after four. Michiko had to be to work at six, hardly sufficient time for what I—and I hoped she—had in mind. "Not a lot of time."

"Not enough." Her smile confirmed what I felt, while her eyes reflected my disappointment.

"How about we go somewhere, have a beer, and talk about the vineyard," Ned suggested. "It's still a go, isn't it?"

"It's a go," I said. "But this is Sunday in Coyote Springs, not San Francisco."

He wagged his head. "What you're telling me is the bars are all closed. Oh, wait. There are no bars." He clicked his tongue.

"The Officers Club on base is open," Michiko said.

"Ugh," Ned groaned.

I was plodding my way across the courtyard toward the carriage house when two people emerged from the breezeway, blocking my access to the elevator. The woman in front held a microphone. The brawny guy behind her had a TV camera mounted on his right shoulder.

"Jason Crow—" she marched aggressively toward me "—why do you think your father was murdered? Do you know who did it and why?" She thrust the mic like a sword in front of her.

Obviously my announcement was out, which was what I wanted, to put the murderer on alert. I considered giving an interview, but I had two problems. I didn't know this woman, didn't know what agenda she might have, and I didn't want to get trapped into revealing how little real evidence I had to substantiate my claim. Better, I decided, to keep people guessing.

"No comment."

"The police were confident yesterday he took his own life. What new evidence do you have to prove he was murdered?"

"I said, no comment."

"Do you have a particular suspect in mind? What kind of proof do you have against him . . . or her?"

"I have no comment to make. Please get out of my way."

Zack interposed himself between the reporter and me. Michiko crowded her from the other side. Ned brushed past me and blocked the cameraman's view.

"Hey, watch out, buddy," the guy exclaimed, as he danced under the weight of his heavy video camera.

I raised my hands. "I have nothing to say. Please leave."

"This is a parking lot," the reporter objected. "We have a right—"

"Wrong," Zack shot back. "This is private property, and you've been asked to leave. I suggest you do so before I call the police and have you arrested for trespassing."

"You can't do that."

"Wanna bet?"

It took another minute of verbal jousting, but they packed up and left.

"Probably won't be the last," Ned said. "Come on. Let's go to the O club for a beer. At least on base you won't have to dodge reporters."

"I don't want a beer," I objected. I wanted to go home with Michiko.

"Then have a coke," Ned argued.

Michiko slipped her hand into mine. "He's right. You need to get away from here for a while. I wish there were more time, but—"

She didn't have to finish. I'd been dreaming of being alone with her for so long. I considered asking her to take me to her place where we'd be assured privacy, but getting into and out of her little MG with my long, ungainly legs would be impossible, and she'd have to bring me back before going to work, further limiting our time together. Damn it, I didn't want constraints on our first opportunity for intimacy, and I didn't want every move I made to be a logistical nightmare. I wanted my life back.

"Okay," I agreed because there wasn't much in the way of alternatives.

"You go with Zack and Ned," she said. "I'll run home, change into my uniform and join you there."

A minute later she was driving away in her MG, and I was lifting my dead legs, one at a time, into the back seat of the Packard.

The Air Policeman on duty waved us through the south gate of the base.

I found stateside officers clubs to be anachronisms, holdovers from a time when being a military officer was reserved for white "gentlemen," when the officer corps had a monopoly on education and sometimes literacy, when a commission was reserved mostly for the sons of the elite, the well-bred. Those days were gone, but the exclusive clubs still existed.

The O club on Coyote AFB was neither shabby nor elegant, only badly designed, a hodge-podge of several buildings. The main bar was neo-Greek, the dining room quasi-colonial, and the ballroom split-level. On Sunday afternoon, it was a museum.

The lounge was off the lobby. The long bar had a brass foot rail. No way could I sit on one of the high stools, however. Fortunately tables lined the opposite wall. We sat at the nearest one which happened to be half-hidden behind a cluster of potted plants.

Zack went to the bar and brought back drafts for him and Ned and a Seven-Up for me.

Michiko joined us a few minutes later wearing her white nurse's uniform. The fake foliage was apparently more effective than I realized, because she scanned the room twice before finally spying us. Ned got up and escorted her to the table—something I would have done without thinking in the past—and took her drink request to the bar.

She bent over me, placed a hand on my left cheek and kissed me softly on the right temple. Her delicate scent was sparking synapses in my confused brain. I wanted the rest of the world to go away.

Ned placed her coke on the table. "Come on, Zack." He picked up his beer mug. "Let's go sit at the bar and give these two some privacy."

I should have protested, but I didn't.

"What have the three of you been talking about?" she asked after sipping through her straw.

"Trying to figure out how it was done."

"Did you?"

"No." I rotated my nearly untouched glass of Seven-Up. "But I will."

She nodded, head bowed, then raised it. "You promised the other night to give me the lowdown on why your dad and Brayton Spites were enemies. Now that I've met him . . . interesting man, I must say . . . how about filling me in?"

CHAPTER TWENTY-ONE

I debated how much I should reveal. It would all come out eventually, and I wanted to be the one to tell her when the time came. Not yet though. I leaned back in the chair and splayed my hands on the tabletop

"Until twelve years ago Dad worked for Spites as his accountant and financial manager. Spites has a reputation for shoddy construction. No one buys a second Spites house."

"Is that why your father left him?"

I shook my head. "Only partially. There was an incident. One of Spites' cracker-boxes caught fire, resulting in the deaths of a young mother and her three-month-old baby."

"Oh, my God. How terrible."

"The fire marshal blamed frayed wiring on a toaster. Dad talked to the father who was working at the time the blaze started. He swore the appliances were all new, wedding presents hardly more than a year old. Dad poked around the burned-out house to look for himself and came away convinced the source of the fire was actually a defect in the structure's internal wiring."

"What did he do?"

"Unfortunately, he couldn't prove anything because Spites had the charred wreckage bulldozed the very next day. The grieving father became understandably agitated, made emotional public threats of legal action, even got a lawyer in Abilene who was willing to represent him on a contingency basis. Before they could do anything, however, the grieving father was killed in a hit-and-run."

Michiko frowned at me. "An accident?"

"Dad didn't think so, but there were no witnesses, no evidence. They never found the car, for instance."

"So he quit working for Spites?"

"He didn't have any choice." I rotated the base of my sweaty glass. "Dad couldn't continue to draw a paycheck from a man he believed to be responsible for the deaths of three people, including a baby."

"Is that when he opened the *Crow's Nest*?"

I shook my head. "First he went to work for Pete Schmidt who'd just opened a steakhouse on North Heyward. It was a big change for Dad. His background was in construction, not food service."

"Pete Schmidt." She bit her lip. "Any relation to Delman Schmidt, the guy in Saigon . . . who—" She didn't have to finish. The guy who died a few feet away from me, who probably saved my life, or what was left of it.

"Dad found out later Delman was Pete's son by his first wife."

I remembered the guy's response when I asked him if he was related to Pete. "Not so's you'd notice."

"Delman's mom died when he was small," I went on. "Pete was on active-duty in Korea at the time, so her parents raised Delman. Apparently Pete and his in-laws didn't get along all that well. If Delman ever came to see his father at the steakhouse, it wasn't while I was there. He recognized me from playing football, but I didn't recognize him."

"Had your father ever met him?"

"He said Pete talked about his boy, sounded real proud of him, called him Buddy, but Dad said he couldn't remember ever meeting him."

"Is that where your father met George?"

I nodded. "George was Pete's head waiter. He tried to tell Pete to stop giving everything away too, but to no avail. My dad and George finally gave up, left Pete and opened their own restaurant. Pete cried foul, of course."

"Was George a full partner from the beginning?"

"Yep. Dad handled the business side and George ran food service, but they kept the partnership under wraps. George was afraid it would hurt them if it got out."

"Did Spites know they were partners?"

"I'm sure he did."

"But he didn't make any trouble?"

I took a drink of my Seven-Up. "I suspect he was afraid his former accountant might have a trump card up his sleeve to use against him. Plus, they weren't competing for the same market. I don't think it was until Dad and George bought the old Brayton mansion and turned it into the *Crow's Nest* that Spites began to see Dad as a business threat."

Michiko's mouth had fallen open. "Did you say Brayton mansion?"

I chuckled. "Brayton was his mother's maiden name. The family went bankrupt in the Depression and was forced to sell it. When I was a kid it was a rooming house. It had been empty for probably five years when Dad and George bought and restored it."

"Has Spites ever commented about it once being his family's home?"

"Only one time that I'm aware of." I took another sip of my drink. "Dad had finished the renovations. He and George were about to have the grand opening, when Spites expressed concern to the zoning commission that the house, having been built before there was a building code, didn't meet current commercial safety standards. All of a sudden there were inspectors all over the place checking wiring, plumbing and structural compliance."

"Sort of like the letter to the IRS?" she asked.

I nodded. "Now you know why Dad's first reaction would have been to blame Spites."

"Did your father confront him? About the inspectors, I mean."

I couldn't help smiling. "He knew better. Blaming Spites would only have made Dad look petty and vindictive. He chose another tack. Instead of treating the inspectors like the enemy, he fully cooperated with them. In the end they publicly praised the quality of the work he'd done."

Michiko grinned. "Was that the end of it?"

"It might have been, but with the success of the *Crow's Nest,* Dad was suddenly in demand for old building restoration. During my junior year in college, he actively campaigned against Spites for restoration jobs. He won the civic auditorium project, came in on time and on budget. Spites got the theater project and, as usual, he milked it, ran into cost overruns and schedule delays. That wouldn't have been so bad, but then, when it was nearly finished, half the ceiling caved in, injuring a workman. As a result, the council turned the project over to Dad for completion, and the city filed a suit against Spites to recover the funds it lost."

"I couldn't help noticing," Michiko said, "your reaction when the mayor said your father was considering running for his office. Why did that surprise you?"

"Because he'd been asked before and had always refused."

"And he hadn't said anything to you about it," she concluded.

I'd have to remember never to try to keep anything from this woman. She read me too well. "It also makes me wonder if it's true."

"If it is, why would he have been considering it now?"

"Good question. The office is largely ceremonial, but it wields considerable public influence. The only issue I can think of that might get Dad fully involved is the proposed mall."

"Explain that to me."

"Spites wants to clear land southwest of the city and build there. That'd mean two things, extending utilities, especially water, outside the present city limits, and it would draw traffic away from the downtown area. Dad isn't . . . wasn't against expansion. It's inevitable, but he felt our first obligation was to protect and conserve our limited resources, and not threaten the livelihoods of the established businesses that have been so important to our community."

"So he wanted to turn the downtown area into a mall instead of building a new one."

"He was concerned about the inner city blight that's ruining so many cities."

Just then we heard the bartender greet a new arrival.

"Evening, Colonel, how ya doing today?"

As he spoke, the bartender poured the newcomer a drink—a tall glass half full of ice, two shots of vodka, tonic and a lime wedge.

Zack had told me about this character. Lieutenant Colonel Mortimer Bartholomew, United States Army retired, now a civil servant working in base supply. The drink the barkeep was fixing was known as a "Bart."

CHAPTER TWENTY-TWO

Tall, narrow-chested and scrawny, the colonel walked with a simian gait, his long arms dangling rather than swinging as he moved ponderously on spidery legs. He was about sixty, with a shiny skull, fringed with close-cut white hair. His splayed red nose was all the more conspicuous because the rest of his face, though coarse and mealy, was pasty white. His focus was exclusively on the bar, so he didn't see Michiko and me behind the palm fronds.

He slipped onto a stool at the near corner of the bar, not ten feet from where we sat, removed a twenty-dollar bill from his wallet and instructed the bartender to refill Zack's and Ned's glasses. Zack glanced my way, an amused smirk on his face. He'd been through this ritual before and knew better than to argue.

"Thank you, Colonel," Zack said in a voice that carried. "That's very kind of you."

"I don't believe I've met the gentleman with you." I could imagine the disapproving scowl on the old man's face. Mustaches were frowned upon, flamboyant ones doubly so.

"Colonel Bartholomew, sir, may I introduce my friend, Ned Herman."

No stranger to the protocol dearly beloved by the senior generation, and something of a ham in any case, Ned played his appointed part, went over to the old man with an outstretched hand and showed all the deference an inferior should to an elder.

"Colonel, I'm very pleased to meet you, sir."

"You're not in the military."

"Not now. I'm using the GI bill to attend graduate school in Austin."

Michiko placed her hand over mine. I looked over to see the amusement on her face. Every club had its characters, those daring, unsung heroes who'd singlehandedly saved the republic, its pontificators with expert opinions on every subject.

"Humph. Put a head on it," Bart commanded. The bartender added another shot of vodka. The colonel took a sip, smacked his lips. "Saw the thing in the paper about your friend Crow," he told Zack. "Too bad. Should have expected something like that, I reckon, getting cozy with niggers. Either have one of them shoot you or drive you to shoot yourself."

Zack stiffened, glanced my way.

From a previous conversation with him, I knew Bart was originally from Mississippi, of an old but war-impoverished family—the conflict in question being the War Between the States. His accent was still markedly Dixie rather than Texan, though he hadn't lived in the Magnolia State in more than thirty years. He'd been residing in Coyote Springs since his retirement from active duty ten years earlier. Zack had also told me Bart's attitudes toward race and women made George Wallace and Lester Maddox look like hot-pink liberals.

I considered getting up, approaching the bar and introducing myself. It would have been interesting to get the man's reaction, but I was more interested in hearing what else he had to say. Bart was a windbag, but the old goat might reveal something useful. Drunks and little children could be invaluable founts of information.

I shook my head in a signal for Zack to let it go.

Michiko squeezed my fingers. I gave her a weak smile.

Zack quaffed his beer.

"People seem to think if you give them whatever they want 'cause they been deprived," Bart grumbled, "everything'll be fine. Doesn't work that way. But you can't tell them do-gooders. That steakhouse won't last long now. Can't expect that crippled son of his to run it. The help'll rob the place blind before long. For all I know it might have already, and that's why Crow shot himself."

The anger in Zack's face was unmistakable. He took a deep breath, no doubt in preparation for an explosion, but again I signaled for him not to. He stared at me as if I were crazy, but I wanted to hear more.

"Been to the *Crow's Nest*?" Ned asked conversationally. His back was to me, but I caught a glimpse of the expression on his face as he swiveled toward the old man.

"Oh, a couple times. Not bad. Big steaks, but the quality isn't really that good. Still, it's the best in town since Pete Schmidt's place closed. His were the best, not as big looking, mind you, but thicker and half the platter wasn't fat and gristle."

Bart swallowed some of his drink before continuing. "Pete was regular Army, you know. Quartermaster Corps. Medically retired as a major, lost a foot to frostbite in Korea."

"Was he from around here?" Ned asked.

"Llano and damn proud of it. Texas proud. Could give you history from the Republic to the present. Name all the governors, things like that. Had a boy in the Air Corps, officer, doing real good, real proud of him.

Pete and his lady had a ranch out north of town. Sprawling place, big house, huge pecan orchard. Used to hire wetbacks to thrash and gather. Told me he could live on the income from the pecan trees alone."

Zack lit a cigarette and smiled at me through the smoke. We knew that wasn't true.

"Raised his own cattle for his restaurant too," Bart continued. "Place was always packed. Sharp businessman. 'Til he got double-crossed."

"Oh?" Ned raised an eyebrow.

"Where do you think Crow and the nigger learned the business?"

Michiko started to rise, but I tugged on her hand. "Let him go," I whispered.

"But—"

I put a finger to her lips, urging silence. "Not yet."

"They used to work for Pete," Bart rambled on. "Elsbeth was a good waiter, I'll grant you that. Knew his place 'til he took up with Crow. Then he got uppity. Walked out with Crow and ruined the man who gave him a good livelihood."

"You don't believe in competition?" Zack barely managed to control the tone of his voice. I shot him another warning glance.

"Competition? Is that what you call disloyalty?" He took out a cigarette, lit it, took a puff, and ground it out. Zack inhaled his own butt much more deeply.

"Can't expect loyalty from those people. Stupid to try. Put a top on it," he ordered the bartender, who poured another shot of vodka and squeezed another wedge of lime.

"What happened to him?" Ned asked.

"Died about a year ago," the old man said. "His business went bust 'cause he was stabbed in the back. Got depressed. Stayed out at the ranch 'til his wife had to take him up to the Vet's hospital in Big Spring. Diabetes, I hear. Died up there."

"His wife still live around here?"

"Passed away a few months after he did. That's what disloyalty does."

The old colonel tapped the rim of his glass and watched as the bartender added more vodka and lime.

"Pete was sharp on public relations. Always gave a ten-percent discount to the military. Used to stop by the club here and hand out complimentary dinner tickets for two. Didn't cost you a dime to eat there unless you wanted something extra like dessert. You had to pay for that, and for drinks, of course. Gave me a ticket every time he came in."

"Sounds like he was giving away most of his profits," Ned commented as the bartender topped the old man's drink again. At the colonel's insistence, he also poured the two young men another beer, despite their protests.

"Pete could afford it, what with the oil."

"Oil?" Ned's brows shot up.

Zack audibly groaned.

"Told me himself, in confidence, of course, there was oil on the place. Was fixing to drill a well when his health broke. Your pal Crow ended up getting the ranch too. Bought it for his crippled son. Smart move, I reckon. The boy can't play football with no legs. This way he can live on the oil income."

I climbed to my feet and pulled back Michiko's chair when she stood.

"You guys ready to leave?" I came out from behind the mini-forest.

Zack slipped off his stool. Ned did the same.

Bartholomew looked up at me. It took a moment before recognition dawned. Then pasty white went even paler.

"I'm Jason Crow." I extended my hand. He took it because it was there. "I've heard a good deal about you, Colonel. I know now at least some of it's true." I reached for a bar napkin and asked the bartender for a pen. "For LC Bartholomew," I wrote, then under it: "Free dinner for 2." I signed my name and placed it on the bar beside the old man's glass. "You let me know now if there's too much gristle."

Sucking in their cheeks, Zack and Ned abandoned their latest round of untouched beers and walked toward the lobby. Michiko and I followed. It wasn't until we were halfway to the door that I heard Colonel Bartholomew finally say something. "Jesus wept and cried."

"That miserable old bigot," Ned snarled as we made our way under the long canvas awning to the curb where Michiko had parked her MG beside the Packard.

"Why'd you give him a free meal?" she asked.

"It was that or punch his lights out. I don't think Dad would have wanted me to do that. It sure wouldn't have changed his mind about anything."

"You think a free meal will?" Ned challenged.

"He won't cash it in," Michiko said derisively.

"Oh, yes, he will," I countered, "after he shows it around and tells everyone we're great friends."

"The old sot," Zack muttered. "I bet he and Pete got along fine. Made the ranch sound like Tara. And that crap about oil! Typical pipedream."

"You sure?" Ned asked.

I laughed. The lure of oil was like the lure of gold. "If there was oil on the place you can be sure Dad would have told us. Besides, if the land had oil, Schmidt would never have gone bankrupt."

We reached the curb.

"By the time he leaves the club," Zack said, "his glass will be full of lime wedges and straight vodka. The bartenders take bets on his consumption. Every afternoon after work, he puts away an average of six shots and buys five more rounds for other people."

"And he drinks vodka because it won't leave a smell on his breath." Ned guffawed. "I sure wouldn't want his club bill."

"Apparently neither does his wife. I saw her once," Zack said. "A barrel of a woman. Came storming into the bar and dragged him out by the ear."

Ned and Zack exchanged glances, got into the Packard and started it up. The air conditioning compressor kicked in.

I draped my wrists lightly on Michiko's shoulders and would have given her a kiss if a car hadn't driven by. "I'll see you tomorrow."

She nodded. "I'm sorry I dragged you here, Jason, sorry you had to hear that. Don't pay any attention to the old coot."

"What old coot?" I smiled, or tried to. "Tomorrow."

I sat sideways in the rear seat of the Packard, very much aware of my legs stretched across the leather upholstery, my mind rummaging over the encounter with the retired Army colonel, trying to sort the truth from the distortions and the lies.

"Is that the way people saw Dad? As a backstabber, a parasite?"

CHAPTER TWENTY-THREE

"People respected your father because he was successful and honest," Zack assured me.

"Pete Schmidt obviously didn't feel that way. The few times I met him he seemed a bit pompous, but he was friendly enough. He never mentioned having a son."

"Delman?" Ned asked.

I heard his reluctance in saying the name. I also knew the story of how he and Zack had found me three days after the Tet offensive started. Zack, Delman and I had been in the O club game room when the Viet Cong attacked. Zack and I had helped a couple of guys who'd been injured, then I left to get medics. When they arrived and I wasn't with them, Zack went outside to find me and ended up getting struck by flying debris. He woke up three days later in the Tan Son Nhut hospital. He asked about Delman and me, but nobody knew anything about us, so he called Ned, my hooch mate on base. Together they searched for me.

Somewhere between the club and the hospital where I would have been headed, they came across a partially collapsed sandbag bunker. There Zack found my hat, which started him digging. He found Delman first. His body was already starting to decompose. The sight and smell were enough to make Ned bolt to the side and puke his guts out. Not a pleasant memory. Zack had persevered in his search, however, and a few minutes later found me in a tunnel of rubble, barely alive.

The night of the Tet offensive, January 31, 1968, changed my life forever. The last thing I recalled was running out of the officers club to find a medic. I had no recollection of the bunker, of being shot, of Delman putting the tourniquets on my legs.

I was suddenly aware of Zack staring at me in the rearview mirror.

"Bart said Pete's son was an officer." I cleared my throat. "But Delman was enlisted. Remember how nervous he was about going to the O club with us?"

"The old fart got a lot of things wrong," Zack pointed out, "like him being in the Air Corps. It's been the Air Force for over twenty years. Then there's the huge pecan orchard and—"

"They sound like a pair," Ned commented. "Bart's sure George will run the *Nest* into the ground trying to manage it by himself."

"As is Grover Reed, our lawyer." I snorted. "People underestimate George. He's tougher and smarter than they realize. Everybody credits Dad with defying convention by going into partnership with a black man. They don't realize George was the one taking the risks. If it hadn't worked out, Dad would've been commended for his noble intentions. George would've suffered rebuke socially, emotionally and economically."

When we arrived at the carriage house, Zack asked if I wanted him to go upstairs and get my wheelchair. I did, but instead I strode to the elevator and rode up, while he and Ned took the stairs. Vanity would carry me just so far, however. In this case, to the bedroom, where I removed the offensive devices, donned a pair of jeans, pinned up the legs, and rolled into the office.

Ned had seen me legless at Willy, but he still averted his eyes, an automatic reflex, not intended to offend. It was a reminder nevertheless that the sight of me was discomfiting, even to friends.

Zack brought out a tray of cold cuts from the kitchen. We fixed ourselves sandwiches. I parked myself behind the desk.

"Okay," Ned said after taking a couple of healthy bites of his Dagwood, "you've announced to the world that your father was murdered. So tell me how you think it went down."

I recited the information I had in the same staccato fashion Burker had used.

Zack took up the cause. "We know the weapon came from the gun case." The three of us automatically turned to the tall, glass-fronted cabinet. "The police found the only key in Mr. Crow's pants pocket."

"I can't imagine him handing his killer the gun," Ned said between bites, "then sitting there and letting himself be executed. It doesn't make sense."

Executed. The same word I'd used.

Zack and I had been over all this the night before. More than once. Without resolution. I was missing something. Maybe Ned's fresh perspective would give me a new insight.

"Mr. Crow could have left the keys on the desk, then stepped out of the room," Zack suggested.

"Why?" Ned wasn't buying it.

"To go to the bathroom?"

Ned's mustache twitched with annoyance. "Somebody comes to visit him in the middle of the night. Why would he put his keys on the desk? For that matter, why would he even have them out? Then, sometime during this mysterious visit, he excuses himself to use the can. The murderer opens the cabinet and removes the gun. Crow comes back, the killer shoots him in the head, places the weapon in his hand and returns the keys to his pocket, right? Why?"

Zack looked at him. "Why what?"

"Why did he put the keys back in Crow's pocket instead of leaving them on the desk where he'd found them? By the way, I was in the office with him more than once. I don't remember him ever leaving his keys on the desk. Do you?"

"No," Zack admitted.

"Or maybe this mysterious visitor showed interest in the guns, and Crow opened the cabinet to let him examine them more closely. Then for whatever reason, he leaves the room. Doesn't seem very likely, but let's leave that for a minute. Was the gun usually kept loaded?"

"No," I said emphatically.

"So the killer had to get the gun out of the cabinet, find the ammunition—where was it kept? In the bottom drawer?"

Zack and I stared at each other, then at him.

"Don't look at me that way. It's the first place anybody would search," Ned said with a shake of his head. "So the murderer gets the gun from the cabinet, locates the ammo, loads the gun and closes the cabinet to make things look normal—all in the time it takes the old man to relieve himself—"

"Unless he had the ammo on him when he arrived," Zack suggested.

"In which case—" Ned lifted his iced tea glass "—it would definitely have been premeditated murder, not just a momentary, impulsive decision." He drank. "But if the murderer came here with the intent of killing Crow, why all the complications? Why not go up to his room, shoot him with a Saturday night special, leave and take the gun with him? Bury it somewhere or throw it in the river or the lake where it would never be found?"

"I don't know," I said, venting my frustration. "I can't explain those things. But there has to be an explanation. There simply was no reason for my father to kill himself."

Ned fixed a second monster sandwich. Zack and I passed. We covered familiar ground—again—over the next fifteen minutes.

"*Monty Python and the Holy Grail* is playing at the Starlight," Ned announced. "I hear it's hilarious. You guys want to go?"

I had no intention of putting on my legs again, and though I wouldn't need them at the drive-in, I had no desire to take a chance on having to use a public restroom, sitting legless in my wheelchair. "Not me."

Zack declined as well. Ned left. All of a sudden I had time on my hands.

"I'm going down to the carpentry shop," I said. "I need to keep busy, do something. I thought I'd make a mantle clock for Debbie and Aaron as a wedding present."

He nodded. "Good idea. Want help?"

"Thanks, but I'd like to do this myself."

"In that case, I'm going to gas and clean up the Packard."

I was perched on a stool at the band saw with a stack of seasoned mesquite boards at my elbow, when Burker entered. I switched off the machine, swiveled around and lifted my goggles to my forehead.

For a careless moment, he stared. I doubted he was aware of swallowing hard. "I . . . I thought I'd let you know the autopsy results are in."

I knew what the verdict was without being told, but for some perverse reason I wanted him to say the word.

"Suicide."

I picked up the top plank, placed a square along the edge.

"You don't accept it though, do you?" I didn't respond. "Heard you told everybody your father was murdered."

I made a mark on an uneven edge. "He was."

Burker moved to the other end of the workbench, hefted his butt onto the stool there. "I've given you my reasons, the evidence that supports suicide. What've you got to support your theory?"

"My father had no reason to kill himself. On the contrary, he had every reason to live. I was coming home. We had plans to do things together. Plus, there's no way he'd kill himself using my gun."

Burker picked up a screw driver, went through the motions of examining it. "Look, Jason, we're not friends. Never have been. Probably never will be, but I've always respected your talent on the football field and your intelligence. You were good. Damn good. What's happened . . . well, it's a shame."

"I don't want your pity, Burker."

"Good, because you won't get any from me, but I will tell you I'm disappointed in you. You're smart. That's why I expected you to be more objective about what's happened. Let me give you another tidbit of information, another fact for you to consider. There were powder marks on your father's right hand. He pulled the trigger."

I wanted to shut out the world and the image he was forcing on me, of a gun held to my father's head and the trigger being pulled.

"What about the body?" I asked, "And my father's personal effects?"

"Body's been released to Eldrige's Funeral Home. I'll bring his personal stuff by tomorrow."

After he left, I remained in the shop, patiently planing boards to precise tolerances, cutting them with equal care, then fitting them meticulously in place. All the while my mind kept racing through the day's events. So much had happened. So much I didn't understand. A question surfaced. Something that didn't fit. *The Joint* wasn't the type of place where Bubba was likely to hang out. So what was he doing there on a Sunday morning?

CHAPTER TWENTY-FOUR

I lay in my bed that night, recalling the smirk on Bubba's face as he looked down at my plastic limbs, Burker's revulsion in the woodshop at the sight of me sitting on the stool without them. I thought about the band saw cutting through mesquite. Did it sound like the bone saw cutting off my legs? I was massaging my left stump as I drifted off to sleep.

I'm woozy. Where am I? *I try to raise my head. It feels leaden. Who is this man?*

"Lie back, lieutenant, and be still. I'm Dr. Weatherby. You're in the recovery room at the Tan Son Nhut hospital. Do you understand what I'm saying?"

I blink my eyes and mumble, "Tan Son Nhut hospital."

"Do you remember what happened?"

I try to think. "Saigon. Dinner on the barge. Met guy from home." The words come out as a croak.

"Do you remember being at the officers club?"

"Rockets."

"Yes. There was an attack. You were injured."

I stare up at him. What he's about to tell me isn't good. I can feel it, but I have to know. "How bad, doc?"

"You were shot in the calves of both legs. The wounds themselves weren't all that serious and wouldn't have been life threatening if you'd received immediate medical attention. Someone put tourniquets around your thighs to stop the bleeding. They wouldn't have caused any serious damage either, if they'd been promptly removed. Unfortunately three days went by before anyone found you."

He pauses. He doesn't want to continue. I can see it in his eyes. I don't want him to either, but . . . "Go on."

"Here's the good news, son. Whoever put on those tourniquets saved your life. You'd have bled out otherwise."

"The bad news?"

"They were on too long. They cut off circulation. Gangrene set in. There was no way to save them. We had to amputate both your legs above the knees. I'm sorry."

"Oh, God! My legs." I try to raise myself up. I want to look. It can't be true. My

legs must be there. They have to be.

The doctor gently puts his hand on my shoulder. "Take it easy, son."

I collapse onto the mattress. He cut off my legs. He shouldn't have done that. I need them to play football. And Michiko. I can't go to her . . . Wait. He cut off my legs. What else did he cut off? Oh, please God! No. Please.

I look up. I can barely see the man through my tears. "What else? What else did you cut off?"

"You're fine, lieutenant. Just your legs."

"Will I be able to walk, doc?"

"As soon as you heal from surgery, we'll start your physical therapy. That's when we'll be able to evaluate how complete a recovery you'll make."

He's not answering my question. Because he doesn't want to tell me the truth. Oh, God!

CHAPTER TWENTY-FIVE

Coyote Springs, Texas, Monday, August 26, 1968

The clock on my bedside table said 8:03 when I awoke to the smell of coffee brewing and the sound of the shower running. It reminded me of the monsoon rains in Vietnam.

Among the things I'd learned from the surgeon who'd amputated my legs was that I'd been hit at close range from behind with American issue .38 caliber bullets. Considering I was unarmed, it was hardly surprising that I'd be running away from gunfire. The VC often used our own weapons against us, which explained the American ammo. It could even have been friendly fire that caught me. Something like thirty percent of war casualties were the result of friendly fire.

The big question was who had put on the tourniquets. The logical answer was Delman Schmidt, the guy from Coyote Springs who Zack and I had met in Saigon and later invited to the Officers Club. His body had been found a few feet from mine. He'd been shot in the chest, and according to the doctor, had undoubtedly died within seconds.

But this was no time to be thinking of Vietnam and dead comrades.

In the office I found the telephone number for Joe Gutierrez, a local contractor and invited him to give me an estimate on drilling at least three new water wells on the Schmidt place. He agreed to get out there soon, maybe that day, and take a look at the situation.

Zack had left the morning paper on my desk. I was reading about Arthur Ashe's victory in the U.S. Singles Tennis Open the day before—the first black man to win the tournament—when I heard the familiar clatter of Michiko's wooden wedges on the stairs. In the past we'd rarely locked the outside door, but we did now. I wheeled out and let her in.

She greeted me with a kiss on the lips that sent tingling sensations pooling in my lap. Straightening, she grinned, aware, I had no doubt, of the affect she had on me. After pouring herself a cup of coffee, she settled on the couch in the office and tucked her long legs under her. God, she was beautiful!

"How's the IG going?"

She made a face. "They're driving us all crazy. The hospital commander's threatening to put us on twelve-hour shifts. As if exhaustion and low morale will accomplish anything."

I chuckled. "All leaves are cancelled until morale improves." It was a standing joke about military illogic. The strange part was that it sometimes worked.

Zack joined us, a mug of coffee in hand.

"I'll drop you off at Eldridge's," he said, "then come back here and see what the tax auditors have to say. If you finish at the undertakers before I get there, maybe Aaron can bring you back."

A reminder of how dependent I was on other people. At what point would Zack begin to resent being my batman and chauffeur?

"I'll drive you," Michiko offered.

"Thanks, but I don't think I can fit into that MG of yours." It was very low and cramped. I wasn't sure I could have gotten into it with two real legs, much less dead appendages. "You think you'll be that long?" I asked Zack.

He read my mind. "Relax. We'll get through the audit just fine. That doesn't mean they won't have a few quibbles to justify their efforts. I'll finish up with them as quickly as I can."

"I want to stop by the *Gazette* and see Mrs. Collins. I have a few questions I'd like to ask her."

"Since you don't need me at the funeral home," Michiko interrupted. "Why don't I visit with Mrs. Collins—"

I looked at her. "You?"

Rather than show umbrage at my tone, she used another ploy. She sucked in her cheeks and pouted her lips, knowing it was a gesture I found sexy. "Why not? It'll be a good opportunity for me to practice my English," she said, imitating a Japanese accent. "I'm sure she'll help me with the hard words."

I laughed and realized it felt both wonderful and like a betrayal. "Actually there's something else I was fixing to ask you to do, but there's no reason you can't do both."

Zack left a minute later to start the Packard and turn on the AC. I was about to get dressed, when Mrs. Flores, the cleaning lady arrived. She offered her condolences. I introduced Michiko. The women, who were so very different, nodded greetings.

"I didn't know if I should come," Mrs. Flores said, "if you still want me to clean."

"I'd appreciate it if you would. I'll be staying here for the time being." I started to wheel out from behind the desk, then realized that the hobi coat covered my hips but left my stumps exposed. Mrs. Flores had seen me legless several times, but I'd always been fully dressed. The first time she'd observed me pensively, then gone on with her work. After that she'd shown no discomfort in my presence, simply accepting me the way I was. I wished more people could be as open-minded.

Retreating back behind the desk, I asked her to water the house plants for me, something my father had always done himself. "By the way, are they all here?"

She looked around. "Yes. Why?"

"Just wondered. Do you know if Dad repotted any of them recently?"

Her brows drew together. "I don't think so." She wanted to question why I was asking, but refrained.

"How about starting in my father's bedroom, while I get dressed?"

She nodded and went through the passage to the small inner chamber. I wheeled across the hall. Michiko followed.

"Close the door," I told her nervously. We'd arrived at a crucial moment. She'd never seen my stumps. She was a nurse. Undoubtedly she'd seen men in worse condition than I was, but she hadn't been emotionally involved with them. We'd been intimate in Japan before I went to Vietnam, but I'd had two good legs then. How would she react to me now? "I need you to stand by while I put on my prosthetics."

"All right."

It was a strange sensation, part embarrassment, part stimulation that had my hands shaking as I rolled the compression socks on my "residual limbs." She watched as I lowered the stumps into the prosthetic harnesses, repositioned and finally secured them. What was going through her mind, I wondered. When I finished dressing, she smiled.

"You're doing great, Jason." Her eyes were moist, and suddenly so were mine.

A few minutes later I took my usual seat in the back of the Packard. George, Aaron and Debbie were already at the funeral home when Zack dropped me off. I'd phoned Mom that morning and invited her to join us, even offered to pick her up, but she'd declined. "Whatever you decide is fine, Jason."

The funeral director asked a series of predictable questions. Everyone turned to me for answers, further recognition that I'd become the head of the family. The graveside service would be tomorrow. I wondered if the killer would be there, and if I'd be able to spot him. What did a murderer look like?

CHAPTER TWENTY-SIX

We were just breaking up at the funeral parlor, and I was about to get into Aaron's yellow Skylark convertible—he was long legged too, so there was enough room in the front seat for me—when Zack pulled up. Dad could have gotten a new car long ago, but he loved the fin-tailed behemoth and, up to a couple of years ago, my brother had been around to maintain it. Leon had his shortcomings, but no one ever doubted his instinctive capacity for things mechanical, automobiles being at the top of the list. The perpetual grease under his fingernails used to drive my mother crazy.

"That was quick," I remarked as Zack was getting out of the car.

"Not a talkative lot," he grumbled, opened the back door for me, then added, "But I was able to confirm they'll be packing up today and leaving for Austin. The head of the team had a couple of recommendations but no significant adverse findings."

I dragged my legs across the rear seat and leaned against the passenger-side door. "I don't suppose he told you why they were here to begin with," I said once we were underway.

Zack chuckled. "The guy in charge could give lawyers lessons on being tight-lipped. I did get the impression he felt his time had been wasted though."

"Which suggests we were set up."

Zack shrugged. "We'll probably never know."

It was only three blocks to the lawyer's office. Getting in and out of the car took me longer than the drive over. I could have walked the short distance, but I would have been drenched with sweat from the August heat, and my stumps would have been raw. I would also have undoubtedly attracted attention as I swung the ungainly limbs in arcs along the street. With more therapy I'd gain better control of the articulated knees and maybe someday be able to stroll more naturally—I hoped—but not today.

Grover Reed greeted me with a firm handshake. "I wasn't expecting you."

"Is that a problem?" I asked.

"The business I have to discuss is with Mr. Merchant."

"Oh," I tried to act nonchalant. "I figured you wanted to talk to both of us about our partnership."

"I'm sorry, Jason, but what I have to say to Zack is legally confidential, privileged."

"How long will it take?" Zack asked. "Perhaps Jason can just wait out here."

"We could be a while. It might be better if you took him home and came back."

Reed's disparaging remarks about George yesterday and his talking about me now in the third person was beginning to tick me off. On the other hand, I had imposed myself where I hadn't been invited.

"I'll wait here," I said, aware I was putting my friend on the spot.

Zack stroked his chin. "I'll try not to be too long."

I shuffled off to an upholstered chair, lowered myself into it and picked up a magazine. The lawyer wasn't pleased with my obstinacy, but there wasn't much he could do about it. He ushered Zack into his private office and closed the door.

It opened a minute later and I was invited to join them.

"I hope you understand, Jason," Reed said, "this was nothing personal, but I have a responsibility—"

"I completely understand," I told him as I gripped the chair arms and lowered myself into it. "Thanks for letting me sit in."

"It was Zack's call. Actually this works out better because I need to discuss your father's will with you too." He asked if we'd like coffee. I accepted as a sort of a peace offering.

"Since y'all were away last week—" Reed addressed himself exclusively to Zack after he sat behind his desk "—I didn't know if Theo had informed you he'd made you executor of his will."

Zack shook his head. "He broached the subject several months ago, but I didn't know he'd actually done it."

"When did he make this change?" I asked.

"As a matter of fact, it was just this past week. As you probably know, George Elsbeth was the previous executor."

The timing seemed ominous. I sipped my coffee.

"I've never done this before," Zack said. "What does it entail?"

"You control the distribution of Mr. Crow's assets. All of them," Reed replied. "Let me summarize the document, and you can ask any questions."

He settled back more comfortably in his leather chair. "After a few minor cash bequests to several long-time employees, Theo's half of the *Crow's Nest* is divided equally among his wife Julia, his daughter Debbie, his son Leon, and George Elsbeth."

"What about Jason?" Zack asked.

"I'll get to him in a minute."

"That gives Mr. Elsbeth controlling interest," I noted.

"Correct. Previously your father's fifty percent was split between your mother and you three children." Reed again addressed Zack. "Also under the new will, all earnings, if any, for Debbie and Leon are to be held in trust by you for five years. Debbie can get her share sooner if she marries, but Leon's is to be withheld until he is determined to be drug-free for at least three consecutive years."

Zack frowned.

Reed went on. "Restoration, Inc., Mr. Crow's building restoration business, goes to you and Jason jointly. That hasn't changed from the old will. All cash assets, including life insurance paid directly into the estate, amount to about fifty thousand dollars which is divided as follows:

"Five thousand to Aaron Elsbeth for his education. That's not a stipulation, however. Aaron can spend the money anyway he wants. Theo was simply expressing a preference for its use."

Zack nodded his understanding.

"Another five thousand goes to Debbie for her education. Use of this money, like the earnings from the *Crow's Nest*, is controlled by you for five years or until she marries. You determine what constitutes educational expenses: for example, buying a car for her to drive back and forth to school would be acceptable, but the expenditures have to be related in some way to her formal education."

Again Zack nodded.

"Five thousand also goes to Leon, but this money, like the earnings from the *Crow's Nest*, is strictly controlled by you. The money can be used for his rehabilitation or in any other way you deem appropriate for Leon's benefit, but you cannot give funds directly to him."

I asked if my father knew for sure that Leon was on drugs.

"Several of his comments implied it," the lawyer said, "and the condition of the bequest, different from the former outright grant, suggests it."

In other words, yes.

"However, that isn't the delicate part," Reed said, this time to me. "As you may know, your grandfather left the ranch to your mother but with your father as trustee on behalf of you and your siblings. In Theo's former will, he terminated his role as trustee upon his death and turned the family ranch over to his wife, in addition to giving her a cash bequest of twenty-five thousand dollars. In this new will, he lays claim as Julia's husband to half ownership of the ranch, something he'd never done before, and he leaves intact his status as trustee for the other half. He bequeaths to you, Jason, his half of the ranch and the trusteeship for the other. In other words, you have sole and complete control of the entire ranch. He makes only one stipulation, that your mother be allowed to reside there for the rest of her life. In addition, instead of a cash bequest, the twenty-five thousand dollars is to be put into an annuity that will guarantee her an income for life."

I understood now what Dad had meant when he said he'd make sure mom's church never got the ranch. Even if they tried to contest these provisions, it would take them a very long time and cost them a lot of money.

"That's the tricky part," Reed continued, addressing me. "Your father was taking a calculated risk that your brother and sister won't contest distribution of the assets. Except for the ranch, he's left nothing to you. Nominally you and Zack each receive half of Restoration, Inc., his minor construction and refurbishing company, but that's essentially an ad hoc business with few capital assets. In effect, he's left you his good name, that's all."

"So if Mrs. Crow challenges this will to get the ranch," Zack concluded, "it'll be at Jason's expense."

Reed nodded. "Theo was counting on her unwillingness to go that far. Except for his small government disability check and any savings he might have, Jason has been left penniless. Even his interest in the ranch won't make him wealthy, since he can't sell it without the concurrence of all parties concerned and must in that event share the proceeds. He'll still have to work for a living."

I could see how ugly the situation might get: a neurotic mother fighting her crippled son for a piece of property. Not a heart-warming tale. Dad was counting on that. He was using me, using my handicap as a weapon against my mother and her church. I should be offended, outraged. The last thing I wanted was to be regarded as an object of pity, and that was what this will did. Yet I also understood what my father intended, squeezing good out of bad, advantage out of misfortune.

"Actually, Julia has very little to complain about," Reed went on. "She has a place to live and, between the annuity and her share of the earnings from the steakhouse, an adequate income. Of course, if the *Crow's Nest* falters or goes out of business, she'll be financially pressed." The lawyer regarded me. "Your father was counting on you to support your mother from ranch income or whatever other sources you might develop."

"If she had sued for a divorce," I asked, "what would have been her chances of getting controlling interest in the ranch?"

Reed looked surprised.

"You didn't know she'd asked Dad for a divorce?"

"Your father mentioned her wanting to donate the ranch to her church, but he didn't say anything about a divorce."

"When was this?" I asked.

Reed pondered. "Tuesday. He called late Monday afternoon to make an appointment and came by the next morning. Since your grandfather left the ranch to both of them equally, it couldn't be sold or given away by either of them separately, so your father was satisfied the church wouldn't get it during his lifetime. He wanted to make sure she wasn't able to give it away in the event of his untimely death."

Had he had a premonition? "Untimely death? Were those his words?"

"As a matter of fact, they were. He never discounted the possibility of being hit by a truck or choking on a piece of his own steak."

But he wasn't hit by a truck or . . .

"Divorce," I reminded him. "Could she have gotten the ranch in a divorce settlement?"

He canted his head in a noncommittal shrug. "Since it was her family's place, she'd certainly have had a strong negotiating position—full title to her family's ranch, for example, in exchange for waiving all claim to her share of the *Crow's Nest*."

"Did my father give you any indication he was contemplating suicide?"

Reed didn't seem surprised by the question. "Not even remotely."

"Don't the altered provisions of the will suggest it?" Zack asked.

I looked over at him, wondering if he was changing his mind about murder.

"Not really," Reed answered. "Theo reviewed his will every year and often made little adjustments to it—amounts of cash bequeathed, the names of employees he wanted remembered, that sort of thing."

Zack's forehead furrowed. "You've accounted for only forty of the fifty thousand dollars. What about the other ten?"

I'd lost track of the cash bequests, but my friend the accountant obviously hadn't.

"It goes to you," Reed told him. "If the will is challenged, you may get to earn every penny of it."

"One more thing," I said. "Were you aware the IRS is auditing the *Crow's Nest*?"

"No, I wasn't. When did that start?"

"Tuesday."

"Your father didn't say anything to me about it," Reed said. "Probably just routine."

"Apparently he suspected it was because of a letter being sent to the IRS accusing him of some sort of illegal dealings."

"It's possible, of course—the letter, I mean. But your father said nothing to me about it, and I'm sure he would have if he'd been concerned."

"Is there anything illegal going on?" I asked.

Reed smiled broadly. "You ought to know better than ask me a question like that. For one thing it would breach confidentiality. For another, I doubt you'd believe a lawyer's answer anyway." He laughed. "No, Jason, there was nothing illegal going on that I'm aware of. Your father was an honest man. I'll stake my reputation on it."

When we left Reed's building, my head was buzzing. The sudden change in my father's will at my mother's expense. Giving George Elsbeth majority control of the steakhouse, but removing him from executorship. Putting Leon under Zack's virtual guardianship. Did Leon know about this? How would he react when he found out?

CHAPTER TWENTY-SEVEN

By the time Michiko entered my father's office, it was well past noon. I'd removed my legs and was seated in my wheelchair behind the desk. Zack sat across from me. Michiko kissed me on the cheek, then settled into the armchair opposite Zack.

"Learn anything from Helga Collins?" I asked her.

"Did you know your father and Brayton Spites had a verbal confrontation at the city council meeting Friday?"

I didn't. "Tell me about it."

"Apparently Spites formally requested the extension of city services to the area he wants to develop. Your father reminded the council that taxpayers have a right to demand a return on their investment. He questioned whether the project would enhance the quality of life in Coyote Springs, or draw commerce away from long-established downtown merchants and line the pockets of the developers?"

"Sounded like Dad was on a roll."

"Helga said the chamber was perfectly quiet. One of the amenities of this city, your father pointed out, is the abundance of parks and playgrounds. He asked if Spites' project would include public recreational facilities. Spites alluded to designs for a community center with a swimming pool and tennis courts, but your father stopped him and repeated the question until Spites had to admit the plans were for private facilities, not public."

Spites should have known better than to try to bamboozle Theodore Crow. I could imagine Dad telling me about this episode. We'd have shared a good laugh over it.

"That was when your father brought up Spites' failure to complete the civic theater and the expense it incurred," Michiko went on, "the shoddy workmanship that resulted in a young worker being permanently crippled and the public reputation of Spites as a charlatan and a fraud."

"Wow! Pretty strong stuff," Zack commented.

"Helga said everyone was stunned. It amounted to a personal attack, something your father had never done before. Spites threatened to sue him for slander and defamation of character. Theo replied that truth is a positive defense, and at least his accusations were in the open, not ugly letters sent in the dark of night."

"Maybe the IRS audit was bothering him more than he admitted," Zack suggested.

"Didn't Spites do essentially the same thing when he called in building inspectors after the restoration of the *Nest* was completed years ago?" Michiko asked me. "Sounds like your dad had had enough."

"What did Helga say about Bubba?" I asked.

"Nothing good. Brayton is capable of using violence by proxy—she mentioned the hit-and-run following the house fire that killed the young mother and child —but Bubba seems to enjoy the hands-on variety."

The incident at *The Joint* confirmed that. "What about drugs?"

It was a confluence of factors that had drawn me to the hypothesis that Bubba might be into drugs. The name of the place, *The Joint*, while probably no more than a play on words, had started my mind going. A joint. Marijuana. Leon had admitted to smoking pot, and he had been seen near there on a Sunday morning. Bubba, who wasn't a student, was also there on a Sunday morning. Dad had taught me to be suspicious of coincidences.

"You're right," Michiko said. "Mrs. Collins's heard that Bubba deals drugs, but doesn't use them himself, which she described as a rare display of intelligence on his part."

So maybe I'd been right. The one consolation I could take was that apparently my brother had been there to buy, not to sell.

"I keep wondering though if the *Crow's Nest* could have anything to do with your father's death," Michiko said.

"Because it had been the Brayton family home? Doesn't seem likely," I replied. "The Spites family lost the place at least thirty years ago. After that it was sold and resold half a dozen times, getting more run down with each change of owner. If Spites wanted it, he could have bought it for a song long before Dad did."

Zack raised a forefinger. "I wonder if Spites ever made a bid on the place. If he did and lost out, it might mean something."

"How can we find out?" I asked.

"Nancy Brewster's an investigative journalist. She might be able to dig up some information."

"But what does it mean if he never bid on the place?" Michiko asked.

I considered the question. "Only that he wasn't interested in it at the time. Remember, when Dad bought the house it was falling down. Now it's a landmark."

"I don't really see Brayton giving a hoot," Zack said. "But what about Bubba? Surely he knows it used to be in his family. It could very well be sticking in his craw."

I couldn't imagine Bubba being the least bit interested in a Victorian house either, but I'd missed or misjudged so much I didn't want to completely discount the possibility.

"I learned something else," Michiko said, addressing me. "Helga was in love with your father."

"What?" I gaped. "You're not serious."

"She was in love with him, Jason. Yesterday you saw a woman who admired and respected your father. Today I saw a woman who was having a hard time keeping it all together when she spoke about him."

"Are you suggesting they were more than . . . friends?" Zack asked.

Michiko shrugged. "I don't know what may have been going on between them. All I can tell you is she cared for him in a way that went beyond ordinary friendship."

Another surprise. I asked Michiko if she'd had time to talk to the neighbors and if any of them had seen or heard anything the night my father was killed.

Her dark eyes saddened but never left mine. "I believe I know when he died."

I braced the arms of the chair and straightening. I had a terrible urge to scratch my right knee. "How? When?"

"3:40 a.m."

"Why?"

"Like a lot of old people, Mrs. Chenak in the Gothic house across the street, doesn't sleep very soundly. She said she was awakened abruptly Friday night by the kid next door setting off a firecracker. Apparently he's in and out at all hours of the day and night and does all sorts of outrageous things. A couple minutes later he set off another one."

"I've met him," Zack said. "Struck me as a pretty normal teenager."

"I'm just repeating what she told me. Anyway," Michiko continued, "she says her bedside clock said 3:40. She was about to call the cops when she heard his VW driving away. Since he was leaving, she figured it wouldn't do any good to report him."

Zack glanced at me, then asked Michiko, "Did you talk to the kid? What does he say?"

"Denies everything, setting off the firecrackers, even being out."

"Mrs. Chenak heard two firecrackers?" I asked, puzzled.

"She wasn't exactly sure. The first one, the one that woke her, could have been a door slamming, but she's certain the second noise was a firecracker."

"Then she heard him leave," I mumbled slowly. "Did she hear him return?"

Michiko shook her head. "Says she finally got up around six. By then his car was in the driveway. She was surprised she hadn't heard him come back, because no other car sounds like a VW."

Leon drove a Volkswagen.

CHAPTER TWENTY-EIGHT

A few minutes later Ned strolled into the office wearing snug cut-offs and a skin tight T-shirt. For a moment I caught myself staring at his thickly muscled legs. Mine had been like that. A football player's legs, hard, powerful. He'd stopped by earlier, he said, but found no one around, so he'd gone to the gym on base to work out.

"They let you play with their dumbbells?" Zack asked.

To Ned's quizzical expression, I shrugged.

"All it took was the mention of your name, Tiny Tim." He grinned. "They're very sympathetic toward ninety-seven-pound weaklings."

"Watch it, buddy. I don't play the ukulele and I don't sing falsetto," Zack countered.

Ned gaped at him, then we all laughed. I was amazed at how good it felt.

"When do we start work on the vineyard?" he asked me.

I hadn't forgotten about our project. Confirmation at UT on Friday that vinifera grapes, the European varieties used for making wine, would grow in West Texas had been the reason for our trip to Austin, a detour that had given my father's killer the opportunity to strike. The notion that my failure to come home that night had led to my father's murder was ridiculous, but I couldn't get it out of my head. If I'd been here, maybe the killer wouldn't have shown up. On the other hand, what could I have done in the middle of the night? Walk in on him? Only if swinging my butt across the floor counted as walking. Even then, I'd have been helpless to interfere. Perhaps I, too, would have been killed. Would that be better than living the way I was without even my father's presence?

"As long as you're here," I said, trying to lighten my tone to match my friend's, "you might as well start earning your reputation as our viticulture expert."

Ned went to gas up, check the tires and oil and generally baby his new shiny Karmann Ghia. Meanwhile Zack and I proceeded in the Packard out to the Schmidt ranch. I'd changed into work clothes, a faded-denim shirt and an old pair of jeans, the legs tucked under me. I took out the notepad I always carried on a job and reviewed the list of things to do before the place was ready for our vineyard: clear away the mesquite and prickly pear cactus, build tool and storage sheds, install an irrigation system, and put in rows of poles and wire for the grape vines.

We took Heyward Street north toward the Coliseum, veered east, then north again, continued on another five miles to a dirt road and turned onto the Schmidt ranch. Zack got out and opened the gate, swung it in and jumped behind the wheel. For a few seconds I envied, even resented his careless mobility. I'd had that once, in spades, but I never would again.

The driveway ran straight through a thicket of scrub for a hundred yards, over a rise, then descended to a single-lane plank bridge that crossed a wide bar ditch. Beyond it the road rose gradually to a house set in a grove of old live oak trees. The fissure in the land was invisible from the highway. The illusion was that the road ran directly to the house.

The place was typical West Texas cattle country. Mesquite and cactus, bare dirt and rock. Zack and I knew what we wanted to do with the land, but what about the house? The building was probably sixty years old, a single story, shingle-roofed, dilapidated clapboard structure. There was a ramp at the end of the sagging front porch, and steps that didn't look particularly safe.

A hundred yards behind the house was the pecan orchard Colonel Bart had mentioned. Twenty-five mature trees, half of them dead. What remained wouldn't earn more than pocket change.

"You sure you still want to go through with our plans for the ranch and vineyard?" I asked Zack.

"Don't you?"

I hesitated to say what I was thinking, what I feared. "Did Dad put you up to this?"

Zack looked over at me. He didn't like the implication, what it said about all three of us. I bowed my head.

"If you remember," he said steadily, "we talked about being partners long before we went into the Air Force. Nothing's changed, Jason. I was serious then. I'm serious now. And just in case there's any question in your mind, your legs . . . or lack of them, have nothing to do with it."

He opened the car's electric windows and lit a cigarette.

I was being paranoid again. The shrinks had warned me.

"I keep waiting to wake up, Zack. I feel guilty for being handicapped, as if it were my own fault, and an equally unreasonable suspicion that someone is responsible for crippling me."

He sucked smoke deep into his lungs, let it out through his nose before finally replying. "Survivors experience guilt too, you know. For being whole when other people aren't."

I swiveled around to fully face my friend. "Dad said when you came home you apologized for not finding me sooner. I guess these last few months have been pretty rough on you too." I paused. "Zack, this isn't the way I ever imagined I'd have to spend the rest of my life. But because of you I'm still alive. I can only thank you for that."

In the silence that followed, a persistent breeze wafted its way across us through the open car windows. The sun was high, a scorcher, the sky clear. Soon we'd feel the first refreshing coolness of autumn and the cleansing chill of winter. The cycle would go on.

"I've been thinking about the house," I finally said. "How about we restore it as a simple, classic West Texas ranch house and use it as an office and tasting room?"

"It needs a lot of work." But I could hear enthusiasm for the challenge in his voice.

"Well," I said, "we are in the renovation business. We might as well start with this place. Nothing to lose. If worse comes to worse we can always burn the place down."

"We can call it Theo House."

A lump formed in my throat. "I think he'd like that."

At a distant sound of a vehicle, I looked toward the road.

Ned's Karmann Ghia raised a swirl of dust as it plunged into the gully, bumped over the narrow wooden bridge and roared up to join us. He bounced out of the sports car with the energy of a puppy eager to play.

I told him about Theo House. He approved. On our first trip here, when Zack and I were talking only about raising cattle, Ned had shown no particular interest in the building, the neglected pecan orchard or the land itself, until he'd found the dried-up grapevines along the garden fence. I'd laughed when he suggested we plant a vineyard. Now he wanted a closer look at this "Chateau Crow."

The wrap-around porch made the modest four-room house appear bigger than it was. The front door opened directly into the living room. Two small, high windows flanked a painted-brick fireplace on the left. The kitchen was straight ahead and connected to the master bedroom beside it. A second bedroom opened off the living room. There were no closets, and the only bathroom had been created by enclosing half of the back porch.

The place had never been luxurious, but for some dirt-poor settlers this had probably been a dream come true. The humbleness of the plain wooden porch posts and rattly old windows with their thin wavy panes were very different from the imposing columns and beveled-glass casements of the *Crow's Nest.* I wondered which house had meant more to its original owners.

Back outside, we reviewed plans for our initial experimental acre of vines.

"That'll handle six hundred cuttings," Ned said.

"Which will yield about five tons of grapes," Zack noted.

"Double that," I corrected him, "since we'll be planting vinifera." I'd done careful research after Ned piqued my interest. The statistics still amazed me.

Ned was skimming a handful of powdery dirt from the surface of the dry hardpan at his feet, when a new cloud of dust funneled down to the bridge. Half a minute later a twenty-year-old Chevy pickup reappeared and bumped toward us. The engine coughed and dieseled when the driver turned it off.

Joe Gutierrez was a small wiry man with acne scars marring an otherwise pleasant Hispanic face. In his mid-forties, he'd been born and raised in Coyote Springs, as had several generations before him, yet Spanish was his first language, giving him a subtle, musical accent in English. He owned a fair-size collection of heavy equipment, most of which looked like renegades from a junk yard. Zack and I had worked with him on a couple of restoration projects years before and knew looks could be deceiving. His equipment was in tiptop operating condition.

He put out his hand to Zack then came to me, shook my hand and offered his condolences on the death of my father. It was the first time he'd seen me in several years, but he seemed completely unfazed by my missing legs. If he thought the idea of starting a vineyard in Coyote Springs was crazy, he gave no indication of it. I introduced him to Ned.

We spent more time at the Schmidt ranch than I'd intended, but the excitement of planning the vineyard, discussing cattle and sheep raising, costs of fencing, stock tanks and witching for water was a welcome distraction from the reality of my father's death.

When we got back to the carriage house just after four. Michiko was in the office wearing her nurse's whites. George had let her in. I put my arm around her slim waist as she bent to kiss me. I explained where we'd been.

"Do you like roses?" Ned asked her.

"Sure, why do you ask?"

"Roses and grape are susceptible to pretty much the same diseases, but roses show signs of distress sooner, so we'll plant some throughout the vineyard. I'll even let you pick them," he told her with a wink.

I had just wheeled behind the desk when we heard unfamiliar plodding steps on the stairs. Zack went to the entryway and returned a minute later with Clyde Burker.

CHAPTER TWENTY-NINE

The detective placed a brown cardboard box on the coffee table. I introduced Ned and Michiko. Burker paid scant attention to Ned as they shook hands. He had eyes only for Michiko, who virtually ignored him.

"I understand you're taking over the old Schmidt place," Burker said in his strong West Texas twang. "Place is pretty run-down. Ole Pete wasn't much of a rancher. His love was the steakhouse up on North Heyward."

He plopped heavily into the chair at the corner of the desk.

"Pete's old lady, Velma . . . now she was something else," he rambled on. "Reckon the only soft spot she had, besides Pete, was for that boy of hers."

"You mean Delman?" I asked.

"Was that his name? I only heard her refer to him as Buddy. Didn't live around here. Was in the service somewheres. I stopped her for drunk driving the day she died. Often wondered if taking her in that afternoon instead of seeing her home would've saved her life."

So he played the what-if game too. What if he'd taken her in? What if I hadn't gone to the officers club the night the Tet offensive started? What if I'd come home as planned Friday afternoon?

"I felt sorry for her," Burker went on. "The ranch had been auctioned off. The steakhouse was closed. Pete was dead. They say he lost a leg before he died. Diabetes." Burker suddenly glanced at me, got out a handkerchief and wiped his forehead and the sweatband of his Stetson.

"I reckon it was the booze," he rushed on. "They both drank like fish. Anyway, she died that night. I suppose you could say the booze killed her too. That and the pills."

I fidgeted in my seat. "Did you come here to talk about Pete Schmidt?"

Burker took a deep breath, pushed himself up from the chair, went over to the box and removed a large manila envelope, which he placed on the desk in front of me. "A copy of the medical examiner's official report. Figured you'd want to see it."

I extracted the death certificate. At the bottom, in the block entitled Manner of Death, there were several choices including Homicide and

Pending Investigation. The checkmark was beside Suicide. I slammed the papers down.

Burker waved toward the box. "I also brought your father's personal effects."

"What about the gun?"

"It's there."

I was aware of everyone watching me. "What has your investigation turned up?"

"Like you said, your daddy believed in taking care of his things. The gun was well maintained. One shot fired. His fingerprints were the only ones on it."

"You're absolutely certain it was suicide?" Ned asked. Again I heard sympathy in my former hooch mate's voice.

"No question about it."

"Was the M.E. able to determine the time of death?" Michiko asked.

"Can't be certain to the minute. He estimates somewheres between two and four a.m."

I gazed at her, then turned back to Burker. "That's pretty late, isn't it?"

He shook his head. "Depression's a funny thing. Tends to feed on itself, especially in the dark. What time did your daddy usually go to bed?"

"On Fridays? Anywhere between eleven and one."

"He could've had insomnia. As the night got older and darker, he became more depressed. If he'd held on for a couple more hours, the sunrise might've brought him out of it."

I scanned the official document, searching for something, anything, some clue. "How much had he drunk?"

"Only a small trace of alcohol in his bloodstream. He wasn't drunk, but then you said he wasn't much of a drinker."

"How much was left in the bottle?"

Burker looked at me sharply. "Matter of fact, it was empty."

"The bottle was empty, but Dad had only a trace of alcohol in his bloodstream," I repeated. "Does that make sense to you?"

The note of exasperation in his reply was unmistakable. "It only means he'd finished it a couple hours earlier. Or poured the rest down the sink."

I was getting nowhere. He seemed to have a pat answer for everything. I could tell him about Aaron's late visit, about Debbie's pregnancy, but he'd say it helped explain Dad's depression, or worse, it would make Aaron the prime suspect in a murder Burker said hadn't happened.

Ned spoke up. "Jason thinks his father was murdered. Is it possible?"

"I know he does. That's not unusual. Suicide's hard, especially for members of the immediate family. They feel responsible. Some of them never accept it and get really messed up. Others deny it happened."

"My God," I exploded, "to hear you talk, I have a choice of going crazy or being mad. Apparently you're completely close-minded to the chance that I might be right."

"Look, Crow, what I'm saying is you've got to accept reality. Your daddy killed himself. I'm sorry for your sake, but facts are facts."

I wanted so much to spring from my chair, to pace, to . . . run.

"What about Mr. Crow's health?" Michiko asked.

"He had no terminal disease like cancer, if that's what you're thinking." He regarded me with sad eyes. "You're upset, and Lord knows you got every reason to be, after what happened to you. But you're making a big mistake if you're putting stock in the gun he used being yours. Once a man's made up his mind to take his life, the most important thing is that it be quick and painless. Ain't nothing more effective than a bullet—from anybody's gun."

He rose heavily to his feet. "You think I'm callous, but I got to look at the facts. His marriage was over, and your mom was talking about divorce."

I raised my hand to stop him. "How do you know that?"

"I told you I was gonna investigate. I talked to a member of her church. Understand your daddy refused, but it still means his marriage had failed. Your brother disgraced himself," Burker continued, "dodging the draft, then getting mixed up with drugs. The business here's receiving a surprise audit. Hell, the IRS is unnerving for any of us, even if we ain't successful businessmen."

I had to grant Burker grudging respect. He'd done his homework. "Are you suggesting my father was in trouble with the government?"

"No, I'm not—" he was clearly exasperated "—but lawyers and tax collectors—and cops," he added, "make people nervous, even honest people."

He paused a moment before serving what he probably thought was the crowning blow. "Then there's your sister being involved with a Negro. Aaron Elsbeth may be a credit to his race, but he's still black. I know your daddy was open-minded and made George a partner, but even liberals balk when their daughters are concerned."

Michiko spoke up quickly. "Mr. Burker, from what Jason and Zack have told me, Mr. Crow had a few enemies, like Brayton Spites. I'm not accusing Spites or anyone else, but isn't it possible someone staged this death to look like suicide?"

Burker looked squarely at her. "I'm glad you're not accusing nobody, and I'd be real careful about throwing names like Spites around. He's an influential man in this community, and he can get real nasty when he's riled."

"How about answering her question?" I snapped.

He glared at me, but it seemed more a reflex than personal animus. "Like I told you last night, there were powder marks on your father's hand. He pulled the trigger." He studied me for a moment. "I know it's hard to accept all this. You've been dealt more than your share of problems, but get on with your life. What's past is past."

Except my past would follow me for the rest of my days.

"One final question," I said. "What was my father wearing?"

"Wearing? He was fully dressed. Pants, shirt, shoes and socks. It's all there in the box."

"Doesn't that strike you as odd? A man who went to bed around midnight still fully clothed at three o'clock in the morning?"

"Just means he never went to bed."

"But his bed had been slept in."

Burker shook his head. "You don't know when. It could have been unmade from the night before."

"The cleaning lady, Mrs. Flores, was here that day. She would've made it, if he hadn't."

"Jason, you're grasping at straws."

"And you're ignoring inconvenient facts."

We stared at each other. Michiko broke the tension by asking the detective if he'd be attending the graveside service the next day. He acknowledged he would but probably only briefly. He finally left.

Tight-lipped, I wheeled to the box he'd dropped off. My father's clothes were neatly folded: white shirt, gray pants, black shoes and socks, and a handkerchief. There were three separate manila envelopes, one containing his keys, another his wrist watch and gold wedding ring. The third held the gun.

While Zack put the Smith and Wesson in the safe, I pivoted around to the gun case, opened it with my father's key and examined the weapons. They'd been cleaned, but not recently. Ned opened the bottom drawer for me. There was no way of telling when the cleaning gear had been used last. I'd found dirt in the wastepaper basket but no oily cloth patches.

As for the clothes, I'd checked my father's closet and found the suit Aaron had talked about, the brown pin-stripe. It was on top of the laundry bag of things to go to the cleaners. The tie with the violet accent thread, the only one of its kind, was hanging up. Aaron was right. I would have said it was gray to match the suit. So Dad had had two visitors that night, and he'd gotten out of bed and dressed for the second one.

"By the way—" Ned closed the drawer "—didn't you say your mother was a member of the Church of the Sacrificial Lamb? I ran into a guy at the gym who mentioned it. Excuse me for saying it, but it sounds weird."

"In what way?" I again positioned myself behind the desk.

"They seem to have borrowed ideas from all over. They're opposed to all government service, especially the military, like the Jehovah's Witnesses; have confession and unmarried clergy, like the Catholics; are strict segregationists and believe in a racial hierarchy, like the Mormons. At the top, as you might expect, are the whites, then come the yellow, the red and finally the blacks. I guess I can sort of understand the 'Jesus was white therefore white is best' logic, but I have no idea how they came up with the others. I don't know where you'd fit in, Mich."

She smirked. "I guess that makes me a three-quarters. Gee, Jason, what would our kids be?"

"Just ours," I said without a smile, but I was glowing inside. She wants to have my children! "The head of this church calls himself the High Priest? Any information on him?"

"All this guy knows about him is that his name is Bertram Livingstone."

"Do you think Nancy Brewster might be able to dig up something about this church too?" I asked Zack.

"It sounds like the kind of investigative reporting the press is notorious for."

CHAPTER THIRTY

I had intended for Zack to see Nancy Brewster by himself, but after Michiko went to work at the base hospital and Ned decided to go back to the vineyard, as he was already calling the Schmidt ranch, I became restless. While I showered, put on my legs and clean, more presentable clothes, Zack called ahead to make sure Nancy was home.

We arrived there an hour later. She was standing at the open back door of the gingerbread cottage behind her aunt's two-story house, watched me work myself out of the back seat, then greeted me with a warm smile. The porch had no handrail, so Zack served as a prop as I struggled up the three steps. We went through an old-fashioned kitchen into a living room with a high tin ceiling and polished wood floor. Potted plants hung in the window bay.

She served iced tea laced with mint. "Aunt Helga says you both graduated from CSC with honors."

"They were the best years of my life," Zack said.

"How long were you in the Air Force?"

"A little over three years."

"I thought an Air Force hitch was four years."

"It is," Zack said, "but Ned Herman—you met him yesterday—worked in personnel. After Tet, he asked me what I wanted to do. Naturally, I said come back here. He handled the paperwork so I could get an early release from active duty and complete my military obligation in the reserves. He's not all brawn."

"He also helped Michiko get assigned at Coyote AFB," I added.

"He sounds like a wheeler-dealer," she said.

She started to pour me more iced tea but stopped when I asked, "Was my father having an affair with your aunt?"

"So you know about that?" She resumed pouring.

I do now, I thought. "How serious were they?"

"He was about to ask for a divorce so they could get married."

"Then my mother demanded one herself."

Nancy nodded. "She wanted to give the ranch away. He couldn't grant her a divorce without hurting you . . . and your brother and sister."

"What was your aunt's reaction?"

"Disappointment. She hated having to sneak around."

Being the other woman would have given Helga a motive to kill Mom, I thought, but not Dad. I told Nancy what we knew about the church, passed on the name of the guy Ned had met and asked her if she'd be willing to delve deeper.

"Sounds like the makings of an exposé. Do you think your dad's refusing your mother a divorce could have had anything to do with his death?"

"Like her inheriting the ranch and giving it to them? It's a possibility." One I'd been considering.

"If that's the case, it hasn't worked," Zack added. "Mr. Crow left his interest in the ranch to Jason."

Nancy saw the implications immediately. "Now if she wants to give it to her church, she'll have to fight you to get it. Do you think she will?"

"I don't know. That's why we need to learn more about the church and its leadership."

She frowned. "Is your mother really that dedicated to religion, or is there something else going on?"

I squirmed in my seat. "You mean she might have confessed something to the priest that he's using against her?"

"Like what?" Zack asked. "Leon's all messed up, but that's public knowledge. Debbie's affair with Aaron is hardly a secret, and her pregnancy won't be for long."

"Debbie's pregnant? With Aaron's baby? That does complicate matters." Nancy paused. "Maybe it's the other way around. The church told your mother something they discovered that she feels obligated to keep secret. It wouldn't even have to be true. She'd only have to believe it is."

"There are no limits to lies," I said.

We talked of other things, the vineyard and our plans for ranching the old Schmidt place. Finally it was time to go. I struggled to my feet. She watched, but it was more out of concern than fascination. At the door I shook her hand and held it. "You wrote the column about my father, didn't you?"

She bit her lip. "How'd you know?"

"It wasn't her style."

"But it was her sentiments."

"Thank you." I leaned forward and gave her a kiss on the cheek.

CHAPTER THIRTY-ONE

I settled into my bed. Zack switched off the overhead lights, crawled into the sack across the room. Within a minute he was gently snoring. Despite the long day I was restless. I wanted to get up and walk around, pace the floor, do the casual things I used to do. Instead I closed my eyes and let thoughts and memories drift in and out.

Saigon. Wide boulevards, walled gardens, *fine restaurants. And people. Homesick GIs, hedonistic contractors, native Saigonese, refugees, street people, black marketers, drug dealers, and young girls. Beautiful young girls, Asian and Eurasian, aged beyond their years, selling their bodies in helpless, hopeless degradation. The "Pearl of the Orient" turned rancid.*

I'm stationed at Tan Son Nhut Air Base on the outskirts of the city. It's the major point of embarkation for all of South Vietnam. Zack's assigned to Bien Hoa, only thirty miles away, but tonight's the first time we've gotten to see each other.

We shun the usual game of bar hopping, drinking the swill called Bah-Mi-Bah, buying aggressive prostitutes "Saigon Tea," and go instead to the My Cahn floating restaurant on the river.

"You realize we're breaking all the rules," I tell Zack. "This place's been bombed several times, and the food's open to question."

He scoffs. "I'll take my chances. It's better than GI chow."

An American comes to our table. "Aren't you Jason Crow?" He extends his hand. "Name's Delman Schmidt. I'm from Coyote Springs."

I don't recognize him. "My father used to work for Pete Schmidt. You related to him?"

Delman snorts. "Not so's you'd notice. My folks're good, church-going Christians who don't approve of smoking and drinking and such like." He smiles, puffs on his stogie and orders a bottle of overpriced French wine for the three of us.

We laugh, toast each other's good health and talk about home, always about home.

The old French-colonial city is more of a madhouse than usual this evening as people take advantage of the lunar New Year truce. Since we're all leaving on R&R from Tan Son Nhut early in the morning, I suggest Delman join us for a nightcap at the officer's club on base.

"I'm enlisted," he reminds me.

"You're in civilian clothes. Nobody'll know the difference."

He chuckles. "I heard you guys put your pants on one leg at a time too."

In the club's main bar we buy bottles of beer and wander back to the game room. A few minutes later Delman returns to the main bar. Something he's just said disturbs me, but I can't put my finger on what it is.

I shrug off the feeling of someone walking over my grave. Much better to think about seeing Michiko, imagine touching her, making love to her. I take a deep breath. I have a ring for her in my pocket, if she'll accept it, if she'll marry me. Soon, I tell myself. Soon I'll know.

"Three ball in the corner pocket." I lean over the green-felt table, adjust my stance, then freeze. The familiar shrill whistle above the beat of the rock music in the main bar lasts only seconds, but it's long enough to send an icy shiver down my spine. Oh, God!

"Incoming!" I shout.

A host of obscenities accompanies the mad scuffle of feet as everyone hits the deck.

I crouch against the side of the fat-legged pool table, arms and hands tented over my head. I can't breathe. My heart pounds like a pile-driver during the long eerie silence that finally terminates in a teeth-rattling explosion. Not a direct hit, but close enough to make the tin building shudder. Close enough it jars my bones, rocks tables, spills drinks and tumbles steel beer cans to the chipped asphalt-tile floor. The rocket's concussion drums my ears. Acrid dust pours down from the raw wooden rafters, clogs my nostrils, blurs my vision. The band in the other room stops playing. Beatles's harmony dies, replaced by shouted commands and the high-pitched screams of bar girls.

A second explosion. The earth trembles. I shake.

Damn it, I don't want to be here. I'm supposed to be on R&R in Japan. With Michiko.

Peering across the foggy sea of prostrate figures, I watch a one-armed bandit topple in slow motion, smashing into a tray of beer bottles and dirty glasses. I cover my face as razor-sharp shards spew in every direction. Behind me I hear a heavy thump and an agonized yowl of pain.

"My eyes!" the man in front of me screams. "My eyes!"

Sweet Jesus.

"Stay still," commands Zack from across the room.

I bolt to the injured man a moment before my friend reaches him. A tow-headed second lieutenant has his hands cupped over his face. Blood streams between his fingers, down his wrists, staining his dirty green fatigues an uglier brown.

"Take your hands away," Zack orders. The man slowly complies.

Rapier points of glass protrude from blue eyes that will never see again. I taste my gorge rise.

"My legs," a voice behind me cries out. "Somebody help me."

"I've got this one," Zack assures me. "See what you can do for the other guy."

I leave the blind man. An Army major lies sprawled face down, the calves of his legs pinned under the game room's second billiard table. I motion to a captain and lieutenant colonel in flight suits. "I'll lift. You pull him out." No one argues.

Spreading my feet, bending my knees, arching my shoulders and filling my lungs with the room's contaminated air, I clasp one corner of the massive slate table and slowly raise it. The wounded man's wails catapult into an agonized shriek as his crushed extremities are dragged across the debris-littered floor.

"He's free," the senior officer huffs.

I lower the table with a thud, glance at the victim's blood-soaked pants and wonder if a surgeon will be able to salvage the mangled limbs.

That could have been me. Don't think about death and maiming. Stop shaking.

I survey the room. Dazed officers and civilian contractors are picking themselves up, brushing themselves off. A few cuts, a few scrapes, everyone coughing, but as far as I can determine, no other serious injuries. "You all right?" I call over to Zack.

"Not a scratch."

"Where's Delman?"

"Left just before the VC delivered their calling card," Zack replies over his shoulder. "Said something about seeing a long-lost cousin in the main bar. Check there." He guides the blind lieutenant to a cleared spot on the floor. "We need to get this guy to the hospital. Now."

"I'll call the medics." I step over the game room wreckage, instinctively ducking my head as I go through the doorway to the main bar.

The chaos and litter there are even worse. Young women—they look more like girls—in colorful ao dais, are babbling in tonal Vietnamese. Some are filthy, a few bloody, all terrified. A side door opens. Against the phosphorescent glow of flares illuminating the black sky I see two figures dart by. I start to call out, then the door slams shut.

"You Jason Crow?"

I whirl to face the GI behind the bar. He's hanging up the wall phone. "Yeah—"

"Just got a message for you, Lieutenant. You're to report back to your unit on the double."

It's two o'clock in the morning. How do they even know I'm here?

CHAPTER THIRTY-TWO

Coyote Springs, Texas, Tuesday, August 27, 1968

I woke in the night with a maddening urge to scratch my right knee. I lay there for several minutes massaging the stump, trying to convince damaged nerve ends to give up the bogus sensations. I'd fallen out of bed once in the hospital when I tried in a drug-induced fog to take a step on legs my brain wouldn't accept were no longer there. I was fortunate. The phantom pains I'd been experiencing were annoying but mild, rather than severe and painful. Some guys got hooked on narcotics and pain-killers in an attempt to alleviate the torment. I'd resisted the temptation to use them. I hated feeling lightheaded and out of control.

In the semi-darkness of the room, I kept thinking about the man who had been the dominant influence in my life, the person I looked to for inspiration and guidance and never came away wanting. The man I wanted to be like when I grew up.

Today, in a few hours, I'd bury him.

My musings wandered to him and Helga Collins. How naive I was to not realize Dad had needs too. I took comfort in knowing he'd found someone I respected. I understood now the strange serenity I'd detected in him. Debbie was wrong about his weight loss in the past year. He'd slimmed down because he'd toned up, replaced middle-age flab with firm muscle, not out of grief, but from joy. He'd found a woman who returned his affection.

I thought too about Michiko. I'd waged a torturous war with myself when she first came into my hospital room in Wilford Hall. Stuck in my wheelchair, unable to stand, to hold her in my arms, or touch her in the casual manner lovers do, I wasn't sure which was worse, being with her or being away from her. What I did know was that I couldn't cripple her with my handicap. I tried to push her away. Subconsciously I must have been aware I was testing her, making her prove she really loved me, not felt sorry for me.

"Love isn't a handicap," she assured me. "It raises us above our limitations."

This past week, standing in front of a full-length mirror, I'd begun to hope maybe she was right. I was able to strap on make-believe limbs and stand with my arms around her. Yet something still separated us. Not my missing legs. At least not for her. How could I ask her to love me when I loathed myself?

You can walk if you really want to.

I understood now that Dad wasn't talking about putting one foot in front of the other, at least not solely. He was telling me I was still me, with legs or without.

My lack of self-confidence was having an impact on Michiko's relationship with Zack as well. They'd been friendly enough in Japan, but since Tet, she'd grown cold, at times hostile, to him. Why? Did she resent his wholeness? Did she hold him responsible for what happened to me? The idea was preposterous. How could he have searched for me sooner than he had when he was himself in the hospital with a concussion? Zack saved my life, but after three days no one could have saved my legs. The damage had been done within twelve hours of the tourniquets being applied.

I performed my exercises impatiently that morning. I was restless and needed to get moving. I didn't want the day to start. I just wanted it to be over. I hurried through my shower and emerged to find Zack had fixed us a breakfast of scrambled eggs, toast and coffee. I wasn't hungry, yet I sat at my father's desk and consumed what was served without ever tasting it.

The hearse would be arriving in less than an hour. I was getting ready to cross over to the bedroom when my brother appeared in the doorway. He'd trimmed his beard, exposing his cleft chin.

"Jay, I'm sorry about the other day. I shouldn't have said what I did, not to you."

"It was the shock," I assured him.

"You said I don't like you. It's not true. It's just . . . I feel so stupid and clumsy around you. You're always in control. If what happened to you happened to me . . . I think I'd rather die than . . ." He blushed furiously. "See? I'm forever saying stupid things."

"Not stupid, Lee. Honest. I also told you I'd like to be your friend."

He bowed his head. "I'd like that too."

I had questions about *The Joint* on Sunday, about his plans for the future.

"I need to get dressed," I announced and started to maneuver around the side of the desk.

A year ago I would have invited him into the bedroom so we could talk while I got dressed. I didn't now. Leon was uncomfortable enough at the sight of me fully clothed. So many things that had once been natural and spontaneous had been taken away from me when the surgeon amputated my legs. Friends, family, opportunity.

Leon went downstairs.

Twenty-five minutes later, wearing my legs and a western-cut medium-blue suit, I took the elevator to ground level and was relieved to find my brother sitting on the bench under the staircase. I lowered myself to the seat beside him, aware of his discomfort at the concentration I had to use in performing such a routine act. Zack clattered down the stairs, saw us and occupied himself with inspecting the raised bed of pink hydrangeas at the foot of the staircase. The plant George had mentioned Saturday night that kids had disturbed, had shriveled and died.

"What's happened to us, Lee? We've grown so far apart."

My brother shook his head. "We've never been like real twins, have we? We don't look alike, think alike, act alike."

"But we used to be closer."

"Maybe we've grown apart simply because we're different."

I decided this was not the time to get philosophical or to pussyfoot around subjects. "Are you still using hard drugs?"

To my relief, he didn't take offense. "I was for a while, but I'm off them now."

"It didn't smell that way Saturday," Zack interjected.

Leon looked over at him and scoffed. "That? That was just a little pot Kern picked up. Pot's no worse than booze. In fact, it's better. You don't get a hangover from it, and it isn't fattening."

"It's still illegal," I pointed out. "Illegal enough to get you busted."

"Not unless you're dealing."

"And you're not?"

"No, I'm not," Leon replied, the temper that seemed always just below the surface beginning to rise.

With that, Zack announced he wanted to change his tie and went upstairs.

Once he was gone, Leon asked, "What would you do if you found out somebody you knew was gay?"

What a sad anti-word, I thought, and what a strange time to bring up the subject. "Nothing. It would be his business, not mine."

"Would you remain his friend?"

"Why not?"

"You wouldn't feel compromised?"

"Why should I? It doesn't change who I am."

"Would you want to know, if he was a friend of yours?"

I wondered where this conversation was leading. Was Leon trying to tell me he was homosexual? He'd never dated much, but . . .

"If it was going to be an issue," I replied. "But basically what consenting adults do in private is their business, as long as there's no third-party victim."

Could this be what Mom had discovered and wanted kept secret? I didn't believe it. The revelation might be scandalous but hardly worth the family ranch.

Hearing Zack coming down the wooden steps, Leon dropped the subject as quickly as he'd raised it.

"I've made a lot of mistakes, Jay."

"We all have."

"You've got your honor."

"At a cost."

"The price isn't important. Honor is."

I thought of what Dad had told me all those years ago when I'd been cheated out of the high school class presidency. *We can't control what other people do. We can only act honorably in our own lives.*

"If I had one thing to do differently," my brother continued, "I'd go over there and take my chances."

"Do you think the war's justified then?" Zack asked. He'd changed his dark-blue tie for a black one.

Leon faltered, annoyed at the interruption. "No, I don't."

"I think I've finally come to agree with you," Zack admitted. "Unfortunately, people in power don't take unwashed, long-haired, dope-heads very seriously." What had started out as a sympathetic statement was turning into acrimony. "Aiding and abetting the enemy won't stop the war. It'll just get more people killed and crippled."

The veins in Leon's neck stood out. "Are you calling me a traitor? Are you blaming me for what happened to Jay?"

I cut in. "He didn't mean it that way, Lee. Look, you may be right about the war, I don't know myself anymore. That's not relevant at the moment."

"No, he's dead." Leon got up and stood in front of me. "There won't be any more recriminations from him." He glared at Zack. "And I won't take any from you."

For a change, Zack kept his mouth shut and after a few moments of tense silence, Leon sat down again.

"I'm moving back to the family ranch, Lee," I announced. "For Mom's sake. Why don't you come live with us? We both need you, and the ranch, well, it's sort of neutral turf. Our memories and associations with it are happy ones. Help me with Mom. Let's try to be a family again."

My brother's reply was sad, resigned. "It's a nice thought, Jay, but it won't work. Too much has happened to Mom, to you and to me. We had some good times there when Gramps was alive, but that was a long time ago. We're not kids anymore. It's better to leave the good memories where they are. We can't go back."

He rose, paced, spun around and faced me.

"I'm leaving, Jay. As soon as Dad's estate is settled and I get my share, I'm returning to Central America. It's my home now. You should see the jungles. They're beautiful, so full of wildlife." I winced at the thought of tropical jungle, but he didn't notice. "And my friends are there. I teach them English. My Spanish has gotten pretty good too."

"You're leaving?" Zack shot a worried glance at me.

"I don't belong here anymore. I came back to see Jay and get some money. You don't really need me, and I'm tired of looking over my shoulder to see if I'm about to be arrested as a draft dodger . . . or pot-head," he added, with a touch of sarcasm. "You have your world here. You don't deserve the shame of my presence."

"I'm not ashamed of you, Lee. Give things a chance to work themselves out. You haven't been here even a month."

"It's enough. I'm leaving."

"Don't go," Zack implored. "It'll look like you're running away again."

The limousines were pulling into the courtyard.

"Right," Leon said obstinately. He got up and walked away.

"Wait," I cried out, as I struggled to my feet.

CHAPTER THIRTY-THREE

I plodded heavily around the corner of the carriage house, the tight, constricting prostheses agonizing in the summer heat. Leon stood in the courtyard with the Elsbeths, Debbie and Michiko, but he didn't appear any more comfortable with them than they were with him.

I'd arranged for the hearse containing my father's casket to come to the *Crow's Nest* to lead the cortege from there. George tried, through watery eyes, to offer a consoling smile, but the effort only made the torment on his face more heart-wrenching. Dad had touched so many lives so deeply. Some people had welcomed my declaration that he'd been murdered, because it meant he hadn't abandoned them, hadn't proclaimed they didn't count in his life. If there had been any lingering doubt in my mind that he was murdered—there wasn't—it would have fled at that moment. I did matter to my father, and so did these people. We had been his world, part of his identity and individuality.

"Your friend Cole called," George told me. "He ran into car problems in Dorr, said he'll get here as soon as he can."

"Damn that piece of junk he's driving," Zack muttered.

My brother overheard the comment and perked up. "He's still having trouble with the Volvo? He shouldn't be. I back flushed the radiator a couple of times when he was here. That should have cleared up the problem."

"He told me about it Friday night," Ned commented. "Did you change the thermostat?"

"Where was I supposed to get a thermostat on a Sunday?" Leon snapped.

"You have a point."

Limousine assignments had already been decided: Mom, Leon, Debbie and I in the first car, followed by George, Zack, Aaron and Michiko in the second. Except Mom wasn't here. My sister had driven out to the ranch that morning to pick her up, but Mom insisted on meeting us at the cemetery.

"Every time I go out there," Debbie complained, "no matter what I say, she takes offense."

"Does she know about you and Aaron?" Leon asked.

She shrugged. "I've always gone alone. She's never said anything, and I figure she would if she knew."

I watched my brother. His sullen expression suggested something besides Zack's remarks were bothering him. He said he'd come back for money. What money? Certainly not an inheritance. He wasn't earning much as a grease monkey. Did he need money for something in particular?

An escort of off-duty motorcycle policemen accompanied our cortege to the cemetery. It was a rare summer day in West Texas. The air was still. High clouds, overcast from horizon to horizon, sealed in what little moisture the arid land gave up, producing a closeness that was oppressive.

A large number of people had already assembled in the shade of the spreading live oak trees. The flutter of white handkerchiefs being used as fans reminded me of little birds trapped in cages. Was one of the people standing patiently in the sultry shadows the person who'd murdered my father and cut off yet another part of my life? I saw familiar faces: the mayor, members of the city council, Helga Collins, Nancy Brewster, our family physician, our attorney, *Crow's Nest* employees present and past. I shuffled, nearly stumbled, on the uneven turf, heard indrawn breaths and caught the strained expressions on people's faces.

Will he fall? What should I do if he does?

We were in place under a canvas awning when my mother arrived accompanied by a clean-cut young man wearing a black suit, white shirt and black tie. He hung back as she approached us. I took her hands, gazed into her red, watery blue eyes beneath a coarse black veil. I saw nothing there, no emotion. This cold detachment was so out of character it frightened me. I kissed her lightly on the cheek.

Rabbi Symunts stepped to the head of the casket. A middle-aged man with an air of contentment reflected in his ordinary features, he spoke slowly, comfortingly, even joyfully, about the deceased, not as a memory, but as a companion still by our sides. When he finished, he nodded to me. I took a stiff step forward and recited from memory a piece written by Canon Henry Scott Holland more than half a century before.

Death is nothing at all.
I have only slipped away into the next room.
I am I, and you are you.
Whatever we meant to each other,
That we are still.
Call me by my old familiar name,

Speak to me in the easy way you always used.
Put no difference in your tone,
Wear no forced air of solemnity or sorrow.
Laugh as we always laughed
At the little jokes we enjoyed together.
Play, smile, think of me, pray for me.
Let my name be ever the household word that it always was.
Let it be spoken without effort,
Without the ghost of a shadow in it.
Life means all that it ever meant.
It is the same as it ever was
There is absolute unbroken continuity.
What is death but a negligible accident?
Why should I be out of mind
Because I am out of sight;
I am waiting for you, for an interval,
Somewhere very near
Just around the corner.
All is well.
Nothing is past; nothing is lost
One brief moment and all will be as it was before
How we shall laugh at the trouble of parting when we meet again!

I felt my father's presence so powerfully, so painfully, that when I looked up I expected to see him standing there, smiling.

As the casket was lowered into the ground, people approached in single file, bent down and threw the traditional handful of dirt into the grave. Zack picked up a second fistful and offered it to me. It was an ancient symbol. Bury the body, put it to rest. But there could be no rest for me until the dead man's murderer was found. I had no intention of ever forgetting the one person, who more than any other, had molded my life.

My mother was returning to her car with her escort when Brayton Spites, who'd come late, stepped in front of her. She took his outstretched hands and clutched his arms as he kissed her on the cheek.

The painful lump in my throat receded as hot rage consumed me.

CHAPTER THIRTY-FOUR

I wished Spites hadn't come to the cemetery, that he wasn't a shadow in my life. To my relief he didn't linger. After greeting my mother he returned to his idling car and drove away. The showdown that I sensed was inevitable was for the present averted.

The reception that followed in the Crystal Room was brief, considering the number of people who attended. Many of those who hadn't stopped by on Sunday brought food now. It was all carefully laid out on the sideboard, though few seemed interested in partaking of it. Most shook hands with the bereaved, said the appropriate words of sympathy and left. A few shared a drink or a plate of food with a fellow mourner. Helga Collins and Nancy Brewster didn't make an appearance. In a private word to me at the cemetery, Helga said only that she hoped to see me soon.

My mother chose a seat near the door, close enough for people to stop by, but remote enough to discourage any lingering. Her young male escort sat silently at her elbow. I had already introduced myself and prevailed upon the guy to do the same. I had then made it a point to write his name down in my pocket notepad. Brother Steven, as he called himself, tried to act blasé, but I could see he was unnerved by the action, which was exactly my intent.

After the last visitor had left, the Crows and the Elsbeths moved into the parlor for the reading of the will. Brother Steven parked himself in a chair in the hall within view of the door. Michiko and Ned remained in the Crystal Room. He did his best to distract and amuse her with the sad tale of how he'd gotten stopped for speeding in Jordan but talked his way out of a ticket, because the cop was into bodybuilding too. Her smile wasn't very convincing.

By unspoken consensus I was placed at the head of the long table where, less than two weeks before, my father had presided over a festive celebration. I was struck by how the change in vantage point wrought differences in perspective. I'd experienced the same sensation when I'd found myself looking up from the confines of a bed or wheelchair. It had seemed impossible initially that I'd ever be able to walk on what the surgeons had left me.

"Failure is more honorable than never having tried," my father had reminded me.

So I'd persevered, but the victory seemed as hollow now as my new limbs. I'd willingly abandon them and accept life in a wheelchair if doing so would bring my father back.

Our family attorney, Grover Reed, sat on my right. He seemed inspired by the occasion to be pedantically laborious in reading the complex will and explaining its provisions. From my new position, I watched the reactions of the people at the table.

George, sitting at the far end, nodded slightly when Zack was named executor. Obviously he knew about the change. He also showed no surprise when Reed told him he'd been given control of the finest steakhouse in West Texas. His sole response was to murmur the price was too high.

His son Aaron, sitting quietly next to Debbie, seemed genuinely surprised by his bequest. He said nothing, however, only reached for Debbie's hand and squeezed it.

My sister listened passively when her name was mentioned, showed concern, even anger, at being placed under Zack's guardianship—until she heard that her inheritance would be turned over to her when she married.

Through all this, Leon slumped in his chair, sulky and pouting—until the lawyer explained Zack's role in controlling his inheritance. Then the brooding features turned crimson with outrage. I braced myself for the explosion I knew was coming. But it didn't.

On my left, my mother sat lethargically, as if she weren't listening. The black veil she'd insisted on wearing, even indoors, had gone awry, making her appear drunk. Black was not her color. In the artificial light of the dark-paneled room she looked old and brittle, her sallow complexion taking on a greenish tinge. She asked no questions. When the reading and the explanations were completed, she took a crumpled envelope from her handbag and passed it quietly to me, then stood up.

"Even in death he mocks me," she muttered. Seeing Debbie sitting beside Aaron, her hand in his, she frowned at her daughter. "You're more like your father than I realized."

Mom left. I would have run after her if I could have. Through the open door, I saw Brother Steven follow her. No one else moved, as though they understood the drama was not yet over. Indeed, her departure galvanized Leon into action.

"You bastard," he growled at Zack sitting directly across from him. "Little king of the mountain."

"Leon, please," Debbie pleaded.

He gave her a withering glance that made her recoil into silence, then he bolted from his seat and started for the door. Just short of it he spun around, venom in his eyes. "You may be my brother's keeper," he shouted at Zack, "but you're not mine."

I called out to him and leaned forward, my hands clasping the table as I pulled myself to my feet.

"Let him go, Jason," Debbie said. "There's no reasoning with him when he's like this. Give him time to cool off."

She was right, but I wanted to rant at the feeling of impotent rage welling up inside me.

George relieved the tension by inviting everyone to the other room for a drink. Reed politely declined, said his farewells and left. In the Crystal Room, we found Cole Wainton sitting with Michiko and Ned. He apologized to me for missing the interment.

After everyone had been served a drink, George asked me if I'd received my telephone call.

"What phone call?"

"Sorry, I forgot to tell you earlier. A man rang twice this morning. His voice sounded familiar, Mexican I think, but I couldn't place it, and he wouldn't leave his name."

"What did he say?"

"Just that he had to talk to you personally."

"If it's important," Cole assured me, "he'll call back."

"Probably Joe Gutierrez," Zack said.

The group was breaking up, but before anybody got away Michiko invited everyone to her place for dinner. She'd been promising to prepare an authentic Japanese meal for some time. George declined. He simply wasn't up to it. Debbie and Aaron thanked Michiko with obvious regret, but they were attending a civil rights meeting that evening. Ned accepted without hesitation. Cole asked that it be an early evening since he had a long, mechanically uncertain drive home. We agreed to meet at Michiko's house at five o'clock.

Zack and I returned to the carriage house alone. I'd quietly slipped the envelope my mother had given me into my jacket pocket while she was leaving. Leon's outburst had distracted people's attention enough afterward that no one mentioned it.

Only now did I examine the standard letter-size envelope postmarked Coyote Springs, dated June 6th, 1966—more than two years earlier. Inside was a single sheet of ordinary paper, obviously much handled. I wondered how many times my mother had taken it out and read it. I perused the short, typewritten message in the middle of the page:

TC loves nigger women's black bodies.

Ask him about Lavinia.

I tasted bile. Surely this was not the cause of the split between my parents? It was incredible that my mother could give credence to this kind of malicious garbage.

I removed my coat and tie, then asked Zack to drive me to the family ranch to see her. I wanted to remove my legs as well, but decided wearing them would make her more comfortable.

As I sat once more in the back seat of the Packard, I found myself thinking, not of Mom, but of Lavinia. Aaron's mother had been a beautiful woman, tall and slim with fine features. She came from the British Caribbean and spoke with an accent that echoed more closely that of Helga Collins than a southern drawl or West Texas twang. Lavinia had played piano in their local Negro church and encouraged, even inspired, Aaron's musical talent.

Less than a year after Zack and I went into the service, she was diagnosed with cervical cancer and died a few months later. My father had kept me apprised of the tragic events, but it was from Debbie that I learned how depressed Aaron became after his mother's death. Looking back now, I realized it must have been during that period they'd been drawn to each other as lovers.

Considering how much George had loved Lavinia, it came as no surprise that he hadn't remarried.

"Joy," my father once said, "can bring people together, but pain binds them forever."

Studying the hate letter in my hand, I knew from the postmark it had been sent after Lavinia's death. What I didn't understand was why or by whom? Perhaps my mother could tell me.

CHAPTER THIRTY-FIVE

The drive to the ranch was a waste of time. My mother wasn't there. I called to a couple of Mexican workers mending the fence near the house. Self-conscious about the Spanish I hadn't used in several years, I nevertheless learned she hadn't returned that afternoon and, of course, they had no idea where she might be or when she'd be back. A detour to Leon's place was no more productive. Neither he nor his pea-green VW were there.

We arrived at the carriage house to find Ned Herman leaning against his Karmann Ghia.

Zack and Ned waited in the office, while I crossed the hall to remove my legs and change clothes. Before doing so, however, on an impulse I suggested to Zack that he call Nancy and invite her to the dinner at Michiko's. "Tell her to wear something comfortable, since she'll be sitting on the floor."

Twenty minutes later I settled into the front seat of the Packard. Ned followed in his car. When we arrived at her cottage, Nancy was rocking on the front-porch glider, wearing an ankle-length floral skirt and an old fashioned white lace blouse. Her auburn hair was gathered atop her head with tortoise-shell combs. Zack seemed fascinated by the archaic style and complimented her on it.

I had him stop in front of Michiko's house so Nancy could go in through the front door. Ned pulled to the curb behind us. I watched as Michiko greeted them with a deep Japanese bow, her white tabi-ed feet held modestly together. She was wearing a pale-green summer kimono with red and white blossoms below knee level. The obi was maroon. Her shiny black hair was piled high, exposing her slender neck. With her pale complexion and dark almond eyes, she was the classic Japanese beauty, the charming hostess whose singular concern was the pleasure and comfort of her guests.

The house consisted of a small living room, a tiny kitchen, two little bedrooms and a single bath. My first renovation project with Zack a couple of weekends ago had been to cut long thin wooden strips, notch them, and paint them with black gloss enamel. They formed a grid on the stark white-papered walls of the living room and one bedroom. Michiko had covered the worn carpet with tatami mats, and Zack had hung Japanese lanterns over the light fixtures. An oriental screen concealed the door to the kitchen and formed a small alcove where a low, black-lacquer chest held a severe arrangement of dried flowers.

The tape deck, neatly ensconced in the hall closet, was playing koto music. The stark, deceptively simple, almost primitive plucked instrument—the sound reminded me of a banjo— was entrancing.

After Ned, Nancy and Michiko had gone inside, Zack pulled around to the driveway at the rear of the house. I used my wheelchair to get to the back door, but there I left it. I was just coming from behind the screen, pendulating my legless body across the room to the low round table when Nancy saw me and complimented us on the beauty of the room. Her easy acceptance of my physical condition made me exhale with relief. She'd passed a crucial test.

Cole was the last to arrive. He'd had his car's cooling system back flushed one more time, the thermostat replaced, and the fluid levels checked in preparation for his return drive to Austin. He took a place by the wall between Ned and Nancy.

"You didn't say the other night if you were going into civil or criminal law," Ned commented to him.

When Cole had announced he'd be attending law school at UT, Ned had been scathing. "The second oldest profession. At least the first one gives its clients pleasure."

"I think you look like the criminal type," Zack said.

Cole laughed. "Thanks a lot."

"I don't know," Ned joined in. "Criminal law is cut and dried. If you steal, cut off your hand. If you kill, chop off your head. An eye for an eye, a tooth for a tooth. Civil law is a much more fun. 'I don't like you, so I'm going to screw . . . er . . . sue you.'"

Cole stroked his beard in mock seriousness. "Don't get mad, get even, huh? Sounds like good advice to me."

"Hey, guys, lighten up." I said with a laugh and accepted a hot wet hand cloth from the tray Michiko was passing around.

Taking advantage of the gas jet in the living room baseboard that was used for a space heater in winter, Michiko had run a rubber hose to a portable burner so she could cook at the table Japanese style.

Our first course was crispy fried vegetable tempura. She seemed a little surprised when Ned liked it. "You strike me as the meat-and-potatoes type."

"It beats West Texas fare," he mocked, "where an hors d'oeuvres is potted meat on a saltine."

I rolled my eyes. Cole frowned.

The second course was Sukiyaki which Michiko pronounced Sk'yaki, served with transparent soba noodles. Cole passed up the raw egg she offered to go on it, but Nancy, undaunted, accepted.

Green tea was also served, but after one sip, Cole commented that it tasted like spinach water, and he didn't like spinach. "Got any beer?"

"How about sake?" Michiko asked.

"Oh, no." He laughed. "Once was enough. Beer I can handle."

Nancy was instantly alert. "Do I smell a war story here?"

I grinned and invited Zack to tell the tale.

"Jason and I had been stationed in Japan several months," he began, "when Cole came through on his way to Danang."

"Cole was Zack's training officer in OTS," I pointed out.

Zack took up the narrative. "Cole's first question when he found out I was from Coyote Springs was to ask if I knew the guy who'd won the *Texas College Athlete of the Year Award.* Jason was pretty well known, not just in Texas but nationally. There was a lot of talk about him playing for the Dallas Cowboys."

My glory days, I ruminated, filled with a bright future.

Zack went on. "When I told him Jason was my best friend, Cole said he'd like to meet him some time."

"The opportunity didn't come until Japan," Cole added. "In one day I had four firsts. My introduction to the Land of the Rising Sun, meeting Jason, discovering sake and falling in love with Michiko. I quickly learned to respect the first three and that I was doomed to a broken heart over the fourth."

Michiko demurely reached over, took Cole's right hand in both of hers, batted her eyelashes and said in a mocking accent, "Don't butterfly me, G.I."

Everybody laughed at the reference to Madame Butterfly, the opera in which an American officer uses a young Japanese girl, then abandons her.

Zack clucked his tongue. "Who's telling this anyway?"

"Sorry," Cole mumbled contritely. "Go on."

"I better explain," Zack said. "Japanese side streets are very narrow. Some have only catwalks on one side or no sidewalks at all. They're sort of like tunnels."

"They're not the only hazards," Cole added, chuckling. "Let me tell you, the kamikazes are alive and well and humoring their death wishes as taxi drivers."

This time Michiko grinned at me. For a moment the present slipped away. It was like old times, the group of us talking over each other, Michiko and I making subtle eye contact.

"I think we've got the picture." Ned fidgeted, showing all the signs of boredom at having to listen to a familiar story. "Three intoxicated GIs staggering through narrow alleys where murderous hackeys sport. Go on."

Zack ignored the sarcasm. "We'd just finished a round of sake in a stand bar, and tight-wad Cole here was reluctantly picking up the tab. Jason was about to step into the street. I was right behind him."

"Behind him?" Cole interjected, "you were right on his butt."

"All of a sudden," Zack continued unfazed, "Cole grabs me by my shirt collar and yanks me back."

Cole took up the narrative. "I heard a car screaming down the street and was sure Jason was about to walk right in front of it. He was too big for me to manhandle the way I had little Zack here, so I did the next best thing. I gave him the biggest shove I could."

"It was a good one, all right," I agreed. "Sent me sailing clear across the street. You should've seen the expression on the driver's face." I laughed.

"It didn't seem so funny at the time," Zack said. "Jason and I walked away without a scratch, but poor Cole only narrowly escaped getting himself killed."

"Ahem—" Cole coughed "—the cab barely touched me."

"You could have fooled us," Zack rejoined with a loud snort. He turned to the others. "He was screaming in pain."

"The one thing we could be sure of," I added, "was that his vocal chords hadn't been damaged."

"They're exaggerating, of course."

"Uh-huh." Zack grinned.

"We had to commandeer the offending taxi," I said, "and rush Cole to the American hospital at Tachikawa."

"The next day," Cole said, "after these two lugs had sobered up, they paid me a visit and—"

"And found him in great torment—" Zack went on melodramatically "—with a sprained ankle."

"My only consolation—" Cole reached over, and this time gathered Michiko's hand in his "—was this beautiful Eurasian Florence Nightingale."

She fluttered her eyelashes. They both laughed.

"But Jason," Cole continued, "is so much against pain and suffering, he took her away from me so she wouldn't have to witness it."

"So that's how you met," Nancy said.

Michiko slipped her hand out of Cole's. "Karma." She gazed at me, then poured hot sake into tiny cups.

"Frankly," Zack said to Cole, "I don't think you ever had a chance."

Cole smiled. "Against a six-foot-six All American quarterback? Are you kidding?"

The silence that followed could have been very uncomfortable if it had lasted more than a second.

"Here, try this." Michiko handed Nancy one of the shallow cups.

As I watched and waited for Nancy's reaction, I realized Cole's thoughtless remark was actually a compliment. For the moment he'd forgotten I was no longer a football hero. So had I. In my mind I was walking down the halls of Tachikawa hospital in excited anticipation of seeing the most beautiful woman I'd ever encountered.

"This doesn't taste so lethal." Nancy took a second sip.

Cole smirked. "Wait till you try to stand up."

Zack asked Michiko about the inspection at the hospital.

She huffed. "Some narcotics haven't been properly accounted for, so the inspectors are having a field day. Now they're attacking the filing system. My boss has me sifting through old medical records, most of which should have been destroyed or retired ages ago."

Nancy helped Michiko clear the table.

"Do you still think your father was murdered?" Cole asked me, when they'd resumed their seats.

"Definitely," I replied, the relaxation I'd begun to enjoy, vanishing.

"Jason, how?" Michiko asked. "The police say—"

"I asked you the other day if you thought my father killed himself. You said no. Were you just humoring me?"

She knelt demurely, a good Japanese woman, but her firm reply came from her American half. "No, I wasn't humoring you. I still find it incredible your father would take his own life, but incredible doesn't mean impossible."

"And lack of evidence doesn't constitute positive proof," I retorted more sharply than she deserved.

Cole shook his head. Nancy asked how the reading of the will had gone. I gave her a brief outline of its terms.

"I don't understand why your father didn't make you executor," Michiko said to me as she poured a fresh pot of hot tea.

"The way the will's written, if I understand it correctly," Cole explained, "Jason's only security is his possession of the family ranch. Making him executor would weaken his position if his mother decides to challenge the will in court. He wouldn't be able to claim poverty or helpless dependence if he were in control of large sums of money. Also, the opposition could, and probably would, say he was in no position to supervise his brother's activities from a wheelchair. They might even use his handicap to question his competence."

"That's ridiculous."

"Cole's right," I said. "Dad knew what he was doing. Can you imagine what it would have been like for George if he'd remained executor? Mom's church would contest every decision he made and drive him to a nervous breakdown, then claim it proved he was incompetent to handle the responsibility. In fact, Zack, you might be in for the same treatment."

"What about the Schmidt place? Who gets that?" Cole asked.

"The vineyard? Oh, I already own that," Zack said. "Mr. Crow mentioned in one of his letters to me in 'Nam that it was being auctioned off and that it would probably go cheap. I wrote back and said I was interested in buying it if the price was right, and that I'd send him a power of attorney to represent me. But time ran out. Apparently somebody else was interested in it too, so Mr. Crow bought it in his own name. We finally transferred title last week. I'd had to wait for my Gold Flow funds to come through."

"Gold Flow?" Nancy asked.

"The government's worried about GIs overseas spending too much money there," Zack explained, "and contributing to our balance of payments problem. So they allow service members stationed outside the US to put up to ten-thousand dollars in a special account that pays ten percent interest, but you can't take the money out until you come back to the states."

"Sounds like a good deal," Nancy commented.

"But I thought you were partners," Michiko said.

"We are," I told her. "We signed the papers last Monday too."

The meal over, Cole stood up, stretched and began to say his good-byes.

"See you this weekend?" I asked.

"You're going ahead with your Labor Day barbecue then? I figured—"

"It's traditional and it's been advertised for weeks."

"But—" Michiko started.

"Dad would want us to."

"Good for you," Cole said. "I'm sure he'd like that. I'll definitely be here if I can get a new car by then. By the way—" he paused "—my offer stands. If you can use extra capital, count me in. I'd rather invest with friends than have money sit idly in the bank."

"Thanks, Cole. We'll keep it in mind." I didn't want to commit or discuss it further now, especially with Ned scowling at me.

Cole kissed Michiko on the cheek, told Nancy he'd enjoyed meeting her, shook hands with Zack, Ned and me and departed.

As soon as the door closed, Ned spoke up. "You're going to let him invest in the vineyard?"

"Too bad you couldn't stick around Friday," I told him. "It took a while, but we finally convinced him we weren't crazy."

"Where would he get that kind of dough?"

"He told us his mother died last year and left him a big insurance policy, and he has his Gold Flow savings from 'Nam as well as the GI bill for school."

"And now he has a part-time job with a law firm," Zack added. "So he's not hurting."

I could hear Ned's thinking: *I should be the one investing.*

"Which reminds me," he said, "I was able to track down the real estate agent who handled the sale of the *Crow's Nest* to your father. She said as far as she knows no one had made an offer on the place in years. She was sure Spites never had. Word would definitely have gotten around."

That seemed to rule out the *Nest* as a motive for Brayton Spites to murder his archenemy. Or did it?

Two hours later, Ned left, Zack drove Nancy home, and I found myself alone with Michiko.

CHAPTER THIRTY-SIX

She lay snugly against my chest. We'd been quiet for some minutes, our breaths in sync, and it seemed to me our heartbeats too.

"Are you sure?" I finally asked. "Really sure?"

She raised her head and peered at me in the shadowy stillness of her bedroom, a soft, conspiratorial smile coming to her lips. "Did I hold back?"

Impulsively I tightened my hold on her. "If you did, God help me. I won't survive your letting go."

I felt the jiggle of her naked breast against my bare skin as she chuckled. "Me, neither." She gazed into my eyes. "I'm sure, Jason. No reservations. No doubts. No regrets. I want to spend the rest of my life with you."

I closed my eyes.

"Jason?" her voice was soft, gentle, understanding. "Jason, look at me." I opened my eyes. "It's going to be all right. You'll be all right. We are. I love you. Nothing else matters."

We kissed. I began to stir.

The phone rang.

I wanted to let it ring, and from the expression on her face, she was tempted as well. Telephone calls at ten o'clock at night didn't bode well.

"It might be the hospital," she murmured unhappily. She'd wrangled the night off in spite of the IG's visit, but favors of that sort always came with strings attached.

"Hello."

I watched the expression on her face slam from annoyance to tight-lipped anger. She handed me the instrument. "It's Zack."

"What's the matter? What's happened?" I asked into the receiver.

"I'm sorry to call you," he said, his tone echoing his apology. "I wouldn't, except—"

"Just tell me, Zack."

"I talked to Nancy about the church. It's not good, but when I got home Cole called me from Austin."

"Cole? Why—"

"He found out some things about the high priest. He and the church are under investigation. They've already been banned in several states. What I'm hearing is scary, Jason. I don't think it's a good idea for you to leave your mother alone with them."

"Why?"

"Nancy spoke to a woman whose son had to be sent to California for de-programming after he'd been rescued from the Church of the Sacrificial Lamb. For one thing, this so-called church uses drugs to control people."

"What kind of drugs?" I could feel Michiko staring at me.

"Uppers, downers, hallucinogens like LSD and peyote. On older recruits, like your mom, it's mostly soporifics like opium."

"Opium?" Drugs would explain my mother's mood swings, her essential lethargy.

"There's more. Nancy's informant heard about two people who died and left their entire estates to the church. One was a man in his mid-twenties who'd inherited a couple of oil wells after his parents were killed in a small-plane crash. He died very suddenly of a heart attack."

Guys in their twenties might lose a leg or two in an accident or war, I reflected, but even in battle they didn't often have heart attacks. "And the other person?"

"A suicide. A middle-aged woman whose husband and daughter died in an automobile accident was inconsolable until the Church came along and saved her. Then suddenly, three months later she took an overdose of sleeping pills after making out a new will that disinherited her brother and sister and left everything to the Church. The family's contesting the will because the estate turned out to be worth about two-and-a-half million dollars."

"Come pick me up."

"Now?"

"Yes, damn it. Now."

"Do . . . Do you want me to bring your legs?"

"I don't have time for that." I paused for less than a heartbeat. "But bring a gun." We hung up simultaneously.

Michiko's eyes were wide, troubled. "What's going on, Jason?"

What little I knew seemed flimsy on retelling, but I trusted Zack's instincts. He'd saved my life.

When he arrived at Michiko's house less than fifteen minutes later, she and I weren't arguing exactly, but we were having a heated discussion. She wanted to come with me. I wouldn't let her. She finally relented when I explained what I needed her to do.

"Okay, what else can you tell me about this church?" I asked Zack, as we pulled away from Michiko's house.

Thick clouds made the black night starless. Distant flashes of lightning in the southwest punctuated the tense drive out to the family ranch.

"You don't join the church," he said. "It joins you."

"Excuse me?"

"You can't go to them and say you want to become a member. It's more like a secret society. They identify potential candidates, then convince them they can be admitted to the ranks of the righteous if they meet the church's rigid standards. You can imagine how they select their candidates. Victims is a better word. From what this woman told Nancy, the high priest has novices confess their most intimate secrets and fears in minute detail to him personally."

The changes in my mother were beginning to make sense now.

"At first it's a great consolation to have someone listen sympathetically and grant you forgiveness."

"Until it becomes a weapon used against you," I said.

"Exactly. A condition for being absolved of one's sins is to do something you don't want to do, like giving up smoking or drinking or eating junk food."

"Sounds reasonable," I said, though I wasn't buying it.

"Ah, but here's the twist. Afterwards, as a penance, you're asked as a sign of submission to the will of the Lord and obedience to his church, to do the very thing you were asked to abstain from. So if you confess to doubts about the church, its rules or the wisdom of somebody in it, you're commanded to smoke a couple of cigarettes just when you thought you were over the craving. Or take a drink right after you got dried out. Or eat a box of chocolates when you'd finally lost the twenty pounds you'd been trying to shed for the last ten years."

"Brain washing," I mumbled. "What about finances?"

"Nancy doesn't have any specific figures, but her source reckoned they're already worth millions. New members start off tithing ten percent."

"Start off?"

"It goes up from there. By the time this woman pried her son away from the church, he was not only turning over all his earnings, he was stealing cash and jewelry from her to give them."

"How did he justify this behavior?" I asked.

"Claimed he was doing the work of the Lord. Thanks to her aunt's connections, Nancy was able to find out the church doesn't have any large amounts in local banks. However, a clerk at Coyote National said they've been known to take out certified checks in the four, even five figure range, payable to a numbered account, probably in Switzerland." Zack turned onto the county road. "Nancy thinks she might have a blockbuster on her hands."

"Tell her to be careful. These people don't sound like they'll take kindly to being investigated." I braced my hand on the dashboard as Zack bounced onto the rough county road leading to the ranch. He gripped the wheel tighter as we skidded through a bend. Once again I wished I were driving. "You said Cole called," I reminded him.

"A few minutes after I got back from Nancy's place. The connection was bad. Probably this thunderstorm. I had to cut the connection and call him back. Heard him perfectly the second time. Anyway, before he left Coyote Springs he phoned his sponsor in the law office where he's been hired, and asked if the guy knew anything about the Church of the Sacrificial Lamb. To Cole's surprise he did."

"So what was he able to tell you?" I asked impatiently.

"He confirmed the name of the high priest is Bertram Livingstone, alias about six others. I wrote them down. He's fifty-five years old and served time in California ten years ago for fraud and embezzlement, a bunko artist who specialized in bilking old folks out of their life savings."

"Nice," I said sarcastically.

"That's not all. The deacon in the Church, Hal Halbert, also with a bunch of aliases, was tried and acquitted for manslaughter about fifteen years ago. Then, five years later he was convicted of aggravated assault and rape. He did his time in Folsom—with Livingstone."

"Maybe Nancy ought to back off."

Zack went on. "The church's currently under legal scrutiny in Austin, which is how this guy was able to get so much info so quickly. It's already been banned in California and Arizona, and there's talk of removing their federal tax-exempt status. Several civil charges, including unlawful detention, are pending. Cole promised to keep digging."

I let out a breath. "I'm glad you called me."

"I didn't want to."

"I didn't want you to either, believe me, but I'm glad you did."

We arrived at the ranch turnoff.

"Mom's in more danger than I realized." I should have looked deeper into the church and been stronger in opposing what I knew was a sham.

"What would they have to gain now?" Zack asked. "The ranch is yours, not hers. Hurting her won't do them any good."

"Unless they want to put pressure on me through her."

"Hold her hostage?"

"Apparently they're capable of it. In a sense they already have. Under normal circumstances contesting my father's will would take years and draw attention. This way—"

"Seems to me," Zack said, "anonymity would serve them better." He paused. "Unless they have reason to believe the ranch is more valuable than you think it is. Then the price might be worth it."

"If you mean oil, I can assure you there isn't any, and Mom knows it. Gramps had geologists all over the place years ago. I remember how disappointed they were."

"Maybe she hasn't told them, or they don't believe her."

The gate stood open. Our tires crunched on the coarse caliche road up to the house. The same black Chrysler sedan that had been there on Sunday morning was parked beside my mother's old pickup. But this was the middle of the night.

Zack pulled around to the back of the house.

CHAPTER THIRTY-SEVEN

Zack removed my wheelchair from the trunk and expanded it. I heaved myself into it. No one came out to greet us, though lights were on and our approach must have been heard.

The kitchen door wasn't locked. I hastened through to the living room and found myself smack dab into the middle of a prayer meeting. My mother and two men were kneeling in the center of all the clutter holding hands. One was the muscle-bound "Popeye" I'd met Sunday. The other was considerably older. I recognized him from my first visit home. They ignored me until Mom raised her head, stared at my stumps and burst into tears. The two men continued their psalm recitation.

"Your prayers," I told the high priest, "won't do you any good. You won't get this ranch."

All flesh and no brawn, he rose laboriously to his feet. "Young man, it is not for you to tell us the ways of the Lord."

"Then I won't," I responded, "but let me tell you the way of one man. Get out."

"We are your mother's guests." He spoke in that ponderous tone that had so irritated my sister. "Honor thy father and thy mother, sayeth the Lord."

"Neither shalt thou take the Lord's name in vain," I quoted right back at him. "My mother has the right to live in this house if she chooses. But I own it and the land it occupies. You're not welcome. I'm ordering you to leave."

No one moved.

"If you don't, I'll call the sheriff and have you evicted, and I'll file charges against you. Your Lord may forgive trespassers, but I don't. Get out. NOW!" I bellowed.

"You're making a mistake, young man, but I'll not argue with you. Sister Julia deserves better from her sons, but the ways of the Lord are often strange."

"They are indeed. Don't ever set foot on this ranch again, Mr. Livingstone." I watched for a reaction from the false prophet to my using his name. I detected none. "Tomorrow I'll apply for a restraining order permanently barring you and all members of your church from coming on my land or any other property belonging to me. I hope you know I'm not making an idle threat."

The high priest turned to my mother. "Sister Julia, the Lord still has great hope for you. Do not despair in serving Him. Come with us and let us be a help and consolation unto you, a haven in the name of the Lord. Let not the sinners be a distraction to the wonders of His mighty deeds."

"Mom, look at me," I commanded.

Nervously she turned, her gaze instantly drawn to my missing limbs before she raised her brimming eyes to meet mine.

"Mom—" my voice was thick but gentle "—I'm your son. I love you, and I know you love me. These people have tried to make you doubt my love. I don't believe they've succeeded. Let me prove it."

I glanced over at the empty sideboard in the dining room, then motioned to Zack. "Go out to their car," I said. "I saw some boxes in the back seat. Check them. I think you'll find they contain china and silver."

"How dare you!" the high priest shouted. "You have no right to search my vehicle. This is illegal."

"If they do—" I addressed Zack "—remove them." I turned to the priest. "Those antiques are my sister's property, left to her by our grandfather. If my mother suggested you could take them, she was mistaken."

I hadn't recognized the significance of her cleaning the treasured family heirlooms when we'd come out Saturday to break the news of my father's death.

The younger man started following Zack to the door.

"Hold it, Popeye," I called out. "You're not going anywhere."

"The hell I ain't—" He turned to look at me, but froze when he saw I had a revolver leveled directly at him. At my request, Zack had brought it from the safe in the office. I'd slipped it into the back of my waistband just before we'd gotten out of the car.

"Go ahead," I told Zack. "They won't interfere."

"This is outrageous," the high priest declared.

I said, "Both of you sit on the couch."

Popeye was prepared to argue, but the priest put a hand on his forearm and nodded for him to comply. He was smart enough to realize I wasn't bluffing. What, after all, did I have to lose? Who would prosecute a legless cripple for defending his grieving mother against intruders? I had no intention of killing them, but I might shoot them in the legs.

While we sat staring at each other, the gun held firmly in my hand, I watched the con boss calculating. In the end, Zack made three trips from the sedan to the kitchen, and the high priest did nothing. I asked my mother, whose face was buried in her hands, "Do you still want to go with these people, Mom?"

"We'll wait for you," the fat man said.

"Not here, you won't. Get out of this house and off this property. If my mother goes to you it'll be of her own volition and without this place. It should be interesting to see how caring you are then."

I wasn't about to let her go with this charlatan in any case, but I sensed if I had to forcibly detain her, the rift between us might become unbridgeable.

She didn't elect to stay as much as to not go. The others walked out without further argument. I handed the gun to my friend. He went onto the porch to watch them drive away. By the time he rejoined us minutes later, my mother stood stiffly next to me, the small piece of luggage I'd asked her to pack at her feet. I held her hand.

Zack carried the suitcase to the car. Mom and I sat in the back seat. Encircling her in my arms, I tried to calm her, but even when I succeeded, it wasn't for very long. A moment later she was again nearly hysterical. Zack made sure the ranch gate was locked securely behind us.

Rain clouds had been building all evening. The heavens were so low, they seemed within reach. The air felt alive and charged. It reeked of ozone. The storm struck. Thunder shook the earth seconds after each brilliant flash of lightening. To my tormented mother it must have seemed like the wrath of God, the God she was so completely convinced she'd failed.

It was past midnight by the time we arrived at Clover Hospital. At my request, Michiko had contacted our family physician and explained my suspicions. Both of them were waiting for us at the emergency entrance. It took only a few minutes to admit my mother for "nervous exhaustion." After repeated assurances that I'd be back to see her the next day, she allowed herself to be led away by the doctor and a nurse.

Already late for her shift, Michiko left me as reluctantly as my mother had.

Rain pelted the windshield in great heavy splats as Zack and I drove to the carriage house. A Texas twelve-inch rainfall—twelve inches between each drop. Then the squall stopped as abruptly as it had begun. Seconds later, the sky opened and great wind-whipped silvery sheets of rain swept down.

Zack planned to park the Packard in the middle stall of the garage. Its rear door opened directly under the stairs in front of the elevator. That way I could stay dry. But when he raised the overhead door, he found the space already occupied by an old blue Ford pickup. He examined it quickly.

"It's yours," he told me after jumping back behind the wheel of the

Packard.

"What?" I gaped at him. "What are you talking about?"

He was dripping wet. "Just before dinner Sunday, Leon told your dad he'd found a used truck he wanted to fix it up for you with manual controls. I didn't realize he'd actually done it."

I remembered my brother's question when we went to see him Saturday to inform him Dad was dead. "So that's why he asked if I was out driving around. Where is he, Zack?"

The car buffeted in the violent wind, while Zack told me of his earlier fruitless visit to Leon's place.

As I settled into bed, I thought about my mother and wondered if I'd ever get her back. Dad was physically gone. Now Mom was emotionally separated. I felt closer to my kid sister than ever, but Debbie's focus was on the father of her child and soon would be on the baby. They were all in for difficult years, and I vowed to help them in any way I could, just as Dad would have.

But what about Leon? As twins we should be the closest of all. Instead we seemed to be worlds apart. Where was he? Off somewhere getting high on drugs? Why?

I remembered the smell of pot.

CHAPTER THIRTY-EIGHT

Cole told us to meet him at a lounge called Chambers. Now we're waiting for him to show up. I look around. A chic new dancehall patronized by junior executives and college kids with rich daddies. None of them look like spaced-out freaks, but I'm sure I caught a whiff of pot when we came in. Zack moves a couple of chairs out of my way as I strut across the crowded floor to a table against a far wall. Nobody pays any attention. What a wonderful feeling!

We sit down. Ned's studying the body English of a couple of guys in hip-tight bellbottoms playing a pinball machine in the corner. When he realizes I'm watching him, he picks up the wine card tented on the table. "Classy place. Your friend has good tastes." He studies the selections. "Or at least expensive."

A waitress wearing a leather mini-skirt, undersized vest and cowboy hat comes to our table, appraises Ned with a glance, gives Zack a pass and focuses mascara-lined blue eyes on me. I smile. It's nice to be admired. I wonder what her reaction would be if she knew my legs are hollow.

"Who's got the membership?" she asks.

Ned groans. "Somebody ought to tell Texas Prohibition's been repealed."

"We're waiting for a friend," I say. "I don't know his number but—Ah, here he is."

Several people greet Cole as he stands in the doorway. He sees us, waves them off and weaves his way toward us. I introduce Cole to Ned. While they're shaking hands, the waitress withdraws to the bar and a young man appears at our table. He's wearing tan bells, a maroon blazer, a light-blue shirt and an outrageous psychedelic tie of red-and-green swirls.

"Hi, Mr. Wainton. I thought I saw your gray zephyr outside." He speaks with a tenor lisp, gives me the once-over, then smiles as he zeroes in on Ned's impressive muscles.

Annoyed by the obvious interest, Ned holds up the wine list. "Do you really have a '64 Piesporter Goldtroepfchen Spaetlaeser?"

"Easy for you to say," Cole quips.

"It goes against the rule of German wines being good only in odd-numbered years," Ned explains.

"Bring us a bottle, Bruce," Cole says.

A guy wearing frayed jeans, a long-sleeve paisley shirt and a necklace of small shells, comes toward the table. "Hey, Cole— "

"Not now, Mouse. I'll get with you later."

The guy frowns. "Oh, okay. Don't forget." He moves reluctantly back toward the bar.

"Friend of yours?" Ned asks.

"He's thinking of enlisting and wants the lowdown."

Zack chuckles. "I wish him luck."

"How do you know so much about wines?" Cole asks Ned.

"I come from a family of vintners in California."

I recount our visit to UT and the plans Zack and I have to start a vineyard.

"In West Texas?" Cole scoffs, then looks from Zack to me and back again. "You're not serious? What are you going to call it, Coyote Caverns?"

"Hey, that's not bad," Ned remarks to me. "You can call the table wine Coyote Caverns and reserve the Chateau Crow label for the vintage stuff." But I can tell he's more than a little annoyed. He doesn't like being mocked. "What's this about a gray zephyr?" he asks Cole.

"I bought a used Volvo." Cole snorts and shakes his head. "It should be yellow like the lemon it is."

The car resembles a 1941 Ford. Originally cherry red, the roof and hood have faded to a mottled pink and gray.

"What's wrong with it?"

Cole shrugs. "Overheating mostly. Jason's brother back-flushed the radiator for me last Sunday and for a while it ran fine, then yesterday it started acting up again."

"Could be the thermostat," Ned opines.

"What're you driving?" Cole asks.

Ned grins. "Got me a new Karmann Ghia."

"Ah, the poor man's sports car."

Ouch! Ned's about to retort when Bruce reappeared.

"Where'd you ever get that tie?" Zack asks, while Ned examines the wine label. "Man, you must be colorblind."

The waiter simpers. "Actually, I am."

"Oops, sorry."

Ned embarks on an elaborate wine ceremony. He opens the bottle, hands me the cork to sniff, decants a sample into his glass and tastes it, then pours for the rest of us. It's a bit sweet for my palate, but so what? I'm in a public place, enjoying myself like everybody else.

A guy in a suit and tie comes to the table and addresses Cole. "Got your quote, man. We need to talk."

"Not now," Cole says, clearly annoyed. "This isn't the time. If you'll excuse us."

"Whatever you say. Just don't wait too long, dude. There are others— "

Cole raises an eyebrow. The guy takes the hint, turns on his heel and saunters over to the bar.

"Don't tell me he's thinking of enlisting," Ned jabs.

"I made the mistake the other day of telling Cole I'm looking for another car." A minute later he invites us all to dinner at Chez Pierre. Ned declines. He has to drive to Midland to meet someone.

"She must be pretty special," Zack comments, "for you to pass up a free meal."

Ned smiles. "Actually it's a guy I'm going to see, an oilman I want to talk to about exploration for a paper I'm writing in my geology class."

For my part, I'm eager to get home, to show Dad what I've accomplished, to share a good laugh with him at the naysayers who thought I'd never be able to walk, to get on with our ranching and wine-growing venture. But the lure of a "normal" night out is like a siren song. I ask Zack if he'd mind driving home so late at night if we hang around for dinner. Cole suggests we stay at his place and go back in the morning. I hesitate. I don't want Cole to see me without legs. It's that illusion of normalcy thing.

"I have a spare bedroom with two beds and its own separate bath," he says, apparently sensing my discomfort. "You and Zack will have privacy."

I call Dad to let him know our plans have changed.

CHAPTER THIRTY-NINE

Coyote Springs, Texas, Wednesday, August 28, 1968

The night was too short, my dreams too chaotic, disturbing. In my waking moments my head swam with images of my parents. I knew what my mother's guilty secret was. I'd figured it out a long time ago. Now we'd have to face it together.

I had no doubt the Church of the Sacrificial Lamb was capable of murder. Had they killed my father, and if so, how could I prove it? But there were other questions as well. What unwitting part had my mother played in his death? What lasting effect would knowledge of her culpability have on her already precarious mental state and on our relationship?

It had rained sporadically during the night. I'd heard the rumble of distant thunder. While Zack continued to snore softly on the other side of the room I pulled my chair around, got into it and wheeled to my father's office. I was looking for something. I just didn't know what.

The desk offered no clues. The bookcases were crammed with volumes, any of which could hold a piece of paper with an explanation for his death written on it, but I doubted it. I parked my chair by the narrow hallway to my father's bedroom, lowered myself to the carpet and once again hand walked through the passage. I scanned the small room, contemplated the bookcases, the pictures, the albums and scrap books, talismans of Dad's love and caring. Yet I felt no warmth radiating from them, heard no whispered consolation. It was as if I were sitting inside a black-and-white movie, and the objects around me were museum artifacts from a different world, a by-gone age. Melancholy engulfed me.

I escaped back to the office. Color returned. Here I could feel my father's presence, his closeness. Here the living man was real in my mind. I couldn't have explained why I smiled, but I did.

You can walk if you really want to.

Back in my chair, I gripped the wheel rims and crossed the hall and let the day begin.

After our usual morning exercises, Zack and I discussed the day's plans over English muffins and coffee, then he stood by while I put on my legs. My heart pounded with excitement as I rode the elevator down to *my* truck. It must already have been there when we came back from San Antonio, a surprise gift from my brother. Poor Leon. His generosity had been overshadowed by our father's death.

I walked slowly around the pick-up, backed myself onto the driver's seat and adjusted my ungainly legs into the space under the dashboard. There wasn't much room because of the mechanism running under the steering column to the foot pedals.

I examined the controls, tried them in place, then started the engine. Cautiously I backed out of the bay. Zack climbed in beside me. I pulled onto the side street, elated by this new-found feeling of being in control.

My first stop was Leon's place, but there was no sign of him or his car. I decided to drive to the vineyard.

I stopped at the crest of the ranch driveway and looked down into the narrow ravine below. Joe Gutierrez's trailer was parked on the far side of the bridge. A row of fuel drums sat on the edge of the embankment, a convenient way to gravity feed the ancient dozer and front loader parked nearby. Pleased with the signs of progress, I crossed the gully, executed a U-turn, returned to the main road and proceeded to my family's ranch.

The inside of the house looked even worse in the daylight than it had the night before. Things were scattered about without any discernible pattern. A thin layer of dust covered everything.

I was convinced now my mother had been regularly and systematically drugged. It was the only explanation for her downhearted moods and her personality change, from easy-going to chronic depression. Zack and I searched for narcotics. An hour later we'd gathered an elaborate stock of bottles and boxes: decongestants, cough medicines, headache remedies, antiseptics, diuretics and laxatives, as well as a variety of prescription medications, some dating back to my grandfather. None appeared unusual, but her doctor said to bring whatever we could find.

"I'll be surprised if there's anything here." I pulled away from the house. "If the church used drugs, the high priest would have been careful not to leave any around.. I'm guessing they were administered as part of some religious ritual."

"Or one of the church members could have been slipping them into her coffee to tea."

I drove to Clover Hospital, dropped the collection off at the lab, then checked my mother's room. She was sound asleep. I left without waking her.

My next stop was our lawyer's office. It took only a few minutes to explain what I wanted—a restraining order banning the high priest and members of his church from all Crow property and from having any contact with my mother.

The attorney asked a few questions, then said he didn't anticipate a problem since my mother was under a doctor's care.

Half an hour later I pulled up in front of Brayton Spites' office.

CHAPTER FORTY

Spites stood behind his big, imitation mahogany desk and welcomed me the way he probably greeted prospective clients—oozing milk and honey. He offered me the easy chair in front of his desk and looked puzzled when I motioned for Zack to bring up a straight backed wooden chair from a corner of the room. I could have explained my difficulty with low seats, but it was enough that Spites had lost the first skirmish. Not only had I taken over his office, but he no longer had the psychological advantage of looking down on me from a higher position.

"What can I do for you, Jason? I'm sure this isn't a social call."

"First of all, let me thank you for your kind words the other day and for the card and flowers you sent. It was very thoughtful of you. Mr. Elsbeth was deeply touched by your sentiments."

The smirk on Spites' face was unmistakable. "I think you know they weren't intended for Mr. Elsbeth, but I did mean them. Your father and I weren't exactly friends, but I respected him. I always knew where I stood with Theodore Crow. He was an honorable man, perhaps the only truly honorable man I've ever known."

His comment, and the sincerity with which he said it, surprised me. For once I found myself willing to believe him. "I'm trying to recreate my father's movements last week. I noticed on his calendar you were scheduled to see him on Saturday at two o'clock."

Spites pressed back into his Naugahyde throne. "As it turned out, I wasn't here in town. I went to Brady on Friday and decided to stay overnight with friends. I didn't return until after three Saturday afternoon when I learned of his unfortunate passing."

He was furnishing an alibi for the time of the murder without even being asked. Interesting. "Why did you want to see Dad?"

He extended his long fingers and toyed with a letter opener. "You've got it backwards. He wanted to see me. He called me earlier in the week and said he'd like to talk to me about trading properties. As you know, I own a few acres southwest of town. Your father was interested in trading the Schmidt place for it."

My right stump began to tingle. It would've been nice if it were a barometer of something, a lie detector, for instance, but it wasn't. Just damaged nerve endings fussing. I concentrated on what Spites was saying. He could only be referring to the area proposed for the new mall.

"When did my father suggest this?"

"It was either Monday or Tuesday. He called to ask if I'd be interested. I said I was willing to listen."

"What were your thoughts on the matter?"

He shrugged. "We might've been able to work something out. My land is worth considerably more than the old Schmidt place, of course, so there'd have to be some cash adjustment."

"The Schmidt place was a working ranch with a house and good water," Zack pointed out.

Spites laughed. "Perhaps once, but not anymore." His smile deepened the lines around his dark eyes. "The house isn't worth bothering with. As for the wells . . . They can go dry. On the other hand, my land is much closer to the city and will appreciate in value when the mall is approved."

"*If* it's approved," I reminded him.

"It will be."

"Are you aware that Mr. Crow didn't own the Schmidt place?" Zack asked.

Again the expansive smile. "Yes, Mr. Merchant, I am. After all, it's a matter of public record, isn't it? I'm also aware of your relationship with the family, so when Theo brought up the subject, I assumed he was acting as your agent. Are you telling me now he wasn't?"

"When was the last time you spoke to my father?" I asked before Zack could reply.

"Let me see—" Spites steepled his fingers "—it must have been Friday. You may have heard we had a bit of a spat at the meeting of the city council. Theo is . . . was interested in restoring the downtown area. Restoration is . . . was his business. I understand self-interest, Jason. Mine is in new construction. I want this city to expand and grow. But getting back to your question, the last private conversation I had with him was Thursday afternoon when I called him to see if we could reach some sort of agreement."

"So you were interested," I pounced.

"Like I said, I was willing to listen."

"You say you called him. Where?" I asked.

"At his office, of course."

"That number's unlisted," Zack said.

Spites chortled. "Theo and I didn't see eye to eye on a lot of things, Mr. Merchant, but we did talk to each other."

I remembered the other blue pickup parked across the street from the *Nest* Saturday when we came home, the flash of sunlight reflecting off the bottom of a beer can, and the smirk on the face of the driver holding it.

"Did you, by any chance, ask your son to keep your appointment on Saturday when you realized you wouldn't be able to?"

"Harden?" Spites looked puzzled. "Why would I ask him?"

"He's not involved in your business dealings?"

Spites was clearly not pleased with the question. "I don't know what concern that is of yours."

"Just curious because he was parked outside the *Crow's Nest* when I got home on Saturday." I could see this was news to Brayton, but he didn't comment. "I understand you're planning to run for mayor."

His features relaxed at the change of subject. "I'm considering it." Again the broad smile.

Zack asked, "What do you think your chances are?"

"It's much too early to tell."

"Did you know my father was considering running too?" I asked.

"Was he?"

It was my turn to chuckle. "The mayor and several city council members told me so themselves. It's hard to believe that you, who are so well connected, weren't aware of it."

Brayton Spites was not one to blush. "Theodore's name has been bandied about for mayor for at least ten years. He's always turned the nomination down. I had no reason to believe those rumors now."

"Except for one thing."

"What's that?"

"You're running too."

Like Bubba, Brayton Spites seemed uncertain how to take my comments. "That's all in the past," he said. "Theo's not a threat to me anymore."

I refused to let the hurt show. "Last Friday my father accused you in public of writing letters. What was he talking about?"

"I have no idea."

"They wouldn't have been to the IRS, would they?"

For a second the other man's face went blank in what I judged to be genuine shock, then he let out a snort. "I have no idea what you're talking about, Jason. I can assure you I don't write unsolicited letters to the IRS. I don't like the tax collector any more than you do."

I wondered how much more interrogation the man behind the desk would tolerate. I had no official status. The police had declared my father's death a suicide. My impression though, was that Brayton Spites was sizing me up as much as I was him.

"Has your son told you about what happened at *The Joint* on Sunday?"

Spites took a deep breath. "I hope we don't have any more incidents like that."

"I do too. But just so you know where I'm coming from, Mr. Spites, let me give you fair warning. If your son ever attacks me or mine again, I won't hesitate to take legal action against him. You've been able to protect his unlawful activities in the past. You won't be able to do so in the future."

"That sounds like a threat, Jason, as well as slander." Spites glared at me with intimidating intensity. "I'll excuse your ill-advised words this time, as the emotionalism of a man in mourning, but next time—"

"No, Mr. Spites." I refused to break eye contact and wanted desperately to bounce to my feet as a way of adding emphasis to my words. "My failure to act decisively on Sunday was the result of a temporary distraction, but the loss of my father won't cloud my judgment in the future or deter me from carrying out my responsibilities."

I levered myself up as smoothly as I could. "Good day, sir."

He remained seated.

I was aware of Zack watching me a few minutes later as I adjusted myself behind the wheel of the truck, swiveled in the seat to look over my shoulder and backed out of the diagonal parking space to join the flow of traffic.

"We've learned a few things from this visit," I said a block later. "First, Spites knows our private telephone number, so he could've called in the middle of the night and arranged a meeting." I wondered if Burker would be willing to check telephone records to see if Spites called Dad that night. "Advance notice of a visit would also explain Dad's being dressed rather than in his bathrobe."

"But why kill him?" Zack asked. "They've been sparing for years without a hint of physical violence."

"I don't know," I admitted. "Second, we do know, however, that Spites has an alibi for the time of the murder."

"Might be interesting to see," Zack said, "how difficult it'd be to break it. Brayton Spites isn't exactly known for his honesty."

"Good point. Third, Dad didn't cancel the Saturday meeting, which means he fully expected us to be back by noon. He wouldn't have discussed the Schmidt place without having us present."

We were almost home when Zack swiveled in his seat toward me. "You knew Spites was lying back there. Why didn't you call him on it?"

I turned left on Davis. "He's always been a convincing liar. Dad used to say the secret to a successful lie is that it's more true than false. Because you see the essential truth of a statement, you either assume the details are correct or you conveniently discount errors as unimportant." I maneuvered around a slow moving Lincoln driven by a purple-haired woman who could barely see over the steering wheel. "Most of what Spites said was true. So what was the lie?"

"Your father calling him about a land trade. It's backwards. Spites called your father."

"Why?"

"Your father wouldn't initiate a discussion about the Schmidt ranch without talking to us first. Besides, if he wanted to negotiate a swap, he'd go to Spites immediately, not ask him to come to him almost a week later. That wasn't his style."

I nodded. "Anything else?"

Zack thought a minute. "By offering your father—or us, which as far as Spites is concerned amounted to the same thing—a piece of the action, he was hoping to get your father to drop the inner-city development bond issue. That'd leave the field wide open for the mall development project."

"Bingo."

But there was another question bouncing around in my mind that I didn't voice: why, with my father dead, was Spites still interested in the Schmidt place?

CHAPTER FORTY-ONE

It wasn't until Zack and I returned to the carriage house that I realized I was hungry. George saw to it that our refrigerator was perpetually stocked. Zack rummaged and found cold roasted chicken, macaroni salad and pickled beets. He piled them, along with wheat bread and a couple of apples, on a tray and carried it to the office. We were only a few minutes into our lunch when we heard a tap on the door.

"I saw you drive up," George said. "It's good to see you behind the wheel again, Jason." But the positive note lasted only a moment. "Debbie told us about your ma. Is she going to be all right?"

I'd called my sister that morning while Zack was out running. She'd assured me I'd done the right thing. "The doc says she's in no danger physically," I told him. "Her mind's another matter."

"She gave you something yesterday. What was it?"

So he'd noticed. I wasn't surprised. "I think you already know."

He nodded. "The letter. I'd hoped she'd destroyed it. I should've torn it up when she showed it to me."

"When was that?"

"A couple of days after she received it."

More than two years ago. It had obviously been festering in my mother's mind all that time. Had it poisoned George's as well? "Did you believe it?"

"Not for a second. But your ma did." He slouched in front of the desk, a weary man.

I waved him to his usual seat. "Is that why they broke up?"

"It was only an excuse." George sat uneasily at first, then paused and settled back. He'd spent many a pleasant hour there, planning, talking, laughing with my father. Zack brought him a glass of iced tea. "Your folks were already having problems. For lots of reasons. She took her pa's dying hard. Before that, Theo's quitting Spites' outfit because of that young woman and her baby getting killed in the fire upset her real bad—him leaving Spites, I mean. You saw them yesterday at the cemetery. I think she's still taken with him." He took a deep breath. "Then we opened our first steakhouse. She wasn't happy about Theo being partners with a colored man."

"I'm sorry she hurt you."

George waved the apology away. "Your pa was a good man." The words were thick. He cleared his throat. "Anyway, your ma got that letter, and it seemed to confirm her worst suspicions. But . . . there's something else."

George took a badly stained white envelope from his pocket and put it on the desk. His name and address were typed in the center. No return address. Postmarked Coyote Springs, Aug. 19, 1968, less than two weeks ago. Inside was a single piece of common white stationery with one line typed on it.

"*TC loved your nigger wife.*" It was unsigned.

The viciousness of it tightened my jaw. "Who else has seen this?"

"Only your pa. He said it wasn't worth discussing. I agreed and threw it away. That's why it's all stained, but then I thought maybe I could find out who sent it."

"Did you?"

"Not until Theo had that argument with Spites and accused him of sending vicious letters."

I'd assumed Dad was referring to the IRS. Now I had to wonder. I recalled the condescending arrogance on Spites' face when I mentioned George. Too bad I hadn't known about this letter an hour ago. Did Spites send it? It didn't seem his style.

"How long has Dad been seeing Helga Collins?"

"So you know about that. He wondered if you did." George looked uncomfortable, like a schoolboy being asked to snitch on a pal. "They were friends a long time, ever since your ma moved out to the ranch."

"You mean even before I went into the Air Force?"

George shook his head. "Just friends then. It wasn't till this last year that they became . . . closer. He tried to be discreet."

"He succeeded. Michiko was the one who figured it out."

A nod. "Your pa was fixing to ask Julia for a divorce when we got word about you getting wounded, so he put it off. With you coming home and doing so well, he decided he could finally make the break—he was sure you'd understand. Then your ma ruined everything by saying she wanted to divorce him to get the ranch."

"He told you all this?"

"We were friends, Jason. I wouldn't be telling you any of this, except . . . he's gone. He was furious with your ma. On account of that church he couldn't marry Helga, because it would mean losing the ranch for you, and he wouldn't do that. Your grandpa wanted it to stay in the family. Your pa refused to let that high priest get it instead."

"You knew about the will then?"

He nodded. "He was worried about whether it would work. I told him it wouldn't if he left me as executor. I reckon he just wanted me to tell him it was all right to change it. It was me who suggested Zack."

"Did Dad expect to die?"

The man sitting across from me became very still, like prey that freezes at a threatening sound. Slowly he raised his head and looked squarely into my eyes. "Your pa was murdered, Jason. I knew it the moment I saw him lying there across the desk. Theo wouldn't kill himself. Not him. It scares me. Not for myself. But what if it's because of Aaron and Debbie? I don't want anything to happen to them."

I recalled my sister's words. "We were counting on his support." That was another reason why Dad would not have killed himself. He'd want to be here for them, just as he wanted to be here for me.

George left a minute later. I decided it was time for me to talk with my mother. Alone.

CHAPTER FORTY-TWO

There was plenty to keep Zack busy if we were going to get serious about starting our vineyard. Cole said new ventures inevitably took more capital than expected. Big surprises could be avoided, however, with good planning. So while Zack stayed in the office and developed our strategic plan, complete with lists and schedules of things to do, I drove back to the hospital. By myself. My newly recovered sense of independence raised my spirits in spite of the mission ahead of me.

In the days, weeks and months since that fateful night in Vietnam, I'd had very little time alone. Someone was almost constantly with me, a nurse, a doctor, an orderly, therapists, other patients. Yet the loneliness of feeling disconnected from ordinary people had never gone away. Now for the first time I was actually on my own, doing something, going somewhere without another person at my elbow. The feeling was euphoric.

My mother was sitting up in bed staring blankly at a soap opera on TV when I walked into her room. For a second her empty face lit up when she saw me, then clouded over again. The nurse had told me she'd spent most of the day sleeping or crying.

"I've failed." Her eyes were red and wet. "Your father was right. I have to give up the church."

I reached over and took her hand. "That won't be hard now. They'd already given you up, hadn't they?"

She stared at me as if annoyed by my perceptiveness. "When you showed up last night, they were excommunicating me because I wouldn't take you to court over the will."

"You knew about it beforehand, didn't you?" Like George, she hadn't been shocked at the reading.

"You really are your father's son," she said, this time with a hint of approval. "He told me what he was doing last Wednesday."

"After you went to him asking for a divorce."

"Yes."

Had he also told her about Helga? Or did she already know? "Mom, there are some things I have to ask you."

She pulled her knees up under the covers and hugged them, bracing herself for what was coming.

"That letter you received about Lavinia and Dad. Do you know who sent it?"

She shook her head. "I didn't then. It wasn't until later when Velma called me."

I'd heard the name before. But where? In what connection?

"Velma Schmidt," she explained, "Pete's wife. You met her when your father worked for him. She was trash."

Burker mentioning stopping her the day she died for driving under the influence. But that was last year.

"She wrote it?" I'd assumed the same person wrote both letters, but Velma Schmidt was dead when the second letter had been sent to George. Two different writers, both saying essentially the same thing in nearly the same words. It was too much to be a coincidence. Either the same person wrote both letters, or the second knew about the first. The question still applied. Why send them at all?

"She called me out of the blue late one night," my mother went on. "She'd been drinking, said she pitied me, being married to a nigger-lover who was only interested in money. But this time, she said, his greed would backfire."

I winced at the facility with which my mother used such ugly words. "What did she mean?"

"There wasn't any oil on their place, but only she and Pete knew it. They'd kept that little secret all to themselves. She was telling me now only because it didn't make any difference anymore. Your father would soon find out. Let's see him get out of this one, she taunted and laughed. I hung up on her. That was the night she died."

"Did she actually say she'd written the letter?"

Mom narrowed her eyes in concentration. "I don't remember."

So it could have been sent by Spites. Dad had bought the Schmidt place quickly because someone else—he didn't know who—was trying to buy it. I realized now it must have been Spites, and for one reason only: oil. Did it also give him a motive for murder if, contrary to what he said, he didn't know Zack owned the land? After all, the transfer had only taken place on Monday morning.

"When you received the letter, did you have any reason to believe it?"

"No," she mumbled. "I had no reason."

"But you wanted to believe it. Why?"

"Do you have any idea what it's like living with someone who's perfect? Someone who never has doubts about what's right and wrong. He didn't need me, Jason. He didn't need anyone."

Obviously she didn't know about Helga. "Did you get any other letters like that?"

She shook her head.

"Mom—" I stroked her cold hand "—why did you agree to give the ranch to the Church?"

"I had to. He told me it was the only way."

"He? The high priest?"

She nodded.

"The only way to what, Mother?"

"To make amends."

"Amends for what?" I hated having to pry every word out of her, but I didn't have a choice. The subject had been festering too long. It needed to be expunged.

"For the past," she said. "For the terrible sin I committed."

"The high priest said you had to give him the ranch in order to make amends for something you'd done years ago, something no one knew about, except you and now the priest?"

"Yes."

"What was that, Mom?"

She didn't answer.

"Was it that you were pregnant when Dad married you? That Theodore Crow isn't my biological father?"

CHAPTER FORTY-THREE

My mother covered her mouth with her hands as tears streamed down her cheeks. "Who told you that?" she cried, her words laced with fear.

"Mom, I figured it out a long time ago."

I was a junior in high school, the star quarterback on the football team. We'd played Midland. I'd scored three touchdowns, the last one in the final thirty seconds of the game, putting us over the top. My picture had been plastered on the front page of the *Gazette*. The local hero. It was serendipity that in the lower right-hand corner on the same page they'd also printed a smaller headshot of Brayton Spites, who'd recently announced his candidacy for a seat on the city council.

I'd never given a thought to the possibility that he and I might look alike. Why should I? But in those two pictures, the resemblance was uncanny. A couple of guys in school razed me about it. I studied those photos for days. I knew Spites and my mother had gone to high school together. It didn't take a genius to figure out the rest.

"Jason, I never wanted you to know."

"I understand that, Mom. I haven't said a word to anyone about it—"

"Oh God, did he tell you?" I knew who the *he* referred to. Dad.

"No one told me."

"You can't imagine how painful it is to know you're indebted to a man like Theo, especially when you're constantly reminded of how he saved you from disgrace."

"Dad did that?" It didn't sound at all like my father.

"Not Theo, your grandfather. When he got mad, he'd bring it up to me."

I remembered Gramps holding his son-in-law in high esteem.

"Theo really loved you, Jason," she said, "but he must have despised me for what I'd done to him."

"You mean he didn't know you were pregnant when he married you?"

She bit her lip and looked away.

"Tell me, Mom."

Her reply, when it came, was little more than a murmur. I had to strain to hear it.

"He knew. I'd been going with Brayton for months, years really, and we always had a good time, but he was only interested in having fun, and I . . . I wanted more. I met Theo when I was working at the canteen downtown. He'd asked me out a couple of times, but I always said no. Then one day I decided Bray needed competition. I wanted to make him jealous, so I went with Theo to the barbecue at the Wohlhofer place. I knew Bray would be there.

"Then something happened. I realized I liked being with Theo. He was so considerate and polite, treated me like a lady and didn't take me for granted. He didn't have much money, but he had enough to buy me a single rose when he took me out. We didn't even kiss on the first date.

"On the fourth date though, we . . . " She looked away. "He had a curfew, so he dropped me off at my girlfriend's house in town afterwards. Ten minutes later Bray showed up, jealous as all get-out. I tried to tell him Theo didn't mean anything to me." She lowered her head. The words were barely audible. "He wanted me to prove it."

I hadn't missed the look on my mother's face as she told me all this. Embarrassment, shame, but for a moment or two there was also a smile on her lips.

"It wasn't until six weeks later I realized I was pregnant. I assumed it was Brayton's baby, since Theo had used a condom. I went to Bray, but he refused to marry me. I was terrified. It was bad enough I'd be pregnant when I got married, but the thought of not being married when the baby came was . . . "

"So you went to Theo and told him it was his baby."

"It could have been," she insisted defensively. "Much later I found out I was carrying twins. Still, I figured they were both Brayton's."

"But we aren't, are we?"

I'd done the research after the pictures appeared in the paper. It was uncommon, but not impossible for fraternal twins to have different fathers. Had my mother not been intimate with two men within hours of each other, it wasn't likely to happen. But she'd just admitted she'd done just that. I didn't want to think about what that said about her. She was my mother. That was all that mattered.

"You knew Dad wasn't my father."

Her only acknowledgment was to keep her head down and mumble, "You must hate me."

"I don't hate you, Mom. I'm not the first child to be conceived out of wedlock."

When I'd figured out my mother had been sleeping with two men at the same time, I'd mourned my loss of respect for her. Now I could only feel sorry for her. The truth was, both my parents bewildered me. Judging from what the mayor's wife had said Sunday afternoon, it was an open secret that Julia wanted to marry Brayton Spites. Theo must have realized he might not be the father of the child she was carrying.

Dad was the same age then as I was now, a young, healthy male of twenty-five. Mom had been beautiful, and there was a war going on. Yet, I knew the man I proudly called my father had loved her once. I could remember a time when she'd been fun to be around. I was amazed she could still feel anything positive for the man who'd abandoned her, while dealing so negatively with the man who'd given her his name.

I drove back to the carriage house in a trough of depression. There was only one man I'd ever call my father. Now he was dead, and I couldn't ignore the possibility that the person responsible for killing him might indeed be the man who'd given me life.

Zack was hanging up the phone when I entered the office.

"That was George. He just heard over the radio that Kern Flores was killed last night in a motorcycle accident out on Spillway Road." Zack reached for a cigarette, then changed his mind. "George also said he's sure now it was Flores who'd been trying to call you yesterday before we went to the cemetery. He said at the time he thought he'd recognized the voice, that it was Hispanic."

I thought it might be Joe Gutierrez and had planned to call him later. Then I forgot.

Kern Flores. The cleaning woman's son, the guy who'd been at Leon's place on Saturday when we'd gone to tell him about Dad's death. "Was Flores alone? Leon wasn't—"

"I asked the same question. The report only mentioned one victim. Do you want to call Burker to make sure?"

I thought aloud. "If Leon had been involved, we would've heard by now. I don't know how close they were, but even if they were only casual friends, Kern's death on top of Dad's is bound to upset him. I've got to find him."

While I descended in the elevator, Zack confirmed Flores's address.

With Zack in the passenger seat I drove past Leon's place first—he wasn't there—then to the filling station where he worked. A middle-aged man with grimy hands, greasy coveralls and an unlit cigar stub stuck in the corner of his mouth was working a gas pump. Without moving the butt, he said it was Leon's day off, then disappeared inside to make change for his customer.

A teenager standing by a water faucet, pretending to adjust the hose nozzle, had been watching out of the corner of his eye. "You're his brother, ain't you?" The boy came over and stood on the pump platform so he could look down into the cab. He seemed disappointed to see two legs there.

"Yes," I replied.

"Thought so. That friend of his, Bubba Spites' cousin, got hisself killed last night on that old bike of his. Your brother might be over at his place."

I became very quiet.

Zack filled in the pause before it lasted too long. "On Pepper Street?"

"Yeah, lived with his old lady," the teenager answered.

"Thanks, we'll check there."

"You bet." The kid watched intently as I manipulated the truck controls.

I steered very slowly around the corner to a convenience store and parked.

"Did you know Flores was Spites' nephew?" My mind was working furiously on this new information.

"Nope," Zack answered, equally astonished.

"Do you think Dad knew?"

Zack thought a moment. "The kid at the gas station did, so your father must have."

Another one of those little details Dad never mentioned.

"Any ideas?" Zack asked.

"A bunch. But first we need to confirm Flores really was Bubba's cousin."

There was a telephone booth at the end of the building. Zack called the *Nest.* No answer. He tried George at home, but again received no answer. Finally, he called Helga Collins.

"Kern Flores was Bubba's cousin all right," Zack told me when he returned to the truck. "His mother, Portia Lou Flores, nee Spites, the woman who cleans the carriage house, is Brayton's sister."

"Let's think about this." I restarted the engine. "Kern Flores is Brayton Spites' nephew and works at the *Nest.* Kern's doing drugs and is a friend of Leon, who admits he's using pot. Leon's working as a grease monkey. Kern is . . . or was . . . a dishwasher earning minimum wage. How're they supporting their habits?"

Zack had no answer.

I drummed my fingers on the steering wheel. "Kern's cousin Bubba is suspected of dealing drugs. Conclusion: Bubba's supplying Flores with drugs. Why? In exchange for information his old man can use against Dad?"

"Makes sense when you consider that right after Kern got fired, the *Nest* receives a surprise audit."

I waited for a traffic light to change. "Kern's getting fired last Sunday and the auditors showing up on Tuesday can't be related. Even the IRS doesn't move that fast, but it could've been the result of information Kern passed to Spites earlier."

"Or his mother did. Shortly after that, your father's murdered. Why? If Spites had already received information he could use against your dad, why kill him?"

"Unless we have it backwards. Maybe Kern or his mother learned that Dad had something on Spites—"

"Like Bubba dealing drugs? Or Brayton being involved in trafficking?"

"That'd make more sense. I guess I'm just not comfortable with the idea of Bubba having enough brains to run a narcotics ring by himself. I wonder if Kern was high when he died."

Zack put his hand to his breast pocket for his cigarettes and came away empty. With a frown he folded his arms. "Is Kern's death simply bad luck when playing Russian roulette with drugs and cycles, or could he have been murdered too?"

"You're voicing exactly what I've been thinking."

"If so, why? Is his death related to your father's?"

I turned toward the east side of town.

"There's one other question we need to ask," he added.

"Where does Leon fit into all this?" I responded unhappily. "He doesn't deny using pot. He even admitted yesterday that Kern was his supplier." I remained silent for several minutes. "Zack, I can't accept Leon's being knowingly involved in Dad's death. He's no killer."

"It's possible, though, he got himself involved in a lifestyle that contributed to your father's death."

It was a reasonable conjecture that more than worried me. If my brother was even indirectly responsible for my father's death, I didn't think I could ever forgive him.

I pulled up in front of the Flores address on Pepper Street.

CHAPTER FORTY-FOUR

The house was a low-income rental and a world apart from the elegance of Spites' residence across town. Zack got out and rang the bell. No response. The listing single-car garage behind the house stood open and empty. I drove back downtown, pulled into the police station parking lot, and walked in the broiling sun to the entrance.

The desk sergeant greeted me by name. "Sorry to hear about your dad."

I thanked him and asked to see Detective Burker.

"He has someone with him right now. He should be free in a couple minutes. Coming to the games this year? Sure could have used you on the football team last season. Have you seen the record?"

Did the guy not know I'd never play football again? "Yeah, lousy."

"That's putting it mildly. You ought to come out and coach this year. They need someone with your experience."

It was an idea I'd never even considered. "I can just imagine the stunned expression on their faces when they see the coach has no legs."

"Kids'll surprise you. After fifty minutes of running sprints, pushing barriers and hopping through tires, they won't even notice, probably forget to hold the door for you too."

I was shocked to realize I was grinning. Someone saw me as Jason Crow, football player, not Jason Crow, double-amputee. The illusion of normalcy gained by wearing prosthetics no doubt helped, but this guy knew I was a double amputee and didn't care. He saw me for what I could contribute, not for what I'd lost.

We talked about the upcoming season, about the strengths and weaknesses of some of the returning players, then the phone rang and our conversation ended, but not the hopeful glow I felt inside. I shuffled away from the desk.

The waiting area was poorly lit, barren and depressing. The tubular-steel furniture gave it a temporary, improvised atmosphere. I picked up a dog-eared copy of Newsweek. The feature article was about the narcotics charges brought against a ring of senior officers in Southeast Asia. One of them was Cole's old boss, who insisted his subordinates had sabotaged him. I was sick of hearing about drugs and the corruption they bred.

I'd just tossed the magazine aside when I heard voices coming down the hall. A moment later a woman stepped into the lobby. She stopped short, and I think I probably stared. Janet Weaver, now Janet Burker. I hadn't seen her since graduation. She wasn't one of the people who'd stopped by to welcome me home when I visited Coyote Springs for the first time a few months ago. The truth is, I almost didn't recognize her. The svelte bleach blonde was still blonde, but the hair was cut shorter and looked coarser. She'd also put on about fifty pounds.

My father had taught me to stand when a woman entered a room and old habits were hard to overcome. I struggled to my feet. "Hello, Jan."

After visibly swallowing she found her voice. "Hello, Jason. Sorry about your dad."

"Thanks."

Silence. We gazed at each other, both of us uncomfortable.

"I heard you were walking," she finally said. At least she didn't say she was sorry to hear about what happened to me.

"Still pretty clumsy." I tried to sound nonchalant, casual.

"You'll get better." Her eyes were locked on mine. I'd hurt her, and for that I was sorry. But I didn't regret the breakup, only the way it had come about. If I hadn't rejected her when I did, would she still be my girlfriend? The question seemed best left unasked.

More silence.

"What do you want, Crow?"

Janet jumped. She'd forgotten her husband was standing behind her. I'd seen him but ignored him. Indeed, old habits were hard to break.

"Take care of yourself." Janet brushed past me and walked out the door.

Burker scowled at her retreating figure, then regarded me. "I assume you're here to see me."

"If you have a few minutes."

"Come on." He turned and retreated down the hallway.

His office was as depressing as the lobby, but more cluttered. He motioned me to a metal-frame armchair. I sat. Zack stood in the corner. Burker offered coffee. I declined. Zack declined. Burker sat and laced his fingers across his ample belly. "What's on your mind?"

"Kern Flores was killed last night. What can you tell me about it?"

"Why're you interested in him?"

"His mother is our cleaning lady, and he used to work at the *Nest*."

"That so? Used to?"

"Dad fired him Sunday before last," I said.

"What for?"

"Caught him with a joint."

"Marijuana? Fired him for that? I'm impressed."

"The rules are plain," I said. "No drugs and no drinking on duty. Get caught, get fired."

"Good for him. If fewer people were willing to tolerate that sort of behavior, maybe we'd have less of it." He studied me. After half a minute I could see his attitude changing. I didn't bother to ask myself why. "What do you want to know?"

"Was his death an accident?"

"Definitely. Motorcycles are dangerous under the best conditions. Last night it rained. You ever ride a cycle?"

"Yeah, in 'Nam," I said. But I never would again.

"Then you know what a slick road's like on a bike. On top of that, he had enough junk in him to fly without an airplane."

"What was he on?" Zack asked.

"Don't know the details yet. The doc says it was more than pot. You need a scorecard to keep up with the junk hippies, draft-dodgers and idiots are putting inside themselves these days."

I didn't miss the reference to draft-dodgers. "Any idea where he got it?"

Burker shrugged his massive shoulders. "Who knows? The stuff goes through here like water through a sieve."

"Can't be cheap," Zack commented. "Where'd he get the money?"

"Hard to say. Petty theft probably."

"Did he have a record?" I asked.

"Not yet. But the price of addiction doesn't go down with volume sales, it goes up." Burker tasted his coffee, made a face and put it aside. "Before long he would've been breaking and entering to steal TV's and hi-fi's. Just a matter of time." He shook his head. "If they don't jump out of the Ironwood Hotel or try to do wheelies in the rain on a motorcycle, they get their brains so fried they're not good for much more'n spoon feeding."

I listened passively to the policeman's harangue. It sounded like Burker knew about the friendship between Kern and Leon? Did he know or suspect Leon was also using hard drugs? Was he trying to warn me what to expect for my brother?

"I've heard," Zack ventured, "Bubba Spites is dealing."

Burker grabbed a cigar from his shirt pocket and lit it. "Look, what I'm about to tell you doesn't go outside this room. Clear?"

CHAPTER FORTY-FIVE

"Bubba's a bum." Burker met my eyes. "We know that. We also know there's big bucks in dope, and more than that, there's power. Bubba Spites thrives on power just like his old man. Without evidence that'll stand up in court though, I can't do squat. If I bring charges and they don't stick, his daddy'll have me for lunch, and," he emphasized, "the punk will still be doing his thing."

"Assuming for a moment Bubba is dealing," I said, "do you think his father is?"

"Like father, like son? Except in this case it would be the other way around? To be honest, I don't think so. Brayton's a tough customer—no question about that—who isn't afraid to use force, but—" he paused "—I don't know if this'll make sense, but he's more inclined to cheat fair and square."

I crooked an eyebrow. "Care to explain that?"

"Let's see. He makes a business deal to build a house or renovate a theater for the lowest possible price. Then he uses every trick in the book to cheat on it. So the houses are shoddy and the renovations fall apart. To his way of thinking, you get what you pay for. When you accept the low bid, you're saying you want to buy cheap."

Burker missed the ashtray on the desk and spilled ashes on the floor. Stepping on them with his boot, he continued. "Cheap and cheat are only one letter different. For him cheating on a contract is standard business practice. Let the buyer beware. A wetback tries to run off on him before his contract's up, Brayton'll have him beat up. If he tries it again he'll get his legs broke. To Brayton that's standard practice. Both he and the Mexican know the rules."

Burker examined the end of his cigar. "Drugs are different. There's no line to ride there, no acceptable defense. No legal trick to hide behind. You get my meaning?"

"I think so," I said. "And Bubba?"

"Different ball game altogether. I can get along with Brayton, even give him grudging respect sometimes. But Bubba? He's rotten."

"How do the two get along?" Zack asked.

"On the surface, like father and son. But Brayton knows what Bubba is, and he don't like it. Maybe at one time he entertained notions of his son redeeming the Spites' name, becoming a famous lawyer or a doctor or something. Now . . . I think he might even be afraid of him."

"Afraid of his own son? Why do you say that?"

"I can't explain exactly. It's just that in a few of the scrapes Bubba's gotten himself into—fights mostly—I get the feeling the old man's bailed him out because he didn't dare not to."

"You figure Bubba has something on him?"

"Hell, Daddy ain't no saint. I'll wager seventy-five percent of his business dealings have shady stamped all over them. Bubba undoubtedly knows about a few skeletons in the closet, enough to make life real uncomfortable for his old man, if you know what I mean."

I jumped in. "You almost caught him the other day, didn't you?"

Burker tried to look unruffled, but his eyes gave him away. "You want to tell me what you're talking about?"

"It didn't mean anything to me at the time," I admitted. "Aaron said when he went to *The Joint* Sunday, Bubba was inside alone, his friends outside. He was waiting for someone. When the slug fest started, the cops magically appeared."

Burker listened.

"Then miraculously you show up. Afterward, you did your damnedest to sweep the incident under the rug." I smiled. "It was a stake-out, wasn't it?"

Burker frowned. "We've had *The Joint* under surveillance for a while. I was in the kitchen. Had a squad car standing by. Whoever Bubba was supposed to meet hadn't showed up, and when the fists started flying I blew the whistle. That's why it all happened so quick." Burker studied the tip of his dead cigar and relit it. "Well, the cover on that place's shot to hell now. If you figured it out, Spites probably did too."

"You do wonders for my self-esteem," I said, but the bitterness I might once have felt was missing.

Burker spoke through a cloud of blue smoke. "Look, Jason, don't underestimate Bubba Spites. He may act the dumb country boy, but he's slick and he's clever. Sometimes that's more important than being smart."

Maybe more dangerous too. "Let's talk about something else," I said. "Kern Flores was Bubba's cousin. How did they get along?"

"And was Bubba supplying Kern and your brother?" Burker added emphatically. "I guess we ought to put all our cards on the table. The answer's no. Bubba and Kern didn't get along. Only a few weeks ago Bubba humiliated Flores in public, poking fun at his Mexican accent and questioning his manhood. There was no love lost between them. As a matter of fact, Flores was lucky he was the victim of only a verbal assault.

One of Bubba's favorite pastimes is gay-bashing. He can be pretty vicious."

So that's who Leon was referring to the other day when he asked me about having a friend who was gay.

Burker went on, "As for your brother's involvement with Bubba, I just don't know. I can tell you they've turned up in the same places a few times. Your brother has a reputation for using hard drugs. Up till last night, Flores didn't. I'd caught him with a joint once or twice, but that's not unusual these days. I've picked up a lot of kids for possession. The penalties for casual use are so extreme—five years in prison—I don't normally run them in unless I suspect they're dealing."

"And my brother?"

"He's clean so far. Until I catch him."

I thanked Burker for his time and worked my way to my feet.

It took only a few minutes to drive from the police station to Leon's house. I didn't have to remind Zack that in addition to commenting on the quick response of the police, Aaron had also said he stopped at *The Joint* because he thought he'd seen Leon there. I felt confident Burker didn't know that, and I wasn't about to volunteer the information. It troubled me nevertheless. Along with Aaron's late night visit to the carriage house, it added up to two things about Aaron I'd withheld from the police. At this point, however, I was becoming more anxious to find my brother. If Leon was really on more than pot, there was no telling what he might do—or what might happen to him.

His pad appeared abandoned. The faded pea-green VW was still missing and there was no answer to my knock on the door. I turned the knob. It was locked.

"A plastic card will probably buy our way in," Zack said.

I nodded and looked down the deserted street while Zack used his laminated military ID to jimmy the snap lock. It took him less than a minute.

The place was a mess. Clothes, presumably clean, hung out of drawers. More clothes, presumably dirty, were strewn over the floor and bed.

"Do you think he's still on the hard stuff?" Zack asked.

I remembered the long-sleeve shirts with the cuffs rolled up to just below the elbows. To hide needle marks? He claimed to have quit. For all his flaws, he'd never lied to me. "I don't know. Let's see what we can find."

I went to the tiny kitchen area. Leftover food on the counter reeked. I found what we were looking for almost immediately in a canister: white powder in a plastic bag underneath a half-used two-pound sack of flour. I knew the plastic bag didn't contain flour when I saw the hypodermic needle with it. I took a crumpled paper bag from a stack in a drawer and put the contraband in it, then called out to Zack to ask if he'd found anything.

"Only this," came a muffled reply.

I stuck my head through the doorway. Zack was sitting on the side of the bed, leaning over the bottom drawer of a chifforobe, holding a pistol. He looked up and handed it to me. I automatically checked it. It was clean and loaded. Leon, like our father, would have kept the gun clean. Dad wouldn't have kept it loaded, however. I put it in another paper sack.

"See if you can find any ammo, cleaning paraphernalia, anything. We'll take that too."

There wasn't any.

"I'll leave him a note." I didn't expect it to do any good, but I took a page from my notepad and scribbled a message asking Leon to call me. I wedged it in a crack on the outside of the door as we left.

From Leon's place, I drove in brooding silence to the family ranch. Events had taken a sickening turn. My brother had suddenly become the prime suspect in our father's murder.

"You know," Zack said, as we bounced onto the dirt road, "I've heard George tell the story so many times about your brother's carelessness with the gun and how he almost killed your father, but I never thought about the weapon itself."

"I figured he'd gotten rid of it long ago," I admitted.

When we arrived at the ranch house, I led the way into the den, a room bigger than the living room with a high, open-beamed ceiling. I walked over to the French doors on the right of the stone fireplace, looked up at the doorframe and pointed to what at first glance appeared to be another knot in the varnished knotty-pine molding.

Zack opened his pocket knife.

"You'll need something to stand on," I said. It was just out of my reach, but I wasn't about to try to climb on anything.

Zack moved a stiff wooden chair over to use as a stool. "You had identical pistols, didn't you?" He nearly jumped up on the seat.

"Gramps always gave us the same presents so there wouldn't be any jealousy, and no, I can't tell you positively if the one I saw the other day was mine or Leon's. That's what we're here to find out."

Zack fingered the puncture in the wooden molding. "The slug's still here."

It had gone in at an angle and was deeply embedded. The old, dry yellow pine had hardened with age. "Take your time digging it out," I urged him. "Try not to further scar it."

When he was finished, he cleaned up the wood chips on the floor and returned the chair to its place. We left the house immediately.

"You've figured out how your father was murdered, haven't you?" he asked me after he'd locked the ranch gate.

"I think so."

CHAPTER FORTY-SIX

I dropped Zack off at the carriage house. He knew what to do. Meanwhile, I was desperate to find my brother. I needed straight answers. I returned to Pepper Street to see if he might be at Kern's house. The VW wasn't there, but this time Mrs. Flores's aging Plymouth was parked at the curb. Perhaps she knew where to find Leon. I saw the window shade on the right move as I struggled up the three wooden steps. A moment later the tired, red-eyed woman opened the door.

Lou Flores was a plain woman who seemed very aware of her fifty years. Knowing now that she was Brayton Spites' sister and my biological aunt, I looked at her more closely, but found no physical resemblance between her and Brayton or myself. She lacked her brother's height. Her eyes were hazel rather than dark brown or black—like mine—and there was no hint of the Indian blood we shared. Her hair was multi-colored, with various tones of brown, gray, even auburn.

"I heard about your son's accident," I said through the rusty screen door. "I wanted to tell you how sorry I am."

"That's very kind of you," she responded. Did she know we were related?

"It's a terrible loss for you."

She pushed the screen door open and invited me in. I wanted only to find Leon, but as I looked at the loneliness in the grieving mother's swollen eyes, I wondered if anyone besides the police had been to see her.

The living room was small, clean and spoke of shabby poverty. She made no apologies for it as she went to a chair facing a little portable TV, probably her regular place. I settled on the lumpy couch while she lit a cigarette from a half-empty pack on the coffee table. The ashtray in front of her was overflowing. So was an equally large one at her elbow.

"He was your only child?"

She nodded. "Maybe if his father hadn't been sick, things would've been different."

Without prompting, she told me about herself, perhaps more than she wanted to, and I suspected more than she'd told anyone in a long time. She'd been a library assistant when she met Hector Flores. He was seven years her junior, had little formal education and was supporting a big family in Mexico.

They became friends. One day he asked her to marry him. She knew it was so he could stay north of the border, but she was already over thirty, reclusive and far from pretty. Knowing there was also little likelihood of anyone else ever asking for her hand, she accepted.

"He was a good man," she said. "He worked hard. He was honest. He was kind and gentle. I grew to love him. I think he cared for me too."

Soon after Kern was born, however, Hector was diagnosed with Multiple Sclerosis. He was young, the disease was aggressive and there was nothing that could be done. "He wanted to go back to his family in Mexico, so we moved to Monterey."

Kern was five then. He was almost fifteen when his father died.

"I guess it was a mistake coming back here." She seemed to be talking to herself as much as to me. "I thought it'd be better for him to grow up as an American, but we'd been away too long. He doesn't . . . didn't fit in here. Maybe he wouldn't have fit anywhere."

She lit a fresh cigarette from the stub of the old one.

"My brother was furious with me for marrying a Mexican, but I thought with Hector gone, he might be more understanding when I came back. I'd even named Kern after him. That's Brayton's first name, you know."

I nodded and she went on. "It didn't make any difference. As far as he was concerned, I'd married beneath me and disgraced him. That's why he'd married Lauren instead of your mother. Lauren was a state senator's daughter." She looked up at me in panicky embarrassment.

"I know." I let her draw her own conclusions about what I was referring to. "So Dad was aware of who you were when he hired you and your son?"

"From years ago. Your father was a kind man. I can't understand why— He apologized when he fired Kern because of the marijuana, said Kern had been a big help to him and that if he promised to stay clean, he'd take him back."

"Did you tell your son?"

"He wasn't interested. He had his photography and a part-time job as a janitor at the Lazy J Motel, said he could make more money taking pictures than washing dishes."

The Lazy J was a cluster of tiny cabins on the north end of town, one of the early motor hotels. Its wholesome days were far behind it. I remembered the envelope full of photos Kern had been carrying when he raced out of Leon's place on Saturday.

"I didn't realize your son was a photographer," I said. "I'd like to see some of his work."

For a moment her dull eyes brightened, but the sparkle quickly faded to wariness. "He took his camera whenever he went out and spent hours in his darkroom. He used to do a lot of landscapes. I don't know what he's been doing lately." She looked at me anxiously. "They're all in his room if you really want to see them. I haven't been able to go in there yet."

She led me to a medium-sized bedroom that was typical of a teenager's, slovenly and not very clean, except there was a poster of a muscle man where there should have been a Playboy centerfold. I could see why she didn't often go in there.

She pointed to the right door of the two in the far wall. "That's his darkroom."

She'd given her son the master bedroom with its separate bath and small walk-in closet. The three-quarter bath was filled with an array of photographic supplies, equipment, cameras and lenses, including an expensive zoom telephoto.

"Did he buy all this himself?" The cramped space contained thousands of dollars' worth of equipment.

"He put all his spare money into photography."

I asked where he kept his photos. She pointed to a trunk at the foot of the bed. I was unable to kneel. If I'd tried to bend over the low chest without a cane or some other support I would have fallen flat on my face. Fortunately there was a wooden kitchen chair opposite it which I dragged closer.

I sat and opened the chest. The top tray held a few articles of clothing, cheap souvenirs, and a couple of nudist magazines. Removing the tray, I found a cardboard box containing three manila envelopes. I opened the top one and found what could only be described as male pornography.

I caught the look of anguish on Mrs. Flores's face as she moved away to the window and stared out into a weed-choked backyard. Cigarette ashes fell undisturbed on the floor at her feet. I wished I could spare her further pain, but I'd come this far. I had to go on.

The pictures in the second envelope were completely different, well composed, sharply focused prints of West Texas countryside—abandoned prairie houses with tortured windmills, mesquite trees with prickly pear cactus clumped tightly beneath them. I sensed an almost eerie hunger for peace and tranquility in them. The negatives were in little packets, separate from the prints.

I was about to call Mrs. Flores's attention to these beautiful scenes, but decided to open the last envelope first. It was another collection of naked bodies, not all male. This time there were also negatives. I realized the contents of the first envelope hadn't been taken by Kern. They were posed. The subjects in the third batch were almost certainly unaware of the camera. These pictures were more than pornography. They were the grist of blackmail. I recognized some of the people, one in particular: Bubba Spites.

I nearly stopped. There was no particular reason for me to look under the box, but that was where I found the single grease-proof envelope containing 35mm negatives and contact prints.

I held them up to the light. The images were tiny, a series of pictures taken in rapid succession somewhere within sight of the Coliseum. In the foreground two stocky men were holding something between them. There was a third figure half hidden off to the side. The images were too small for me to recognize faces, but I knew who they were.

I put those pictures in the bottom of the box, covered them with the two manila envelopes of human subjects and the nudist magazines and left the landscapes in the tray.

I held out the cardboard box. "May I take these?" I asked the heartsick mother who was still smoking by the window.

She turned to me, a look of disillusionment on her face. "Take them all if they interest you." She tightened her mouth. "I'm sorry, Jason. I know you're not like that. Yes, please get rid of them."

I needed to explain but this wasn't the time. I took the box and followed her out to the front room.

She lit another cigarette and said through the smoke, "He told me once he'd never get married. I thought it was because he was afraid of his father's illness, that it might happen to him, but I guess he had other reasons too." This was probably as close as she could come to admitting her son was homosexual.

"How long had he been using drugs?" I asked.

"I don't know. He smoked marijuana sometimes. I was afraid he'd get hooked, but he said a little pot once in a while wasn't addicting. I didn't know about the opium."

Bells went off in my head. "Opium?"

"That's what the police told me a little while ago."

"Where did he get it?"

"I have no idea. I never saw his friends, except for Leon."

"Do you think he was supplying Kern?"

"Oh, no," she said. "People say ugly things about your brother because of . . . the war, but it's not fair. He's very kind."

"Has he been by to see you?"

"No," she said, clearly disappointed. "I'm sure he's very upset."

"What are you going to do now?" I asked at the front door.

"Now? I don't know. Stay here, I guess."

"Forget about this." I tapped the box under my arm. "Go take a look at the other pictures. Your son was a very talented and sensitive photographer, something of an artist with a camera. I think you'll be very pleased and proud of what you see."

Her eyes instantly filled with tears. "Thank you for coming, Jason. Thank you very much."

CHAPTER FORTY-SEVEN

I took a detour by my brother's place on my way back to the carriage house. I wasn't surprised that his car still wasn't there, but I was worried. Leon wasn't weak, and he wasn't a coward, as many people liked to label him. He'd shown the courage to oppose my father on more than one occasion as well as the fortitude to go off to Canada and later Central America on his own. Unfortunately, neither activity demonstrated sound reasoning. It wasn't that Leon wasn't smart. He tested out with an IQ higher than mine, but he was too prone to let emotion override his common sense. Drug use could only complicate matters, especially with so much going on. Dad's death. Now Kern's. Both of them tragic. Both suspicious.

Another complication was sitting in a box on the seat next to me, photographs that suggested unsavory conduct, fraught with danger, if they were being used for blackmail. How aware was Leon of what Kern was doing? More frightening was how involved he might be. A lot was riding on what Zack was able to find out.

The steel-and-plastic devices clamped on what was left of my legs were beginning to hurt. Easy fix: remove them and use my wheelchair. Unfortunately doing so would reduce my mobility considerably at a time when I couldn't afford the luxury of sitting around.

When I arrived back at the carriage house, Michiko's little red MG was parked in the courtyard. Last night with her . . . But this wasn't the time to be thinking about what we'd shared.

I rode the elevator up, the box tucked under my arm, and found her sitting in the corner of the couch in the office, her legs folded under her, an open book in her hand. I placed the box on the near corner of the desk.

"Where've you been?" She put the book aside, rose, sauntered over and put her arms around me. I almost tottered, unbalanced by the feel and scent of her. "I've been so worried."

We touched lips. I dared not go further. "How long have you been here?" I gently relinquished body contact.

"About twenty minutes." She gazed up at me, but didn't move out of the way. "I have a few hours off. I thought we might—" She kissed me again. I knew exactly what she had in mind. "I realize my car is hard for you to get in and out of, but—"

"I'm driving my own truck now."

Her mouth fell open. I told her about the pickup my brother had fitted out with hand controls for me.

"Oh, Jason, that's wonderful."

It was, and I wanted to share the joy I felt with her, but other realities kept getting in the way. "Yeah." I stepped to the bookcase behind the desk and started opening the wall safe. "How did you get in?"

"George was over at the *Nest*." She pointed to the box. "What's that?"

"So you haven't seen Zack?"

"I thought he was with you."

"He went out to the base."I had the wall safe open by then. The bag of drugs we'd recovered from Leon's place was inside, but the gun Burker had returned to me wasn't, nor was the matching revolver Zack and I had taken from Leon's smelly room.

She studied me. "What's going on, Jason?"

I was transferring the envelopes into the safe and about to answer her question when the phone rang.

She picked it up. "Leon? Jason's been looking all over for you. Zack? No he's not here, but Jason is. You want to talk to him?"

I watched her from the other end of the desk. "Is that Lee? Where is he?" I started shuffling around the back of the desk toward her, my left hand extended for the receiver.

Michiko lifted a finger to stop me. "Yes, I understand. Wait a second. Jason wants to talk to you." She held out the instrument to me.

I grabbed it, pressed it to my ear. "Lee? Where are you? We need—"

The line went dead. I stared at the instrument and would have called him back had I known where he was.

"What did he say?" I asked Michiko.

"He wanted to talk to Zack. Only Zack. Said he was going to the Schmidt ranch, insisted Zack meet him there. At once. He was very emphatic that it had to be now, right away."

To confront him over his inheritance probably. "Why the Schmidt place?"

"He didn't say, but he was adamant that Zack meet him there at the house." Her tone softened with concern. "He sounded funny, Jason."

"Funny?" I returned to the safe, closed the door, spun the dial. "Funny how?"

"He was very excited. He said . . . this is Leon. I want to talk to Zack. When I told him Zack wasn't here but you were, he yelled that he didn't want to talk to you, that Zack had to meet him at the Schmidt place. Right away. Alone. He was very insistent. Zack had to come alone."

Something was definitely wrong. I labored toward the doorway. "Wait here for Zack. He shouldn't be much longer. When he gets back, tell him to meet Leon and me at the vineyard."

"Can't I just leave a note and come with you?"

"I have to talk to Lee alone. Please, Michiko, it has to be just the two of us."

"But—"

"I'm sorry, sweetheart. I don't have time to explain right now, but I will later. I promise." I opened the outside door and stepped onto the landing. "Just tell Zack, please."

The elevator door opened as soon as I pushed the button. I kissed Michiko hurriedly on the cheek and stepped inside. She stared at me with worry in her eyes, as the door closed. At the bottom I wanted so badly to be able to run to my truck, or at least move faster. My stumps felt raw from sweat.

Thanks to my brother's mechanical skills, the pickup started without a hitch. I thought of Cole's cranky Volvo. Over the next twenty minutes I pushed the speed envelope, traveling not quite enough over the limit for a cop to stop me. I had a terrible feeling I couldn't afford the delay a ticket would cost.

I bounced onto the coarse road leading to the Schmidt ranch, the sense of foreboding increasing, my attention drawn to the squat house in the distance, with Leon's bug parked in front. Why had he chosen this particular place to confront Zack?

At the crest of the ridge overlooking the bar ditch, I stared down at what looked like a construction site. It had changed since my last visit here. Gutierrez's crew had already cleared the immediate area. Dry brush was piled in several heaps. More fuel drums lined the far rim. In the late afternoon stillness, I could smell them.

I made my descent to the bridge and drove onto the narrow wooden structure. I was midway across when I heard the crack of splintering wood. The bridge was giving way. Should I slow down or speed up? Before I could react, the truck shifted, dropped. A board sprang up, impaled the radiator. The engine stopped. Steam billowed, blinding the windshield.

My heart began to pound. No need to panic, I told myself.

I tried to open the door. A creaking sound. The cab tilted. I had the precarious sensation of being in a pile of pick-up sticks. More cracks, pops. I felt the platform sway. The front end tilted more steeply downward. I braced my arms against the steering wheel to hold myself upright.

My mind raced with questions. The window was my only escape.

A groan, followed by a raw squeal of metal against something. Bridge bolts? Rivets? Braces? The truck dropped, then bounced, as if on springs. A wooden side beam went airborne, as if fired from a bow. It spun and twisted like a demented javelin, slammed into the end barrel on the cusp of the opposite bank and set off a chain reaction.

One by one, like so many bottles of beer on the wall, the barrels tipped and plunged into the narrow gorge below me. The sharp stench invaded the cab, my nostrils. My psyche. I hung suspended over a shimmering pool of gasoline.

Don't panic.

I had to get out of the cab. Again I tried to open the door, but it remained jammed shut. Another crack. I glanced up, felt the truck seesaw. Stabilize.

For how long? I sat motionless, afraid to move, afraid to breathe.

No, damn it! I hadn't come this far to die like this.

I braced my hands on the steering wheel. The steam had dissipated. Now the pungent smell of gasoline embraced me.

Another grinding squeal. The truck tilted, seeking a new balance point. It toppled forward. My chest slammed against the steering wheel, and my head bounced off the windshield.

CHAPTER FORTY-EIGHT

I feel dizzy, lightheaded.

"Jason."

What's that smell?

"Jason, wake up."

Where am I? Am I in a gas station? Leon? What am I doing here? I was in the officers club. Where's Delman?

"Jason, you have to wake up. I need you to help me."

The major. The pool table crushed his legs. They'll have to cut them off now. Poor guy. Imagine having to go through life with no legs.

"Jason, damn it, wake up."

It's okay, Zack. I'll go get the medics. They'll have to cut off his legs.

"Jason, wake up. Now. You can do it if you really want to."

You think so, Dad? You really think so? They say I can't, but if you say so.

"Jason I'm going to pull you through the window, but you have to help me. Wake up and help me."

"Zack?" My head hurt. I opened my eyes. "Where am I?"

"You've had an accident."

With a red Corvette. The girl is pinned under the dashboard. She's bleeding. I can't get her out. I can't leave her to go for help either. Stop the bleeding. I have to stop the bleeding. A tourniquet? No, no, her legs are paralyzed, but they're not bleeding. It's her side. Pressure. Apply pressure to the wound.

"Jason, wake up and stay awake. It's important, very important that you stay awake. You have to help me. Your pickup's stuck. I have to pull you through the window."

I opened my eyes again. Yes, it was Zack. "Where are we?"

"On the Schmidt ranch. Your truck's pinned on the bridge. I can't open the doors. Your right boot's caught under the brake pedal. Can you get it loose?"

I was draped over the steering wheel. Yes, I could see my right boot under the pedal. I used my hands to move the leg, but nothing happened. *I can't feel my legs. Why can't I feel my legs? They won't move.*

"Jason, I'm going to pull—"

"Please don't cut off my legs. Please. Not again."

"Jason, you have to wake up and pay attention. I'll have to pull you through the window, but first you have to get your boot out from under the pedal. Hurry. There isn't much time."

"Is that gasoline I smell?"

"Yes . . . hurry up, Jason. We have to get your boot out from under the brake pedal. Can you do that?"

Suddenly, I understood where I was. *I'm going to die. I don't want to die. I can't let Zack die.* I reached down with both hands and tried to twist the empty leg, but the boot wouldn't move. "Wait."

"There isn't much time, Jason. Hurry."

I unbuckled my belt, unzipped the fly, managed to get the pants down past my hips. I released the harnesses, levered myself toward the open window. I felt my stumps separate from the prostheses.

"Get out of here," I warned Zack. "I can pull myself through."

He said something and disappeared. At least he was escaping. The fumes were starting to water my eyes. *Run, Zack. Run.* How long would it be, I wondered, before the pool beneath me exploded? Would I die quickly? Or would I be slowly roasted to death?

Calisthenics and pumping iron were paying off. I clawed my way through the window. Or maybe it was the adrenaline rush of pure terror. My legs stayed in the cab. Zack stood at the edge of the narrow bridge, waiting for me.

"Go! Get out of here!" I yelled, as I dangled half-in, half-out of the truck window.

"Put your arms around my neck. Don't argue," he ordered. "Just do it."

I wanted to argue. I wanted to beg, cajole, order him to save himself. But any delay would only doom him. Was it only the fumes rising from the pool that had my eyes watering? *You don't have to die, Zack. Run.*

I clung to his shoulders, aware for the first time in years how small he was. Five foot-two Zack Merchant carrying a legless former six-foot-six football player on his back. He sidestepped along the edge of the bridge, clinging to the side of the truck bed. At the end he had to bend nearly in half to carry me. Step by step. To the end of the tortured platform. Onto the dirt roadbed.

"Put me down," I said in his ear.

"No."

He carried me up the hill one unsteady footstep at a time. I could see Michiko there, wringing her hands.

We approached the ridgeline. I glanced back over my shoulder at the same time I heard a sharp squeak. I caught the briefest glimpse of the truck shifting. Then came the nearly simultaneous explosion and concussion.

CHAPTER FORTY-NINE

We were virtually lifted over the crest. Zack collapsed onto the ground with me on top of him. I rolled off his back as quickly as I could and tried to take inventory of the situation.

Zack was panting. Michiko was silent but I could see her breathing. Relief skittered through me. As far as I could tell no one was bleeding.

"Zack, you all right?"

"Yeah, how about you? Michiko?"

"Okay." She was out of breath.

"Zack, you saved my life," I said. "Again."

"I'll put it on your tab."

I shook my head in disbelief of the man's raw courage. "Where are your glasses?"

He shrugged. "Must have dropped them somewhere along the way."

"They can be replaced."

"I had it all wrong." We both turned to Michiko who was struggling to get into a sitting position. "All wrong."

"Had what wrong?" I asked.

She didn't answer, just kept repeating the same words.

Behind us, black smoke mushroomed from monstrous orange and yellow flames. It was no longer just a petroleum fire. The creosoted wood of the rotten bridge and the cleared brush piled nearby were blazing. The combination added billowing clouds of grayish white smoke and sickening, acrid fumes.

I looked down at myself. In my underwear, my stumps naked, exposed. I was about to try to pull down the end of my shirt to cover myself when I remembered.

"Leon!"

In all the turmoil, I'd forgotten about my brother. He was the reason we were here.

Zack rose slowly to his feet and climbed a little uncertainly up the steep rise to the summit of the bar ditch levee. "His car's still over by the house. No sign of him though." He redirected his gaze. "The Packard's too close to the fire. It's out of commission. Want me to carry you to the house, to Leon?"

"I'll just slow you down. You and Michiko check on him. I'll wait here."

Not that I had much choice. Without a wheelchair, my only alternative was to drag myself there, but that'd be slow and torturous. The dry ground was like gravel. Hot gravel. By the time I reached the house my hands would be bloody and my backside worse. Most of all, I knew there was nothing I could do when I got there.

A useless, legless cripple.

After they left at a jog for the house, I carefully pawed my way up to where Zack had stood. Shielding the sun from my eyes, I watched the two of them circle the fire, cross the dry gully "downstream," dash to the house and disappear inside.

Depression threatened to overwhelm me. I should be there, actively participating in whatever needed to be done. The minutes lengthened. I fidgeted. Michiko reappeared, ran to the passenger side of the ugly green bug and opened the door. Zack emerged onto the porch cradling Leon in his arms. As far as I could see my brother was unconscious. Unconscious or dead?

He can't be dead. Zack wouldn't have any reason to carry him out if he's dead.

He positioned the limp body in the back seat of the car and ran around to the driver's side while Michiko squeezed herself in the back seat with Leon.

I heard the engine sputter to life. Zack gave the fire a wide berth and crossed the bar ditch at its shallowest point, so he wouldn't bottom out.

He pulled alongside me, slammed on the brakes, leaned across the empty passenger seat and swung open the door. I'd barely hoisted myself inside before he popped the clutch and we sped away.

"What's wrong with him?" I shouted to Michiko as we thrummed over the cattle guard.

"OD'd." She held up a syringe.

"Is he going to make it?"

"I don't know." No equivocation or mealy-mouth platitude. "I hope so."

So did I.

The dirty, slime-green contraption didn't look like it could do thirty miles an hour, but Leon was a mechanic. The engine howled. We approached the city and the first signs of traffic. Zack planted his hand on the tinny horn and careened around a slow-moving delivery van. We reached North Heyward, and cars pulled out of our way. I saw a flashing red light behind us. Zack didn't slow. The patrol car pulled alongside.

I leaned out of the window and shouted, "Hospital."

The trooper bolted ahead and led the way, siren wailing.

Alerted by the police radio call, the emergency room staff at Clover was waiting. I heaved the passenger door open wide, dropped onto the scorching, gritty pavement, and clawed my way frantically to the curb. Startled medical personnel rushed toward me.

"Not me. Him!" I pointed to the limp body in the back of the Volkswagen. Within minutes, they had Leon on a gurney and rolling through the entrance. Michiko ran alongside. Zack grabbed a wheelchair from just inside the doorway, held it for me as I hoisted myself into it, then pushed me at a run through the stark white-tiled corridors.

"I've got it," I shouted over my shoulder and took control of the chair. "Call the fire department."

The emergency room had a rainbow of medical gowns clustered in a curtained alcove. Michiko handed the syringe to a white-smocked man. She was coolly professional now. I wheeled back and forth in a frenzy, trying to see around people.

"Will he be all right?" I kept asking.

"Get him out of here," a rotund, middle-aged man with a stethoscope in his ears shouted at no one in particular as he bent over his comatose patient.

Zack pulled my wheelchair out of the hubbub.

I resisted. "No." But I had to relent.

"Everything that can be done is being done," Zack insisted in my ear.

"I know." I forced myself to take a long, deep breath. "I can't let Leon die too."

A nurse handed me a folded white top sheet to cover myself. I felt like I was at the bottom of a barrel, trapped, helpless. I'd been fooling myself, thinking things would get better.

We're not quitters, you and I.

But at that moment quitting was so tempting.

Aaron and Debbie arrived with George. At Zack's request, Aaron had stopped at the carriage house and brought my wheelchair, and to Zack's relief, his spare glasses, black-framed GI goggles he never used because they made him look like a myopic accountant.

Aaron asked about Leon, George about the events that had brought us there. Debbie was the most distraught. I tried to reassure her Leon would be all right, but my own anxiety didn't make me very convincing. Aaron instinctively put his arm around her, earning a shocked expression from a passing white woman. The two paid no attention.

Zack and I retired to the men's room to clean up. I thanked him for saving my life a second time—and my brother's. Zack Merchant had risked a horrible death to save me. I could never repay him for that, and I told him so. The gratitude would always be there, a new bond.

When we rejoined the others, Nancy Brewster was among them. Michiko gave me a shaky embrace and announced that Leon was still unconscious.

CHAPTER FIFTY

I was at loose ends. Another incident in a series of events I hadn't anticipated. Should I have? There were no coincidences. Every action had a cause and effect. I'd known, belatedly to be sure, that my brother had a problem with drugs. I should have been less accepting of his claim that he was off them. Druggies lied. Except that for all his faults, I'd never known my brother to lie to me. Which left the question of what had driven him to go from being "clean" to overdosing?

I separated myself from the others, not interested in yet another repetition of facts that offered no enlightenment. I needed to think, to figure things out, so I parked my wheelchair in a dim alcove adjacent to the waiting area. A few minutes later I heard voices, and started to move on, granting the speakers the privacy they obviously wanted, when I recognized them.

"Zack, I'm ashamed of the way I've been treating you," Michiko said. "I know now how wrong I've been. You saved Jason's life today. You didn't hesitate. You didn't think about yourself."

"He's my friend, Michiko. I couldn't just stand there."

"You risked your life for him. My God, you could have been burned to death!" I pictured her with head bowed.

I gripped the rims of my wheels and was about to join them when she continued.

"The way I've treated you . . . I don't know if you'll ever be able to forgive me. I . . . When I saw Jason in Japan," she went on, "after he'd been evacuated from Vietnam, I thought how unfair it all was . . . "

"And you wished it had happened to me instead," Zack said calmly.

"No." But her protest was too sharp, too quick to be convincing.

"Do you think you're the only one? I see it in the faces of a lot of people. Little Zack's legs are so short he wouldn't miss them, but big strong Jason, he's different."

"No," she cried again. "No. I'd never wish that on anyone. Oh, Zack, I've made such a mess of this."

Did I hear a sob? Was Michiko crying? My fingers tightened on the wheels of my chair.

"A little while after I arrived here from Japan," she went on, her voice thick, "and saw how miserable Jason was, and how hard you pushed him, I got scared. The therapists kept downplaying the possibility that he'd ever be able to walk, and you kept insisting he could."

"I was following his father's lead. Theo admitted he sometimes had doubts whether Jason would be able to walk, but he said it was better for him to try and fail than not try at all, not know if it was possible. Theo believed that failing isn't being a failure. Not trying is."

"I was afraid if Jason wasn't able to walk, he'd never recover from letting his father down. I was afraid it would destroy him—" her voice choked "—and I'd lose him."

"Then you don't know him very well."

A long moment of silence followed. Finally, Michiko asked, "Please forgive me, Zack. Please don't hate me."

"I don't hate you, Michiko."

I was about to turn the corner, let them know I'd been listening and assure Michiko that Zack really was my friend, but I decided not to violate the privacy of their moment. Instead, I retreated to the main waiting area and wheeled over to the corner where Debbie was holding hands with Aaron.

"When did Leon start using drugs?" I asked my sister, "and why?"

She shook her head. "I don't know exactly. Daddy used to send Leon money when he was in Canada, until Dad found out Leon was smoking pot and hashish, or whatever it is they smoke up there. I don't know who told Dad. It might have been Leon himself. It'd be just like him."

I didn't realize my father had been supporting my fugitive brother, but I wasn't surprised either. Dad was disappointed in Leon, but he wouldn't turn his back on him, just as he wouldn't have abandoned me. Never.

Debbie went on, "Sometime after that Leon met a group of missionaries on home leave from Costa Rica who talked him into joining them there."

A druggie paradise.

"Leon worked in an orphanage," my sister continued. "Jason, the letters he sent me describing the conditions were heart-wrenching. He kept asking for money to help out." She gazed at me, her expression softening. "He came back here to see you, Jason, but he also wanted to raise funds for the orphanage. He swore he was clean."

So that was what he'd meant about returning to get money. "Why didn't anybody tell me about this?"

"I wanted to," she acknowledged, "but Daddy asked me to hold off for a while. He said you'd just told him about the orphanage you'd visited outside Saigon, and that you had enough demons to battle for the time being. You didn't need to hear more stories about dying babies."

I'd seen them, smelled death. Dad was right. That probably wouldn't have been a good time to remind me. "Did Zack know about the orphanage?"

She shook her head. "No. Leon was sure he'd pass it on to you, and Leon wanted to tell you himself."

At least Zack hadn't been holding out on me. This helped explain the animosity between him and my brother. "So Dad refused to give Lee financial support."

"He said he'd be glad to help the orphanage, and he'd match any money Leon earned or raised, but only if Leon turned it over to him so he could send it all directly to the orphanage. That way he could be sure Leon wasn't spending it on drugs."

"Did Leon agree?"

"Not happily, but he agreed."

I could imagine the tension between them.

Michiko and Zack rejoined us then. She'd been crying, and Zack looked wrung out. He'd come close to death today and expended more energy in saving two lives than he probably used in a week of running.

I extended my hand and Michiko came over and clasped it. Zack sat cattycorner to George.

I returned my attention to my sister. "What was it between Dad and Lee? Why couldn't they get along?"

"You don't know about Brayton Spites?"

"That he's my biological father? Yes, I know."

Zack and George exchanged embarrassed glances.

I laughed. "Did you really think I wouldn't draw the same, obvious conclusion half the town's drawn?"

"You never said anything," Debbie commented.

"Why should I?" Did she and Zack realize Leon and I had different biological fathers, that Leon really was Theo's son?

"We were afraid of what you'd think of your pa if you found out," George added.

I had my answer. They saw Dad as a cuckold, instead of Mom as . . . well . . . loose.

"I'll tell you the same thing I told Mom. There's only one man I'll ever call my father. I proudly bear his name."

Debbie kissed me on the cheek. "We should have realized."

I rephrased my question. "Is that why Lee and Dad didn't get along?"

"Remember when pictures of you and Spites were both on the front page of the paper? Leon instantly realized you looked like Spites." She shrugged. "He asked Daddy if the two of you were his kids. All Daddy would say was that we were all his children and that he loved us equally. Leon felt he was being patronized and got mad, called Daddy a fool."

I shook my head. It all had the terrible ring of truth.

"Right after that," my sister continued, "was the incident with the gun when it went off and almost hit Daddy. Leon hadn't done it intentionally of course, but the look he saw on Daddy's face . . . like he wasn't sure, really bothered Leon. What could he say? If Daddy actually thought he had tried to shoot him, telling him otherwise wouldn't make any difference."

"So Leon said nothing." I remembered my brother running out of the house in a panic. "Things were never the same after that."

I should have gone after him. I could have reasoned with him. He would have listened to me. Or would he? He'd obviously confided more in Debbie than he did in me.

I wheeled to the nurse's station for a progress report on my brother and found our family physician there. Leon wasn't likely to come around for at least twelve hours, he told me, then gave me the results of the lab tests. They'd found cannabis, opium and morphine in Leon's blood system.

"Addicts sometimes compound drugs to enhance their effects," he explained. "Unfortunately it also increases the danger of overdose and complications. Your brother's extremely lucky. If you hadn't found him when you did, he'd probably be dead by now."

I thought of Zack finding me in Vietnam. Timing was everything. "Any idea where he might have gotten the drugs?"

The doctor shrugged. "The cops are in a better position to answer that. I can tell you though that marijuana's as easy to get these days as a pack of cigarettes. Morphine's a little more difficult, unless you're in the medical profession or pharmaceutical business. There's also a brisk trade in stolen drugs, barbiturates, amphetamines and a variety of other substances."

Michiko had said there was an investigation at the base hospital over missing narcotics. Was that the source of the morphine?

"Opium, of course, is illegal," he went on. "This is only the second case I know of around here. We occasionally run across LSD, but mostly what we see is cocaine from Central and South America."

"Opium conjures up images of smoke-filled Oriental dens," I said.

"That's the usual way it's taken—inhaled. Water pipes, I'm told, have become very popular in California."

Leon had taken morphine by injection. He'd admitted to me he occasionally smoked pot, but he'd sworn he was off the hard stuff. Why would he be truthful about one drug and lie about the other? It didn't make sense, especially since he'd never lied to me before. So I had to wonder if he'd injected himself or if he'd had help.

"Marijuana's inhaled and so is opium, right?" I didn't wait for a response. "Could the two be put together in a joint?"

The doctor thought a moment. "I suppose so."

That meant Leon could have been given a stoked-up joint without knowing it, in which case his ODing hadn't been intentional or accidental. He'd been set up. Is that what had happened with Kern Flores?

"How long would the combination take to knock a person out?" I asked.

"It'd depend on how much was inhaled. Assuming a single joint and the usual pop of opium, not more than a few minutes, I should think."

"Would those amounts be fatal?" I asked.

"Probably not, but your brother had also taken morphine."

"And morphine is injected," I said. "Why would he do that if he was already high?"

"By the time he injected himself, he could have been coming down. Reality gets distorted under the influence of these substances. He might not have had any idea what he was doing."

"Did you find any other indications he'd been shooting up lately?"

"There were some old track marks, but nothing recent, except this one shot, of course. He was clumsy with it. Under the circumstances, I suppose that's understandable."

"Last question," I said. "The other case you ran into: was it Kern Flores?"

The good doctor pursed his lips, then said good-bye without directly answering the question.

CHAPTER FIFTY-ONE

Since my brother wasn't likely to wake up for hours, I suggested everyone go home. "I'll stay here with him."

"You've been through enough today," Aaron objected. "Get some rest. I'll stay. Debbie can relieve me in the morning."

Grateful for the respite, I thanked him and accepted his offer. Zack left a list of telephone numbers at the front desk where we could be reached.

After gassing up Leon's car, we took Michiko back to the carriage house for her MG. She had to report for the midnight shift in an hour. She too was emotionally drained. Staying alert through the wee hours wouldn't be easy.

"I'm sorry about your legs," she said.

I laughed. Once again the option had been *your life or your limbs.* This time I'd consciously chosen life. As Zack had said, living without legs was better than not living at all. "That's the advantage of the steel and plastic variety," I said. "They're replaceable." Though when I'd be able to get another pair was anybody's guess. How do you explain to bureaucrats that prosthetics you'd been issued less than a week earlier had been destroyed in a fire and you needed new ones?

She kissed me on the cheek. "I love you." She gave Zack a kiss as well. "Thank you for being his friend." Then she climbed into her tiny sports car and drove away.

Upstairs Zack locked the outside door. Only after I got away from the hospital and its varied smells did I realize I reeked of the fire. Zack no doubt did as well. I let him shower first, since he could be in and out faster than I could. Afterward I put on my hobi coat and took to my wheelchair. Sleep could wait.

"How did you make out on base this afternoon?" I asked.

Before moving back to the carriage house, Zack had shared bachelor officer quarters with a lieutenant who was a gun enthusiast. The guy now lived off base in a house that was a small arsenal, complete with a mini ballistics lab. He'd stopped by the *Crow's Nest* on Sunday to convey his condolences and offer any help he might be able to give. I doubted he'd expected to be taken up on it.

"I told him what I had," Zack explained, "two guns and one slug, and that I wanted to know which gun it had come from. I'd already made a mark on the bottom of the one we'd taken from Leon's pad. The lieutenant asked me three times if he was tampering with evidence. I told him honestly that he wasn't. After all, no crime had been committed when your brother accidentally discharged one of those pistols years ago."

Some people would call it equivocating or hair-splitting, but what choice did we have, since Burker refused to acknowledge my father had been murdered or to investigate further? I also had to recognize that what we learned would probably not be admissible in court. Even if we had been able to get Burker in on it, I suspected a good defense lawyer would be able to discredit our efforts on a technicality.

"He asked me if I was going to explain to him what it was all about," Zack said. "I told him yes but not now."

"He was okay with that?"

"Surprised me too."

"So what were the results?" I held my breath.

"The weapon that killed your father was the one Leon misfired in the den years ago, not the one from the cabinet." Zack looked me straight in the eye. "Your father was not killed with your gun, Jason."

I exhaled. It helped my argument that Dad would never have used my gun to kill himself, but that too was a technicality. It appeared to be mine, and as I'd so vividly learned, appearances mattered. The question now was who had pulled the trigger of my brother's revolver.

"I found something else you need to see," I told Zack after we'd crossed over to the office and he'd brought us each a bottle of Coors beer.

I couldn't reach the safe from my wheelchair, so I asked Zack to remove the envelopes I'd retrieved from Mrs. Flores. I explained where and how I'd discovered them.

"Burker had scoffed when I suggested Kern Flores might have met with foul play." I examined the small prints with a magnifying glass. "I wonder what he'd say if he saw these."

"They certainly go beyond the harmless curiosity of a young man with unconventional interests," Zack noted on studying them.

The sex shots destroyed Bubba's image as a macho bully. The others established a link between him and the Church of the Sacrificial Lamb. I didn't know what a professional photo analysis might disclose, but I felt sure I was looking at Bubba making a drug delivery to the high priest. Those pictures set Bubba up for blackmail by his cousin on two counts and posed a threat to the church as well.

Zack returned the photos to the safe and locked it.

"What happened at the bridge?" he asked me. "You have a blow-out or a mechanical problem? Did the hand controls mess you up?"

"The bridge was sabotaged. It had to be. It fell apart as soon as I rolled onto it. It had been solid enough when I drove over it earlier today, and Joe Gutierrez had undoubtedly used it since then. Joe's conscientious, especially about safety. If the bridge had shown signs of stress, he would've cordoned it off."

How difficult would it have been to undermine it? Probably not very, especially with all the heavy equipment available. Pulling one or two of the supporting beams out of alignment would likely be enough, and it wouldn't show from above.

We moved back to the bedroom and sat on our beds across from each other.

"Was Leon already there when you arrived?" Zack asked.

"His car was parked where you saw it."

"Do you think he . . ." He let the sentence hang.

"Booby-trapped the bridge?" He certainly had the mechanical know-how. I shook my head. "It wasn't Lee. He isn't that devious. He was set up, too. And I wasn't the intended victim. You were."

Zack scowled. "Me? Why do you say that?"

"The call Michiko answered at the carriage house was for you, not me. The caller was clear about that. Whoever it was hung up the moment I got on the line, because he knew I'd recognize he wasn't Leon. Michiko said he sounded funny. She hasn't known my brother long enough to be sure of his voice on the phone. The caller also referred to me as Jason. Leon always calls me Jay, just like I always call him Lee. No, the invitation was specifically for you."

Zack didn't argue, but he did look bewildered.

"There were a couple of other points I should've picked up on," I said. "Let's assume for a moment Leon did want to meet with you, give you a hard time and try to talk you into releasing his inheritance money to him. There are any number of places he could have asked you to meet him. Why choose the Schmidt ranch, which, as far as I know, he's never been to? Why confront you on what amounts to your turf?"

Zack frowned. "Okay, why?"

"Because the killer was familiar with it and knew he could set up an accident there that wasn't likely to be questioned."

"Makes sense," he said tentatively, "but why would anyone want to kill me?"

"Because you own the Schmidt ranch. If you were to die, what would happen to it?"

Zack's brows drew together. "You'd get it."

After seeing so much death, we were both careful to have current wills. Mine was complicated, because I had a family. Zack didn't, so his was straightforward: everything came to me.

"The likely assumption would be that I'd want to sell the place," I said. "Not only is it not worth much, but it would then have had bad associations for me if you'd died there."

"I still don't understand why anyone would want to kill me over an essentially worthless piece of land."

"Suppose the killer doesn't know it's worthless."

Zack shook his head. "You mean oil. It's always about oil, isn't it? But there isn't—"

"Everybody knows Schmidt had the place surveyed, but only Pete, his wife Velma, and later my mother knew it came up dry. On the contrary, Pete and Velma told everyone just the opposite, that it was oil-rich."

Zack paused, then nodded. "So you think your dad was murdered for the same reason—to get the Schmidt ranch?"

"It was common knowledge he bought it. I'm willing to bet, regardless of what he said, Brayton Spites didn't know he'd transferred title to you earlier in the week until we told him."

"But he knows now—"

"Which gives him a motive to get you out of the way. He knows now you own the land, but he still doesn't know it's worthless."

Zack nodded. "I can't see Brayton booby trapping the bridge though."

"How about Bubba?" I asked. "You heard Burker. Bubba's vicious. He wouldn't hesitate to kill you or my brother . . . or Kern Flores, especially if one of them was blackmailing him."

"The photos," he said. "Yes, it all fits."

"Like father and son."

By now it was well past midnight and the exhaustion wrought by a day of terror and anxiety—and a bottle of beer—was taking its toll. I pulled down the covers and slid under the sheet.

"So where do we go from here?" Zack got up to turn off the overhead light. "What do we do now?"

"Wait until my brother comes around. Maybe tomorrow he'll be able to tell us who his supplier is."

CHAPTER FIFTY-TWO

Coyote Springs, Texas, Thursday, August 29, 1968

I awoke to the sound of the shower, which meant Zack had already gone for his morning run. The clock by my bed said it was almost nine. I couldn't remember the last time I'd slept that late.

I called the hospital. My brother was stable but still unconscious, no change from the previous night. I did my exercises while Zack made the coffee and fixed breakfast. We hadn't gotten around to eating the night before, so we were both famished. I was also restless and on edge. My world was too full of unanswered questions. I was reduced to my wheelchair again, dependent on others to transport me from one location to another. I hated it, but I also refused to sit around and do nothing. The question was: what could I do? What should I do?

Do something.

Still using Leon's bug, Zack and I rode out to the vineyard. The devastation from the fire had been contained, thanks to alert neighbors and a quick response by the volunteer fire department, but the bridge was little more than charcoal, my truck a black shell. Several pieces of equipment belonging to Joe Gutierrez were toast. The front end of the Packard was blistered, the tires melted. Was my father's car salvageable? I hoped so. I'd have it towed to the ranch later. Maybe Leon could restore it.

I sat impatiently in the VW while Zack climbed and groped through the debris for any indication that the accident had been engineered, but he was no expert at arson investigation. Besides, the fire had probably destroyed any evidence.

Back in town, he dropped me off at the hospital before returning to the carriage house to clean up.

Debbie was in the waiting room when I rolled in. She'd relieved Aaron a couple hours earlier. Leon was still in intensive care. My sister and I had a rare opportunity to talk privately.

She asked what had happened at the Schmidt place. I told her, but made it all sound like the accident it appeared to be, a weak old wooden structure collapsing from age and fatigue, Leon inadvertently taking an overdose of narcotics.

She didn't need to know, not yet, that someone had tried to kill him and Zack.

I went to my mother's room. The tox screen the doctor had ordered the night before proved a waste of time. Whatever the church had been administering had washed out of her system. I stayed with her for a while. She didn't comment on my using my wheelchair instead of walking. After she slipped off to sleep, I returned to Leon's floor.

Burker was there talking to my sister and getting her upset.

"What's going on?" I demanded.

"Checking on your brother. He's facing charges for possession and use of controlled substances. The district attorney's also considering referring him to federal authorities for draft evasion."

I'd had enough. "Be very careful in pursuing those charges, Detective Burker."

He stared at me, the old hostility back. "Is that a threat?"

"I wouldn't think of threatening an officer of the law," I said, using sarcasm to mask my fury. "But I might offer advice to save him from embarrassing himself."

He glared, not saying a word, and waited.

"You've been aware of my brother's presence in Coyote Springs for weeks. You could have picked him up at any time at his residence, at his job or at the *Crow's Nest*. You know, or at least have suspicions about who his supplier is, but you've done nothing to apprehend him. Instead, you single out the injured party for punishment when he's most defenseless. Seems to me that's the methodology of a lazy and incompetent cop who wants to put notches in his belt without doing any work."

I watched his fat face turn dark red. I'd hit my mark and it felt good. I also knew I'd advanced from passive irritant to active enemy. I didn't care. He wasn't a friend. I hoped he understood I wouldn't be a victim.

Debbie was biting her lips when Burker turned and stomped out.

"Was that wise?" Zack asked. I'd been only vaguely aware of his joining us while I was staring my nemesis down.

"Probably not. On the other hand, if he's as effective as an enemy as he's been as an ally, I don't have much to worry about."

I wheeled to the nurses' station and asked to use the phone. Grover Reed, our attorney, answered personally and agreed to see me in fifteen minutes. Debbie promised to call me at his office if there was any change in Leon's condition.

On the drive to the lawyer's office, Zack told me Ned had called from Austin.

"He'll be arriving tomorrow morning for the Labor Day bash. In the meantime he wanted us to know he's made arrangements with several wine growers in California to ship a variety of cuttings for the vineyard."

"Did you tell him what happened yesterday?"

"No," Zack said, "but I gave him Cole's telephone number and suggested he see if our aspiring lawyer wants to join him, rather than drive that clunker of his."

"What did he say?" My impression was that the two Austinites weren't particularly fond of each other.

"He laughed and said he would."

We pulled up in front of Grover Reed's office. I had to shift over to the driver's seat so Zack could get my wheelchair out of the back. VWs, we'd discovered, were not wheelchair-friendly. I ignored the attorney's nervous stare at my lap when he greeted us in his reception area. In his office with the door closed I explained the situation and my need for his help to protect my brother.

"He's probably safe," Reed assured me, "while he's in the hospital. That doesn't mean, however, that a bench warrant hasn't been issued for his arrest as soon as he's released."

"Suppose he volunteers to go into rehab?"

"The first hurdle will be the district attorney. I can probably convince him to leave your brother alone, but I must tell you, alienating Burker didn't help."

I instructed Reed to coordinate arrangements for my brother to be transferred to a drug rehabilitation center as soon as Clover released him. If all went well, Leon would be out of the state before the cops knew he was gone. Fortunately, Zack could pay the expenses out of Leon's trust fund. That didn't mitigate the fact I'd let my temper get the best of me, and instead of protecting my brother, I'd put him in more jeopardy. If he ended up going to prison, I'd have it on my conscience for the rest of my life.

We were just concluding our business with Reed when Debbie telephoned. Leon was waking up.

I'd assumed—erroneously as it turned out—that when my brother regained consciousness he'd be able to answer my questions. All he did, however, was jabber nonsense, whisper, shout, cry, plead, even sing in his delirium. The nurse who came in to check on him said it could be hours, even days, before he showed any semblance of rationality. Watching him writhe against the restraints holding his arms, legs and waist was painful, especially when I considered his next stop might be a federal prison.

"Leon, who gave you the drugs?" I asked when he finally seemed to recognize me. All I got in reply was statements about being sorry.

"Why did you go out to the Schmidt place?" I received no answer that made sense.

"What about the gun?" I asked sometime later.

"The gun? I took it with me to Canada." He giggled.

"Did Kern know about it?"

Leon's eyes sprang open and a grin lighted up his features. "He wants to learn to shoot it." The movements continued unabated, rhythmically now. "He borrowed it. So he could practice. Promised to bring it back."

Was that what Kern had wanted to tell me? That he'd taken the gun, that he'd given it to someone else? Who?

Leon began crying. "Kern's dead." He sobbed like a child before his tears turned to anger. "I knew something would happen. I told him not to take those pictures of Bubba . . ."

The crying stopped abruptly. For a moment he seemed in control of his faculties. He looked me in the eye. "He was a good kid, Jay, but he had a lot of problems. He saw his daddy get sick and die, and it was going to happen to him."

"What about the pictures by the coliseum?"

"My idea." Leon seemed proud of himself. "I saw what was happening to Mom. Dad didn't know they were giving her drugs, but I did. I didn't like them doing that. That's why we took the pictures. I wanted to give Daddy proof."

"Did Dad see them?"

"Kern had just developed them and brought them to show me, when you came to tell me he was dead."

Leon seemed then to realize what he'd said. He stared at me, his big, hazel eyes red and wet. "Daddy's dead," he moaned.

"He loved you, Lee."

Leon was transferred from intensive care to a regular hospital room a few minutes later. I stayed with him for a while, finally emerged late in the afternoon to find Michiko waiting for me with Zack. She came over and kissed me.

We discussed plans for the evening. She had to be back to work at midnight. I wanted so much to spend the hours until then with her, but I was being selfish. She needed sleep. I suggested she call me in the morning at the end of her shift.

Zack and I returned to the carriage house. The past few days had been emotionally and physically draining, yet I was restless. I needed to keep my hands busy and decided to stop off in the carpentry shop and work on the clock for Debbie and Aaron.

"There's something gnawing at the back of my mind," I told Zack. "A fact I'm missing, a relationship that doesn't quite fit."

CHAPTER FIFTY-THREE

As I listened to Zack climbing the stairs, I kept thinking about something my father used to say, that emotion and intuition can tell us something is wrong, but they can't tell us what. Only logic can do that. What was the logical connection I was missing? Or was I making the mistake of combining pieces that didn't belong to the same puzzle?

Two people had died violently in the last four days. Were their deaths related, or was I jumping to an unreasonable conclusion? They hadn't died the same way. One was apparently a suicide, the other an accident. Or was it only an apparent accident? The two dead men knew each other. What were the chances of it being a coincidence? Zero.

I heard a thud overhead, as if Zack had slammed his fist against the wall. In anger? Frustration? Another sound, this time from our bedroom. Violent temper tantrums weren't like Zack. I wheeled to the door, turned left toward the elevator and came to an abrupt halt.

Bubba's truck was parked on the side street. Of course, the photos! Bubba must have found out I'd gotten them from Kern's mother, Bubba's aunt, Lou Flores, and had come looking for me to get them back and found Zack instead, alone. I'd bet on my friend in a fair fight anytime, but the disparity in size between the two belligerents wasn't fair. The man who'd staked his life to save mine was in mortal danger. What could I do about it?

Not bound into the room, pick up the blob and toss him over the balcony rail, as I once might have done. The incident at *The Joint* proved that even standing on two legs I wasn't much good in a fight.

Okay, I told myself, *you're handicapped, but you're not helpless.*

The elevator was too noisy. It would alert them I was coming. I rolled to the foot of the stairs. The clatter of feet on the wooden steps had always been a klaxon announcing the arrival of visitors. But I didn't have feet. I locked the chair's brakes, slipped off the seat and ascended the flight without making a sound.

Too low to see through the window in the outside door at the top of the landing, I listened for perhaps five seconds, then turned the knob in the blind, not knowing what I'd find on the other side. From the bedroom I could hear Bubba's voice, silky with sarcasm. "Where's your sawed-off friend, squirt?"

"He's not here." Zack's words were constricted, as if he were being strangled.

I slipped inside and closed the door silently behind me. Thank God, Dad didn't tolerate squeaky hinges.

"In that case," Bubba said, "I guess you'll just have to give me what I want all by your lonesome."

The bedroom door was partially open. Fortunately, Bubba had his back to it. I'd have to move quietly, but slithering across the polished floor on my butt didn't make any noise.

"Now, runt," Bubba continued, "I want them pictures."

"What pictures?" Zack asked, his voice a pinched squeal.

"No games, little man." There was a sudden crash and thump. Through the half-open door, I saw Zack tumble across the room, his wiry body slamming against the side of my bed. He lay momentarily dazed, motionless. I wasn't sure if he was really hurt or only pretending.

"You know what pictures I'm talking about," Bubba growled, "the ones your buddy stole from old lady Flores."

Zack climbed very slowly off the floor, but instead of retreating from his assailant, he moved toward him, out of my view. Was it a sign he'd seen me? "I don't know what you mean."

"I said no games," Bubba repeated. I heard wheezing in his voice. He was fat and out of shape. "Your legless boyfriend took pictures from dear Auntie Portia's house. I want them. Now."

"They're not here," Zack answered.

"Where are they then, peewee?"

I slithered across the waxed asphalt tile to the office and eased the door closed behind me. Zack was obviously stalling for time. How long could he hold out? I reached for the phone. No dial tone. I fought off panic.

The rifles were still locked in the gun case, the key in the safe. I'd tried picking the lock the other day and failed. This was no time for another experiment. Breaking the glass would leave me in a sea of shards and bring Bubba faster than I could get one of the weapons out and loaded.

The revolvers were in the wall safe. So were the pictures. Bubba had already killed Kern for them. He wouldn't hesitate to kill again. I was determined not to lose this evidence. If Bubba walked in while the safe was open, there wasn't much I could do to defend myself or safeguard the photographs, nor could I be sure Zack would be in a condition to do anything. But I had to take the chance.

The first problem was getting to the safe itself. I pushed my father's leather chair over to the bookcase and pulled myself up into it. I couldn't even reach the back of the shelf where the safe was.

Judging by the muffled sounds coming from across the hall, it wouldn't be much longer before Bubba lost all patience and did something drastic.

I began removing books from the lower shelves and placed them under me. It seemed to take forever to get high enough to reach the safe dial. Learning to walk on artificial limbs had honed my sense of balance, but being perched on a wobbly stack of slippery books on the swiveling leather chair was still precarious. If the chair rotated or the books slid out from under me, I'd fall with a crash, maybe injure myself, and the enraged fat man across the hall would have me at his mercy.

I was tense but my hands were steady. Time sped by. Another crash came from the other room. Zack was putting up a good fight but . . .

I dialed the combination. The safe didn't open.

Did I have the numbers right? Out of sequence? I spun the dial again extra carefully this time. Precious seconds raced by. Sweat trickled down my back. The safe clicked open.

I reached for one of the guns. It felt cold, heavy and familiar in my hand. Images of combat, of firefights flashed through my mind. My stomach muscles clenched. My stumps prickled maddeningly. The moment passed. I tightened my grip on the stock of the weapon and removed it from the safe.

Thank God Zack had left the bullets in the bag with them. There were only four. That'd have to be enough. Quickly I locked the safe, loaded the weapon and tucked it into the back of my waistband.

Cautiously I dismantled the shaky tower of books, lowered myself to the floor and clawed my way across the rug to the door. I listened a second, then inched it open.

I could see Zack in the other room. Bubba's flabby body had him squashed against the closet door so tightly his feet dangled off the floor. Fatso had one hand clutching Zack's shirt. The other thrust a large, shiny hunting knife under his chin. Zack's cheek was bright with blood.

"Out at the ranch," Zack barely wheezed as Bubba dug the knife point against his throat. "We took them out to the ranch for safe keeping."

"Then, runt, that's where we're going."

Bubba released his hold and backed up. Zack slumped forward and started to fall to the floor. Spites grabbed Zack's bloody shirt and shoved him in front of him. I'd scurried into the open doorway of the dim kitchen. The two men emerged. Bubba held Zack in a half nelson, forcing him toward the outside door.

"Hold it right there."

"What the—" Bubba swung around, dragging Zack painfully with him as a shield. He stopped in mid phrase, a huge grin brightening his puffy face when he saw me legless on the floor.

"Let him go," I ordered. The condition of Bubba's face told me Zack had given as good as he'd got.

"Still playing the big man, ain't you?" Bubba snarled. "You don't look real big to me now, crip, not from where I'm *standing*." He emphasized the last word and laughed. "I wish my daddy could see his model of manhood now." He seemed unimpressed by the gun in my hand, totally confident I wouldn't use it.

"You're a much bigger target than Zack," I said. "You can't hide behind him."

"But I can cut his throat."

CHAPTER FIFTY-FOUR

"Unless you let him go unharmed," I said, "you're a dead man. If you doubt me—" I fired a round that went whizzing within inches of Bubba's head, shattering the window behind him "—think again."

Movement ceased. Even breathing. Only time marched on.

"Let him go," I repeated, my words soft, menacing.

Bubba considered another few seconds, then released his grip.

Zack tore himself away from my line of fire. He didn't seem sure whether I'd pull the trigger again, this time not avoiding my target.

Still Bubba didn't quite lose his swagger, though my gun was pointed directly at him. I stared into his brown eyes, the eyes of my half-brother. If it hadn't been for the shot I'd already fired, I was sure he would've stomped over and kick me solidly between my stumps.

"What about the pictures?" he asked, then added with defiance, "Look, Crow, I ain't no faggot. That greaser was queer. All I done was let him do what he wanted to do. I never touched the friggin' fairy." He spat on the floor.

Like his father, Bubba Spites knew how to wrap lies in truth. It was true Kern Flores was homosexual, and it seemed equally likely Bubba was not. What the photos showed was not so much deviant sex on Bubba's part as the humiliation of the guy kneeling at his feet.

"Your daddy may not mind you hanging around with queers," Bubba said, "but mine does. Just give me the friggin' pictures."

I couldn't help smile as I watched the bully sweat.

It took the police only a few minutes to respond to the sound of the gunshot, which was one of the reasons I'd fired. When they arrived, they were stunned at the sight of a legless man sitting on the floor pointing a revolver at Bubba Spites. I, however, didn't give them time to stare. I explained that Mr. Harden Spites had broken in and attacked Mr. Zack Merchant, who had the bruises to prove it. I demanded Spites be placed under immediate arrest and that Clyde Burker be summoned. The older of the two policemen seemed relieved at the mention of the detective's name and sent the other cop down to the patrol car to radio in the request.

Burker showed up twenty minutes later, his shirt tail sticking out. He didn't like what he saw, but I was consoled by one thing—he was looking at me, not my missing legs. Explanations followed in the office while Bubba sat on the floor in the foyer, his hands cuffed behind his back.

Five minutes after Bubba was loaded into the paddy wagon, Burker drove Zack, still in his blood-stained shirt, and me to the police station to make formal statements. There, Zack called Nancy. She arrived within minutes, notebook in hand, ready for her first big scoop.

Brayton Spites showed up not long after. His dark-brown eyes locked on mine. In the end, he broke the contact. Neither of us said a word.

Zack had turned both sets of photos over to Burker. The small prints didn't mean much without an explanation. On the other hand, the regular size ones of Bubba with his cousin needed no elaboration.

Bubba's dread of his father's reaction had been well founded. When Brayton saw the pictures, he leveled a look of pure contempt at his son, one filled with such malevolence that for a moment everyone in the room seemed to fear physical violence against the younger man.

"Has he made any statements?" Brayton asked coldly.

"No, not yet," Burker replied.

Bubba started to say something, but his father held up a hand stiffly, his glare impaling. "Not a word," he commanded. "Do you hear me? If you say one single word, you're on your own."

Bubba nodded. His father telephoned a lawyer who appeared fifteen minutes later, demanded a private consultation with his client and confirmed Bubba's refusal to make a statement.

Back in his office, Burker closed the door.

"Just so there's no misunderstanding, Crow—" he settled into his swivel chair, his voice ringing with authority "—let me explain how I see things. Your father died the other night as a result of a single gunshot to the head. It had all the appearances of suicide. You later insisted it was murder, but when I asked for proof, you gave me only vague statements that your father wouldn't have killed himself. I felt sorry for you, and I'm not going to apologize for that. What's happened to you is tragic. You talked the other day about being patronized. Well, Jason Crow, that's just what you've been doing with me, and I don't like it any better than you do."

I frowned at the overweight detective behind the cluttered desk, but refused to squirm. "On the other hand," I countered, "you didn't inspire much confidence by playing the bad cop. Perhaps if you'd acted like an intelligent, competent police officer, I would've treated you like one."

Burker worked his jaw as he studied me for a long minute. "Now that we've got that out of our systems, let's go over recent events." He took a deep breath. "Your father died early Saturday morning. Every indication pointed to suicide. Kern Flores, who up until the previous week had been employed at the *Crow's Nest*, died a few days later in a motorcycle accident while under the influence of drugs. Then your brother, also a known drug user with a reputation for a violent temper, OD'd. You and your friend almost got killed rescuing him. Now Bubba Spites, a less than model citizen, breaks into your apartment to steal salacious photographs you have of him." Burker looked at me. "Have I got it right so far?"

"Go on."

"We've suspected Bubba Spites of dealing drugs for some time, but we've been unable to prove it. The photos you've just given us could change that—*if* they stand up in court."

"They were voluntarily given to me by a person who had legal possession of them," I said.

"Good point. Bubba's sexual adventures will embarrass him—and his father—but they won't put him in jail. If the other pictures substantiate drug dealing, they might."

"Only might?" Zack asked.

Burker regarded us both. "Let's get something straight. If the photos show Bubba passing something to the high priest they still mean nothing unless we know what that something is. Which means one of the parties will have to tell us. You can be sure this high priest character, Livingstone, isn't going to confess, so that means Bubba will have to. Problem there is that for him to say it was drugs, he'll have to incriminate himself, and he's not about to do that. Unless—" he raised a pudgy finger to forestall Zack's interruption "—he can work a deal with the DA. Right now, apprehending a nationally sought-after cult leader is more important than nailing a local small-time drug peddler."

"Even if he was responsible for Kern Flores's death?" I asked.

"Prove it."

Zack and I sat silently mulling over the situation.

"So Bubba gets off scot-free," I said. Burker was right, and maybe the DA was too, given the choices they had, but it rankled nevertheless.

"Maybe. Maybe not. No telling what will result when lawyers get together to decide how many notches they want on their belts." Burker and I stared each other down until Zack asked:

"What about the assault on me?"

"You can swear out a complaint against him," the detective said, "but it'll still be up to the discretion of the DA whether he wants to prosecute. My guess is he won't. You can take Bubba to civil court, of course. No jail time, but I reckon you can make yourself a nice piece of change from his old man for your pain and suffering, and to make the matter go away."

Zack huffed. We could talk about it later.

"In either case," Burker said ominously, "you've made a couple of mighty dangerous enemies."

Zack and I left the police station a few minutes later, no closer to our goal. We had details the detective didn't have, but they still weren't enough to establish who'd murdered my father or why, and turning the information over to Burker would make my brother the prime suspect. I didn't, for example, tell him about Leon's gun and how it had been switched with mine. I came away feeling only one thing had been accomplished: Burker acknowledged my father might have been murdered.

Upon our return to the carriage house I persuaded Zack to indulge in a long hot shower. He'd taken a serious beating from fat boy. Tomorrow he'd be hurting even worse. I needed to clean up too, but I could wait. When I finally did emerge from the bathroom half an hour after entering it, I was surprised to find my friend still awake and nursing a snifter of Courvoisier. He had one waiting for me on my bedside table as well.

I thanked him. "No Grand Marnier?"

"I've sworn off."

I pulled myself onto my bed. "Let's review. Means. Motive. And opportunity."

CHAPTER FIFTY-FIVE

We started with Brayton Spites.

"Assuming he really is responsible for the death of the guy whose wife and child were killed in that house fire," I said, "Spites is capable of premeditated homicide—"

"By proxy," Zack pointed out. "He probably didn't run down the guy himself. Too dangerous. And you noted yourself he furnished an alibi for the time of your dad's death without even being prompted. If he used a hired killer, it might be next to impossible to find him."

"Or her," I said. "A woman visitor would explain Dad's getting fully dressed. You're right though, a professional hit man really complicates matters, but we can still give Spites credit for means and opportunity. It's motive that I don't buy. I can't seriously believe Brayton Spites would kill my father. Not over land or money. I think he was telling the truth yesterday when he said he respected Dad, even envied him."

"Envy and jealousy are age-old motives for murder," Zack reminded me.

"When they lead to hatred," I agreed. "For all their contentiousness, I don't think Dad and Spites hated each other. In a strange sort of way they were flip sides of the same coin, rather than opposites."

Zack frowned, then gave me a cockeyed grin. He understood what I meant, even though I wasn't expressing myself very well.

"How about to protect his name or his son then?"

I shook my head. "Brayton isn't naïve. He's arrogant and self-important, but not to the extent of thinking his name's worth killing anybody over. Definitely not my father. As for his son, I think Brayton would hang Bubba out to dry before he'd kill for him."

"How about Bubba then?"

"Oh, I have no doubt he's capable of murder, but is he capable of subtlety? He'd beat a man to death, maybe even torture him and listen to him scream, but I can't see him staging a scene to look like a suicide, complete with champagne. He'd be more likely to trash the place."

Zack snickered. "Okay, subtle isn't a Bubba quality. How about the Church of the Sacrificial Lamb? One of its members could easily have made contact with Kern to get their hands on the gun, using sex or narcotics as an enticement."

I frowned and swirled the brandy in the crystal snifter. "Definite possibilities. If a church representative, perhaps even the high priest himself, called in advance and asked to see Dad—maybe on the pretext of a crisis with Mom—Dad would have gotten dressed. Means and opportunity. The champagne doesn't quite fit though—"

"Unless the killer was cool enough to search the place after murdering your dad, found the open bubbly, poured out what remained and left the empty bottle to make it look like he'd been drinking alone."

I considered it. "That would explain the M.E. finding only a trace of alcohol in Dad's bloodstream. As for motive, the ranch, whether they believe it has oil on it or not, is valuable property."

"Bottom line," Zack said, "we can't eliminate the church. Is there anyone we definitely can eliminate?"

"Cole, since we stayed with him. By the way, I never noticed before how much you snore when you're drinking. You cut several cords of wood Friday night."

"Sorry. Let's hope cognac doesn't have the same effect." He took a sip from his snifter. "How about Ned?"

I hated to think that my old hooch mate might be involved, but if I was going to be thorough and objective, I had to consider him.

"His trip to Midland gives him opportunity, and he'd been to the *Nest* often enough to have met Kern and obtained the gun. Means. As for motive—"

"The vineyard, of course," Zack said without hesitation. "He wants a part of it so badly he can taste it. You saw his reaction when he found out Cole had offered us financial backing."

"He wasn't happy about it," I acknowledged.

"I think he feels cheated."

I had to agree. "He also didn't know about Dad transferring title of the property to you until Tuesday night. And the next day there was an attempt on your life."

For a moment neither of us spoke.

"So he goes on the list of possibles," Zack finally concluded.

I nodded. "Yet . . . " But I didn't finish the sentence. Saying I didn't want him to be my father's killer was pointless. This exercise was to eliminate the impossibles so that only the possibles remained.

"How about closer to home?" Zack asked. "If we're going to be thorough—"

"We have to consider everyone." I knew he was referring to George, Aaron, even Debbie and my mother.

"Means, motive and opportunity," Zack recited. "We only have to eliminate one element, and the other two elements don't matter."

"George had no motive to kill Dad." I hadn't forgotten about the letters, but the first one had been sent years ago. The timing was off. "There was no animus between them, Zack. I'm certain of it. They were successful business partners, but mostly they were best friends. George would have died to protect Dad and vice versa."

To that I would have to add that George had no reason to harbor any ill feelings towards me. Killing Dad the night before I was finally coming home would have been adding sadistic cruelty to murder. No, George was out.

"I agree," Zack said. "What about Aaron? He had means and opportunity, and if, contrary to what he told us, your father forbade his marrying Debbie and said he wanted her to get an abortion—"

"No." I was emphatic. "Dad would never want Debbie to abort a child, and he genuinely liked Aaron. I think the meeting between them took place essentially the way Aaron described it." I paused. "If I'm wrong about this, Zack, if Aaron and Debbie or my mother are involved in any way, there's no hope in this world."

"So where does that leave us?"

"With the church and Ned for sure, and I suppose, Brayton and Bubba, if only by proxy." My mind ran through the list of people who were in any way associated with my family and friends and the *Crow's* Nest.

"My gut tells me we're still missing someone, something, but my brain doesn't seem to be able to connect the dots. The answer's here somewhere, Zack. It has to be."

CHAPTER FIFTY-SIX

We finally turned out the lights.The room was in darkness. I should have been sleeping, but my mind wasn't willing to slow down. So much had happened in the last days and months. It was hard for me to realize that my world would never be the same as it had been, that my future wouldn't be anything like what I'd expected.

My best friend took a beating this evening. He didn't complain. He didn't blame it on me, even though it wouldn't have happened if I hadn't taken those pictures from Mrs. Flores.

Zack's always been reliable, a good friend . . .

I'm running out of the officers club *toward the flight line. My heart's pounding. I'm worried about Zack. If one rocket can hit the club, what's to keep others from finding the same target? And where's Delman? He seems to have disappeared. I don't want to think about the guy who got blinded or the one whose legs were crushed.*

I guess I won't be going on R&R after all. Michiko. Beautiful Michiko. I want so much to put my ring on her finger, to hear her tell me she'll marry me, be my wife, that we'll spend the rest of our lives together.

I haven't told anyone about my plans to propose to her, not Dad, not even Zack. I doubt he'll be surprised. He teased me enough about going bonkers over her, when we were in Japan. He was right too. One look and I knew she was the girl for me. Dad'll love her. She has charm and intelligence and a wonderful sense of humor. I'm not sure what to expect from Mom, but Dad'll bring her around.

There's a bunker ahead. Or the remnants of one. Must have taken a direct hit. It's half caved in. The flight line isn't far away. If I run directly across it I can get to my outfit in less than half the time it'd take to circle it. I still don't understand how they knew I was at the club.

What's that? A voice? Someone's calling me?

I come to a halt. Look around. There it is again. Somebody's calling my name. The voice's familiar. It's coming from the bunker.

I get closer. Delman? What're you doing here? He's smiling. He starts to say something—Bud? But?—points behind me. I hear the gunshot. My ears ring. His eyes have gone wide. They flash in utter amazement before they go dark with searing pain. My God, he's been shot. Blood blossoms on his shirt. He crumples to the ground. Is he still alive? I've got to help him. Delman. I kneel at his side, place my index finger to his carotid artery. I can't feel a pulse.

Something just hit me. Is the roof caving in? I'd better get the hell out of here. Oh, another blow. I'm falling forward. My head. What hit me? Have I been shot too? I'm going to hurt like hell in a moment. I try to turn. Who? But . . .

CHAPTER FIFTY-SEVEN

Coyote Springs, Texas, Friday, August 30, 1968

Zack was too sore the next morning from Bubba Spites' beating to run his daily three, so while I did my calisthenics, he went over to the *Nest* and called the telephone company to get our cut lines repaired.

Half an hour later he and I rode down in the elevator. George and his staff were busy setting up smokers on the side lawn for the Labor Day barbecue. Beef brisket, chicken and sausage. The air was redolent with their mouthwatering aromas.

"I'm glad you decided to go ahead with the barbecue," I told George. "Dad would have wanted the tradition to continue."

"I keep telling myself that," he replied somberly, "but it won't be the same without him."

He was right. Dad loved playing host, greeting people, showing them around. He had a prodigious memory for names and faces.

Still using Leon's car, Zack dropped me off at the hospital to check on my mother and brother. Mom was sleeping, so I didn't disturb her. Leon was awake but far from rational. Physically he was out of danger, but his mental functions were still uncertain. I hoped with all my heart he'd recover from his ordeal. Everybody urged patience.

I was wheeling out of his room to return to my mother's, when a candy-striper called to me. "You have a phone call, Mr. Crow. Do you want me to have the switchboard transfer it to your brother's room?"

"I'll take it at the nurses' station, if that's all right." At the high counter I grabbed the receiver.

"Cole called," Zack told me. "He and Ned just got into town. They drove caravan style. Cole's bought a new car. Wouldn't tell me what kind though. Wants it to be a surprise." Then he added, trying to make it sound like an afterthought, "Cole says Ned's gay. Is he?"

"Ned? I lived with the guy for almost a year in Vietnam, Zack. If he's gay, it's news to me. What makes Cole say that?"

"He claims the tip-off was the way that color-blind waiter at *Chambers* came on to Ned last Friday. Says they can always spot each other. Anyway," Zack went on, "Ned wants me to meet him out at the vineyard.

To discuss the cuttings he's getting for us, I guess. He's going to be in for a shock when he sees the place. Gotta run. Talk to you later." He broke the connection before I had a chance to reply.

Why would Cole say Ned was gay? I sat there at the nurses' station, my mind buzzing. *Chambers*. The color-blind waiter with the psychedelic tie. The gray zephyr.

My hooch mate had never said or done anything to suggest he might be homosexual, but now I had to consider the possibility. He was a body builder who liked to show off his muscles. He flirted with groups of females, as he'd done at the reception Sunday afternoon, yet I'd never known him to go out on a date or talk about a girlfriend. At Tan Son Nhut he hadn't indulged in the favorite GI pastime of going downtown and buying bargirls Saigon Tea. Nor had I, but that was because I had Michiko waiting for me.

"Mr. Crow?"

Dad? I looked up.

"Are you all right?" The nurse was studying me with concern. The phone instrument, still in my hand, was beeping.

"Sorry." I handed it to her. "Daydreaming." Or a nightmare.

I was still parked in the same spot when Aaron showed up a few minutes later to sit with Leon. Debbie promised to relieve him around noon. With my future brother-in-law on hand and Leon sound asleep, I decided to check on my mother again, this time wake her if necessary to answers my questions.

Leon was convinced she was being drugged. Nancy's investigation confirmed the church used narcotics as a means of controlling and manipulating its members. Yet the tox screen had come back negative. Did Mom realize she was being doped? How were the drugs being administered? Maybe if we knew the how we'd be able to determine the what. And if it turned out Mom and Leon had received the same combination of narcotics, it would point to the church as the culprit—or the church's supplier. Bubba? I felt like I was on a treadmill, covering the same ground over and over again but getting nowhere.

My mind kept coming back to Zack's telephone call and Cole's claim that Ned was gay. My brother had asked me whether I'd want to be told if a friend was gay. I'd thought for a minute he might be referring to himself. Later I realized he was talking about Kern. But why would Leon ask me about Kern? We were no more than nodding acquaintances. Could Leon in fact have been referring to Ned?

If Ned was gay, he'd been damn discreet about it, but suppose he was. Means, motive and opportunity. Kern was gay and had access to Leon's gun, the gun, we now knew, that had been used to kill Dad. Means.

Ned had driven to Midland, a hundred-plus miles past Coyote Springs. He could easily have come back later, however, killed Dad and returned to Midland without ever being missed. The old lady in the gothic house behind the *Nest* had heard a VW drive away. The Karmann Ghia was a VW with a different body. Opportunity. The motive would be to get the Schmidt ranch. But why? What made that particular piece of land important enough to kill for? It didn't make sense unless . . .

A crazy notion struck me. I thought of the dream I'd had the night before.

Delman had gone off to see a "long-lost cousin," a term that might refer to an actual relative but didn't necessarily have to. In my dream—or was it a memory?—just before he'd been shot Delman had pointed to someone behind me and said Bud or But. I'd been assuming Delman and Buddy were the same person. Suppose they weren't. We knew Delman was dead. Suppose Buddy was still alive. Could Ned be Buddy?

I was still mulling these possibilities when I reached my mother's room. Housekeeping was in with her. I could have requested they leave while I visited, but decided to come back later. I needed to think. If Ned was Buddy, he certainly had a motive for getting the Schmidt ranch—his ranch. Means, motive and opportunity.

I returned to Leon's floor. The same volunteer hailed me the moment I emerged from the elevator.

"You had another telephone call, Mr. Crow. I transferred it to your brother's room. I thought you were there with him. The uh . . . other man," she said tentatively, "took it. I hope that was—"

"Who was it?"

"A woman. She told me her name . . . I'll think of it in a minute."

"That's okay. I'll check with Aaron."

"Michiko called," he told me as soon as I entered the room. "Said she'd found part of Pete Schmidt's medical record. Apparently the files are a real mess. From what she's been able to piece together so far, it appears Burker and Colonel Bartholomew were both right. Pete lost a foot to frostbite in Korea, then, just before he died in the VA hospital in Big Spring they had to remove the lower part of his other leg."

A chill ran down my spine. Pete Schmidt was a double amputee when he died.

I returned to the nurse's station. "May I use the phone?" I asked. "A local call." I had one other detail I wanted Michiko to check. Who was listed as Pete's emergency point of contact?

After two rings the base operator answered and connected me to Michiko's extension at the hospital.

A female voice answered. "Oh, hi, Jason. Michiko left a few minutes ago. Someone called her. I thought it was you. Must have been serious, 'cause she went stark still, then said she'd meet you . . . well, whoever it was . . . at the ranch in twenty minutes. He must've offered to pick her up, because she said okay, she'd meet him outside in two."

A ranch twenty minutes away. That could be only one place. My heart began to pound.

"Then Michiko ran to the boss, told her she had to leave immediately, that it was an emergency. I can tell you, the major wasn't happy about letting her go, not with the IG here, but Michiko was in tears."

My hand tightened on the receiver. Michiko crying? An emergency?

"Did you see who picked her up?"

"No. He stayed in the car, one of those sporty German things."

Just then Lou Flores—Bubba's aunt—stepped off the elevator. In that split second all the pieces fell into place.

"What color was the car?" I asked the voice at the other end of the line.

"Green, I think. Why do you—"

I raced back to my brother's room. Aaron looked up from the chair on the far side of the bed.

"Let's go," I said

He jumped up. "Where to?"

"The Schmidt ranch to prevent a murder."

CHAPTER FIFTY-EIGHT

Aaron had to drive his Skylark in a wide circle around the blackened pit where Zack and I had nearly met a fiery end. As I looked at the three cars parked outside of the ranch house, I wondered how I could have been so dense.

Aaron skidded to a halt in front of the peeling building. With the convertible's top down, all he had to do was lift my chair over the side and expand it. In a near panic I transferred to the seat. My back was soaked with perspiration. Aaron pushed me up the porch ramp at a run.

The front door was open.

Zack stood in the middle of the living room, a gun pointed at Ned.

"Thank God you're here," Cole said from the far side of the room. He was standing beside and slightly behind Michiko. Her beautiful face was as pale and stoic as I'd ever seen it. Not a tear in sight now. There was compassion in her almond eyes—and fatalism. It unnerved me.

I looked at Zack's strained expression, at the bewilderment and fear etched on Ned's features.

"Zack says it was Ned who killed your father." Cole frowned. "But why, Zack?"

"For this place. For the oil," Zack said. "Except the joke's on him. There isn't any oil."

I wheeled myself slowly in front of the fireplace and turned toward the others. They all pivoted to face me. Zack and Ned were on my right, Cole and Michiko on my left. Aaron remained in the doorway, a dark sentinel against the glare of the afternoon sun.

"Zack's right," I said. "The geological survey Pete requested came back negative, but after all the bragging he'd done, he was too proud to admit it, even to Buddy. Do you really think Velma would've let this place go if there was oil on it? She was the only other person who knew the truth. Unfortunately, she didn't get around to informing her son either."

"Then how do *you* know?" Cole asked.

"Velma called my mother the night she died to tell her my father'd been suckered."

"So," Zack said to Ned, "the murders were for nothing."

"God damn it, Zack, what the hell are you talking about?" Ned's jangled nerves made his voice shrill. "What murders?"

"Mr. Crow and Kern Flores."

"There's one detail you missed," I told my best friend. "Look outside."

Zack's brows drew together, but a small step to one side was enough for him to glance through one of the dirty windows at the vehicles parked in front of the house. Leon's VW, Ned's Karmann Ghia and Cole's new car. It took only a couple of seconds for him to make the connection.

"Oh, my God." The gun in his hand drooped.

"What is it?" Ned peered outside. "I don't see—"

"The car," Zack mumbled.

"What car?" Ned demanded. "Damn it, what the hell are you two talking about?"

"The green Porsche," I said.

"Cole's new car? What about it?" Ned still didn't understand. "What's it got to do with—"

"His Volvo was hemmed in by our Packard all Friday night, when we stayed with him," I said. "We didn't know he also had a Porsche."

"I still don't . . . "

"While we slept in Cole's upstairs bedroom," I explained, "Cole drove to Coyote Springs in his Porsche, killed Dad, then returned to Austin in time to serve us morning coffee.

I rocked my wheelchair nervously forward and back, forward and back. Cole didn't say a word, but ridicule glistened in his eyes.

"Cole thought Dad owned this ranch." I leveled my next words at him. "You figured with my father dead, you'd be able to pick the place up cheap."

"I hadn't intended to leave the Porsche parked in front of the house Saturday morning," Cole's tone was patronizing. He was enjoying himself. "But I was running a little bit late."

"Yes," I said, "and I bet I know why. The speed trap in Jordan."

"It doesn't matter. None of you will live to explain any of it." Abruptly, he wrapped his left arm around Michiko's neck and pressed the pistol he'd kept hidden in his right hand to her temple.

Ned gasped. "Wha—"

I stopped breathing. My pulse quickened.

Instinctively Michiko clutched her assailant's forearm.

That was when I saw it. "Oh, God!" My heart pounded in my chest. The stumps of my missing legs felt like they were on fire.

"What?" Zack asked.

"The ring," I whispered. "The ring I bought in Saigon. The one I'd had in my pocket when I ran into the bunker."

Michiko's eyes went wide and her jaw dropped with sudden horrified understanding.

Cole had been there. He'd been at Tan Son Nhut, the major point of embarkation for all of South Vietnam. I understood now. I could finally see things clearly. Cole was the "cousin" Delman had seen in the main bar of the officers club. It was Cole and Delman I'd glimpsed silhouetted against the flares in the night sky.

"Cole killed Delman." I remembered the absolute astonishment on Delman's face before the pain of the bullet registered, a split second before he fell dead at my feet.

"It was Cole who . . . shot me, then put on the tourniquets." It was Cole who made me *a legless cripple.*

Zack groaned as the truth penetrated.

Cole chuckled at my dawning awareness. He gazed at my lap, pleased with his handiwork.

Unbearable hatred and molten rage swept through me at that moment. Because of him my athletic career was destroyed. Because of him my father was dead.

"Zack," Cole said with smug calmness, "put your gun on the floor." When Zack hesitated, Cole shouted, "Now!" Then he grinned and said softly, "Or I'll kill Michiko."

My friend obeyed. As he bent down, he glanced at my *residual limbs.* On straightening we made a heartbeat of eye contact.

I brought him to you, it said. *I did this to you. Forgive me. Please, forgive me.*

Cole ordered the other three men to line up in front of the fireplace behind me. Aaron stalled, but like Ned and Zack, he had no choice.

Cole stared down at me, alone in the middle of the room. I wondered why I'd never before noticed the insanity in his eyes—or the sadism. "I'm sorry you came out here, Jason. I was hoping to let you live. I was looking forward to watching you cope with the loss of your friends. It would've been fun listening to you trying to defend your bosom pals after they were found naked and dead of drug overdoses. I would've tried to console you, of course."

"My God," Ned exclaimed, "you're mad. You're stark, raving mad."

Cole seemed not to hear him. "But this is probably just as well," he said. "Eventually you'd have figured it out, then I'd have had to kill you too. This is more efficient. Get down on the floor."

I studied the cold, contemptuous face, then shrugged as if it made no difference. If he hadn't had his arm around Michiko, it probably wouldn't have. Except for her, there was nothing left for me. My father was dead. My life was ruined. I locked the wheels of the chair and lowered myself to the dusty floor. "You're outnumbered, you know."

He laughed. "But nobody here is faster than a speeding bullet."

You're right, Dad. I'm not Superman.

"Zack, fold up the chair and lay it on its side," Cole ordered.

Again my friend complied. At Cole's further prompting, Zack pushed it out of the way. I was left isolated in the center of the room. *Cole's legless cripple.*

His eyes sparkled with glee. "As for you, *boy*," he growled at Aaron, giving him a disdainful sneer, "I hadn't expected you either." Cole's attention, however, remained fixated on me as I tucked my empty pants legs under me. "Since you're here though, I'll just have to kill you too. But then, what's another dead nigger?"

I looked up. "You're a loser, Cole Wainton, just like your old sot of a mother, and as big a fool as Pete."

With my back to the others, I couldn't coordinate a plan of action, but I did see Michiko in front of me shift her hand. I had a good idea what she was about to do. Cole's concentration was again locked on me. I meant to keep it there.

Dramatically, I clutched the ends of my stumps. "These aren't important." I glared up at him. "I'll dance on your grave."

The condescending expression on his face had morphed into a mask of pure malevolence, when suddenly he let out a yowl and slackened his hold on Michiko. Blood streamed from the long scratch she'd torn into his arm with the ring she'd reversed on her finger.

The light shifted. Aaron lunged forward with an ear-splitting roar. Michiko rammed her elbow into Cole's solar plexus. He let out an oomph and tilted forward. The gun in his hand went off. Aaron fell to his hands and knees.

"Stop!" Cole righted himself and pointed the gun directly at Michiko's head.

My pulse pounded in my ears.

Cole studied his fallen attacker. Aaron looked up at him. Their gazes met. Cole carefully leveled the pistol at the black man's skull.

Zack and I shouted simultaneously. In that instant's distraction, Aaron sprang. His joined fists smashed into the gun a split second before it discharged. Ned screamed and tumbled to the floor. Zack joined the wrestling match for the .38. A third shot rang out, shattering a window pane.

I vaulted forward on my stubbie legs and hugged Cole's knees. Michiko spread her arms in a whirling arc that made direct contact with his face. I heard the crunch of nose cartilage. He staggered, lost balance, toppled backward, but instantly flipped onto his belly, elbows under him, ready to spring. I scrambled onto his back, caged one arm under his chin.

The other I pressed against the base of his neck, locking it in a vise.

I sucked air through my nostrils in long, violent bursts. My muscles tightened. My mouth was dry with the bitter taste of venom. All the grief and humiliation I'd suffered was now cradled within my grasp. It would take only a small jerk of my arms to break the man's neck.

Gradually, I became aware of the silence around me. I glanced up. Aaron had seized the gun from Cole. Zack had reclaimed the Smith and Wesson. Ned was on the floor curled in a fetal position. Michiko was applying pressure to the wound in his side. Blood oozed between her fingers. Everybody watched and waited. No one said a word, and I realized they wouldn't stop me. They were giving me permission to end my tormentor's life. My arm muscles began to contract. I heard the choking gurgle they produced.

I had no idea how much time elapsed before I felt the tears streaming down my face. Hot tears for the man who'd been my staunchest champion, my wisest mentor, my father. Tears of despair, of hopeless craving for the physical wholeness I'd never again experience, and finally what my father would have called tears of love for the simple gift of life itself.

I let go.

Zack and Aaron snatched Cole's limp body off the floor and hauled him roughly into a corner. The fight was gone. Michiko tore the ring off her finger and flung it at him.

I didn't hear the police cars pulling up outside. I looked on, as if viewing a silent movie, while Clyde Burker directed two uniformed policemen to take bloody-faced and bloody-armed Cole Wainton into custody.

Zack righted my wheelchair. I was bereft of strength. He and Aaron each hooked their arms under my elbows and lifted me into it.

The room was shrouded in afternoon shadow. Michiko stood before me, her face tear-stained, her lips pinched. Somehow, for just an instant, we managed to smile at each other.

A full hour elapsed before I got a chance to thank Burker for his act of faith in responding to Mrs. Flores' phone call. She'd stopped by the hospital to visit Leon and had no idea what was going on when I hastily called to her to phone the detective and request he come to the Schmidt ranch immediately.

"I figured you must have been desperate to call me," Burker said.

By that time Ned and Cole had been taken in separate ambulances to Clover Hospital. Burker then asked Zack, Aaron, Michiko and me to come to the police station to answer a few questions. A few turned into a torrent. What I learned was that Cole had called Michiko and told her that Ned was Velma's son, that he was desperate to get the Schmidt ranch, and that he'd kill me if necessary. Ned had already tried to kill Zack, Cole told her, by sabotaging the bridge, and now he was meeting me out at the place.

Cole invited her to go with him to try to rescue me. Then, just as they were arriving at the house, he gave her the ring and told her to put it on as a sign to Ned that she and I were engaged. Ned, he claimed, was infatuated with her. She'd have to convince him that if he really loved her he'd let me go. It didn't seem like it would work, Michiko admitted, but everything was happening so fast, and she was willing to do anything to protect me. It wasn't until I saw the ring and identified it that she began to understand what was really happening.

Burker continued to pepper us with questions, which we answered candidly. When he started asking them again, however, I balked. "That's enough for today."

"I'm almost finished."

"Correction. You are finished." I gripped the rims of my chair. At his frown, I said, "Clyde, I'll answer all your questions, fully and unequivocally. I might even answer them twice, but not now. It's been a difficult day. I'm tired and I'm leaving."

I rotated toward the door.

Burker started to object, then relaxed his posture. "Would the three of you mind waiting outside for a minute?" he asked Michiko, Zack and Aaron. At their expressions of doubt and concern, he added, "Promise. Just a minute."

I nodded to them. After closing the door Burker settled his rump against the edge of his desk and crossed his arms.

"I just want to tell you I'm sorry about what's happened to you and your family, but especially to you, now that I know the circumstances. There are bad people in this world. I know you don't want pity. I'm not giving any. But I do offer you my respect."

He paused. Fumbled nervously with his hands. "I want you to know too that I hold no hard feelings about our past personal differences."

I bowed my head, then looked up. "It's I who owe you and Janet an apology. I was a strutting peacock, full of myself. You deserved better from me as a teammate. She deserved better from me as a man. I failed you both. I'm sorry."

I wasn't sure which of us made the first move, but we shook hands firmly. I doubted Janet would be as forgiving as her husband, and I doubted Clyde Burker and I would ever be close friends, but that was all right. Considering the complexity of the situation, it was probably just as well.

He opened the door for me and I wheeled myself out.

I wasn't surprised to see Debbie holding Aaron's hand or Nancy standing beside Zack, but I was taken aback when we left the building to encounter a slew of reporters camped in the parking lot. I was in no mood for another marathon of questions, so I extended a public thanks to Detective Burker and the other members of the police department for apprehending the man who had ruined so many lives.

"Including yours," one reporter prompted. Everyone went still.

"No," I said. "I refuse to give him that power. My father taught me to never quit, to make the best of the life God gave me. That's exactly what I intend to do."

Aaron and my sister left for his garage apartment. Zack escorted Nancy to her cottage. And I went home with Michiko.

CHAPTER FIFTY-NINE

Coyote Springs, Texas, Saturday, August 31, 1968

Michiko and I arrived at the *Nest* a little after eleven o'clock the following morning. The night we'd spent together had been emotional on both our parts, but it had also been the most sensual and fulfilling in my life. I had no doubt she loved me, that she accepted me the way I was, that we were a union of more than bodies. I was a man. She was a woman. I loved her more than life itself.

The *Crow's Nest* had been closed for seven days. Now on the eighth day tables and chairs were set up on the front and side lawns for the Texas barbecue that would officially mark its reopening at noon.

Rather than pull into the courtyard, I asked Michiko to tool up the circular driveway in front of the restored mansion. I couldn't remember the last time I'd used the front door, but somehow the symbolism of it was important to me. She halted the MG at the base of the ramp Dad had installed to the wrap-around porch, got out and untied the wheelchair lashed over the spare tire behind us. The wheels locked, I transferred to the seat, then I tugged her down and kissed her on the mouth.

She started to reciprocate, pulled away and actually blushed. "Jason, not now."

I laughed with liberating delight. "Definitely later."

Everybody was in the parlor: Zack, George, Debbie, Aaron, Nancy and Ned. He'd spent a few hours in the emergency room the day before and then been released. The wound he'd received had been bloody and would probably leave a scar. Fortunately it hadn't done any more than cosmetic damage. The atmosphere wasn't festive so much as imbued with a feeling of relief that a crisis was past. On the sideboard, chafing dishes sent up little puffs of steam with the familiar smells of smoked brisket, baked potatoes, green beans, pinto beans and yeast rolls. A large bowl of crisp salad sat on a draped table along with another chafing dish, this one emitting the sweet aroma of warm peach cobbler.

My father's place at the head of the table was vacant. His high-back armchair had been relegated to the corner. With considerable reluctance I wheeled myself into its place. While Michiko poured us both glasses of iced tea and sat on my right.

"I imagine Zack, Aaron and Ned have filled you in on what happened yesterday," I said.

"Thank God you're all right." Debbie held onto Aaron's arm with both hands. "That everyone's all right. If I'd lost you—"

Nods as people drank tea.

"When did you begin to suspect Cole?" Nancy asked me.

"Not until Mrs. Flores stepped off the elevator at the hospital yesterday to visit Leon. I know her as Lou Flores. Bubba calls her Aunt Portia. Her full name is Portia Lou Spites Flores."

"I talked to Clyde Burker a little while ago," Zack said. "He took your advice and checked with the highway patrol in Jordan. You were right. Cole was running late Saturday morning because he received a speeding ticket there in his Porsche at 4:15, coming *from* Coyote Springs."

"I wish he'd received it going *to*," I commented. "He undoubtedly would have aborted his mission."

"You'll drive yourself crazy playing the what-if game," George warned me from his usual place at the far end of the table. That would change, I vowed. This was his table now.

"I know," I said. There were so many what-ifs to choose from. If George hadn't recounted the story about Leon carelessly letting his gun go off in Gramps's study. If I hadn't decided to stop at UT on the way home. If we hadn't accepted Cole's dinner invitation. "So many little hints that something was wrong—if I'd paid attention."

"We," Zack corrected me. "You weren't alone, Kemosabe."

"Such as?" Nancy prompted.

"At *Chambers* where we met for drinks," Zack said, "the waiter referred to Cole's car as a gray zephyr. We took it as joke, because his red Volvo was faded down to the gray primer."

"In fact," I explained, "the waiter was referring to Ned's red Karmann Ghia, confusing it with Cole's green Porsche, an easy enough mistake for someone unfamiliar with foreign cars. Since the guy was color blind, he saw red and green as gray."

"As soon as Jason pointed out the Porsche yesterday afternoon," added Zack, "I understood immediately what had happened, maybe because I almost ran into it twice the morning we left Austin in my hung-over state."

"You hadn't had any more to drink than I had," I told him. "You were drugged. Cole knew you were fond of Grand Marnier, so he spiked it to insure you didn't get up during the night. He was confident I wouldn't be leaving the second floor."

"You told Burker yesterday that Cole was dealing drugs," Aaron said.

"How did you know that?"

"Hindsight's a wonderful thing," I replied. "As soon as Cole walked into *Chambers* Friday, people started coming up to him, showing unusual familiarity, even by Texas standards, to someone who had supposedly only been in town a few days. Cole gave them the brush off, but they didn't seem to mind. The truth is they were drug customers."

"If you think about the characters who came up to him," Zack said, "they should have been a clue. Druggies."

I shrugged. "We see what we expect to see. We weren't thinking of Cole as a dealer."

"He was also spending money hand over fist," Zack noted. "He bought us pricey wine that he didn't drink, splurged on dinner in the most expensive restaurant in town, yet he drove a clunker."

"When he came to my verbal rescue at *The Joint*," I said, "he addressed Bubba as Mr. Spites, though no one had mentioned his last name. And Bubba, equally shocked at seeing Cole with me, addressed him sarcastically as 'sir,' not a normal Bubba term by any means."

If I hadn't been so preoccupied with the humiliation of being knocked down and called a legless cripple, I might have picked up on those things. "Bubba also called Cole Mr. Mouthpiece, an allusion to his being a law student, which he wouldn't have known if they were strangers."

"Burker later admitted he'd had *The Joint* under surveillance," Zack said, "because he suspected Bubba might be meeting his supplier. He was, Cole. Which was why Cole was so aggressive in confronting Bubba and shutting him up."

"I didn't realize how much Cole had changed his appearance from his active duty days until I saw Zack wearing old, black-rimmed GI glasses. Still, even then Cole was careful to avoid people as much as possible. The reception on Sunday, for example, and Dad's funeral on Tuesday, because he was afraid somebody might recognize him."

Nancy poured herself more iced tea, then stood and went around the table replenishing everybody else's.

"His explanation for getting out of the service didn't ring true either," I continued. "Cole was the epitome of the *lifer*, not because he was naïve about military service, but because he understood the system and how to manipulate it."

"The system didn't fail him," Zack said. "He'd failed the system."

I nodded. "When the D.A. checks Air Force records, I'm willing to bet they discover he resigned under threat of court martial because he was implicated in drug trafficking."

"How was he able to make your father's death look like suicide?"

Nancy asked.

"Dad wasn't foolhardy. With a gun pointed at him, he would've complied with an assailant's demands and tried to reason with him. In this case, I think Cole simply put Leon's gun to Dad's temple and pulled the trigger."

Did dad know he was about to die and why? It saddened me that I'd never know.

I paused to take a slow sip of iced tea before going on. "Cole had one problem, however. No gunpowder burns on Dad's hand, something a coroner would look for."

"I'd never have thought of that," Nancy said. "I would have just put the gun in his hand to get fingerprints on it."

I nodded. "Cole knew what he was doing. He used Dad's key to the cabinet and got out *my* gun. Then he filled the wastebasket with dirt from a flower bed downstairs."

"How do you know that?" Nancy challenged.

"Because I found dirt in the wastebasket by the desk Saturday when Zack and I searched the office."

"The dead hydrangeas!" George exclaimed.

"Yes," I said. "Cole put my gun in Dad's hand, squeezed off a round into the wastebasket, then replaced it with Leon's matching revolver. That way there was only one round fired from the fatal weapon. Cole returned the dirt, minus the slug, to the flower bed. But it was late and dark, and he was in a hurry. He didn't put it back carefully enough. The hydrangeas died."

"How did you know there were two shots fired?" Aaron asked.

Michiko explained. "The police reported that Mr. Crow died between 2:00 and 4:00 o'clock. It actually happened at 3:40. That's when the old lady who lives across the street was awakened by the first of two bangs. She thought they were firecrackers."

"The first was the shot that killed Mr. Crow," Zack said. "The second was Jason's gun being fired into the wastebasket."

"How did Cole get Leon's gun?" Aaron asked.

"Kern Flores. Probably in exchange for drugs. I'm sure now it was Kern who called me the day of Dad's funeral to tell me something that involved Cole. It was unfortunate that Cole happened to be there when George mentioned the calls from someone with a Spanish accent. I figured it was Joe Gutierrez. Cole realized it was Kern and killed him."

"So Kern's death wasn't an accident," Debbie said.

"An accident that was engineered," I replied. "Kern could connect Cole with Leon's gun and possibly with supplying the high priest with narcotics. Kern had to be silenced. My guess is Cole furnished him with a joint fortified with opium, as he had Leon. Unaware of its true strength, Kern ended up killing himself, which was what Cole had hoped for."

"Cold blooded, bastard," Aaron muttered.

"But . . . didn't you say Cole saved your life in Japan?" Nancy asked.

"Actually he was trying to kill me. I realize that now. He said himself he didn't see the taxi coming, he only heard it. He'd arrived in Japan that day and had forgotten they drive on the left side of the road. He thought he was pushing me into the path of an oncoming taxi, not beyond it."

"He was lucky Japanese drivers are so skillful at dodging people," Michiko said, "or he wouldn't have gotten away with just a sprained ankle. By the way, I checked this morning with the nurse who was reviewing files with me. Captain Cole Wainton, stepson, was listed for emergency notification after Velma."

If only we'd known this from the beginning. But George was right. You could go crazy playing the if-only game.

"What he did to you, Jason," Debbie said, her voice thin and faltering. "Why? How could he be so mean?"

I stared at the table set in front of me. Burker had given the only possible explanation. There are bad people in the world.

"For reasons I don't understand, Cole idolized Pete. Pete had lost a foot from frostbite in the Korean War. When Cole's attempt to kill me in Japan failed and Pete lost the lower part of his other leg to diabetes, I think Cole's sadism took hold. He had a philosophy, don't get mad, get even. Dad wasn't available, but I was, so he decided to even the score by going after me."

"Obviously he'd been planning vengeance for some time," Zack said. "Pete had already gone bust when Cole met me in OTS. His first question when he found out I was from Coyote Springs, was whether I knew the guy from there who'd won the *College Athlete of the Year Award.* Yet he never showed any particular interest in sports, as a player or a fan."

"Parallels," I said. "His mother died of an apparent suicide, so Dad was made to look like a suicide. Pete was a double amputee, so I was made a double amputee."

"Sick," Nancy said.

"He's not sick," Aaron insisted. "He's evil."

More nods. More downcast eyes.

"Thank God it's over." Debbie held tightly to Aaron's hand.

But of course it would never be over. Not for me. Not completely. My father was dead. The career I had been dreaming of since childhood was gone. My legs were gone. Life would never be the same.

"What about Leon?" George asked.

"I spoke to Burker on the phone before I came over here," I said.

"He assures me there won't be any charges brought against him as long as he goes into rehab."

Ned pushed back his chair, rose and walked over to an ice bucket at the end of the side board.

Not champagne, I wanted to shout. *I won't drink champagne.*

He began the ritual of presenting the label to me, a California Riesling. He pulled the cork and offering it to me.

"Ah, yes." I sniffed. "A musky scent reminiscent of tree bark in a summer storm."

Ned raised an eyebrow, poured a little of the wine into my long-stemmed glass.

I swirled it around to release its full bouquet, held it up to the light, took a tentative sip, churned it around in my mouth, swallowed and smacked my lips.

"A pungent hint of vanilla," I announced, "autumnal sea breezes and dried apple, with just a gentle whiff of toasty nuts, sweet cherry, kumquat, baking spices and rain-drenched stones."

Ned laughed along with everybody else. "You don't know what you're talking about any more than I do."

"It sure sounds good though." Zack remarked with an added chuckle.

Ned assumed a formal tone. "Might I conclude, sir, that you approve?"

"Decidedly so, my good man. Pour the stuff."

While Ned went around rationing out the two bottles, I observed the people at the table. They all had their individual challenges. George, to run the restaurant business without his best friend and business partner. Debbie and Aaron to face a world of discrimination. I had mine. I'd lost my legs, but not my ability to go places. I'd make the best of the hand fate had dealt me. I'd never be a quitter.

"I propose a toast." Zack raised his glass. "To life."

To life. My father was physically absent, but his spirit was present. Theodore Crow's wisdom was forever locked deep inside me. I had only to remain true to it.

I reached out and took Michiko's hand. I'd come home.

EPILOGUE

Tuesday, November 19, 1968

The trial of Cole Wainton for the first-degree murders of Theodore Crow and Kern Flores was over. Guilty on both counts. Just before eleven o'clock today, the judge sentenced him to death in the electric chair. Cole would probably never be tried for taking Delman Schmidt's life, but how many times could you execute a man? Undoubtedly he'd appeal both the verdicts and the sentences, which meant I'd be appearing in courtrooms for years to come, presenting myself as the legless cripple he'd made me, the victim of a sadistic killer.

The nightmare of death and mutilation would never be completely over for me, but I was alive and free and deeply in love.

Michiko and the others had gone ahead to the *Crow's Nest.* I planned to meet them there for lunch in a little while, but first I wanted to visit my mother in the psychiatric unit at Clover Hospital. According to her doctors and the staff, she was doing well, making slow progress, but she'd suffered so many blows to her mental stability that I wondered if she'd ever be whole again.

I was turning onto Davis when a new, shiny-red Corvette streaked in front of me. I slammed on the brakes and narrowly missed its rear bumper. The woman driver peeled away without giving me a glance, apparently unaware I was there.

My heart pounded. My palms became slick. The vision of another Corvette careening into my path flashed through my mind. I pulled over to the curb, put the transmission in neutral and set the emergency brake, then took several deep breaths. After a full minute of willing my hammering pulse to subside, I returned to the courthouse. Mom would have to wait.

The bailiff was closing the courtroom door for the lunch recess.

"I need to see Cole Wainton," I told him.

"He's not here, Mr. Crow. They've taken him to the county jail. Not sure you'll be allowed to see him there. Might have to wait till he's transferred to Huntsville."

"Who do I need to talk to?"

"The D.A. I reckon. You can use the phone in my office if you like."

It took some persuasion to get the D.A.'s permission, but when I drove to the jailhouse a few minutes later, the officer in charge was waiting for me. He was sympathetic, but nevertheless questioned the wisdom of my confronting the man who'd killed my father and maimed me. "The D.A. says to give you ten minutes. No more."

"I have only a few questions," I said. "Shouldn't take long. He'll either answer them or he won't."

The jail keeper shrugged. "You won't have to worry about him giving you any trouble, Mr. Crow. He'll be shackled and there'll be two guards with him the whole time."

I thanked him and followed him into a small room that contained only a single table and two chairs. Fifteen minutes that seemed like fifteen hours went by before the prisoner was brought in. Steel chains around his ankles hobbled his steps. His hands were manacled to a waist chain.

We stared at each other. He appeared smaller here than he had in the courtroom. His complexion was sallow. The brilliant blue of his eyes was already fading. The prison garb hung loose and wrinkled, a sharp contrast to the tailored suit he'd been wearing less than an hour before.

One of the guards shoved him roughly into a bolted-down chair on the other side of the table.

"What do you want?" Cole demanded of me.

"To ask a question or two."

He smirked. "Why should I tell you anything?"

I had no response to that. Asking him a question was handing him the weapon of silence.

"Why did you cripple me? It wasn't because of Pete Schmidt, was it? At least not completely."

The amused expression on his face was uninhibited and ugly. "Oh, you finally figured it out. Congratulations." He slouched back against the iron frame, gazed contemptuously at me but said no more.

"It was for Daphne." Not a question, but a statement.

Daphne Higginsson, the driver of the Corvette I'd run into outside Llano four years ago. The accident had left her a paraplegic. Colonel Bartholomew said Pete came from Llano. Another connection I'd missed.

"You were her fiancé, weren't you?"

"We were supposed to get married," he shouted. "You ruined her."

The guard approached, hovered. He didn't have to say anything.

Cole lowered his voice to a hiss. "She was beautiful. Her daddy was rich. We were going to be married. But after the accident she'd lost all sensation. She couldn't feel me. Do you know what it's like to have sex with a woman who can't feel anything? She couldn't walk. She couldn't control herself. She couldn't please me. More than that. She disgusted me. I had no choice but to call off our engagement."

"So she committed suicide."

"That wasn't my fault." His voice was tight, louder. The outrage was still there. "It was on account of you. You destroyed her body. You made her unworthy of me. You stole her from me."

I was about to point out that she was the one who'd been driving recklessly, but he didn't give me a chance.

"Just like you stole Michiko from me," he said. "She was *my* nurse until you walked in, then it was like I wasn't there. The big, rich, handsome star quarterback. Superman. Ha." He sneered, his eyes blazing.

"So you took your revenge."

"My first impulse was to shoot you in the back, let you live the rest of your life not being able to feel anything. Then I saw you help that major in the officers club who got his legs crushed, and I knew what I had to do. I didn't want you to be numb. Better for you to feel and need and know that nobody would ever desire you. What woman would give herself to a guy with no legs, a freak who had to crawl on the floor for the rest of his life?"

The other mystery solved: how my unit knew I was at the officers club. It didn't. The bartender was holding the telephone in his hand when he passed on the information to me, but that wasn't how he'd received it. Cole had told him in person before he disappeared into the night with Delman. He'd already figured out what he was going to do to both of us.

I was sick inside. I'd taken pride in not letting him see me without my prostheses. I'd wanted him to continue to think of me as whole, not deformed. It hadn't occurred to me that he craved seeing me as a *legless cripple*, an object of pity and revulsion. I remembered the way he'd looked at me as I backed up the stairs to his attic bedroom. I'd seen curiosity. Why hadn't I recognized fascination? Because I thought he was my friend. The following morning, after he'd murdered my father, when he came barging into the bedroom with the coffee tray, he'd stared at the pillow I'd thrust in front of me. Why hadn't I recognized the triumph in his gaze? Because I wanted to see compassion, not malice.

"You got your revenge on me," I said. "So why did you have to kill my father too?"

"I'd made you pay for what you did to Daphne. I had to make him pay for what he did to Pete and my mother."

Dad didn't do anything to them, I wanted to scream. *They did it to themselves.*

He strained at the chains binding his wrists to his waist.

"It was all your father's fault. If he hadn't talked you into walking, you'd have spent the rest of your life sitting in a wheelchair or dragging yourself around like the freak I made you. But he ruined everything. I had no choice. I had to kill him. I had to get even. I had to make both of you pay for what I'd lost. Pete. My mother. The ranch. Daphne. Everything."

He was blaming me for my father's death. I wanted to vomit.

"The old bastard wouldn't even give me the satisfaction of dying the way I wanted him to. He took out a bottle of champagne when I walked in. I told him you were on the way, that you were wearing your new legs. He got a picture from his bedroom for me to see. You, standing beside Michiko, your arm around her waist. So damn smug. Nobody could see your legs weren't real."

The illusion of normalcy.

"And she . . . she was looking up at you with adoration in her eyes. Killing him was easy. I walked around the end of the desk to lean over his shoulder and get a better look at the picture. To distract him I told him you were planning to do the Texas Two-Step with Michiko at the barbecue. He was laughing when I took out the gun and blew his brains out. I'd wanted him to suffer first, but at least he was dead."

My throat burned. I couldn't speak. I bowed my head, afraid he'd see on my face, in my eyes the soul-searing agony he'd inflicted. But then I realized something. One of the questions that had been gnawing at me since that Saturday morning was whether my father had discovered his killer's true identity, whether he'd realized the man with him had intentionally crippled me, whether Dad knew he was about to be murdered.

Without intending to, Cole had just answered those questions. Dad had been laughing when the trigger was pulled. My father had died a happy man, proud of me.

I stared at the prisoner on the other side of the table, scanned the barren room and studied him again. I might actually have had a smile on my face when I asked, "Was it worth it?"

His eyes narrowed. "Go to hell, Crow."

"I'm glad I stopped by to say goodbye," I said. "You don't realize it, but you've given me a very special gift today." I didn't tell him what it was.

I surveyed the dingy room once more and rose to my feet.

"I'm leaving now to meet the woman I love, a woman who loves me. Nothing you've done has changed that. We're getting married soon. We plan to have a houseful of kids. I'm surrounded by friends and people who care for me."

I pivoted and closed the short distance to the door, knocked on it and turned back one last time. "Enjoy your prison walls, Cole. I have a feeling you're going to think about me a lot more than I will of you. I'll be too busy raising a family, running a business and experiencing life."

I heard the rattle of his chains as I crossed the threshold. There was a bit of a hitch in my stride but I felt free, freer than I had in a long time. I'd reached the point of acceptance. I'd never take my life for granted. I'd never undervalue the love that surrounded me.

I made a vow too. If there was life after death, my father would look down on me with pride for as long as I lived.

Ken Casper Bio

Ken Casper, aka K. N. Casper, author of more than 25 novels, short stories and articles, figures his writing career started back in the sixth grade when a teacher ordered him to write a "theme" explaining his misbehavior over the previous semester. To his teacher's chagrin, he enjoyed stringing just the right words together to justify his less-than-stellar performance. That's not to say he's been telling tall tales to get out of scrapes ever since, but...

Born and raised in New York City, Ken is now a transplanted Texan. He and Mary, his wife of thirty-five-plus years, own a horse farm in San Angelo. Along with their two dogs, six cats, and eight horses—at last count!—they board and breed horses and Mary teaches English riding. She's a therapeutic riding instructor for the handicapped, as well.

Life is never dull. Their two granddaughters visit several times a year and feel right at home with the Casper menagerie. Grandpa and Mimi do everything they can to make sure their visits will be lifelong fond memories. After all, isn't that what grandparents are for?

CPSIA information can be obtained at www.ICGtesting.com
228377LV00002B/48/P

9 781611 940084